1

SISTERS OF THE
SANDS

THE ACOLYTES SERIES

Sisters of the Sands © 2024 J.B. Villinger

All Rights Reserved. No part of this book may be reproduced in any form or by any electronic or mechanical means including information storage and retrieval systems, without permission in writing from the author. The only exception is by a reviewer, who may quote short excerpts in a review.

This book is a work of fiction. Names, characters, places, and incidents either are products of the author's imagination or are used fictitiously. Any resemblance to actual persons, living or dead, events, or locales is entirely coincidental.

Printed in Australia

Cover and internal design by Shawline Publishing Group Pty Ltd

Images in this book are copyright approved for Shawline Publishing Group Pty Ltd

Illustrations within this book are copyright approved for Shawline Publishing Group Pty Ltd

Illustrations within this book created by Vanessa Novak, @ImShyka

First printing: March 2024

Shawline Publishing Group Pty Ltd

www.shawlinepublishing.com.au

Paperback ISBN 978-1-9231-0139-5

eBook ISBN 978-1-9231-0140-1

Hardback ISBN 978-1-9231-0182-1

Distributed by Shawline Distribution and Lightning Source Global

Shawline Publishing Group acknowledges the traditional owners of the land and pays respects to Elders, past, present and future

A catalogue record for this work is available from the National Library of Australia

1

SISTERS OF THE SANDS

THE ACOLYTES SERIES
J.B. VILLINGER

For giving me the power to dream, imagine
and journey into the unknown,
I dedicate this story to my parents,
Gary and Raylee

Contents

One: You Are a Weapon

Sacet

'I will never understand why you saved her,' my grandfather said from behind the tent wall. 'Stop pretending she's your flesh and blood. She's one of *them*. Sooner or later, she'll snap and hurt your son.'

I crept over the hot sand, careful not to make any noise. I placed my hands on the matted animal-skin wall and leaned closer to hear them talking about me. My family's shadows were visible through the tarp as vague and blurry silhouettes.

Dad gave a gruff sigh. 'I'm sick of having this conversation.'

'Aberym, Sacet is a part of our family now,' my mother chimed in. 'And we will protect her.'

Would I get in trouble if they knew I was listening in? No, I had a right to know.

'I'm not asking to kill her, Enni,' my grandfather replied. 'But she shouldn't be here with our people.'

I gasped, then held my breath as his outline moved closer to the wall I was hiding behind. I knew he hated me, but not that much.

'That's not for you to decide,' my father replied.

My grandfather sighed and I saw his silhouette lower, perhaps to sit. 'Today I spied on her. She used her powers again to make a portal from here all the way to the lake without seeing it. Now, imagine if she had training...'

'She's ten cycles old!' my mother blurted, before adjusting back to a whisper. 'She won't be a part of this war anymore.'

That's right, you tell him! I fought the urge to agree out loud.

'We're not putting a gun in our daughter's hands,' my father added.

'You won't have to,' my grandfather said, standing again and pacing. 'Think about it. She could unite our scattered people with these portals. Our armies could teleport all over the world and strike back against the Dominions.

'I *need* to test how far these portals can go. Maybe there is no limit? Let me take her to the other settlements. We could make a link between our people... for trade at first. And on the way I'll train her to defend herself.'

Mum approached, now face to face with him. 'No.'

My grandfather scoffed. 'Come now, you've babied this weapon long enough. Son? Please see reason.'

I put my hand over my mouth to stifle a cry. *I'm just a weapon to him?* There was an extended silence. I could hear my own heart beating.

'You're getting too old for this,' Dad finally replied. 'You can't fight like you used to. We'll go with you. All of us together, as a family. And only to help *unite* our people.'

Footsteps thudded on the rocky pathway leading up to our tent. I ducked down even lower by the side wall. Another shadow, smaller than the others, ran inside.

'Arleigh?' Mum said. 'What's the matter?'

I could hear my friend panting, unable to speak.

'Where's Eno?' Mum persisted. 'I thought you were taking care of him?'

'I... I can't find him,' she managed between gasps. 'We were playing... and...'

'The river,' my father said, cutting Arleigh short. 'Did you check there?'

The silhouettes rushed out together.

'Where did you last see him?' I heard my mother say as they ran to the village's centre.

I clambered up from my hiding spot by the tent's side and watched them run down the path. Dad, Arleigh, and my grandfather made for the river, while Mum ducked into the other tents to alert the villagers.

Where had my little brother gotten to? If it were me on toddler-duty, he'd be bugging me to climb the cliffs with him again. He wanted to see the wastelands for himself. Maybe that's where he went?

I sprinted down the path towards the east side of the village. As I passed the tents, I received several disparaging stares from the villagers. They must have thought I was up to something, as usual.

Finally clear of the village, I began scaling the winding cliff path as fast as I was able. After scrambling over numerous dirt chunks and boulders, I paused along the cliff ledge to catch my breath.

I turned and peered back down into the canyon. There was a sheer drop below. The settlement, nestled between the canyon's wall and the winding river, was now abuzz with villagers fanning out and searching for Eno. Many headed along the riverbank in both directions.

Would they have shown this much concern for me? Probably not. I clenched my fists.

There was a fresh set of tracks in the sand alongside mine on the winding path, belonging to someone much smaller. Eno. The tracks led to an offshoot of the canyon, the dry chasm. Of course, the one place my parents told me to never go.

I should probably tell someone. I opened my mouth, about to call out to the people below. Wait, if I found him first, maybe the villagers would finally treat me better? Maybe my grandfather would stop hating me? *I* should be the one to bring him back.

I turned my back to the settlement and followed the footprints. The ledge grew narrower and forked into numerous, crumbly paths. The footprints were lost along the rocky ground. He couldn't have climbed out of the canyon yet, surely?

I chose the higher path, keeping as close to the cliff as I could. It wasn't long before I heard the faintest of whimpers coming from below.

'Eno?' I called. I got on my knees and slid closer to the edge to peer over the side, down into the deep chasm. 'Where are you?'

'Sassy!' I heard him call up.

There he was, sitting with his back to the rocks on a lower layer that jutted out from the cliff. There was nowhere for him to go, other than down. Tears had swelled around his blue eyes. His clothes and his normally blonde hair were covered in dirt, no doubt from falling and attempting to climb back up.

'Sassa, I want Mummy,' he pleaded. 'I want Mummy!'

'Don't move!' I shouted, my voice echoing through the chasm. 'I'm coming to get you, okay?'

I was determined to be the one to rescue him. I'd prove how grown up I was, how trustworthy. I stood, backed away from the ledge, closed my eyes and began to twirl my fingers. Picturing both Eno's ledge and my own position in my mind, I strained until all of my muscles went stiff.

Something was off. I had made three portals today, the most I'd ever made. My limbs felt heavy, and sweat beaded on my forehead as I kept straining, but nothing came from my effort. It was no use.

'Sassa!'

'Hold on!' I got back down on my knees and positioned myself on the ledge directly over him as he began to bawl. 'Mummy's on her way, alright? She's coming.'

Eno wasn't that far down, I could reach him. I threw out my hand. 'Eno, grab me. Big sis can pull you up.'

He refused to budge, instead continuing to moan, which echoed off the canyon walls.

'Come on, reach Sassy's hand,' I said, but it didn't motivate him.

A harsh, screeching noise sounded from farther down the chasm. Eno stopped bawling and we both went silent. We knew what it was.

'Eno... take my hand,' I murmured. 'Stand up and reach.'

A new kind of fear had taken my brother. He stood up, eyes wide and tear-filled, and mouth agape but silent.

Scuttling insectoid legs hammered below. The echo made it impossible to know how many of them there were. But then I saw one. The necrolisk rose from the depths of the chasm, the behemoth scaling the wall, as if it were flat ground.

'Eno?' I called, my eyes fixed upon the creature. I felt a brush against my fingertips and looked down to see Eno reaching out. I latched onto his sweaty, dirt-encrusted hand and yanked him up. I grabbed him with both arms and ran towards the village.

The necrolisk reached the ledge and launched itself onto the path, blocking our only way back. Its carapace was covered in spikes and glistening crimson scales. Its sharp head, more teeth than anything else, snapped about and located us. The six legs danced up and down as the creature turned to face us. It raised its gigantic claws high into the air.

I had never seen a live necrolisk up close before. It was far larger than any man from our village. My blood was ice.

It opened its jaws and roared again, pounding my eardrums. My legs refused to move. More scuttling could be heard by the chasm to our side. The creature lowered its head and slowly closed in, as if relishing the kill.

My shaking legs gave way, and I fell with Eno back into the sand. Eno squealed and hid his face into my robes. I kicked at the sand to push us back, but the monster was already looming over us. One of its pincers opened and hovered around my head, preparing to snap shut. The inside was filled with razor-sharp barbs.

There was an explosion and a shower of green blood engulfed us. Eno flew out of my grasp to the side. After clearing the blood from my eyes, I shot back up again. The necrolisk's body was headless, unmoving and slumped against the cliff wall.

On the other side of the chasm, on the highest ledge of the cliffs, our parents stood with their rifles aimed at the fallen monster.

'Sacet, take Eno and get back to the village!' Mum shouted. The canyon repeated her commands over and over.

The scuttling grew louder, and Eno and I saw at least ten more necrolisks ascending the other side of the chasm, right towards Mum and Dad. They noticed them too, and backed away from the ledge.

'Go!' Dad shouted, gesturing back to safety.

They both climbed up and out of the canyon, then ran into the desert wastes and out of sight. Their pursuers reached the canyon's precipice and followed.

Eno was sitting to my side, shaking and not taking his eye off the monster's corpse in front of us. He flicked his hands towards the creature as if he were trying to push it away.

'No! Get away!' he screamed, sobbing as he did so. 'Stop it! Get away!'

As if listening to him, the carcass slowly dangled over the ledge, then slid off, tumbling back down into the chasm's depths.

I still couldn't move. My robes were mottled in the monster's green blood.

A horde of other villagers, many holding weapons, clambered up the rocks towards us. I recognised the white beard of our grandfather leading them. A shrill scream in the distance broke my stupor.

'Mumma?' Eno cried, rising and scanning the other side of the canyon. 'Mummy? Mummy!'

The villagers stopped in their tracks and scanned the other side of the chasm. The gunfire had ceased. Aside from Eno's cries, the canyon went silent.

'Azua!' our grandfather called out, his words echoing along the rocks. 'Azua, are you okay?' He waited for a moment before directing the others. 'Go!'

The villagers hurriedly changed direction, heading down the canyon path to find a way up the other side.

Our grandfather turned back to us and continued the climb. When he reached us he leant down and picked up a now bawling Eno. With Eno tucked in his arms, he looked down at me for a moment and turned back to the path, leaving me to sit alone.

That night, Eno was lying on his pelt-covered bed, not moving, and not as excitable as usual. I crashed onto my own bed and bashed my pillow.

'Thank you for your father's offer, but we're not going with you,' my grandfather said to our visitor at the tent's entrance. 'Tell him we wish the rest of you luck, but we have our own plan.'

Arleigh stood at the parted doorway, confused. 'Well, can I at least say goodbye to Eno... to Sacet?'

My grandfather shook his head. 'We'll say our goodbyes when we part ways in the morning.'

Arleigh hesitated, but nodded, and gave a half-wave to Eno and I.

My grandfather closed the cloth door and stared at the ground. He took a seat on Eno's trunk. 'Why, Sacet? Why did you have to take Eno up there?'

I clambered to the end of my bed and stared at him pleadingly. 'I didn't! I was the one who found him.'

He sneered and shook his head. 'Why do you keep lying to me?'

I smacked the bed. 'I'm not! Why won't you believe me?'

He sighed. The wind howled, rippling the edges of the tent.

I wiped away a tear. 'Why do we have to leave?'

'The village is packing up. We can't stay this close to necrolisks.'

'But why can't we stay with the others?' I shot back. 'It's safer together.'

'I want Mummy and Daddy to come, too,' Eno cried out, breaking his silence. He shot up from his bed and punched his sheets, mimicking me.

Our grandfather closed his eyes and then tried his best to compose himself before looking back at Eno. 'Your mum and dad have gone far away.'

'Don't lie to him,' I said. 'You are the king of lies.'

He stood up from the trunk. 'Sacet, you can't talk to me that way. I'm your grandfather.'

'No, you're not!' I yelled back, throwing myself face-first into my pillow behind me. Tears formed in my eyes and dampened the fabric upon my cheek.

He went quiet. 'What do you remember? Where you came from? What you are?'

'Everything,' I muffled through my pillow.

I could hear Eno get out of his bed and amble over to me. He prodded me in the side. 'Hey, Sassy? Where's Mummy?'

I sat up, tears now flowing freely, and brought Eno onto my bed to hug him. 'They're dead, Eno. They're dead and they're never coming back.' I bawled and held Eno tight.

The toddler wore a far more baffled look than before. 'Ne – ver?'

I shook my head, flinging tears about. 'I heard what you said today. Why did you say those things? I would never hurt Eno! I love him.'

He raised an eyebrow and smirked. 'That was just... you must have misheard.'

'No more lies!' I shouted back. 'You think I'm a weapon.'

'Yeah!' Eno agreed, although not sure to what. 'Bring Mummy back!'

Our grandfather leant over and picked up Eno, then sat back down on the trunk with my brother on his knee. He gave a warm smile, as if defeated. 'You're absolutely right, Sacet. The truth is you *are* a weapon. I will train you to be the deadliest warrior this world has ever seen.'

He lowered his head closer to me. 'But there is one lie I want you to keep and never forget.' He gestured down at his grandson. 'You are his big sister. He is your brother. And we are a family.'

Two: A Bitter Wind

Six cycles later
Bound for the ruins of Teersau

I smashed my closed fists down onto Eno's high guard like a hammer. His incorrect blocking technique started to give way. Every time I hit, he shifted back in the sand closer to the river.

I was too strong for him. My sixteen cycles compared to his ten made a big difference to our sparring; while he had hardly any muscle-tone, I was the strongest I had ever been.

'Keep that guard up, Eno!' Aberym shouted with a cracked voice. 'Fight back, come on!'

Eno's grandfather stood farther up the riverbank, getting angrier at my success and his grandson's lack of progress. He never tried to inspire confidence in me, only his *real* grandchild.

Eno lowered his arms and groaned in pain, so I backed away.

I mirrored his stance and raised my arms as if sparring an invisible opponent. 'Try to angle them. Like this, see?'

His face twisted. 'I'm doing it like that. You're hitting me too hard!'

'Both of you stop!' Aberym called as he trudged down the bank. His long, airy robes dragged a path through the sand.

8

He glanced at both ends of the river-canyon, as well as the cliffs above, probably to make sure no one was watching us. Then he gently patted Eno's shoulder. 'Go refill your bottle and take a swim.'

Eno exhaled and loosened his posture. He leant down to pick up his leather-covered canteen out of the sand, before traipsing down the embankment.

Now that Eno was out of earshot, Aberym shot a loathsome look at me. 'This is your fault. You lack control... restraint.'

I folded my arms and furrowed my brow. 'I'm sparring with him like you sparred against me when I was his age. He won't learn anything if I don't attack with intent. *You* taught me that.'

He gritted his teeth. 'If I say you're going too hard on him, then that's exactly what you're doing!'

I shook my head, rolled my eyes, and smirked, before following in Eno's tracks.

'And where do you think you're going?' he asked, and I stopped mid-stride. 'I didn't say you were finished.'

I glanced over my shoulder and gestured to the water where Eno had now jubilantly submerged himself. 'Can't I get a drink first?'

'No,' he replied, approaching me from behind. 'You're training isn't over. Close your eyes.'

I sighed loudly. 'Not this again, you know I can't open portals anymore.'

'Close them!'

I complied, standing in place. Aberym drew closer. The wind whistled along the canyon walls, and Eno splashed in the water behind me.

'I want you to remember what happened to Eno's parents,' Aberym began.

I peeked at him and sneered. 'They were my parents, too.'

'Enough!' He glanced back at Eno and made sure he wasn't paying attention before continuing, 'I want you to picture them in your mind. Where they died. *How...* they died.'

My lips trembled. 'This is a waste of time.'

'Hold out your hands,' he said. I shook my head. After a brief pause, he latched onto my wrist and yanked it up higher. 'You could have saved them if you had opened a portal.'

I shook my head. 'No, they ran off before I...'

Aberym began to slowly encircle me. 'You knew how to make portals by then, you must have made at least five that day alone. But you froze in the moment it mattered most.'

'You can't put this on me,' I replied.

'Strain your wrists. Open a portal, now!'

I stood motionless and strained, but nothing came. I couldn't even remember what it felt like to open a portal. 'I can't do it.' A kick to the back of my knee forced me to kneel in the sand.

'The necrolisks are coming,' he said in my ear. 'Get up and save them!'

I had enough. I shot up, opened my eyes, and gave a scathing glare. A single tear rolled down my cheek. I quickly wiped it away.

I brushed past him, knocking his shoulder, before stomping back up the embankment and into the cave where we were keeping our gear.

'You can't walk away every time you fail,' Aberym called out, his words echoing through the canyon. 'If you do, your failures will follow you to the ends of this world.'

'Are you awake, Sas?' I heard a faint whisper say.

I rolled on our fur rug to face Eno, who was sitting up. The midnight blue sky outlined his silhouette. The cave's mouth sheltered us.

I looked over to Aberym to make sure he was still asleep. He wasn't snoring, but his eyes were closed.

I sat up too, and watched the dark river outside the cave. 'What's the matter?' I whispered back. 'Can't sleep again? Should we move our rug outside?'

Eno focused into the dark cave. He had always hated confined spaces ever since he was young, hence why we weren't camped deeper in. He shook his head. 'No, it's not that. I don't think Grandpa wanted to make you feel bad today. Whatever he said, I'm sure he's just... trying to help.'

Help? All these cycles, Aberym had downright resented me for losing my abilities. But I didn't want to make that Eno's problem.

'Don't worry about it, okay? It's going to be over soon. When we reach the forest, he'll see how great everything is there, and... maybe we can just...'

Eno shrugged. 'Live a normal life?'

I smiled back and nodded. 'Yeah, a normal life.'

He yawned and laid back onto the rug. 'I'd... like that.' He quickly drifted off again.

I leant over and draped his sheet over him again.

Now awake and reminded of my woes, my mind continued to loop through my doubts and guilt. The dark river's flow seemed to slow.

Outside the Teersau ruins

'We've made it, look,' Aberym said the next afternoon, pointing to the hazy vision on the bright horizon. 'The ruins of Teersau. We have completed our great pilgrimage.'

I plodded up the next dune, pulling Eno up it by the hand. The ruins were flanked on all sides by craggy, dry hills. There was no green to be seen anywhere.

'So that's the promised land? Another endless stretch of desert? Where's the lush trees, the wide rivers and lakes, and the "bountiful wildlife to feast on" you told us about?'

He shook his head. 'The city is on the border of this land. We're in Metus now, as promised. Beyond the hills is the *final* stretch, and then... a great forest, with a network of many rivers and lakes.'

I rolled my eyes. 'How far is it?'

'The next river is two days away.'

Eno moaned. 'I don't have enough in my canteen for that!'

Aberym pointed up at the sky. 'Right there, another L line, see? We're on the right track.'

In the distance was a line of white in the otherwise blue sky. It had a distinct curve about it. Seeing one was considered good luck, although I never understood why. Like a few others I had seen in my lifetime, it hung there, motionless, like a tear in the sky.

Aberym chuckled. 'If your sister could open portals, we could make the trip by nightfall.'

I ignored him as I strode down the next dune. 'And let me guess,' I called back, 'when we get to this paradise, we're going to spend all our time searching for more settlements, right?' I stopped and looked between them.

Aberym stopped too. 'Sacet, your power, when you finally get it working again, will save this world.'

I exhaled. '*Uh-huh*, I thought you'd say that.'

Eno walked past him, avoiding eye contact. When he reached me, we both continued down the dune, focusing on where we stepped.

'Kids,' Aberym called, and we stopped once more. 'When we find a good place to rest, a settlement with food, water and shade, how about we stay longer than usual? You both deserve a rest.'

Eno rolled his eyes. 'Longer than usual, so what... two days instead of one?'

Aberym attempted a smile. 'How about a week?'

I nodded slowly. 'Okay, you promise?'

'I promise,' he replied as he reached us.

Eno looked positively ecstatic. 'Maybe there'll be other kids?' He smiled at me. 'Other kids!'

I smiled back. 'Maybe some my age for once, too.'

Eno wore a mischievous smirk. 'Yeah, I bet you're hoping for all of them to be boys, huh?'

'Shut it!' I tried snatching at him but he ran down the dune ahead of me.

'Well,' Aberym began, pointing to the ruins in the distance, 'let's get there first.'

Eno led our trio with a spring in his step, reinvigorated by the potential of other kids to meet. Aberym and I trailed behind. When our eyes met, I didn't feel my usual hate for him. Was he capable of inspiring me after all?

Three: Descent

In the ruins

The ancient city around us was enormous, but every building had deteriorated from age, leaving only hollow husks ready to collapse. Far more surreal was the lack of sound, light, and the living. The dilapidated structures would have been impressive to see before they were destroyed at the beginning of the Great Gender War.

I chose a spot out in the open, away from crumbled stones, then rolled out my fur blanket, ready for another night under the stars. Aberym decided against a campfire, given our location, something I actually agreed with him on.

Eno dropped his backpack beside me. 'This is your bag, where's mine?'

'No,' I replied, pushing him away. 'That is yours, it has a hole in it, remember?'

'Kids,' Aberym whispered, before shushing us. 'Stay quiet around here. We might not be the only visitors in this place.'

'Other pilgrims like us?' Eno whispered back.

'Necrolisks,' I answered, and Eno's eyes widened in shock.

Aberym sat on a fallen, crumbling column and pulled out the map from his bag. 'We'll be fine if we don't give them a reason to leave their nest and come to the surface. Sacet, sit with me.'

I rolled my eyes as I wandered over. 'More revision? What's the point in remembering the settlements if I can't open portals anymore?'

'Just sit.'

I groaned and plonked down next to him. He unfurled the map and pointed at an unlabelled location in the Unclaimed Wastes.

'Fort Promise,' I answered with a drawl for the thousandth time. Anticipating his next question, I went on to describe the location. 'There's a giant stone statute of their chieftain in the village's centre, and a fountain below filled with flowing spring water.'

Time passed; the sun was setting. Eno stared at the evening stars, probably coming up with stories for them. Meanwhile, Aberym and I were still at it.

He pointed at yet another settlement. 'And tell me what you remember from–' He stopped mid-sentence, for all three of us could hear an odd, whining echo throughout the ruins. It grew louder, coming closer.

An aircraft emerged from the distant rooftops, equipped with bright, swivelling searchlights. It was flying low, and as it approached our courtyard, it slowed and descended. A ramp was already winding down on its rear. We had been spotted.

'Run!' Aberym yelled over the wailing engines.

I snatched up the backpack at my feet, not bothering to pick up anything else, and bolted into the nearest structure with the others. The entrance led to an underground tunnel, which extended into the darkness.

My sweaty hands grasped at the rough stone passage walls as I twisted and weaved around the corners so as to not lose momentum. The ceiling above thundered and shook as a rain of laserfire fizzled through the stone.

Aberym howled from behind, causing Eno and I to stop.

'What is it?' I said as we turned back, my words echoing down the long, narrow passageway. 'Come on!'

He stood, gently swaying from side to side as he stared at Eno. His hand was on his stomach partially covering a growing stain of blood. The old man leant forward and knelt upon the grimy cobblestones. We could see the laser's entry wound, a hole larger than my fist through his clothes.

Eno clenched both his teeth and fists. 'Come on, Grandpa!' He pulled on my arms. 'Quick, portal us all out!'

I shook my head. 'I can't, you *know* I can't!'

'Save him... get out of here!' Aberym implored between choked breaths. He locked onto my eyes. 'You know... what you have to do.'

Our grandfather's coherence was fading fast. A slight reassuring grin grew upon his face, but it was quickly replaced by a pained expression.

Amassing footsteps resonated from beyond the thin veil of dust the chase had stirred.

'I'll slow them down,' our grandfather said. 'Go!'

With great difficulty he searched his belt underneath his tattered robes. He pulled out his last grenade and gave us a nod.

'Grandpa!' Eno screeched.

But he had already pressed down on the grenade's switch. The sound of footsteps rang louder.

I suddenly felt lost. My whole life, I had wanted to be free of the man, but not like this.

'Grandpa, we... we need you...'

'Go! Now!'

I broke out of my transfixion, pulled on Eno's robes, and turned to face the dim corridor ahead. My legs wobbled at first, but I forced myself forward with Eno in tow. We heard our grandfather's final battle cry.

As we ran around the nearest corner, an ear-deafening explosion shook the ground inside the tunnels. Stones and clumps of dirt broke free from the walls. We peeked around the corner to see. The whole chamber was filled with dust. Eno began to weep, and I covered my silent, horrified scream with my hand.

Several figures waded through the dust. Each was clad in the infamous silver armour of the female dominion, with transparent helmets and large rifles. The women saw us and gave chase again.

My eyes widened, and I ripped on Eno's wrist to make him follow. We sprinted into the dark, foreboding labyrinth of passages, with no clue as to where we were going.

More gunshots. The projectiles missed us and ricocheted off the walls. Strange, it wasn't laserfire this time? Maybe darts? They wanted us alive.

Eno pulled on my arm. 'Stop, Sacet!'

I hadn't noticed it in the dark, but we stopped just short of a large hole in the corridor's floor. There was a trickle of water below. We peered down through the gaping black maw and saw a large murky cesspool at the bottom. An ancient sewer system. The putrid black water below us bubbled.

My body was covered in sweat and my heart raced. This was our only escape.

'We have to jump,' I said.

'It's too dark,' he said, backing away. Tears streamed down his cheeks.

We had hesitated at the rim of the hole for too long. The first soldier had rounded the corner with her weapon raised.

'S-stop!' she said. I could see her face clear as day. Her bottom lip trembled as she nervously stepped forward.

I grabbed Eno with both arms and dove in. We leapt just as the rest of the soldiers caught up.

As we fell, I threw my arms across my face and took what I thought would be my last breath of fresh air. We crashed into the cold water, and it felt like falling head-first through a glass window. The impact took my breath away.

I thrashed my limbs to face upright. I latched onto Eno's collar before kicking to the surface.

We both gasped for air and looked up at the tunnel. The only light that illuminated this dark cavern streamed in from above. It was much brighter up there by comparison. A soldier approached the edge and peered down into the abyss.

There was another tunnel entrance on the far side of the chamber, and so with Eno's robes still in my grasp, I began to swim towards it. The smell down here was revolting; it was the smell of decay and mould. As we paddled, my feet touched the floor of the pool, and we waded through the shallows.

Our pursuers were assembled on the rim of the hole, watching us make our escape. Their faint voices echoed into the lower chambers. I couldn't make out what they were saying, but I knew what their discussion was about. Like me, they knew what was down here. But they weren't going to jump.

Eno and I trudged ashore. The air was humid and reeked of death, but we both panted deeply anyway. Adrenaline coursed through me.

I rummaged through my backpack, hoping to find my torch.

'Ahh! This is your bag, see?' I said, opening it and showing him the hole.

Eno was still catching his breath. 'Then where's... yours?'

'You left it up there, didn't you?'

'Me? It was your bag.'

Splash!

Our attention whipped back to the bog. Water spouted in all directions from another impact. I started to panic, my chest thumped once more.

I gestured towards the tunnel. 'Come on!'

As we dashed down the passageway, a bright light shone from the water. It illuminated the path and cast our frantic silhouettes on the broken passageway stones. The tunnel ahead was long and empty. I could almost sense the woman training her weapon upon us.

Click!

We didn't stop running. Had her weapon jammed? No time to speculate.

'Come back!' she yelled instead. She kept the light trained on us. 'Don't go that way!'

But it was too late. We had already rounded the corner and were out of her sight. The soldier sounded young, perhaps close to my age.

I gripped Eno's hand tightly. He was shivering. I paid careful attention as I pulled him through the pitch-black tunnel. I dared not run at full speed as I didn't know what we might crash into in the darkness.

Our pursuer closed in, her light revealing our path again. Holding onto Eno with one hand, I put the other out on the wall to feel my way around. The muck oozed through my fingers. The overpowering stench had grown worse as it wafted in our direction, causing me to retch.

Eno was slowing down. 'I'm scared.'

'I know, I am too,' I replied. 'But I'm not going to let them get to you, okay?'

'It's getting too small in here. I don't want to die. Can't we just surrender?'

I didn't want to think about what they might do to Eno, being a male.

I could barely see him anymore, but I could hear him sobbing, and I could feel his wrist shaking in my hand. This was the worst place a claustrophobe like him could be right now, but we didn't really have a choice.

The light on the walls in front of us flickered and grew brighter. As we passed each corner, the soldier's light guided us clearer than before.

We reached the end of the corridor and entered a cave, its floor covered in bones and mucus. A small shaft of light came in from the cracks in the cavern's ceiling. On the far side of the cavern there was another stone tunnel, but it was much higher than I could reach. We would need to climb to get to safety.

There were small tremors beneath our feet. Eno and I sprinted straight for the wall, each step of our feet crunching the bones of long-dead victims. My clammy hands tried to grab onto the rocks but they were too slippery.

A soldier came out of the stone tunnel behind us and stopped. 'Raise your hands, slowly! I'm going to get you out of here, but you have to trust me.' It was the same hesitant girl from earlier.

It didn't bode well for her if she was trying to capture us this way. I was right earlier; her weapon was malfunctioning. I stepped in front of my brother.

'Sas, you have to teleport us,' Eno whispered as he huddled against the wall.

'I can't!' I snapped back. I looked past the girl to the only exit. The other soldiers hadn't caught up yet.

The shudders of the cave became more obvious. The soldier spun around and gasped as they noticed the bones. 'Come on, quickly!'

One of the monsters erupted from beneath the ground between us. It raised its pincer-like claws into the air. Its shell shook and shivered, as if giddy with the impending bloodshed. Its head dipped towards me. Memories of my last necrolisk encounter flooded back. I couldn't move.

'Get us out of here!' Eno yelled, pushing me in the side. 'You can do it, I know you can!'

We couldn't die like this. I looked up at the tunnel above again.

A scream, followed by a burst of laserfire from the soldier's weapon caused the hideous creature to squeal and turn away from us. Each shot cast a shadow of its curved, segmented torso and spiny legs onto the cavern walls. The shadow's legs skittered up and down as the creature rotated to face her.

A lucky shot to the creature's head downed it for good. She backed away to the where she had entered, but another necrolisk burst from the ground, spraying flecks of dirt everywhere and cutting off her retreat.

I had no choice now; I had to create a portal to safety. I closed my eyes and weaved my fingers in circular motions. The flux of stale air changed around us. I focused both on the collapsed tunnel above and on a point a few steps in front of us.

The soldier screamed again. A pack of the towering creatures congregated around her. The cave trembled as more of them surged out of the hive tunnels nearby. The nearest beast swiped at her, but she narrowly avoided it.

I was ready. The portal opened with an otherworldly hum; a small circle no wider than my body appeared beside us. The wall behind it was obscured, replaced with a view of the collapsed tunnel. All we needed to do now was jump through the hole and we would be teleported up to the tunnel.

The soldier fiddled with some of the switches on her weapon and fired. Instead of more darts, flames burst forth, wreathing the necrolisks and lighting the chamber with intense orange. But the fire only delayed them. She was done for.

'Help me!' she begged as the creatures corralled her towards a wall. 'Please!'

I thrust Eno forward through the floating circle. He tripped into it and landed on the solid ground on the other side. I followed him, jumping through the portal, gripping onto its rim briefly as I landed in the tunnel.

Now that we were safe from the necrolisks, I closed the portal by clenching my fingers back together. We were standing precariously on the broken tunnel's ledge, which was now far above the necrolisks. The doomed soldier's options were waning.

This wasn't right, where was her backup? Why did she sound like she was trying to help us earlier?

One of the largest creatures struck at her with its gigantic claw. The strike shattered off a piece of her chest armour and sent her flying. Her body crashed against the wall with a sickening crack and she fell to the dirt. Her weapon rolled out of her hands onto the now bloodstained cavern floor.

She was still alive. I could save her with another portal if I wanted to. Wait... why? She and her kind were my enemy. I wasn't a soldier like her, not anymore. Her people hunted, killed and enslaved the nomads.

'Sacet?' Eno said, looking up at me, eyes wide. 'What are you thinking?'

I couldn't take my eyes off the helpless girl. What if it was *me* down there? Why couldn't I just walk away from this? It was as if the logical part of my mind had been switched off.

I made my decision. Now that my powers had returned, I felt invigorated. I focused again and twirled my fingers in circles. The air around us whipped through the dark passageway. The necrolisks were gathered around the soldier's lifeless body and raising their claws into the air for the killing blow.

A portal appeared above me and another below the soldier's body. I stared upwards at the circle and braced my arms out in front. The soldier fell through and into my arms. The sharp necrolisk claws snapped and slashed their way into the hole, but they withdrew them as the portal shrank and disappeared.

Four: A Rude Awakening

I paced from one side of the chamber to the other. We had thankfully wound our way up to the surface again and were hiding in one of the ruinous buildings. The soldier was still unconscious, sitting propped up against the cobbled, moss-covered wall. Other than the wind, no sound came from the ruined home's entrance.

We would be much safer now that we were above ground and among the city's ruins. There was nothing up here but ancient buildings and old, undisturbed corpses. They were either bandits or other nomads that had taken the pilgrimage through here like us. They must have been here long before the necrolisks nested, otherwise they would have been picked clean.

Eno was sitting and staring at the floor, close to tears. 'I can't believe he's gone.' He wiped his cheeks and shook his head. 'He... he would want me to be strong. He always said that if we wallowed in sadness...'

I stopped pacing. 'That we'd be lost to the world,' I added. I'm sure he felt the same as me and wanted to burst into tears, but now he was trying to be tougher than usual.

He stood and approached. 'That was the first portal you've made since...'

'I know,' I said. 'I know.'

I looked back at our captive. What was I thinking? More soldiers were going to pursue us now. I didn't even know why I had rescued her; was it because of guilt? I should have just left her to fend for herself. We didn't owe her anything.

'What you did was really nice, Sas,' Eno said as he knelt next to the unconscious soldier and studied her. 'But what if *she* was the one who shot him?'

Eno had matured so fast. I still had memories of changing his clothes for him, and yet here he was, debating whether or not we should murder this girl.

Deep down it felt like my heart was twisting in place. I wanted to cry, but I needed to stay strong for him. I wanted to hurt this girl, to make her pay. But I also wanted to tell my brother about my childhood memories and that this girl was just like me. He'd probably hate me if he knew who I really was.

I knelt beside him. 'We're not killing her... but if we leave her, she probably won't live long without us. I don't know what to do with her.'

'I don't know either,' he said, looking down at the soldier's damaged armour we had removed. He bent down and picked up her leggings. 'This stuff looks a bit small for you.'

'We didn't take them off so I could wear them. Remember what Grandpa said about their tech? Sometimes they put tracking devices in them. Help me throw it all away.'

Eno approached an open window and pelted the leggings towards it. They hit the window's side and dropped back in the room.

'Come on, be serious,' I said with a furrowed brow. 'This isn't a game.'

'I know that!' he yelled, bending down and picking them up again.

I watched him throw the leggings out properly. The armour could be heard tumbling and smacking into the open sewer tunnel outside, back down into the depths. He turned around and stomped back past me, giving me a hurt look. He picked up more pieces, grabbing more than he could realistically carry in one trip.

'I'm sorry for yelling,' I said as I leant down and picked up the soldier's helmet.

I examined it in both hands. Its transparent faceplate was made of a sturdy plastic, smeared with blood. The whole suit seemed to be made of the same plastic, and its silver colour glistened in the light pouring in through the window.

I walked to the window and hurled the helmet as far as I could, letting out a sigh of relief. That was the last of it. Good. With any luck, they would look for us down there instead.

The soldier had a slash wound along her ribs. The necrolisk had cut right through her armour and white undersuit. Strangely, her wound didn't seem that bad, just a dark bruise.

A moan, followed by a whimper, suggested that our new prisoner was awakening. What would I even say to her? Sorry, but you're coming with us now?

The girl was petite. She had much paler skin than my brother and I. Like all her kind, she had probably spent most of her life sheltered in a big steel city, so it was no wonder we were far more tanned. Her shoulder-length auburn hair was longer than my neck-length dark brown locks. I was clearly stronger and taller than she was.

She had two bright blue streaks in her fringe, one hanging on each side of her face. These streaks were a sign of the Female Dominion Military and I think it was for rank. Not that it mattered out here anyway; she could have been their leader for all I cared.

She looked about my age, maybe a bit younger. I wondered if she had once been a child soldier, like I was.

The girl's hazel eyes fluttered open, widening as she realised where she was. Her arms squirmed around as she felt for her surroundings, but were restrained by the cord I had tied around her wrists.

'Our prisoner is awake,' Eno said, rushing back over to her.

'Stay away from her,' I warned as I raised my pocket knife. 'She could still be dangerous.'

'I know that already,' Eno snapped, as he stopped in place and looked back at me with his arms folded.

Ignoring my brother, I walked in closer and gestured the knife towards her. 'Don't try anything... or I *will* use this.'

She ceased to struggle and locked her shaking eyes with me. 'Alright, I'm complying. There's... no need for that.' She shifted her body weight forward so she could stand up.

'You shouldn't get up. You took a pretty nasty... uh,' Eno said as the girl was able to stand up without trouble. 'Oh... I guess... I guess not. You seem fine now.'

Her eyes searched around the chamber. 'What have you done with my armour?'

I glanced at the window behind us and then back at her. 'I threw it down there.'

'I did, too,' Eno said, folding his arms again and eyeing her with a smug expression. 'Now you're easy to stab.'

'My weapon as well?' she asked with raised eyebrows.

'Gone,' I replied. 'Your friends won't find you if that's what you're thinking.'

'What? Then what exactly are you planning on doing with me?' she said with a grimace.

I sneered. 'I suppose *thanking* us for saving your life is out of the question.'

She looked down at her feet, as if embarrassed. 'I... uh... you? How? Why would you save me?'

'I was thinking we could use you as a hostage,' I said before a look of repulsion spread over her face. 'If our enemies came too close, I could threaten to kill you,' I added as I crossed my arms defensively like my brother.

'That makes perfect sense. You nomads are all the same,' she said as she twisted her arms, trying to break free. 'You can forget about a heartfelt thank you, especially since it was you who led me into that nest in the first place.'

I strode up to her and got in her face. 'So what should we have done instead? Turned around and asked you nicely to stop? You were the ones chasing us, remember?'

'I was trying to *save* you.'

'We didn't ask to be saved, least of all by you.'

She shook her head in disbelief. 'Well, none of this matters anyway.' She glanced at the doorway as if expecting to see someone. 'My friends are looking for me right now and they will get the drop on you when you least suspect it.'

I gritted my teeth. 'So you're saying we should just kill you instead?'

'Enough,' Eno interrupted. 'There are necrolisks still around. Are we keeping her or not?'

I locked eyes with him. 'You're right,' I said, sighing. 'You'll draw too much attention if you wear that undersuit and nothing else.' I picked up an old robe from the dusty floor and threw it at our prisoner's feet. 'Put this on.'

She eyed me with contempt. 'And if I refuse?'

I gripped my knife tighter. 'Then you die here. Your friends *might* find you, but it'll be too late by then. Those necrolisks will eventually find us in their territory if we stay. You want to live? Then we need to get out of this city and find somewhere safe in the desert before dark. We need food and water, especially water.'

She bit her lip, mulling over the facts. With her hands still bound, she picked up the shabby clothing and managed to drape it over herself. Her conspicuous Dominion clothing covered, she almost looked like one of us, if it hadn't been for the blue streaks in her fringe.

'Alright, let's go,' I said as I gestured towards the door with my knife.

She hesitated, but slowly made her way to the exit. '*Eck*! It's all mouldy,' she said, breaking her tough façade as she inspected the disgusting garment. 'Is this yours?'

'No. Ask Eno, he found it,' I replied.

'It's his,' he said, pointing towards one of the desiccated corpses in the corner of the chamber.

The girl's eyes widened and she squealed. Was this really what passed for a Female Dominion soldier?

We must have been close to escaping the city. The hot desert wind blew through the stone passage. With my knife pointed towards our captive, I directed her to head left at the next fork.

'We must be getting close now,' I said as the passageway guided us into another large, ruined chamber.

Eno ran off ahead down a different passage and out of sight, before running back and stopping in front of us. 'Nope, not that one,' he said, darting away again.

'Eno, stop running off,' I called. 'There might still be necrolisks around, remember?'

He stopped in his tracks, before rushing back over and huddling by my side.

'So... in the sewer back there, why did you *really* jump in after us?' I asked the soldier as we walked down the corridor. 'I doubt it was because you wanted to rescue us.'

'I didn't lie about that,' she snapped back. 'But it... it is our job to track down you people. And we figured you had something to hide. Do you both have special powers? Are you acolytes? That old man killed himself to stop us getting to you. That was insan–'

I slammed her against the wall. 'Do *NOT* speak about him like you know anything!'

'Whoa, easy...' she said, looking down at the knife pressed against her neck. The blade trembled in my hands.

Up until today, I'd hated no one more than Aberym. But now he was gone, I felt a strange sense of loyalty.

Eno shoved her in the side. 'He was protecting us because we're his family, something you monsters don't get.'

I lowered the knife, turned to the side and tried to compose myself again. 'You have no right.'

She huffed and straightened her robes. 'We only fired on you because we thought you were a bandit group we've been tracking. When we saw you running we switched tactics so we could take all of you alive. If it's any consolation, he almost killed a couple of my friends. How about that?'

'Almost isn't good enough,' Eno replied.

'Look, I'm sorry, okay?' she said with a shrug. 'I didn't want that. I'm guessing he was important to you?'

'He was our gr–grandfather,' I stammered as I cried. 'We've travelled everywhere together. He was all we had left.'

Eno's jaw quivered as he teared up.

I exchanged a look with Eno and waved my hand at her dismissively. 'We don't buy your apology.'

Eno wiped his tears. 'Since when does a soldier like you care about what happens to us in the desert?'

The look in her eyes became furtive. 'It's not my fault if I've never really... spoken to a nomad before. We were told you were all rapists and crazed-mutants... and cannibals.'

Eno stared at her with wide, tear-soaked eyes. 'Let's eat her and prove them right.'

The soldier reeled back, believing him at first. Why was she acting this way all of a sudden? Empathising with us now that she was our prisoner? She'd probably strike when our guard was down.

'That's not funny,' she said, continuing to avoid eye contact. 'And when I said I was sorry, I meant it.'

I wiped my eyes with my sleeve. I was sick of this conversation. I gestured for Eno to join me as I walked towards the other end of the corridor. 'Let's go.'

We left her behind. If she wanted to run, now was a good time.

'Do you have a name?' I called back. 'Or are you just a number to them?'

She nervously looked around at the nearby corridors. 'Uhhh.. it's Tau.'

Eno cleared his eyes, too. 'Tau? That's a stupid name.'

I stopped and glanced over my shoulder. 'I'm Sacet. This is my brother, Eno.'

There was a silence as she continued to weigh up her options.

'We aren't going to eat you,' I said, rolling my eyes.

She gave a long, drawn-out sigh and marched after us.

'Unless we have to,' Eno teased after she caught up.

At the end of the corridor there was an archway leading outside into the desert. A hot, wavy haze emanated from the yellow sand outside. We'd finally found our way out of this wretched place. Our footsteps echoed as we walked through the archway. The glare blinded me for a moment, but my eyes adjusted and the outline of the sand dunes on the horizon became clear.

Now that my portals had returned to me, travelling over the desert would be much easier. How many could I create in a day? I concentrated on the distant sand dunes. I stopped, weaved my fingers in circles, closed my eyes. A zephyr of air swirled underneath my robes.

'Do it, Sas,' Eno said as encouragement, but it sounded more like impatience.

'What are you doing?' Tau asked.

A large ellipse appeared, taller than all of us and wide enough for us to pass through. The portal's destination, the distant dunes, was visible through the window. Its circular edges appeared as a smooth haze.

I stepped through the gate and looked back at Tau's stunned expression. 'Coming?'

'I knew it.'

Five: The Helpless Girl

That night I tried adjusting my sleeping position, but it was no use, these rocks were too uncomfortable. Eno was already fast asleep beside me, and thankfully he was warm enough.

In addition to the sound of running water from the nearby river, I also had Tau's crying to contend with. I gripped my knife, stood, and wrapped the blanket tight around Eno.

Tau sat against a pillar of rock, tied up around it. Other than the robes we had found for her, she didn't have anything else to keep her warm. She had been sobbing quietly, perhaps trying not to wake us.

When she noticed me walking over she stopped and focused on the dark waters. Her newfound silence was betrayed by moonlit tears.

I stopped in front of her and concealed the knife in my robes. 'I'm trying to sleep. What's the matter now?' I whispered, careful not to wake Eno.

She kept staring out at the water. 'Nothing,' she whispered back.

I started back towards my uncomfortable bed.

'Wait,' she said, now looking into my eyes. 'The real reason I jumped was...'

I shrugged. 'What?'

'I jumped because... I had something to prove. To myself, and to my friends. The others weren't going to...'

Was she trying to get on my good side again? 'Why didn't the others help?'

'Because... we weren't supposed to go down into the tunnels. Too much of a risk. That and... most of them don't like me. I'm not a very good soldier.'

I scoffed. 'Well, you hunted us down easily enough.'

She frowned and looked out into the water again. 'Yeah, but I've never made a single kill... or a capture. I had to do it this time.' She shook her head. 'You nomads have always scared me. When I was little, all of my squad sisters were killed by your people. I was all alone and...'

There was a long pause between us, and the cold night air picked up. She shivered. 'Remind me why we can't have a fire again?'

'Air patrols. They always fly over any areas close to fresh water. The fire would draw them here, not just your people but the Male Dominion, too. There's also bandits... and necrolisks.'

She shook her head. 'Alright, alright, I get it. So how do you expect me to sleep, let alone walk through the desert again tomorrow?' she whined, now raising her voice. 'I'm exhausted, I'm freezing, and these rocks are driving into my back!'

Eno stirred and I shot Tau an angry look. 'Keep quiet.'

She followed my gaze. 'Sorry.'

I moved in closer. 'Thanks to you, we lost almost everything in our bags. That blanket is for us and you'll just have to make do.'

She sighed. 'I'm hungry.'

'We all are. We'll go fishing in the morning. Until then, stop complaining.'

'Okay,' she said, looking down at my feet, before lifting her eyes again. 'Why did you save me? I've been going over it in my head, trying to put myself in your position. Dragging me through the desert on the slim chance the Female Dominion catches up with us? I'm just slowing you both down. It doesn't make any sense.'

I smirked. 'I seem to remember you being so sure your friends were going to get "the drop" on me.'

She shrugged. 'Yeah, well, I'm still here, aren't I? So, no more lies. Why did you save me?'

'Hmm, no more lies, huh?' I began, before stopping myself. The real reason I saved her?

She leant forward expectantly. I glanced over at Eno to make sure he was still asleep and then sat down on the raised, fractured bedrock, which was the perfect height.

I gestured over at Eno. 'You have to promise not to tell him, got it?' I whispered.

Her eyebrows raised, intrigued. 'Yes, okay, I promise.'

I sighed and dropped my chin to my chest. 'I used to be in the Female Dominion, like you.'

Tau's eyes blinked rapidly. 'What?'

'It was a long time ago now. I escaped and my family adopted me. They pretended I was really their daughter so that the other nomads wouldn't kill me. But I always knew...'

A smile spread across her face. 'That's... that's *fantastic* news! You can come back home again. Do you remember what city you were from?'

Her question stirred long-dormant memories. I remembered what the bright, silver city looked like, but not its name. And the only person's face that stuck with me after all this time was my trainer's. I remember her being the only kind adult, a mother figure. I hoped she was okay.

I broke away from the fantasy. 'No, but it doesn't matter. I'm never leaving Eno's side. I'm the only family he's got left.'

'But... he isn't your real brother?'

'No, he is. Where I came from means nothing. He is my brother, and I'd do anything to protect him.' I glanced back at Eno again, then back at her. 'I saved you because I saw myself in your position. I couldn't let you die, because if I turned out okay...'

'I'm not a bad person,' Tau said, straightening up against the rock.

I gestured at Eno. 'Well, neither are we. And look at what you've done to our family.' I sighed. 'Look at him, does he look like a cannibal to you?'

Tau shook her head. 'No.'

'If I died, I don't know if he'd survive on his own. And if that happens, I blame you.'

She creased her brow. 'I wasn't the one that killed your grandfather.'

'You may as well have been.'

Tau took a deep breath. 'So where do we go now? What's your plan?'

'We can't stay on the river for too long because everyone else does. So, we continue west.' I stood up and walked over to her. I pulled out my knife, and she panicked.

'You won't survive alone either,' I said. 'If you run, or try to hurt us, I will kill you. I can't guarantee that I'll find food and water for all three of us. You need to pull your weight. In return, I'll one day make sure you get back to your big, safe city, a place where you can forget about what your people *really* do out here. Deal?'

She nodded, and I cut her binds. I waited until she wiped away her tears, then I helped her up and brought her over to Eno. We both lay down next to him, keeping him in the middle. I clenched my knife tightly as I brought the blanket over the three of us.

I could hear the soft swishing of the water in my canteen with each step up the sand dune. It felt light, almost empty. Three days had passed, and the heat rose from all around us. The smell of desert herbs was carried on the stinging wind.

Reaching the top of the ridge, I shielded my eyes from the bright vista. The dry sand in the distance hummed, something the desert did that I'd never gotten used to. There were craggy peaks on the horizon, beyond the vast wasteland before us. There was a hint of green on the cliffs. The great forest was so close.

Eno was keeping up with me, but Tau stumbled and panted from exhaustion. Was this the first time she had traversed the desert without the aid of technology? Her face was bright red, burnt from the sun's harsh rays.

Funny, I wished she had been this feeble when she chased us earlier. Although a well-trained soldier, it was almost laughable how ill-prepared she was for this. That said, we could all use a little water.

Without Aberym, I had no idea where to go next, other than farther west into Metus. Even if I did know, I didn't think I had it in me to follow through on his plan to unite all of the nomadic peoples against the Dominions. Anywhere that had shelter would be fine, a place where we were safe. Perhaps with other good people, but I'd prefer if it was just Eno and I. As for Tau, I still didn't know what to do with her.

'You're *really* slow!' Eno called back.

'We're almost there,' I yelled, hoping to motivate her. 'Ready for another jump?'

A look of relief replaced her fatigued expression, and her pace quickened. 'Can we teleport somewhere with shade this time?' she asked, joining us on top of the ridge. She, too, raised her hand to shelter her eyes from the harsh light. 'Can you make the distance to those mountains?'

'Of course she can,' Eno said.

I looked out to the distant cliffs. 'I have enough energy for a couple more tries, but then it looks like we're walking the rest of the way from there. There's an old forest beyond those hills and more rivers than we would know what to do with.'

'How do you know what's over there?' Tau asked.

I shot an angry look back at her. 'Our grandfather had a map, and we were *trying* to follow it.'

She lowered her brow. 'I said I was sorry!'

I circled my fingers as she spoke. Even though I was tired, I was surprised I was able to conjure this many portals in this amount of time, much more than when I was a kid. Perhaps the stress was just what I needed to get better at this?

As I focused on a point in front of us and one far in the distance, the desert wind picked up and shifted the sands like waves in an ocean. An upright portal opened before us. I looked beside the portal to the green hills, and then back at the portal and saw the same image magnified.

I walked through with Eno, followed by Tau. As I closed the portal, I faced the mountains. We were much closer, but my captive wasn't impressed. She slumped to the ground with an exasperated sigh.

'Break time is it?' I called back.

'Yes... just... give me a chance to rest,' she said, and wiped the sweat off her forehead.

It was just as well. I didn't think I had another portal in me for a while.

Eno gazed at the canteen on my belt. 'I should get more water than her because I'm not complaining, right?'

I eased down into the sand. 'We've only got a little bit left; we need to ration it.'

Eno groaned, collapsed, and rolled onto his back. He stared up at the sky. We sat in silence, listening to desert wind.

'Look!' Eno shouted and pointing into the distant sky. 'More L lines!'

I squinted at the distant skyline and saw two lines crisscrossing each other.

'Grandpa would say that's good luck,' Eno said, smiling at me. 'We're going the right way.'

'Eno, Grandpa wasn't *always* right. L lines are a natural phenomenon, like the wind or... the rain. The sun and moon,' I scoffed.

'Why... are we doing this?' Tau asked.

'What?' Eno replied. 'Travelling? Dying of thirst?'

I glanced at Tau. 'You mean the war?'

Tau closed her eyes and pointed in Eno's general direction. 'No, he got it. As for the war, the men started it almost 600 cycles ago.'

Eno's face screwed up. 'Yeah? Well, *maybe* it's because the women wouldn't stop complaining.'

I could hear a soft buzzing in the distance. I glanced in all directions to find its source.

Tau smirked. 'Or maybe it's because the men are violent, destructive, and stupid?'

Eno sat up again. 'I bet any man can survive in the deserts longer than you can.' He picked up a handful of sand and cast it in her direction.

A dark spot hovered in the distant skyline. An aircraft. Had they already seen us? It was too soon to tell. I didn't have enough energy for another long-distance portal, and it would be foolish to run through the empty wasteland. There was only sand in all directions. I shot up and scouted for something we could hide behind, anything.

Tau noticed my worried expression. 'What is it?' Then she, too, heard the noise and turned towards the aircraft.

'Get down!' I shouted. I ran over and pulled them both behind the dune's ridge.

Tau's stare bounced between me and the craft. Her eyes were wide, and she took quick, shallow breaths. Was she about to run? If she signalled them, it'd be over.

I slowly shook my head. 'Don't.'

She breathed heavily. 'But... it could be my way home?'

'Or it could be the Male Dominion!' I yelled, grabbing her shoulder and forcing her back into the sand. 'Do you know what they'll do to you if you're caught?'

I focused on the horizon. The distant droning was becoming far more distinct. Eno and Tau were now lying on the ground to hide, and so I did the same. Eno grabbed onto my leg tightly.

I started twirling my fingers and mustered up as much strength as I could. The veins in my forehead throbbed. I focused on a point just above all of our heads and another point on the sand.

The two portals opened; the first above us, facing up, and the other on the ground as far away from here as I could make it, facing down. I tried making them as wide as I could by stretching my fingers. This should work. From our side, the portal just showed the sky, but from their point of view, we should be nothing but another patch of sand.

I had opened it just in time for the aircraft to fly over us. Its turbines emitted a high-pitched whirring. As it passed, I examined its sleek frame for the insignia that denoted its faction. An intimidating symbol on its tail was similar to that of a necrolisk's head and claws; it was the Male Dominion.

'You were right, it's them,' Tau confirmed.

The craft abruptly veered left and turned around.

'It's coming back,' I said. 'Down!'

Tau knelt back in the sand.

I shifted the portal above us in the direction of the aircraft with one swift pull, positioning it like a shield. Did they see us? The illusion should've concealed us. I continued to track the aircraft with my portal so that it was always facing them.

The aircraft slowed and the machine let out a sickening hiss. It circled our spot numerous times before landing on the top of the dune above us. The whirring of the turbines slowed, and a mechanical shriek sounded – as if something had been left unoiled. It came from the side of the fuselage.

A long ramp winded down and rested onto the sand. I poked my head to the side of my portal for a better look. Three fully armoured soldiers stepped out the doorway, so I hid again. The men stomped down the ramp.

'Nothing. Honestly, Izuk, this is the last time we put you on scanner duty,' one of the soldiers said in a gravelly voice, muffled by his mask. 'There's nothing here. Get back in the AV!'

'But, sir,' another soldier said. 'I know what I saw. It was bandits!'

I heard the thud of body armour, possibly of someone being punched.

'Get back in the AV. Now!' The other two soldiers walked back up the ramp.

My fingers twitched and my elbow ached. *Hurry up and leave already.*

'Wait,' the leader said, and the footsteps on the ramp halted. I could hear more footsteps in the sand. They were getting closer. 'You were right. There are footprints over here.'

How was I going to get us out of here? This illusion wasn't going to fool them up close. Our grandfather taught me how to fight against unarmed combatants, but this was different. Should I bring the portal down over us to teleport a few dunes over? No, we wouldn't be able to outrun them. I needed to act, and it was now or never.

'What is this thing?'

I threw my hand forward and the portal in front of us flew into the nearest soldier. The sand on the face of the portal smacked into him and flung him over the dune and behind the aircraft. The illusion was broken, and the two remaining men spotted us.

'What the?'

They trained their weapons on us and went to clench their triggers. I wouldn't be able to retrieve the portal in time. This was the end.

Six: Pariah

There was a small pop, a whoosh of air, and then a crack thundered in the distance. In the time it took to blink, one of the soldiers' heads disappeared. A mist of warm blood trickled down over us, the droplets streaming down my cheeks.

The dead man's body collapsed into the sand in front of us and tumbled down the dune. As the body spun down the hill, blood spurted out of the neck, creating a speckled trail that stained the sand dark crimson.

The last soldier gaped at his decapitated comrade and, without hesitation, sprinted back towards the aircraft.

He dove and landed on the ramp. 'No, not me, not me... not me!'

The pilot must have noticed the commotion, for the turbines began to whirr, preparing for take-off. A small gun turret under the nose of the ship sprung to life, and it shifted left and right, seeking a target.

There was a distant thud, followed by another whoosh of air as a projectile smacked into the side of the craft. The rocket exploded on impact, sending debris in all directions. What was left glowed red, flames spewing from every fissure.

A low-pitched creak groaned as the metal frame collapsed and exploded. One of the turbines flung into the air, narrowly whizzing past us. Another loud screech. A massive eruption shot the remaining pieces outwards.

Horrified, I sat in the sand, trying to process it all. I couldn't look away from the decapitated man. My stomach churned. Eno spewed next to me. I tore my attention away from the headless body and observed the still-exploding wreckage.

'Both of you, stay down, okay?' I said.

Cinders and fragments of the ruined aircraft still fell around us. A large plume of smoke drifted upwards and falling ash blackened the scene.

I rose and allowed my gaze to follow the smoke trail left by the devastating projectile. I had found its source.

Approaching from behind the wreckage in the nearby dunes, a group of nomads were running towards us. Were they bandits, here to loot and kill? Would they let Eno and I live? And what would they do when they discovered that Tau was our prisoner? She was still entranced by the carnage in front of us and hadn't noticed the nomads yet.

I lowered myself again. 'Eno, listen to me *very* carefully, nomads are coming. When they see you, raise your hands and let me do the talking. Got it?' He was still stunned, so I grabbed his shoulder and shook him. 'Have you got that?'

He gave the smallest of nods.

Tau's eyes widened. 'Wha–what do I do, Sacet? They'll kill me!'

I adjusted her robes around the collar to conceal her undersuit. 'They cannot know who and what you are. You have to act like one of us.'

Our eyes locked in silence. But then she said, 'My streaks!'

'You're right,' I said, reaching into my bag for my knife. 'They have to go.'

Tau glanced over my shoulder at the approaching strangers. 'Yes, quick!' she said as she knelt down into the sand.

I brought my knife to her forehead, clumped one of the blue streaks together in my hand, sliced it off as close to the hairline as I could, and then started on the other streak. I clenched the cut hair in my palm as Tau rose to her feet and lifted her hood over her head. Where would I dispose of the hair? Should I bury them?

It was too late. Like an apparition, a face emerged and peered through the flames. I scrunched the hairs into my left hand. The man's face was scarred and covered in unkempt, black facial hair. His skin was tanned.

His thick brows were lowered, and when he saw us his frown changed into a wide grin.

He raised his giant rifle. It was camouflaged, had an elongated barrel, and a large scope on its top. The camouflage was consistent with his brown clothing. The man navigated through the wreckage towards us.

Several others followed behind him, spreading around the debris.

'Salvage anything useful!' the man shouted back at them. 'Remember, nothing traceable. Reinforcements are probably already inbound.'

The team of nomads sprang into action; they holstered their weapons and pulled out tools instead. They scavenged the wreck, separating what they could from the burnt and twisted frame. Their leader, satisfied with his instructions, turned his attention back to us.

Eno shot up from the sand and wiped the puke from his mouth. He clenched my right hand with his sticky one, and cowered behind me.

'You three pulled off a convincing job as bait,' he said, continuing to aim at us. 'Now tell me who you are, acolyte. Whose side are you on?'

We all put our hands up.

'Don't shoot!' Eno squealed.

'I – I'm Sacet,' I began, and he raised an eyebrow. I gestured at the others. '... and – and they're –'

'Out with it already, girl!' the man bellowed. 'What are you doing out here? I bet you're FD spies sent to infiltrate us.'

The man positioned his eye closer to the scope as though about to fire. My heart was pounding and I held my breath. I closed my eyes and cringed.

'*Ha*! That look on your faces. Brilliant,' the stranger said before he cackled. His face relaxed with a grin and he lowered his gun. Some of the nomads collecting salvage behind him laughed too. The man pointed at one of the others. 'Rolph, don't you laugh. We all remember how much you cried your first time.'

The rest of the group continued their uproarious laughter, except for the one called Rolph. A few even mimicked what he looked like when he cried.

'*Pwease*,' the man continued to tease. 'I'll do anything... *anything*!'

'So... you're not going to hurt us?' I interrupted, causing the man to turn back.

'We know who you are, Sacet.'

Tau let out a sigh of relief and I managed an appreciative laugh.

'You know us?' I asked. 'How?'

'I was part of your village a long time ago before I decided to make the pilgrimage alone. I used to know your family, too, like little Eno there. I'm surprised you two don't remember me.'

'I'm sorry, but I don't,' I said as he walked over to me with his arms spread wide. 'We thought you were bandits.'

'Us?' he said as he embraced me, pointing towards the others. 'Take advantage of three innocent children travelling alone in the desert? Not on your life. Although I suppose that would defeat the point a little.' He bent to the side and peeked at Eno. 'Besides, I'm sure your bodyguard here would have sprung to your rescue. Right, pal? Eno, last time I saw you, you were still a tiny toddler.'

Eno came out from hiding behind me, but he still gripped tightly to my hand, now as sticky as his.

The man scrutinised Tau up and down, his eyes narrowed and his smile faded.

'Didn't catch your name from your stuttering friend over here. Come here,' he said as he made his way over and embraced her tight, too.

'It's – erm – Tia,' Tau managed with a scrunched face, shrugging him off.

'Tia? Well, Tia, sorry for the scare. It's not my fault that frightening children, and Rolph, comes so naturally to me.'

Confused, Tau gave an awkward smile. '*Ha*, yes. Good one.'

He took a step back. 'How do you fit into this, Tia? Where are you from?'

Tau glanced back at me and was about to respond, but I interrupted. 'We met her in Teersau. She's making the pilgrimage, like us.'

The man's face lit up and he pointed to the green mountains. 'Well, you've made it. Well done! A wise idea travelling together, too. Speaking of which, where's the rest of your village, your family? Your parents, and that old coot, Aberym? I was hoping to swap some stories with him. It's been what, six cycles?'

Eno turned away and kicked the sand.

'Our parents died a long time ago, after you left,' I explained, and his smile changed to a frown again. 'And... our grandfather... the necrolisks in Teersau... he didn't make it.

'Oh, that's terrible. I'm so sorry,' he said, bowing his head in respect. After a long pause, he gave a more reserved smile. 'I've heard some interesting stories about him. I'll tell you a few on our way back, in his honour.'

Eno let go of my hand. 'To where?'

The man turned back to the wreckage. 'Alright, enough faffing about,' he said as he jogged up the dune and cupped his hands around his mouth. 'We're done here. Not enough time for anything else. Grab anything not bolted down, let's head back.'

I led Eno up the dune after him. Maybe things were going to turn out okay after all, so long as they didn't discover Tau's real identity. Tau scanned the empty desert, as if weighing her options again, before following us up the rise.

I caught up to the man. 'So you know our names, but we don't know yours.'

The man turned back to me with another toothy grin. 'My name is too long. How about you just call me Pilgrim? Everyone calls me that.'

'He makes all of us call him that,' one of the women interrupted. 'It's like he thinks he's the only pilgrim here.' She brushed my shoulder. 'Hi, I'm Sabikah. I'll take care of you kids, okay?' She, too, had an enormous rifle stowed on her back. She had long black hair, tanned skin, and a warm smile. Pilgrim grinned even more, if it were possible. 'You can call me anything you like, Sabikah the wise. Sabikah the beautiful. Sabi–'

'Enough!'

The nomads picked up their tools and salvaged materials and slung them over their shoulders. They led us away from the wreckage and back in the direction from which they had come. We scaled up and down several dunes.

'Alright, that's far enough. Tern, scanner,' Pilgrim said.

A man pulled out a strange-looking device and handed it to Pilgrim, who proceeded to flick and poke at some of the controls.

'Scanner?' Tau inquired.

Sabikah turned to face her. 'We need to make sure this stuff isn't being tracked, or we'd lead the Dominion right to our home.'

Upon hearing this, Tau focused on the device and discreetly backed off. The nomads held up the various pieces they had salvaged, and Pilgrim ran the device over them one by one. The scanner made a number of different noises, beeping and clicking as it passed over each piece.

'Sacet, if I may ask, what made you travel so close to the nest anyway?' Pilgrim asked as he continued to scan. It was as if he knew the answer already.

'We didn't,' I lied. 'We went by the safe route, around the outer wall. Something must have made the necrolisks hunt farther out than usual.'

'Hmm, that ain't good if even the necrolisks are becoming more desperate,' Pilgrim said as he finished scanning the last piece of salvage. He raised the device up to his face and squinted the gadget's screen. 'All good, although there's some background noise. Could be that we're still too close to the wreck. Should be fine. Okay, guys, sweep it up.'

Sabikah moved to the back of the group. She threw her hands towards our footprints. The sand churned and sifted until the tracks were erased. She was an acolyte like me. Another man, the one called Tern, sighed, spun around and did the same as his comrade. Two with the same power?

I faced the rocky bluffs I had been eyeing earlier, and then down to Pilgrim by our side.

'Shouldn't be too long. You are going to love it there,' he said.

I glanced back to the other nomads and made sure they weren't looking. 'That's great. We could use a rest,' I said.

I couldn't exactly stop to bury the hair that was still clenched in my left hand, they would have seen me, so I slid it into my bag.

That evening, as we turned into what I hoped would be the last corner of this labyrinthine tunnel, the passageway opened up and revealed a bright cavern. Open skylights allowed in natural light, down onto the simple shacks and sheet metal that made up the nomads' homes.

The shanty settlement must have been here for a long time. There were almost a hundred huts. It was all lit up by torches, evenly spread among the settlement's pathways. It was certainly better than lying on the cold, wet floor of a cave like our usual accommodation.

Tau gasped. 'You hid this whole thing here?'

Eno's jaw had dropped. 'This is... amazing!'

Pilgrim turned back and smiled. 'I knew you'd love it. Welcome to our home.'

The entrance to the town was blocked by a makeshift fence constructed of metal scraps, and the fence was broken up every so often by stalagmites jutting up from the ground. There was a guard patrolling at the top of the main wall – a teenage girl. Another child, not much older than Eno, approached the chain-linked gates to open them for us. The gates scraped along the rocky cave floor as they were drawn back.

I smiled at the boy as we were about to walk through, then stopped in my tracks. His face was horribly disfigured, covered in numerous gruesome scars. A large eyepatch concealed most of the damage.

Eno and I had to deal with the repercussions of this war every day, but seeing what had been done to this child gave me pause. My smile faded and my backpack snagged on the gate. After an awkward tug to release it, I looked back at the boy with an apologetic expression.

Tau noticed him, too, and her amazed expression quickly sank. Once our group was in, the boy closed the gate behind us and resumed his guard duty.

'So, how long were you guys thinking of staying?' Pilgrim asked. 'Because as you can see, we could use all the help we can get around here. That's Teelo – kid lost his mother and an eye to a necrolisk. He's been doing whatever he can to help ever since.'

I glanced back again at the boy, who was now speaking to the girl on the wall. He had something in his hand and was showing it to her, but I couldn't make out what it was.

We continued through the village, reaching the town centre.

'He doesn't have anyone left?' I asked weakly.

Pilgrim shrugged. 'What? Of course he does! You're looking at his new dad. Everyone's family around here... I mean, you know... so long as they aren't trying to kill us.' He turned to Sabikah. 'Isn't that right, sweetie?'

Sabikah smirked. 'You're embarrassing yourself.'

Teelo ran over to us, 'Pilgrim! Guys! Wait up!'

'I told you, Teelo, you can call me Dad, remember? What's gotten you so worked up?'

Teelo pulled up in front of us. 'That girl dropped this, Dad,' he said as he opened his palm and showed a small tuft of blue hair.

How did that get there? I thought I had... no. The rip in my backpack!

Pilgrim walked over to Teelo and plucked the hairs from the boy's hand. He held them up close to his eyes, as if scrutinising their authenticity, then turned to us. His face was now absent of his usual grin... He knew.

'Sacet, Eno and... Tia... it looks like you can't be a part of our family after all.'

There was a rustle of robes as the nomads surrounded us and drew their weapons. One of them came up behind Tau and roughly began to search her. Her hood was wrenched down, revealing her undersuit.

I tugged on Pilgrim's robes. 'Please, she's not a threat, she's our prisoner.'

More villagers exited their dwellings to see what the commotion was about. Soon, a small crowd had formed around us.

Pilgrim shrugged me off and pointed at Tau. 'Take that one to the holding cell until we know what to do with her. And you two, move!' He gestured towards the entrance of the nearest building.

Eno stood close to me again, and we moved without questioning him. I looked back to Tau as she was led away by Sabikah and several others.

Tau glanced over her shoulder as she was led away, eyes bulging and shaking. 'Wait, stop! I'm not one of them anymore, please!'

Pilgrim and the remaining nomads escorted my brother and I towards a large hut. We entered through a curtained doorway, and Tau's wails were drowned out.

'Pilgrim, please. I can explain.'

He pointed into the room and corralled us in. 'Explain to him.'

The room was filled with animal pelts that hung from the walls and carpeted the floor. The walls and ceiling were made from bits of scrap metal crudely welded together. On the far side of the room, an old man slept on a bed covered with more furs. The dank and musky smell was overpowering.

Pilgrim strode ahead and jiggled him awake. 'Elder. Elder Hati? Wake up, this is important.'

Hati awoke with a snort. 'I was sleeping, haven't you any... *urgh*... haven't you any respect for an old man's rest? *Hmm*?'

The old man, decrepit with age, attempted to focus his gaze on us. 'And who might this be?' He struggled to raise a frail arm, pointing a shrivelled finger in our direction.

'This is Sacet, the teleporter I told you about from my old village. Her little brother, Eno, as well. But they have betrayed us.'

'I find that hard to believe,' Hati said. 'Two children as young as they.'

'Elder, they led a Dominion spy into the camp,' Pilgrim continued. 'She's bound to have a tracking device inside of her like the others.'

'What?' I said. 'A tracking device? But – I got rid of her armour. Please! She's *our* prisoner. We'll leave if that's the issue. I promise, I would *kill* her before she could ever tell the Dominion about this place. I swear it!'

The old man cleared his throat. 'Sacet, was it? There's something you're not grasping here. Tracking devices are often implanted inside the body. It doesn't matter if you lead her away. They will know she's been here. You've left a trail for them to follow right to our home.'

The old man's eyes widened. 'Everyone here is in jeopardy. Diyon! Yori! Instruct the others to pack their food and essentials. We need to leave for the cavern lake as soon as we can. Go!'

'Wait!' I interrupted. 'What if she doesn't have a tracking device?'

'We can't take that risk,' Hati replied, raising his hand at the others.

The other two nomads rushed outside and the old man turned his attention back to me. 'As for you two, you're obviously not working for the Dominion, you're just ignorant. In either case, I can't allow the spy to live, knowing what she knows. You, on the other hand, will accompany us to the cavern lake.'

He stared up at Pilgrim, who was still standing by his side. 'Pilgrim, you will need to take the enemy soldier out into the desert as far as you can and execute her.'

Seven: Our People

I wanted to grab Pilgrim and stop him, but instead did nothing as he left the old man's side and hurried out of the tent. I glared at Hati, shocked by his instructions. 'I'm sorry, but you're wrong about her. She isn't a spy.'

Hati sat up in bed and flung his legs over the edge. 'And what makes you so sure?' His whole body trembled as he stood. He took a couple of shaky steps and pointed his gnarled, yellow fingernail at me again. 'She's our enemy, she'd say anything to get back to her people again.'

I couldn't fault Hati's logic, but Tau was different. He didn't know her like we did. Eno and I hung our heads.

Hati looked between us, his sternness quickly turning to pity. 'I need to pack,' he said, turning to a trunk of his belongings. 'Either help me or get out and assist the others.' He shook his head and gestured to the tent's entrance. 'If you're looking for forgiveness, we don't have time. Go.'

We walked out in silence and put the old man behind us. I brought my hand to my forehead as I led Eno along the stony walkway, back to the centre of the settlement.

My whole body tensed and my hands shook. They couldn't do this to her. Growing up, nomads that'd learnt my identity had always treated me with contempt, even wanting me dead, so I knew exactly how Tau must feel right now. It wasn't right.

Eno jogged to keep up. 'What do we do now?'

'We're not going with them. We're leaving.'

'Already? But can't we stay with them for at least a little while?'

I stopped and turned back. 'No, they pointed guns at us, Eno. This is not the kind of village where you and I would be safe. We don't need them.'

'When will it ever be safe?'

I placed my hand on his shoulder. 'Maybe never. But if it's just you and me, we know we can trust each other, right?'

Eno shrugged. 'Yeah, but these are our people.'

I spotted Pilgrim on the far side of a courtyard. He was making his way past various tents, probably to where Tau was being kept.

I pointed in his direction for Eno to see. 'Are they, though? Do you think they're right? That Tau should die?'

Eno shook his head. 'I don't want her to die, even if she is our enemy. I'm not angry at her anymore.'

I changed course and sped up, heading to where we last saw Pilgrim. We continued down the path and passed more shacks.

Eno was now running to keep pace. 'Hey, wait! You want to rescue her, don't you?'

We stopped at a corner. I peeked around the shelter and saw Pilgrim farther down the next path. I glanced back at Eno. 'Keep your voice down! Yes, I want to rescue her. I don't think she's one of them anymore. Maybe we've brought her to our side now?'

'Yeah – hey, yeah! If she fought with us, others might change sides, too. But what about the tracking device thingie?'

'I'm sure that was just in the armour we threw away,' I said hopefully, looking around the corner again, before rounding it.

A couple of the nomads from earlier ran past and hurried into one of the nearby tents. Moments later, they left the tent and ran to the next. News of our arrival had spread, and now all of the villagers were exiting their tents with some of their belongings. The pathways were filling with panicked people.

'Only take what you need!' I heard a man yell in the street.

I spotted Sabikah on a shelter roof. She cupped her hands around her mouth. 'Make your way to the cavern pass!'

I peered through the crowd and saw Pilgrim head into one of the tents at the far end. 'There,' I said, brushing past a couple of villagers.

Eno gestured nervously at all of the armed nomads. 'I don't think they're going to let us just take her back, Sas.'

I pulled on his wrist and we hurried through the crowd. The tent was close.

There was an explosion somewhere nearby, and the entire cavern shook. The rumbling was soon overtaken by screams, which echoed against the enormous dome ceiling. The crowd of terrified villagers ran in every direction, many dropping their belongings.

A hail of laserfire came from the skylights above. Hundreds of male soldiers were perched on the holes' rims, firing down on the village. Many more were rappelling down on cords, dropping onto the shelter roofs with loud bangs. Multiple shelters were ablaze already. Assorted villagers fell dead in the streets.

The nomads quickly counterattacked, firing up back up at them. Several enemy soldiers were shot and they fell through the holes. They plummeted and smacked into the cave floor with sickening, squishy thuds.

Eno and I were stunned, staring at the chaos. There was a deep roar nearby, and I saw Pilgrim burst out of the tent. 'Damned Dominion!' He fired his giant rifle at numerous enemies in the village. Pilgrim didn't even notice us, instead joining the fray in the streets.

I was still holding Eno's wrist, so I pulled him along towards the tent. 'We have to save her and get out of here!' I shouted over the deafening booms and shrieks.

We grazed past several more villagers as they scrambled for cover, and then finally we reached the tent. I pulled the curtain aside, revealing a small winding corridor. We rushed in and let the curtain close behind us.

'Well, well, well,' a deep voice began from around the next corner. 'Already restrained? What a gift.'

Who was he talking to? Eno and I snuck closer. I spotted the man immediately. He was dressed in black armour and his back was turned. A hole at the back of the tent must have been his entrance.

Tau was hanging from the roof, ropes tied around her wrists. She squirmed and moaned, attempting to break free. She noticed me and we locked eyes. I raised a finger to my mouth.

She stopped writhing. 'You don't need to do this. You can free me and... you'll never see me again.'

He approached and brushed her cheek with his fingers. 'Now *why* would I want that?' A nearby explosion outside illuminated the tent interior, revealing his lecherous grin. 'Tell me where the acolyte is and I'll spare your life.'

I scanned the room, hoping to find something I could use. The crude walls were made of shrapnel and were still sharp in places. One large, rusty spike in particular caught my eye.

The man pressed a pistol against Tau's face. 'Three... two...'

With barely a thought, I drew two portals. With one strong pushing motion, I forced the portal that was behind the man towards him. It teleported him to the spike, and then there was sound of ripping flesh.

'*Aaarrghh!*' the impaled man screamed. As he quivered, he looked down at his stomach and saw the shrapnel sticking out of it, the rusted point drenched in blood and gore. He stopped moving and hung there motionless.

Eno and I rushed around the corner and approached Tau. My brother's eyes widened when he saw the impaled man. 'You killed him...'

'I didn't know what to do! I panicked,' I said with a trembling voice.

'It's okay,' Tau interrupted. 'He deserved it. Now please, get me down from here.'

What had I done? I killed a man. I could have just teleported him out into the desert. Why did I do that? My legs were shaking. The gunfire outside was intensifying.

I walked over to Tau, barely able to keep my balance. Thankfully, I still had my bag, so I rifled through it and found my knife. I raised it to Tau's restraints and rapidly cut through. The binds loosened and released.

She stared into my eyes, confused, then sprang forward and hugged me. 'Thank you *so* much. You didn't have to save me but...'

There was another explosion and the blast knocked us all to the ground. A bright red line cut from one side of the hut's roof to the other, followed by an ear-piercing screech as it tore through the scrap metal walls with ease. The beam was giving off an insane amount of heat. I shielded my face with my hands. The blazing energy weapon ceased, but it had left an enormous hole in the front of the hut. We cowered as much of the roof collapsed around us.

Afterwards, we sat back up. Outside the hut, back near the village's centre, a large, bright bubble was coming out of the ground. It was like a shell made of hexagons.

Inside it were two men in black armour. One had his hands to the sides, generating the shield. The second was firing a red laser from his outstretched fingertips, which exited the shield and disintegrated the huts around them. Their menacing black helmets obscured their faces. More acolytes.

They were destroying everything in their path, their bright powers lighting up the cavern around them as they moved. The red beam tore through the buildings and emitted a high-pitched squeal.

Tau pulled me to my feet. 'We need a portal, now!'

She was right, but it was difficult to focus. I thought back to the green hills we had seen earlier in the day. I pictured them exactly as I had seen them, then I twirled my fingers and a portal opened beside us. The thick, burning air was sucked through into the cold, dark night on the other side.

'Let's go!' I said, before noticing that Eno was still crouching on the ground with his hands on his head. 'Come on, Eno.'

Tau dove through first. After pulling Eno up by the arm, he and I followed, leaving the burning building behind. We fell through the portal and crashed face-first into the grass. We rose to our feet, and Eno spat out a mouth full of dirt.

We were outside again, surrounded by trees and foliage. The roaring flames, laserfire, and screams could still be heard through the portal, so I closed it. Everything went silent, replaced with nothing but the wind.

Tau leaned against a tree in the dark. I could hear her sobbing. 'I want to go home... I want to go home.'

Eno slumped against a nearby rock.

If Tau had a tracking device inside her, why was it the men who attacked? None of this made any sense.

Tau glanced back. 'It was my fault, wasn't it?' The moon lit up her distraught face.

'No,' I replied. 'They were after me, the acolyte. It's mine.'

'All those people, so many screams,' Eno said as he covered his ears.

We remained still and silent, listening to the wind rustle through the trees. I'd always thought Eno and I would be overjoyed when we completed the pilgrimage and reached the green. It was nothing like what I imagined.

'We should go back,' Eno said suddenly.

'What?' I screeched.

He pushed away from the rock. 'There could be survivors.'

Tau looked as uncertain as I felt. After seeing the entire settlement in flames, it was doubtful anyone else escaped.

Tau shook her head. 'I can't go back there. I'm sorry.'

I frowned at Eno. 'And I can't make another portal back...'

'You *can't*, or *won't?*' he quickly retorted.

'I'm sorry for what happened, Eno,' I continued, and he faced away from me. 'I know you felt like they were our people, but they weren't.'

Eno turned back around and pointed at Tau. 'They only treated Tau badly. And I would have done the same thing if I didn't know her. They didn't do anything to you or me. You just hate everyone because we've been alone our whole lives, always on the move. You don't trust anyone but us.'

Tau shifted anxiously, unsure of what to say.

I scoffed. 'That's not true.'

'I bet you want to travel forever, so that way it can just be you and me.'

'Why is that a bad thing?'

'Because Grandpa wanted you to help our people with your portals, remember?'

My whole body tightened. 'I'm not going back there and dying for people I hardly know!'

Eno's anger faded. He went completely stone-faced, as if disappointed. 'Grandpa never wanted you to die for them... just to try.' He looked up at the moon to get his bearings, and wandered away from us into the darkness.

I didn't want to admit it, but everything he'd said was right. I had always resented Aberym and his grand plan for me.

Tau approached me as if she was about to say something. She hesitated, then turned away, choosing to follow in Eno's footsteps instead.

I followed them, and the three of us walked in silence, deeper into the forest.

Eight: Fish Out of Water

I ran my fingers through the cold water before wading into the shallows. The night wind was cold but the water felt soothing after all that had happened. Compared to last night under the stars, the shack we had found in the forest behind us would be the perfect place to rest.

Eno was already waist-deep in the river and looking up at the stars. He hadn't said a word to me this morning after our spat the night before, but as the day had progressed, he'd opened up a little. Had he forgiven me already?

Tau, on the other hand, was still sulking by the riverside. Our eyes met and I smiled, but she looked away.

Eventually, she shook her head, groaned, stood and plodded into the water to join us. I tried not to react, focusing instead on the school of harmless silver mantakrill swimming past.

'Can I help?' she asked, following my gaze.

I gestured to the fish. 'You can shoo them in my direction?'

She nodded back and moved in a little more. The two of us squinted at the fish in silence for what felt like the longest time.

'I suppose that's two I owe you now,' she said.

It took a moment for me to realise she was referring to saving her. I smirked. 'Three if you count us lying for you in the desert.'

I trudged deeper and got a solid footing on the riverbed, then began concentrating. A small portal, large enough for a fish, opened underwater, with its destination on the shore, creating a miniature waterfall.

Tau saw a fish and splashed at it, but it stubbornly changed direction. She gave a frustrated grunt before looking up again. 'I'm sorry that things didn't work out with them.' She checked to see if Eno was paying attention, but he was happily swimming farther away. 'You two probably would have been safe there without me. And happier, too.'

Across the ripples of water, I could see the distorted reflection of the moon. It lit up the shallow water a pale white and the speckled stars lapped on the surface like glistening sand.

I swayed the underwater portal from side to side, trying to snare another fish. 'It was for the best.' The fish evaded my trap and swam away.

'Almost got it,' Tau said. 'I know they were ready to kill me but a part of me wishes that I could have just... like... hid there, and lived with you two. Then I could escape this war, not be a part of it. Never have to kill...'

I stopped moving my portals. 'I didn't want to kill last night, but I had no choice. I don't regret it at all.'

Tau smiled. 'I'm glad that you can feel that way.' She gestured over to Eno, still splashing in the water. 'I've been taught to hate them, but I don't see what the big deal is. I couldn't do it if I was ordered to. Pilgrim was friendly. Up until... you know.'

My portal finally snared a fish, and it was teleported to the shore. 'I got it! Quick!'

Tau waded back and rushed over to the flailing fish. She scooped it up with both hands, placed it onto some ripped fabric, then wrapped it up before it could wriggle free. She gestured to the three fish we had caught. 'Will these be enough?'

'Definitely, that's one each,' I said with a grin. 'Let's head back. We're going back to the shack, Eno.'

Eno stomped out of the river, launching the water as much as he could with every stride. Once the three of us were out, we picked up our clothes, my bag, and the fish. We made our way back through the trees to the front of the dilapidated shack.

I reached into my bag for my knife – miraculously, one of the only things I had been able to hold onto without it slipping through the hole.

'I'll prepare the food if you get a fire going,' Tau said, looking down at my knife.

'You've prepared mantakrill before, have you?' I asked.

'I have had some survival training, you know.'

I nodded before cautiously offering my knife to her.

She noticed my hesitation and rolled her eyes. 'You still don't trust me?'

I handed it to her and smiled. 'I'm sorry. I just don't trust anyone easily.'

Eno snatched one of the wrapped fish from Tau. 'That's how we nomads survive.' He brought the fish up his nose to smell, instantly regretted it, then passed it back.

Tau examined the knife more closely. 'It's not even sharp.'

'Grandpa made it out of a rock,' Eno said as he sat down by the campfire and started stamping his feet on the dirt. Tau sat on one of the logs surrounding the long-forgotten fire pit and began scaling the fish on the wood. I placed some of the firewood we gathered in the pit and stuffed some tinder underneath.

Eno ceased his playful stomping and shuffled closer to Tau. 'You said before that men started all this. Did you really mean that?'

I shook my head at him. 'Both sides have their own version of the story, blaming the other.'

'Or maybe one of them is true?' Tau shrugged, before focusing on Eno. 'The story goes that a *very* long time ago, men and women lived together. The world was beautiful back then, too, like this forest, everywhere you went.'

Eno's eyes widened in amazement. 'Woah.'

'But it wasn't a peaceful time.' Tau continued with the fish still in her hand. 'There were these political factions that riled everyone up. They grew and grew until the whole world was split by gender. They were led by the world's most powerful acolytes.'

She placed one hand on her chest. 'Our first queen was named Elysia, and she could heal any wound. Everyone loved her because she kept them healthy. She could even bring back the dead!'

Eno gasped, engrossed by her tale. I had heard all this before.

'When the violence started, the men killed Elysia and that's what started the war. Some of the fights between the acolytes were so big that it messed up the planet's weather and, over a really long time, now it's one big desert.'

Eno stared into the forest, perhaps trying to imagine what it was like back then.

Tau smiled, seeing how her story affected Eno. She sighed. 'I have a confession to make.' She paused and frowned. 'Something I should have told you already. We soldiers are instructed that if we ever get lost, that we would be swiftly rescued. At birth, some of us receive tracking devices surgically implanted into our bodies.'

Eno and I exchanged a nervous glance.

'When you captured me, I was so sure that help was on the way.' She gave a single bemused laugh. 'But they never came. So, I guess I wasn't one of the lucky ones. But now that you two have been so nice to me... I'm kind of... happy they never came.'

She stared into my eyes. 'I'm truly sorry.' She held out the scaled fish and awaited our judgement.

I bit my lip, lost for words. Eno and I were well aware of the possibility of surgical implants, and we had rescued her anyway. But that she had waited until now to say this still bothered me.

'I forgive you,' Eno said before I could react. 'You're one of us now. Right, Sas?'

I approached, swiped the fish from her and turned away. 'I'm going to search inside for some tools.' I trudged up to the shack and stopped at the door before looking back. I took a long, deep breath and tried to clear my head. 'I... forgive you, too.'

I pushed open the door with a loud creak. It was a single room. It must have once been a home for a hunter maybe, but it was now covered in dust and mould. Part of the ceiling had caved in, and the few pieces of furniture left were mostly broken.

I rifled through some nearby drawers as the door closed behind me.

I threw the bare skewer to the side and let out a loud burp. Eno laughed, but Tau wrinkled her nose.

'What?' I said.

'You burped; that's gross,' Tau said with a smile.

I raised an eyebrow. 'So what? It's normal out here, okay? Loosen up.'

Eno bent forward from his seat and strained, but no burp came out. 'Wait, wait.'

Tau rolled her eyes at us. 'Fine, then,' she said before standing up and swallowing her food. 'Boouuwweerrp!' She crossed her arms and smirked.

'Good, I guess,' I said with a laugh.

Eno ceased his efforts to force-burp himself and glanced between us. 'I think Tau has you beat.'

I nodded. 'And you, too, it seems. That was like a necrolisk roar. I thought we were under attack.' The others laughed. I cleared my throat. 'I have another question, how... umm... how do the Dominion have kids?'

'Ewww,' Eno said.

'I mean,' I continued, 'you don't... romance your captives, do you?'

Tau almost spat out her food in surprise. 'I think I'll agree with your brother on this one. No, we don't "romance" them. We assimilate a lot of people, and we also create children with science, in a lab – like I was.'

I pointed at her. 'So, you...?'

She averted her eyes. 'I don't know who my parents are. None of the sisters in my squad do.'

I frowned. 'So, no families.'

'Isn't everyone sad there?' Eno added.

She lowered her skewer and leant back on the seat. 'My sisters are my family. And we have our hormones modified, so we don't have the same nasty urges you desert-dwellers do. Whatever love with a male is like, I'm sure it's overrated,' Tau said, now locking her gaze with me. 'How about you? Do you have first-hand experience in... in that sort of thing?'

'No, nothing like that,' I replied, watching the fire. 'We've never stayed in a place long enough for me to even talk to the boys my age.'

Eno giggled. 'Because none of them want to talk to you.'

My eyes felt like they were going to pop out. I snatched up a nearby twig and pelted it at Eno.

'Oww! That hurt!'

'Go to bed, Eno.'

'What?' He shot up. 'But I'm still eating!'

I pointed at the shack. 'Take your food with you. I'll come along soon. Goodnight.'

'Goodnight, Eno,' Tau said.

He gritted his teeth. 'But I'm not a kid anymore!'

'Go!' I shouted.

'Hmph!' Eno bent down and picked up the last skewer, before storming off to the shack and slamming the door behind him.

'Huh,' Tau began. 'I guess you're like his parent out here.'

I folded my arms and looked away. 'Yeah.'

Tau noticed my irritation. 'Oh. I'm sorry. Is it okay if I ask about them? Your parents?'

I shrugged. 'It's fine. Our parents died when he was little. Eno was very adventurous. One day he wandered off and got stuck in a crevice. I was the one who found him, and a pack of necrolisks ambushed us. Our parents rescued us but... they didn't make it.'

'That's awful,' Tau said, reaching out to my wrist to comfort.

'My grandfather took us both away and taught us how to survive,' I continued.

'To lose your parents that way must have been–' Tau said.

'It's okay, I don't even remember their faces anymore.'

I stared down into the dirt.

'What is it?' she asked.

'Well, it's just that I've been thinking. I want you to stay with us. Permanently. Eno's really warmed up to you and you've said things that lead me to believe–'

'Yes,' Tau interrupted. 'Yes I'd – I'd like that.'

We both smiled and stared into the fire together.

Two figures obscured by mist stood in the distance. They were facing away towards a great, setting sun. I walked over the misty floors towards them, kicking puffs of cloud away with each step. My eyes strained from the brightness, and I shielded them, trying to get a glimpse of my parents.

'Mum! Dad!'

They didn't react. They were facing the sunset, motionless. My pace quickened as I tried to join them, but with every step, the distance expanded. The ground kept shifting backwards faster and faster.

The mist around my legs was clearing, morphing into endless sand dunes instead. I had been here before, running away from something, running for my life.

My parents were hand in hand, on top of the next dune. I wanted to be by their side again. They turned around to face me and I stopped short. Their faces were missing – no nose, no eyes and no mouth, nothing. I couldn't remember what they looked like. I screamed. I had lost them.

A blinding flash of light and everything went blank. Pure whiteness. The floating platform I was standing on faded into view. An endless flat plane of white stretched infinitely in all directions, as did a dark-green stormy sky. The clouds rippled and thunder cracked and boomed.

I wasn't alone. I was standing in a circle with six other dark silhouettes, all of us staring at a strange, floating sphere in the centre. The figures were a mix of men and women, but I couldn't make them out. The woman closest to me was facing away, but her bright, light-blue hair stood out. Who was that?

I shook myself awake from the dream and was drenched by a torrent of rain. I looked up, expecting to see the roof of the shack, but instead was blinded by the morning sky. Was I still dreaming?

I sat up next to Eno in the bed and realised that I was, in fact, awake. The walls and roof of the building had vanished. Three Female Dominion soldiers in silver armour stood where the front door once was, and one of them had her hands outstretched.

'Knock, knock.'

Nine: To Water

I pushed myself out of bed, throwing the covers to the ground. Tau was also awake; she rubbed her eyes and jumped to her feet. Eno hid behind our bed.

The three armoured females stood in front of the entrance to the shack, now reduced to a puddle of water, leaving nothing but the furniture and floorboards under our feet. Like when we first met Tau, the women had their combat armour on, and each had colourful streaks in their fringes.

The woman at the front still had her hands outstretched to where the door had been. She was darker-skinned than the other two. Her hair was similar to mine, but black. She appeared strong and athletic, maybe in her early twenties.

Tau turned to Eno and I and backed away. 'You both need to give up. Please. You could get hurt. They are too powerful for you.' She had a genuine look of fear on her face.

'What?' I said, stalling the situation. 'You want to go back to killing people again with them?' I tried concentrating on a new destination. We needed to leave here right away.

'Sacet, you need to surrender, for your brother's sake,' she said as she walked to the three women and stood by their side.

I couldn't tell if she was she serious, or if she was trying to play them. But I didn't have time to debate.

'I guess this is farewell then,' I said. I turned, throwing my hands in front of me and used all of my strength to open a portal next to Eno.

'Malu!' I heard one of the women yell from behind.

There was a moist, slurping sound as I went to jump, and both Eno and I fell into a pool of waist-high, brown water. The ground had been liquified, a slush of what was once the floorboards. The one called Malu had both her hands flat to the ground. The trail of liquified floorboards and soil led straight back to her hands, its path like a small river. She rose again, and under her gloves I saw that her fingertips were exposed.

The second soldier, a short, brown-haired girl, strutted forward. She was only a child, half the size of the others, and about the same age as Eno. Until now, she'd appeared disinterested in what was going on.

'It isn't going to be that easy,' she said, now giving me her full attention.

She closed one eye and raised her fingers in front of the other, before spreading her thumb and index finger apart. Then she retracted the two closer together again. As I stood in the water, there was a strong pinching force on my body. I couldn't move. I was stuck! The pain caused my portal to close.

Keeping her fingers in front of her open eye, she raised them higher, and I was levitated out of the water. Suspended in mid-air, I struggled against the invisible, vice-like grip she had on me.

The small girl's uninterested face turned to that of maniacal joy. 'There's no point struggling, desert cretin. If I wanted to, I could crush you like an egg.'

There was a much stronger squeeze and I shouted out in pain. Her grin grew wider.

'Sacet!' Eno yelled out from the water below. He waded over, grabbed my legs, and tried to pull me out of the air. 'Let her go!'

Tau moved in closer to the others. 'Please stop. I'm sure she would make a great soldier. She's... she's very resourceful and powerful.'

'Do not speak out of turn, trooper,' the stern woman at the back said. 'I fully intend on allowing her to live. But I want to see what she can do first.'

This woman was middle-aged, tall, slender, and had long, curled blonde hair reaching past her shoulders.

The small girl still hadn't broken her line of sight. 'I'm surprised you haven't asked me to put you down yet.'

Had she been waiting for me to say it? Was she trying to humiliate me?

'Okay... argh... put me down!' I said, barely managing to utter each word through gritted teeth.

'Sure thing,' the girl said as she flung her hand to the side and cackled. I was thrown clear past the trees and down the riverbank, so fast that the wind whistled in my ears.

I splashed into the water, sending out a ripple of waves. I tried standing, but my bare feet slipped on the slime-covered stones on the riverbed. I rose to my feet a second time and faced the women, who were walking down the bank. Tau ran over to Eno and helped him out of the shack's liquified remains.

I was outmatched, but I needed to fight back all the same. I had to get Eno out of here. Somehow, I felt reenergised.

I spun my fingers around, and the breeze along the river intensified. A set of portals opened, one on the riverbank, the other above my enemies' heads.

Bringing my hand down, the portal above plunged down with crushing force. But I wasn't fast enough to get all three. Both the older woman and the younger girl sidestepped. Malu stood her ground and looked straight up.

She brought her hands up. The portal encircled her, pushing her into the ground on the other side, but it didn't crush her. A large puddle had formed underneath the portal on the shoreline. I closed my portals; I had failed.

Malu calmly stepped out of the puddle she had created on the other side. She rested a hand on her hip. 'You're going to have to try a lot harder than that to kill me.'

With this, the child acolyte shook her head. 'This is boring.' She turned back to the blonde-haired woman. 'Verre, can we finish this and go back home?' The Verre woman must have been the one in charge, but that didn't change the girl's attitude. She even spoke to her in a rude tone.

Verre crossed her arms. 'No, Iya. We're not done here yet. You there, girl, I'll make you a deal. If you impress me, I'll let the boy go free. He's of no use to us.'

I raised an eyebrow.

'She's lying!' Eno shouted from Tau's side farther up the bank. 'Portal away, Sas! Run. Let go of me–' Tau had grabbed Eno and muffled him with her hand.

'Don't make them any angrier, they'll kill you,' she said.

I shrugged at Verre. 'As if you would let any of us go.'

She grinned. 'For all you know, my offer could be genuine. But for your impertinence, now you'll need to impress me if you want that little boy to live.' Verre glanced back at Eno and Tau, who suddenly disappeared from where they'd been standing.

'Eno!' I shouted, looking in every direction to find them, before bringing my hate-filled gaze back to Verre. 'What did you do with them?'

She smiled, and the three soldiers went fuzzy, quickly fading from view then back again. Confused, I blinked and refocused my eyes. The women then disappeared from their positions, too. I was alone.

A great force smacked into the side of my jaw. I heard a loud pop. The attack sent my body careening through the air. The shooting pain was immense. I collided with the water and sunk, completely disoriented.

I floated up off the bottom and stood back up with difficulty. I held my throbbing jaw and moaned, but opening my mouth caused even more agony. Was it dislocated?

The water had cleared from my eyes, and I saw all three women beside me in the water. Malu was the closest, with a clenched fist and a furrowed brow. How did they get here so fast?

Verre had her hands on her hips. 'Maybe we should leave both of you dead in the water right here? What could you do about it, hmm?'

I frantically searched for Eno. If I found him I could at least portal him away. So long as he was okay, I didn't care what happened to me.

'You won't find him,' Verre said, realising what I was doing.

I glowered at her. 'Fine, I'll play your game,' I said, every word bringing me pain.

Verre raised a hand to stop the others. 'Let her make the first move.'

The little one sighed.

Malu nodded then gazed back to me. 'Bring it on.'

I slowly reached down into my clothes for my knife and brandished it in front of me. The women stood their ground, unperturbed.

Given how fast they were, I knew I had to make this quick and unexpected. I took a couple of steps back, then imagined the portal I wanted to make. One end would be next to my knife, which I would immediately stab through, and the other end would be in front one of their throats. Then I would rapidly slash the second portal across all three of them.

Verre crossed her arms. 'Well? We're waiting.'

No sooner had she finished her sentence did my portal open. I stabbed through and swiped the other portal as planned. The knife made an audible swish and made contact with all three.

An awkward moment passed where their bodies weren't reacting to my attack. But then all three simply vanished, like they were never there to begin with.

'Hmm, going for the jugular?' Verre's disembodied voice echoed around me.

Suddenly, the entire river was filled with hundreds of copies of Malu. What was going on? Were they even real?

'You have a killer instinct,' Verre's voice continued as the clones slowly closed in on me. 'That's something I can work with...'

The first copy was almost upon me, so I swung the knife portal at her, causing her to instantly disappear like before. Then another came and I stabbed her, too. Then another and another.

'Not too smart, though,' Verre quipped.

After I had cleared several other copies, the illusion suddenly dropped, revealing Verre still by the shoreline. Eno, Iya and Tau were still there, too. Eno had been raised into the air by Iya, and Tau was watching on in horror. Eno kicked and squirmed to no avail.

I stepped forward. 'Let him go!'

A hand grabbed my shoulder and firmly spun me around. It was Malu, the real one. I brought my knife portal towards her in response. Rather than dodge, she raised a palm to the incoming knife. Instead of piercing her hand with it like I expected, the knife turned to water on impact. Then, with the same hand, she grabbed my wrist and pulled me farther into my own portal.

I panicked, trying to wrestle my arm back through, but her grip was too strong. She looked to Verre. Verre nodded, as though granting permission.

With her free hand, Malu leapt forward and punched me square in the nose. I flew back from the force. My arm was freed from her grip and the now closing portal. My eyes watered and blurred as my face stung.

I crashed on the water's surface and plunged under. This was hopeless. I wasn't going to get the better of them. I floated for a moment, battered and bruised, before raising myself onto my knees.

I had to send Eno away from here at least. I struggled to raise my hand towards him and thought of a distant location.

Malu looked to her commanding officer again and shrugged.

Verre sighed. 'She's done.' She made a gesture towards me.

My eyes were getting blurrier. I couldn't make out Eno's features. I couldn't concentrate on where he needed to go.

Malu produced a small weapon from her belt, pointed it at me and fired. A sting hit my neck. My whole body convulsed, then my face hit the water's surface and I blacked out.

Ten: Farthest from the Line

Eno

'Wha... ugh... get away...' I said in a stupor, not able to make sense of my surroundings.

My eyes slowly opened. A needle was sticking out of my arm; a woman in plain, clean, grey clothing had injected me with something. She had white streaks in her hair, and was kneeling down next to me on the metal floor. When she saw that I was awake, she withdrew the needle, got back up and walked away.

'Wait, who are you?' I said, but the woman ignored me.

She knelt down next to an unconscious man who was lying next to me; the room was filled with them. She injected him with the same needle she used on me, and he came to almost immediately, looking at his surroundings with confusion. She stood back up and attended another.

I sat up and saw that a number of men had already been awoken and were standing in rows. Our regular clothes were gone, and instead we all wore the same grey jumpsuit. There was a small green square underneath our feet, big enough for us to stand on.

The room was a large square, with one large door in front of the group. A catwalk, too high to reach, surrounded the room, and fully armoured female guards were patrolling and keeping watch over us. More were on the ground floor as well, their faces concealed by helmets.

Only one soldier didn't wear a helmet. She stood at the front of the room and examined us with a curled lip, a furrowed brow and her arms crossed behind her back. She was the fattest woman I had ever seen. She had a bulbous nose, crooked teeth, and a nasty smirk, one of complete contempt for us. We disgusted her.

'Get up!' an angry voice said as a sharp pain took hold in the back of my neck.

One of the guards had hit me with the butt of her gun and was now aiming it at me. 'Stand up, now!'

I stood as quickly as I could and backed away from her.

'No, stand in the square!' she screeched as she pointed at the ground.

I hurried back over to her and stood on the spot she indicated.

'Stand in the square!' another woman screeched nearby at one of the other prisoners.

There was a loud chime, followed by a calm, friendly, female voice coming from somewhere above us. It echoed throughout the chamber. '*You are now in FDC, the Female Dominion Capital. For your own safety, it is important to follow the rules at all times. The first rule you should observe is to always remain on your green square unless specifically told to leave it. Failure to follow this first, and simplest, rule may result in your immediate execution.*'

My toes were outside the square, so I edged them back in to fit. Did anyone notice? The guard who had told me to stand was still watching me, so I avoided her gaze.

She bent forward, bringing her face close to mine. 'Face forward!'

I put my hands by my sides, stood up straight and faced forward. I started to sob and closed my eyes. Where was Sacet?

'No way, I'm not doing it,' I could hear a man behind me say. He was breathing heavily, as if having a panic attack.

'Stand on the square, now!' one of the soldiers commanded. 'This is your last warning.'

'No, let me out of here! I need to get out,' the man persisted.

Out the corner of my eye, I saw him running past us, through the rows, heading for the big doorway. One of the soldiers chased him. The surly-looking woman at the front rolled her eyes and left her post.

She intercepted the man, standing between him and the door. He stopped in front of her and looked back at the other guard behind him. He sank to his knees and started to beg.

'Please, I have a family, childre–'

The ugly woman brought the pistol she was hiding behind her back to the man's forehead and shot him. The contents of his skull splattered onto the metal floor by the men's feet in the front row.

'Anyone else?' she said, raising her pistol into the air and waving it about. 'Don't forget, you're all expendable. We can always get more of you.'

At that moment, the calm voice echoed around the chambers again, repeating the same message I heard earlier. The guard who chased the man continued her patrolling through the rows as if nothing had happened. Tears now flowed freely down my cheeks.

The ugly woman noticed me and glared, approaching. I tried to contain my weeping, letting out only a whimper or two as she got closer. She stood silently next to me, her hands crossed behind her back, looming over me like a predator.

She brought the barrel of her pistol to my temple.

'Stop crying!' she demanded. 'Do as I say or you'll end up like him.'

I used my sleeve to wipe my cheeks dry, and then my eyes. I let out another whimper, which caused the woman's head to tilt. I had stopped, but my jaw still shivered.

'Tani!' the woman called out, causing me to flinch. 'Are they all awake yet?'

'Yes, ma'am,' a timid voice said from behind me. One of the plain women in grey approached.

'Good,' the ugly woman said. I could tell she was still staring at me, but I didn't dare look away from the front.

'You heard the message,' she continued, louder this time. 'Leaving the green square at any time when you haven't been told to means you die.'

She took her gun away from my head, glanced back at the dead man, and made her way through the rows to the front.

'I am your overseer. Unlike the guards, who just keep you from escaping, I have been charged with taking care of you,' she said as she attempted a motherly smile, which turned out more like a rotten leer. 'But as you'll soon discover, it doesn't matter if you're from the Male Dominion or the desert, if you're a man... or a boy, you are worthless to me. Therefore, the tip of the day is to keep me happy, because I can and will shoot you if it takes my fancy.

'The Prison Quadrant here in the city is a mine, the prisoners its miners. In time, you will be taught everything you need to know. But for now, we're going to get you all settled in. Now *when* I say so, I want you to order yourselves into a single line. Look down at the ground.'

A large red line lit up along the floor, pointed towards the big door.

'Remember that once you've gotten into line, remain silent and facing forward... Go!'

The green squares below our feet disappeared and most of the men started to move. An alarm resounded throughout the facility.

'Five, four, three...' She counted down while aiming her pistol at whoever she thought was farthest from the line.

I rushed over to the line, but there was no room. A hand grabbed my shoulder and pulled me in front of him. I glanced back and saw that it was Pilgrim. He caught my eye, gave me a scared look and gestured for me to face forward.

'Two, one.'

When the last man had gotten in line, the alarm stopped, as if knowing we were all in proper formation.

I faced forward again as the overseer came walking past to inspect us.

'Good,' she said, lowering her gun and smiling. She turned to the guards up on the catwalk. 'Open the gate.'

One of the guards pressed a button on the wall and the big doors opened up by themselves, like magic. I had never seen machinery so complicated, or buildings so sleek and smooth. The ugly woman took her place at the front of the line again.

'Stay on the red line and follow me,' she commanded, leading us through the big doorway.

The next room was narrow, a thin corridor, with more guards stationed on the catwalks above. The line stopped as the man at the front was forced to put his right arm into a white box. The guards shoved the man in closer until his whole arm was in the machine.

A nearby woman, with white streaks in her hair and plain grey clothing, pressed a switch on the machine. The man screamed and fell to his knees as the machine hummed loudly. The machine beeped, and his arm came loose from it, revealing a black mark on his wrist.

I didn't want to stick my arm in that thing. What if there was an accident and it took my arm off completely? I was drenched in sweat but somehow also shivering.

'Kid, just do as they say for now,' Pilgrim whispered to me as the man wailed in agony. 'I'll look out for you, I promise.'

The guards picked the man up off the floor and dragged him forward along the line. The second in line stood still, hesitating. The guards on the catwalk trained their weapons on us. After taking a deep breath, he stepped forward and placed his arm in the machine.

The machine started again, but the man resisted the urge to scream out. He strained and groaned, but didn't yell. The machine beeped again, revealing another still steaming black mark, surrounded by scalded flesh. It wouldn't be long before it was my turn. I gritted my teeth and closed my eyes, trying to hide my fear.

Eleven: Welcome Home

Sacet

My mind spun, and all I could hear was the sound of my heart
thumping. My brother faded into my vision, as did an audience of
others around him, watching him silently cry out. I was looking down
on him from above, but somehow also from the side at the same time.
It was bizarre. I couldn't move, in fact I couldn't feel my own body.
What was happening to me? Eno was trying to pull his arm away from
something. Why was no one helping him?

It all disappeared, turning to black. I opened my eyes and saw
something I wasn't accustomed to. I had been living among the rocks
and sand for most of my life, but now I was sitting in a circular,
perfectly constructed and polished room. I turned in my steel-framed
chair and saw that it had only one door.

The room was small, but still accommodated a table and two chairs.
Although it was well-lit, I couldn't seem to locate the source of the
light. This wasn't real, this all had to be some kind of nightmare.

I leant forward onto the metal table and buried my face into my
arms, but as I did I reminded myself of the pain in my jaw and nose. It
still hurt, but I didn't think they were broken. My arms were covered

in the same undersuit material that Tau wore. The suit covered my whole body.

The back of my neck started to itch. I placed my hand to the source of the discomfort and felt an odd protrusion from my skin. A scarred surface surrounded the lump. Surgery? No stitches? How was it scarred already? What had they done to me?

The door in front of me shuddered open. I raised my head from the table as the tall, uniformed, blonde woman entered the room with her arms behind her back. It was the same middle-aged woman from the river, Verre. She sat in the chair opposite me and folded her hands on the table.

'Welcome back home, Sacet,' she said. 'If I had have known you used to be one of us, I would have treated you much differently at the river. I'm sorry we lost you to the nomads so long ago. Back then, we assumed you were dead, otherwise we would have tried to track you down. I hope the savages didn't torture you?'

She already knew everything about me? Tau must have told her.

She smiled. 'Allow me to formally introduce myself, my name is Verre, but you will call me Matriarch. How are we feeling today?'

It didn't matter how nice she was to me, no matter what she asked, I would never tell her anything of value. I shifted uncomfortably. 'Confused.'

She gave a phoney look of surprise. 'Oh? And why's that?'

I stood up in my chair. 'You know damn well why! Where am I? Where is my brother? What are you going to—'

She shushed me. 'Sit down. All of your questions will be answered in due time. You need to be patient,' she said as I sat back down and folded my arms. 'To answer your first question, you are in a containment chamber. It inhibits your acolyte powers, so any ideas you have of teleporting yourself out of here are pointless. But let's get back on track. How are you feeling, really? How's the jaw?' This brought a smirk to her face. She found this funny?

I glared at her. 'It stings. How did you all move so fast? Super speed or something?'

She smiled, looked back down at her folded hands and closed her eyes. 'Hmmm! Now that would be a good power, wouldn't it? No, no. My powers are illusionary; I create pseudo-physical projections, bending light and sound to show you what I want you to see. In reality, my trooper was standing by your side in the river for quite some time.'

Now it was my turn to be smug. 'Well, I see you for what you really are in here, because neither of us can use our powers, right?'

She raised a single eyebrow. 'Who says I'm in the room with you?'

My eyes widened as her body transformed, turning brown. Her hair fell out, her clothing faded away, and her body hardened and morphed into something horrific. Several new legs sprouted in different directions, and her skin became a hardened carapace. She grew and grew into a necrolisk-like form, towering over me. It was similar to a necrolisk, but also not, a faceless abomination.

The creature's legs stomped on the steel floor as it crept closer. More stomps; there were two more terrifying creatures behind me that hadn't been there before.

I pushed away from the table and stood, unsure of whether I was in danger.

'They're not... not real...'

'Perhaps. Or perhaps not.' Verre's voice echoed from all around me.

The first creature grabbed the table with a claw and tossed it aside like it was nothing; it clattered loudly against the cell wall. If these creatures were real, there was no escape.

'I'm going to ask you questions now,' her voice continued, 'and if I think you're lying, then I'll start to do things like this—'

Eno materialised in one of the room's corners, looking equal parts confused and afraid.

'Eno!'

'Sacet?'

As quickly as he appeared, one of the nearby monster's claws whipped around and punctured through his tiny frame, pinning him to the wall. Blood sprayed everywhere.

I ran to him, not caring what the monster would do to me, but it was already too late. Eno's eyes closed and he slumped forward, going limp on the claw. I tried touching him, but my hands waved through, as though he wasn't even there. It was an illusion, yes, but what if this was really happening to Eno somewhere else?

'Stop it!' I commanded. 'Stop this madness. This is sick.'

'So, you'll answer a few questions for me?' Verre's disembodied voice called out.

My fists clenched. 'If you give my brother back, safe.'

Verre's laughter echoed. 'You're in no position to bargain. You want your brother to live? Then answer my questions.'

I begrudgingly nodded. 'Fine.'

The monsters faded away, as did the table, the chair, and Eno, too. I reached out to the walls to check if they were an illusion, but they were real.

Verre reappeared in the centre of the room, displaying a hard smile. 'Question one: how far can your portals *really* go?'

My racing heart jumped. I couldn't tell her that. If she found out I could portal to anywhere I had been before, they'd force me to use my power against the nomads.

I shrugged. 'I've never thought about it before. I've only ever teleported to things that are fairly close by. If I can't see it, then I can't get there.'

She stared at me for a while, before several large globes of light appeared above our heads, hovering and spiralling. They grew brighter and brighter as they encircled us. Verre was difficult to see, now only a dark silhouette.

'Your brother, he's a little young to be travelling in the desert with you, isn't he?'

I shielded my eyes. 'People like *you* didn't give us a choice.'

'Is he an acolyte, too?'

'What? No. If he was, I bet he'd be killing all of your people right about now,' I replied, and there was another silence.

'... That's a shame. Now, I've decided that you're going to be a soldier for us again. You'll have a great, new home here in the capital city, and you'll follow every rule and order we give you.'

I furrowed my brow. 'I'll never kill for you.'

'Mmmmm, but you have killed, haven't you?' Her silhouette moved closer. 'Tell me what you think of Tau. You seem to be quite fond of her, saving her so much. And why is that? Why would you put your life on the line for her?'

'Because she didn't seem to be... like you people.' I looked down. 'But maybe I was wrong.'

My vision started going black. What was happening? Verre disappeared again. An image of Tau appeared in front of me where Verre had been. She was tied up again on that pole, screaming for help, not able to see me.

'So, if I ask you to kill... hmm, no,' Verre's voice resounded, now booming in my ears. 'But her? What if she wanted you to? Needed you to? Yes? Like... perhaps... that man in the village?'

Tau must have told her about him, too. The images of her washed away, replaced with the gruesome sight of the soldier I had killed, limply hanging from the rusty spike.

'Do you... hate them? What he could have done to her, is that what made you want to kill him?' Her words were phasing in and out, as if they were spoken by hundreds of voices at once.

'No! I was just protecting my friend. I didn't mean to kill him.'

'But you did. You did kill him. Look at what they did to that village as they tried to find you.'

More hallucinations formed onto the dark canvas in front of me, this time of the nomads. They were all lying on the ground, dead, torn to pieces by the red beam of energy, shooting from one side of my sight to the other. Still annihilating the huts throughout the village, even now. The villagers who were still alive screamed and reached towards me, steam rising from their cauterised wounds.

'No, that's not what happened.' The visions were all around me now. 'Enough of these tricks.'

I knew it wasn't real. If I just closed my eyes, maybe I could ignore it? I took a few steps back and felt a wall, then brought my hands to my head.

'I'll ask again. Do you *hate* them?' she said. Her voice was now so distorted she barely sounded like a person at all. 'Wouldn't you like to... punish more of them?'

I just wanted this to stop and so I caved. 'Yes! Yes, now please stop this!' The veil of deception lifted like a curtain from my eyes. The room reappeared; Verre stood beside me with a stern look on her face, and the table and chairs had returned.

Verre moved behind her chair. 'Correct answer.' She clasped her hands behind her back. 'You have an implanted tracking device, so it doesn't matter where you try to hide, we will always be able to find you.' I stroked the scarred flesh on the back of my neck again. So that's what it was. 'It contains an acid capsule. When remotely triggered, it releases its contents and burns through your spinal cord. If you're lucky, it leaves you completely paralysed. Even with the best surgeons, trying to remove it will kill you. If you leave the city, or if you enter a place that is off-limits to you, I merely need to flick a switch and end you.'

I shifted uncomfortably at the thought.

'You will train and fight like one of us again. You'll receive assimilation sessions every day. If you disappoint me, I'll have your little brother killed. And if that doesn't convince you, then I'll just kill *you* instead. You will bow to our queen if you ever get to see her, and you will show the proper respect to your superiors at all times.'

Verre sat back down on her chair, folded her hands onto the table and continued, 'If you honour this agreement, you will live a life of luxury. Everything you need will be provided. I'll even see to it that Tau can help out with showing you around, help you adjust to your new life.

'And one last thing. I'm not entirely convinced you're worth my trouble. You are lucky to be alive. Every day, you should be striving to become stronger and better than what you already are. Prove to me you're worth keeping!'

Verre's body dematerialised in front of me. I spun around and watched as the room transformed from solid walls and floors to metal gratings, a cage.

It wasn't the only cage in here. Other roofless cages were suspended from the ceiling. Each was featureless with no furniture, not even a bed. They contained aimless men, staring at me.

My eyes were drawn up to a catwalk that overlooked all of the cells. Female scientists and guards gazed back down at me. Verre stood in the centre, eyes squinted at me. She had been controlling her illusions from above this whole time.

My cell door shuddered and raised open. The water acolyte that had helped defeat me stepped in and gestured for me to follow.

Back up at the catwalk, Verre still stared down at me. The other women dispersed and began examining the other cells and some nearby equipment. I walked towards the door and left my cell.

I stepped out into a steel corridor and faced the water acolyte, who was still wearing her armour.

She smiled. 'Come this way, Sacet.'

To my side there were three other soldiers. Iya, the child acolyte, was among them. Her arms were crossed and she was pretending to examine the ceiling as if that was more interesting than I was.

The water acolyte put her hand on my shoulder as we walked down the corridor. 'Sorry about punching you in the face. I hope we can still be friends? I'm Malu by the way.'

My nose still hurt from her blow, and now she wanted to be friends? Was she serious? I knew Verre and all her minions were still watching me, so I'd have to play nice.

The other three followed close behind. I admired the sleek chrome the corridor was made from. A bright, neon-red line was lit along our path. I vaguely remembered traversing corridors just like these when I was young.

Malu occasionally looked back at me and gave an awkward smile. 'I've been ordered to show you around the place and get you settled in. If you have any questions, I suppose just ask away?'

We turned left and entered a large chamber with windows, possibly the facility's entrance hall. Through the windows was a starry sky.

'Not feeling like talking, right?' Malu continued. 'Still in a bit of shock from your ordeal? I can honestly tell you, I know the feeling.' She focused on the exit and lowered her voice. 'It's normal.' She smiled again. 'Anyway, let me be the first to welcome you back to FDC, your home.'

As Malu approached the door, it opened to reveal a bright city in front of us. The buildings were enormous. I couldn't see anything desert-like, everything was steel and technology, aside from some distant mountains.

This place was most certainly not my home. If I wanted to portal away and escape, I could do it so easily now. But I remembered my brother, and also the tracking device...

It took me a while to break out of my awe, realising Malu had already started walking down the stairs in front of us.

Iya prodded me from behind. 'Move!'

I made my way down the stairs and caught up with Malu. There was a large station at the bottom of the stairs, with benches for people to sit. There didn't seem to be anyone around except for us.

'Where is my brother?' I asked, my jaw still aching.

'He's safe,' Malu replied, looking back at the facility behind us as we descended. 'So long as you and he both follow instructions, you'll be fine.' She pointed at the city. 'I was told you were from this city once. Do you remember how to get around?'

I shook my head. Aside from a few scattered memories of training, I had essentially purged it from my head long ago.

'Well, the city is broken up into numerous sectors,' she continued. 'In the very centre is the Royal Citadel – that's where our queen lives and commands us from. She has her very own Royal Guard detachment of the military, and only the most loyal of soldiers are chosen for it.'

Towards the centre of the city was the elaborate golden tower of which she spoke.

'Just outside the Citadel is the Residential Rim. It's tradition for the queen to surround herself with her people, and so dormitories and apartment buildings were built encircling it.'

'On the far side of the city is the Commercial Quad, where the civilians usually work.'

There were tall, sleek buildings behind the Citadel tower. Bright neon lights covered the surfaces of the skyscrapers. It was so surreal and alive with colour.

'At the moment we're in the Prison Quad, which includes a massive mining operation underground. That's where your brother is right now.'

'Wait, wait,' I interrupted. 'Eno's underground? He's claustrophobic; you can't keep him down there.'

Iya smirked. 'We can and will.'

Malu ignored Iya, stopping now on the station platform. 'We're about to travel to the Science Quad, that's where you'll receive your assimilation sessions every night.'

She pointed to our left, down the thin pathway connected to the station. The buildings in the direction of the Science Quad were industrious, with black plumes of smoke billowing from their chimney stacks.

'And back over in that direction is the Military Quad. That's where all of the military trains, eats and sleeps,' she said, gesturing to the right side of the station. There was a gigantic grey facility in the distance.

'Although you'll be staying with me in the Residential Rim, so you won't need to worry about that. You'll just do your training there.'

Malu followed my gaze. 'If you ignore the fact that we're at war, it's the safest and nicest place to live in the world... Well, if you're female. No other city on the planet can compare.'

There was a loud groan from behind. Iya stepped forward towards a small pedestal and then pressed a button on it. She shot a frustrated look at the two of us. 'You want to stand here talking all night?'

There was a strange humming sound coming from the right side of the tracks. A hovering vehicle barrelled down the tracks from the right, and the humming grew louder. It slowed, eventually coming to a stop in front of us. Its doors opened.

We entered, ducking our heads to get in. There were several rows of seats, all of them empty. Malu went to the front of the carriage, next to a window, and I sat next to her. Iya and the other two soldiers sat a few rows back. Malu stared out the window at the starry sky. There was a jolt as the vehicle pulled away from the station and rapidly accelerated.

I looked at Malu. 'I have to ask... were you born here?'

She broke away from her stargazing with an insulted look on her face. 'Are you asking because of the colour of my skin?'

'Yes, I'm sorry. It's just that I was told it was rare for Dominion soldiers to have darker skin.'

She sighed and shrugged, as though she had told this story before. 'I was a nomad. It's probably why they asked me to show you around, actually. My family was captured when I was little and I was assimilated like you soon will be. Normally when people ask me that, they mean to offend. I've worked hard to be respected, even feared, and yet my superiors still talk to me like I'll never be good enough.' She looked at me again. 'Sorry, I got a little carried away.'

'No, that's okay,' I said, not sure what else to add.

I looked outside the window at the city as the vehicle hurtled down the track. I couldn't help but notice how sleek and clean the city was compared to a nomad village. Malu folded her hands on her lap.

'Wasn't Tau supposed to help show me around, too?' I asked.

'She's still debriefing, you put her through a lot.'

I lowered my brow. '*I* put *her* through a lot?'

'She's told us everything she can so far.' She gave a sympathetic frown. 'Sorry about your grandfather.'

I angrily averted my eyes. A part of me didn't want to see Tau again after what she did.

Malu brushed my shoulder. 'I can't imagine what you're going through right now but... my mother taught me the nomadic last rites. Tomorrow we could hold a little ceremony for him?'

I attempted a smile. 'Oh. I was never taught that. That would mean a lot, thank you. Is that even allowed?'

'Well... officially, no. But I think you'll find most of the people in this city quite accepting when it comes to belief in the afterlife.' She smirked. 'And if anyone complains, they'll answer to me, okay?'

I nodded.

She stood and held onto the handle railing on the vehicle's ceiling. 'This is our station.' The vehicle came to a stop, its door again rising for us. Malu motioned to the platform, so I stood and one by one we all exited the vehicle. I followed Malu up the steps towards a dark-grey facility next to the station.

My knees weakened. 'Um, this assimilation thing?' I began, hoping Malu might be able to put me at ease.

Malu gently held my shoulder. 'I've taken this procedure myself. So... don't be afraid, at worst you'll turn out like me.'

Iya let out another groan, and I gave a polite smile, which quickly disappeared. In truth, I was terrified. What would this assimilation procedure entail?

'A team of scientists will take care of you,' Malu continued as we walked. 'They use a mixture of acolyte powers and technology to change you for the better. One woman will focus on your mind, she'll change the way you think. Another will focus on your powers, she'll work on awakening your true potential.'

A thought occurred: what if, during their work, these scientists accidentally set off the acid capsule near my spine? I was queasy thinking about it.

We entered the facility and walked down the grey corridors. There were soldiers posted everywhere. Scientists were performing experiments in the various laboratories we passed. One room we passed contained rows of strange white capsules suspended from the ceiling. There seemed to be unconscious children floating inside of them.

'I'll bring you here at the end of every day,' Malu called back.

I realised I had been transfixed on the children, so I quickly caught up with her farther down the corridor.

'They will gently put you to sleep for the procedure,' she continued. 'Then I have the honour of carting your limp, sleeping body back home to your bed. Every morning you'll wake up a better person than you were.'

She stopped and grabbed my shoulder. 'And, if I can give a piece of advice? Don't fight it. The more you resist, the more painful it will be.

The first lesson you'll be taught will just be: don't kill women. I'm sure you already agree with that lesson, right?'

We entered through the doorway at the end of the corridor. A team of scientists were waiting, all eyeing me with intrigue. Each had white streaks in their hair. There were also at least ten soldiers posted around the room. Everyone went silent as I walked in. Malu led me to a table in the room's centre.

I was starting to fade out. I couldn't hear what the scientists were saying. Everything was fuzzy, as if I was going deaf. Satisfied I was being adequately guarded, Malu and Iya backed away to the previous corridor.

The scientists advanced. My body naturally tensed, ready to fight, but I again had to remind myself of what was at stake. They laid me on a table and adjusted some straps around my arms, legs and head so I couldn't move. One of the older scientists picked out a needle from a nearby tray and pressed it into my neck. I didn't fight back; it was hopeless. My mind was going to be taken by these people and I was never going to be the same again.

Twelve: Just an Object

The next morning, I sat up and rubbed my blurry eyes. I needed to throw up. On the other side of the darkened room there was an open door. A ceramic bowl sat on the floor inside of the second room, like a fancy toilet. I didn't care what it was, I threw the warm sheets aside and ran to it. I knelt beside the bowl and tried to vomit, but nothing came up.

Somehow, even though my eyes were closed, I could see my surroundings. It was as if I was outside my own head and looking at myself from afar. I was wearing light-coloured clothing, a floral pattern of white and purple. My brown, neck-length hair, normally unwashed and coarse, had been cleaned and tied up in a neat bun. Even my grubby skin had been cleaned.

The duality of my perception was sickening. I tried throwing up again, and this time it came up with a disgusting taste. I felt awful, unable to concentrate and weakened. With my eyes still closed, my second perception shifted and I saw Tau entering the previous bedroom and switching on the lights. What was happening to me?

Tau wasn't wearing her armour, but rather a more formal military dress instead. She had her blue streaks put back in, too. As she made her way to the bathroom, I brought my sleeve to my mouth and wiped away the sick that still clung to my lips.

She poked her head through the doorway and spotted me bent over the toilet. 'Woah, Sacet, are you okay?'

'Does it look like I'm okay?'

I kept my eyes closed for fear of throwing up again if I opened them. This other perspective was spinning out of control, and I couldn't seem to focus on what I wanted to. I saw everything around me all at the same time, even things that were behind walls.

'Fine. I'm sorry for asking. Is there anything I can do to help?' she said, now upset, as if I was the one responsible for how I felt.

'Look, just... just... give me some time, alright?'

'Sure. We're waiting for you outside when you're ready.'

I was still angry at Tau, but I couldn't recall why.

My second perception watched as she left the room and out into the living area. I was finally able to control this sensation. My mind followed Tau as she sat down at a glass table with Malu, who was reading something. I tried to look farther past the living room, but my vision went fuzzy; it gave me a headache.

What happened last night? All I remembered was being taken to that facility and then... being put to sleep. What did they do to me?

No, more importantly, what did they do to Eno? Where was – that's right, he was underground in the mines, and if I didn't do as they told me, they might kill him.

I was hesitant about opening my eyes, but the sickness-inducing swirls were finally under control. I opened them anyway and saw the brown sick water below me. The smell was awful. I stood, made my way over to the sink and twisted the handle next to the faucet. Leaning down to wash my face, I gargled and spat out the burning sick that was still in my mouth.

'Uck...'

What was this power? Did the scientists boost my abilities this much overnight? Were they expecting this to happen? Malu told me they would only be amplifying my powers, not changing or adding to them. It would be best if I didn't tell anyone about this; the less they knew about what I could really do, the better.

I walked back into the bedroom and faced the closed window. The curtain had darkened the room, but sunlight still leaked from behind it. My second set of eyes saw the balcony behind the window curtain, but I couldn't make out the view from the balcony itself.

Walking over to the window, I parted the curtains and took in the stunning view of the city. The tall buildings were covered with windows and adjoining balconies. There were people moving about inside their homes on the other side of the street.

I opened the glass door, stepped closer to the edge of the balcony and peered down into the streets. They were filled with people walking in all directions. The crowd's discussions and other noises of the city travelled up to my ears. My vision spun and I felt sick again. I withdrew from the balcony and back through the windows into my bedroom.

Raising my hands to cover my eyes, I tried to compose myself. This sickness didn't seem to be going away any time soon. I walked to my bedroom door and tried to focus on what my own two eyes were telling me, rather than these images of my surroundings that bombarded my mind.

I saw what I believed to be, from memory, a light switch. I turned it off and left the room.

The living area was joined with a kitchen and dining area. They were all in one large room, which overlooked the city with a balcony of its own from the dining area. Iya was sitting on an elongated cushioned chair, staring at the ceiling. She had a similar military uniform to Tau. I couldn't see anyone else in the room. Good, that meant my unwanted entourage of guards was shrinking.

'Good morning,' Malu said from the dining table. She, too, wore a uniform. Tau was also sitting at the table.

'Feeling better?' Tau inquired while standing to pull out a chair from the table. 'Have a seat.'

I ambled over to the table and sat in the chair next to them. I was still dizzy and even though I was looking at the table, my second perception was spinning all over the place. Malu put down the strange, see-through device she was reading from to give me her full attention. She gestured around the room. 'So, this is my home. I've been asked to share it with you for a while. You know, until you get with the program and find your own place. Until then, it'll just be you and me. We've got a big day planned. First, we're going to get a bite to eat, then we're heading over to the Military Quad to introduce you to your trainer.'

I shook my head. 'Food? Erm, I don't think I'm ready to eat, I'd rather sit here for a bit.'

'Still not feeling well?' she asked. 'I guess we can stay for a little while and fill you in on things you might not know yet. Do you remember what our streaks all mean?' She pulled on the side of her fringe, which was mostly coloured purple with blue tips.

I shook my head. It had something to do with ranks, but that was all I knew.

Malu relaxed back into her chair and put her feet onto the table. 'First thing you should know is that there is a streak colour and a tip colour. Streaks are for the detachment and tips are for the rank.

'The first streak colour is white; that's for scientists and administrators, the people who run the place. They're not fighters, so they're pretty boring. Next is blue; the basic soldiers, Tau for example. Red streaks are city defence; demolitions or an engineer of some sort. Green are the highly trained special ops teams; stealth and misinformation, that sort of thing. Yellow is the air force.'

Malu put down her feet and faced me with a serious expression: 'And purple? That's for acolytes, you and me... and Iya over there, too.'

Iya still sat in silence, looking around the room at anything but us. Her streaks were purple, too, but with red tips.

'And the tips?' I asked.

'First rank is white: initiate. It's for children or people who have just joined us, like you. After that is blue: trooper. And then red: corporal, they lead squads. Green: officer, they lead units. Yellow is for colonel; there's only six of them in each detachment here in the city and the officers answer to them. Lastly, black tips make you matriarch. There's only six of them, too, one for each detachment.'

It hadn't meant anything to me at the time, but now I remembered Verre's streaks. Like Malu and Iya, Verre had purple streaks in her blonde hair, but her tips were black.

I put my elbows on the table. 'That Verre woman, she's the acolyte matriarch, right? I don't like her... at all.'

Malu grinned. 'Well, that's a shame, because you're going to have to show respect to all of your superiors now. Everyone in this room is your superior at the moment. Although, when you get your white-tipped purple streaks, you will outrank Tau. Acolytes are just more important people than regular ones.' She smirked at Tau.

'Hardly fair,' Tau said.

Malu stood from her chair. 'Are you feeling better yet?' she asked of me. 'I don't know about you but I'm famished. How about you, Iya?'

Iya stood too, looking over to us with glazed eyes. 'Firstly, yes, I'm hungry. I've been telling you that for ages. And secondly, call me by my rank. You should be setting a good example for her.'

'Er... sorry, Corporal. Okay, let's go,' Malu replied.

We got up and made our way out of the apartment and into the corridor. Unlike most of the corridors I had seen so far, which were cold and made of chrome, this one was decorated with smooth carpeting and artsy engravings in the colourful tiled walls.. We followed a long red rug that led down the hall, passing apartment doors as we went and tiny depictions of women performing work, like cooking and building. We reached a staircase and descended it.

Tau caught up alongside me. 'So, uhh, Sacet. About what happened at the river... I feel terrible about it. I honestly was trying to save the both of you. Can you forgive me?'

My heart sank as I imagined where Eno was right now. 'Fine, whatever,' I lied.

'He'll be okay,' Malu added, focusing on the hallway.

Tau leant over as we walked, trying to catch my attention, then smiled. 'That's good because I was hoping we could start over and be proper friends, all of us.'

Malu nodded. 'Sure, I always need people who've got my back.'

Iya snorted. 'I'm only here today under orders.' She gestured towards me. 'To kill this one if she gets out of line.'

Tau looked expectantly at me. I could tell she was feeling guilty about not siding with us.

I shrugged. 'Okay, Tau. But I'm not even sure what I'll be doing around here yet, other than being forcibly brainwashed every night.'

Tau nudged me. 'It won't be as bad as you think. You'll start liking it here soon, I'm sure of it.'

We came to the bottom of the stairs and into a reception hall. It was filled with women coming and going out of the apartment complex. They must have been civilians because none of them had streaks in their hair like Iya, Malu or Tau. They wore clothing and dresses that showed off extravagant colours. Some of them noticed us and avoided eye contact. We left together through the main entrance.

'I've made a morning booking at Alai's,' Malu said as she led us down the street. 'It's close by and I love their food. You'll love it, too. Have you tried them, Corporal? We can get something else if you'd prefer?'

Iya groaned. 'No... and it's fine. Whatever is fine.'

As we walked, I observed the other people passing by on the street. They didn't seem unhappy, but then, did they know what atrocities their military committed around the globe? Could this be what they had planned for the whole world?

The entire place was decorated colourfully, just like the people. The walkways were lined with trees, the buildings and storefronts painted in vivid hues, and even the path below our feet was cut into decorative patterns.

There was art painted on various walls, too, sometimes of soldiers, other times of a smiling old woman wearing pure white robes, surrounded by an aura of gold. Were the townspeople painting all of this?

There was a billboard hanging overhead depicting some sort of huge aircraft on a sky backdrop. On it were the words: New weapons to end the fight.

Malu scoffed when she noticed it. 'It sure would be nice to end the fight, but they've been working on the Coda for cycles now with no end in sight.'

I felt light-headed. There was too much information surrounding me. My second perception swirled and spun out of control. My regular vision blurred and tunnelled. I swayed and collapsed to the ground.

'Sacet? Sacet!'

Tau leapt towards me, attempting to cushion my fall, but I hit the ground anyway.

I needed to get out of this street. I stood carefully. As Tau offered her shoulder for me to lean on, Malu rushed over, appearing concerned. Even Iya was taken aback.

I needed to say something, or they would look further into this. I didn't want them to find out about this new power I had. 'It's fine, I'm fine. I – I'm not taking too well to the procedure, that's all. Can I skip it tonight?'

Malu shook her head. 'Uhh, Sacet, I think we should take you there right now.'

'No!' They leant back at my outburst, so I cleared my throat. 'No it's... alright. More scientists are the *last* thing I need.'

'Could be dehydration?' Tau suggested. 'Or maybe because you haven't eaten in a while?'

I nodded in agreement. 'Yep, that'll be it. Let's keep going to this Alai's you were telling us about.'

Malu seemed hesitant. 'Okay, but if it happens again, we're taking you, no question about it, and I'm *definitely* mentioning this to them. They could be hurting you without you realising it, right?'

'Exactly,' I said. Of course they were hurting me! How much longer could I keep this charade going? I was physically safe here, sure, but I had never been more unhappy, more angry in my entire life. *Eno, I hope you're okay*, I thought.

We arrived at the restaurant; the front sign spelled 'Alai's' in big, fancy letters. As we left the bustle of the city streets I felt a bit more relieved. The loud and crowded mess of the boulevard was instead replaced with the clattering noise of the eatery's customers enjoying their meals.

The unfamiliar yet delicious smelling odours overwhelmed my senses. Sizzling meats in simmering oils made me want to bite the air in front of me. Culinary creations of various colours I had never seen before gave off equal notes of sweet and savoury. The bubbly beverages reminded me of a hazardous chemical, but the allure to try them was powerful. Some meals looked so delicate that the slightest breeze would crumble them.

There weren't many seats left. Was Malu sure she had a booking? Iya stepped forward and glared at the civilians in front of us. Some of the customers who had already finished their food noticed her, stood without speaking and left. They avoided eye contact as they passed us, rushing out of the restaurant.

'I think our table just opened up,' Iya said, sitting down. She pointed to a nearby waitress still serving another group of customers. 'You! Clear this table!' The waitress moved away from the other table and set to work cleaning ours. The other customers didn't even glance in our direction.

Malu sat with Iya on one side and I sat next to Tau. It was good to sit; all of this moving around was still making me sick.

The waitress came back with a glass-like device, similar to the one Malu had in her apartment.

'Wha– What can I serve our most esteemed soldiers today?'

Malu smiled. 'I made a booking under Malu. It was for four people. No hurry.'

Iya leaned back in her chair and stared at the ceiling. 'Don't say that, now they'll take their time.'

The waitress bowed and rushed off, and Malu turned to me. 'So, Sacet, I was thinking that I would introduce you to my mother and sister. They'll give you a warm Nomadic welcome, I'm sure.'

'Oh, that sounds great. Um... what about your father?'

Iya refocused on the conversation and stared at Malu expectantly.

Malu's smile faded, and her eyes darted nervously towards Iya. 'My father and brother are in the Prison Quadrant along with all of the other men.'

I nodded. 'Do you ever get to see them?'

'Sometimes, if I have an assignment there.' She forced a smile. 'To be honest, I'd... rather not talk about them.'

How depressing. Is that how I was going to feel about Eno after the Dominion crushed my spirit?

'How about you, Tau?' I asked. 'How many sisters do you have?'

Tau thought for a moment. 'Tens of thousands, I guess?'

Malu giggled. 'Perhaps what she meant was... how many of them are you close to?'

Tau frowned. 'Oh. Um, three? Tyr, Coleo and Tarsus. I caught up with them last night. They were *really* worried about me.'

'And what about you, Iya?' I said, slightly sarcastically. 'Got any friends?'

Iya leapt across the table, seized my collar and forced me to be face to face with her. 'Listen carefully you imbecilic, petulant, thief of my personal oxygen supply. I don't want to know you. I was happier when I didn't.'

Our noses were almost touching and our eyes locked. She didn't let up. 'I'm not here to help you, and I'm definitely not going to *cry* over the death of your grandpapa, one of my enemies. And if you neglect to call me Corporal again, I will crush your flesh into a paste so fine, I'll use it to flavour the meal they bring me. Clear?'

The whole restaurant was silent, waiting for my response. I would love for nothing more than to fight her right now, to teleport her to the middle of nowhere, but I remembered Eno.

I gritted my teeth. 'Clear.'

She released me and eased back into her seat, staring down anyone that had been watching us. The rest of us waited in silence, avoiding Iya's loathsome gaze.

The waitress thankfully interrupted with a large platter of fruit, vegetables and assorted meats. There was even necrolisk meat on the plate. As it was placed onto the table, Iya sat back up in her chair with excitement and reached for a piece.

'Wait! Uh... Corporal, ma'am,' Malu said as she brought a hand in front of Iya. 'I've asked Alai to prepare a traditional nomadic meal. In this case, a tribute spread, in memory of Sacet's grandfather. I know you don't care but–'

Iya rolled her fingers to speed Malu up. 'Yes, yes. Cast your little magic spell and talk to the dead person already.'

Malu picked up a small, metallic object from the tray and clicked the trigger. A small flame shot out from the top, and she positioned the lighter over the top of a wax candle in the centre. The candle lit and flickered gently.

'Now?' Iya said.

'One last thing,' Malu said. 'Sacet, do you have anything you would like to say in honour of your grandfather's passing?'

Iya rolled her eyes and glared at me.

'Oh. Uh... well, when my parents died, he stepped up to protect me and my little brother. He... he was a smart person and he taught us a lot. Not just about survival but about the world, too.'

I hesitated and Malu smiled. 'It's okay, you're doing great, keep going.'

'He was wise, but he wasn't always a good man,' I said. All three girls, even Iya, stared at me, confused. 'The only thing I admired about him was that he would protect my brother no matter what,' I continued. 'He knew what I really was. He resented me; he blamed me for everything bad that happened around us. The only reason he trained me was because he wanted to use me as a weapon. I always felt like a prisoner, with no free will. Being with my brother made it tolerable.'

Iya's frustrated expression calmed. All three hung on my every word.

'I feel bad because he was the only person Eno could trust, other than me. I had to take his abuse. I pretended like it never got to me.' I wiped the tears from my eyes. 'I hated him... so much.'

After a long pause, Malu sighed. 'Males, am I right?'

Tau reached out her hand to mine. 'You don't have to feel like you're alone anymore. You've got your sisters back.'

Malu smiled. 'Your *original* family.'

I nodded, pretending to be comforted, but truthfully that did little to make me feel better. Still, I could tell they were trying. Was this what it was like to have friends?

Malu gave a small bow. 'And we all honour his passing.' She smiled. 'Now, let's eat!'

Both Malu and Tau picked up a piece of food and began. Iya and I sat a little while longer in silence. I thought she'd be eager to eat, but she blankly stared instead, as though something was weighing on her mind.

Thirteen: An Imperfect Circle

Eno

The restraints around my wrists were too tight, especially after just receiving a tattoo there. I slowly lifted my arms to examine the mark again. The symbol was black and had numbers underneath. It had a little face with eyes, but no mouth or nose. It was surrounded by... arms? Maybe wings? It stung badly.

All I could see was the small, dark holding cell surrounding me. Space was cramped, forcing me to stay seated. I couldn't breathe. My chest was heavy. The walls were closing in. I panted over and over, hoping to get more air. Was it getting darker in here?

The only light came from the small slits in the cell door. Outside the slits, was another cell across from me and a corridor separating us.

The train car jolted again, causing me to shoot up off my seat for a moment. My tattoo smacked into the metal restraints, and it stung even more than before. I couldn't contain my cry. I hoped the guards didn't hear me.

'Please let me out of here,' I whispered. 'Please let me out of here please let me out of here please let—'

'Is that you, Eno?' a voice said from one of the other cells that I couldn't see.

It was Pilgrim, I recognised his voice. Wasn't he worried about the guards? If they caught us talking, I don't know what they would do to us.

'Y-y-yes...' I replied.

'You've got to stay strong, little buddy,' he said. 'I'm going to get you through this. We all are, aren't we guys?'

'That's right,' another voice said to my left.

'Don't cry, kid. Don't give them the satisfaction,' a different voice on the right said.

'Just do your best, buddy,' Pilgrim continued. 'Do you remember the promise I made? What was it?'

'You said you would look out for me,' I replied quietly.

'I meant it.'

I started crying again, but I couldn't wipe my cheeks. 'I'm sorry, Pilgrim.'

'Sorry? What are you sorry for?'

'We thought you were all dead,' I blubbered. 'My sister and I, we did this to your village. It's our fault.'

'Listen to me. It's not your fault. A bunch of us made it out, but I got my stupid self caught afterwards. You didn't do this.'

'Are we going to die in here?'

'We're fighters. They're not going to break our spirits, got it?'

'I... I got it.'

There was stomping outside the cells in the corridor, followed by a sharp electrical crackle.

'Stop talking!' one of the guards said, no doubt electrocuting someone through the small slits in the cell door.

I could hear muffled groans of pain as the shocks continued. Was it Pilgrim? It could have just as easily been any man stuffed in these cells.

There was a shift in the train's momentum and I slumped to the side of my cell. The constant hum of the hovering carriage lowered its pitch; we were slowing down. The guard stopped shocking the man and walked past my cell.

'Let them out,' I could hear the overseer say from the end of the corridor as the train slowed and eventually stopped.

There was a mechanical whir around me as the rusty restraints loosened and lifted up. My cell door squealed open, as did the others.

'Stand up!' one of the guards shouted as the green squares lit up on the ground in front of all of our cells. 'Move to your square, now!'

We stood, almost in unison, and positioned ourselves on our squares, facing into the corridor. The ugly overseer walked down the aisle between us, but stopped when she got to me. There was another mechanical noise as the door at the end of the carriage opened like a ramp.

The overseer pointed at me. 'We've got something special in mind for this one. Take him!'

'Yes, Overseer,' one of the guards said, prodding me from behind.

'I volunteer to do his duties,' Pilgrim said to my side.

'Me, too,' another man said on the other side of the aisle, giving me a quick glance and a smile. He faced forward again before the overseer saw him.

'I don't recall asking for volunteers,' she said in a low, gravelly tone.

Two guards approached each of the men with their long lances and struck them. Blue sparks appeared, and the men convulsed with gritted teeth, slumping to the ground. The overseer watched with a smile as the guards didn't let up.

'Stop it!' I cried out.

The overseer turned back to me and slapped my cheek with the back of her hand, sending me back towards my cell. An alarm sounded throughout the carriage.

'Get back on your square!' she screamed as I landed into the metal door frame. 'Move! Get on it, now!'

My square was flashing red now that I wasn't on it, so I stepped inside it again. The overseer stared me down. The alarm stopped. She pulled out a small, glass-like device and tapped a button, causing the green square at my feet to disappear.

'Number fourteen,' she noted, looking at one of the nearby guards. 'Take the boy.'

Another red line appeared at my feet, leading out of the carriage. The nearest guard grabbed my stinging wrist and pulled me along the line. All the other men had enraged faces, as if they wanted to act out, but couldn't. No one else stepped forward as I was led out of the train carriage, down its ramp and out into the station.

The cavern was vast and open, bigger than any I had ever seen. Glowing, electrified guide wires twisted along thousands of paths. I guessed that's what was powering the trains. Many wound their way around the edges, and coiled up rocky spires in the cavern's centre. Lamps were dotted throughout, lighting the paths and working areas.

The guard hurried me along the red line as we left the platform and down some steps. The overseer's horrid shouts started to fade as we pulled farther away. Was Pilgrim okay?

'Hurry up,' the guard said, jolting my wrist downwards, almost tripping me down the next step.

'Please, why are you doing this? I'm no threat to you, I'm just a kid,' I said.

'You wouldn't be the first,' she said as we reached the bottom of the steps. 'It's better that you grow up caged rather than a free monster.'

There were several men in a quarry-like area, with guards watching over them from the upper levels. Most of the men had gathered around a large stone wall at the bottom of the pit. The area was well-lit, and they had lots of equipment and machinery.

Before entering the site, the guard and I reached the end of the red line. She turned, pointed a small metal device at me and clicked a button, producing an audible beep. Then she pulled me off the line with no alarms to follow.

We made our way down a weaving path before reaching the bottom. All of the men had stopped working, as if they were waiting for us.

The guard shoved me towards the men. 'Here he is. Hopefully he's useful, for *all* your sakes.'

The men all wore the same prison uniform as me. They were mostly older, except for one long-haired boy, who appeared similar in age to my sister.

One of the older men stepped forward. 'Hey there, kid,' he said, putting his arm around my shoulders and walking me over to the other men. He glanced at the soldiers. 'The introductions can wait, we're kind of on a tight schedule here. We've got a job that only someone like *you* can do.'

'What? But I'm just a kid?'

'Exactly,' the man replied, pointing to a small hole in the rocky wall. 'You see this wall here?'

'Yeah?'

'Well, it's not very stable, and if we get the heavy equipment in to laser it up, it might cave in that tunnel.'

'So?'

'*So*, there's a valuable piece of equipment stuck in that hole there and we can't reach it.' He measured his hands apart. 'It's about this big, silver. Rather than just calling it a loss and moving on, we've been told we have to get it back out. If the tunnel caves, then the piece will be crushed. This is where you come in.'

I stepped back. 'Oh, no. No, I can't do that.'

The man leaned in closer so only I could hear. 'You'd better not say that out loud again, not while they're watching us. They'll kill one of us at random if we fail. Please, just try.'

'Is there a problem?' one of the guards said, walking over to us. Her fingers impatiently tapped around her rifle's trigger.

'No, ma'am. No problem at all, right kid?'

I had no choice but to nod. 'Um... right.'

'Hurry it up then,' she said, prodding the other man with her gun.

He led me closer to the wall and leant down to peek through the small hole. 'I don't like it any more than you do,' he said, noticing my anxious expression. 'Here, take this.'

He handed me a small plastic torch then stepped back from the wall, giving me room. I knelt down to get a better look, holding the light out in front. The weak torch barely lit the tiny dark tunnel.

My heart raced. My breath quickened. I already felt like I was running out of air.

I glanced back at the man, but caught sight of the guard advancing closer, so I lay down flat onto the ground and started to crawl in. I was only just thin enough to fit. I shimmied through the narrow gap, but it didn't seem to be getting any wider. The side of the tunnel scraped against my wrist, and I cringed as it stung again. I pulled myself over one jagged stone after another, my torch showing the way. A particularly sharp stone cut my hand open.

I couldn't see the entrance behind me anymore. I wanted to cry again, to scream out, but I didn't want the tunnel to cave in. My lungs heaved and screamed for oxygen.

I held out my torch again and saw something shiny. Pulling myself closer, I reached out to it. I felt around, looking for something to grab onto, and eventually found what seemed to be a handle.

I pulled as hard as I could. It was stuck, like they said. I shimmied closer and tried pulling on it sideways first, grunting as I did so. Nothing worked. There was floating dust everywhere. I wished a strong breeze would come through and blow it all away.

There was a loud rumbling and I could hear small stones shifting and cracking. Vibrations shuddered in the ground beneath me, so I let go of the handle and started shifting backwards as fast as I could. With every push backwards the shaking seemed to intensify.

A pebble fell loose and hit me in the back of my head, rolling off my neck and into my hand.

'Help me!' I screamed, still trying to shift backwards.

'Get out of there!' a voice said from the exit.

There were other muffled voices outside, but I couldn't make out what they were saying. Another tremendous quake took hold and the voices disappeared. I turned over onto my back, closed my eyes and held my hands up to my face, hoping to shield myself.

'No!' I yelled.

The quaking stopped. It was silent. I opened my eyes. The small light shone more clearly now, and I could see that the small tunnel had grown. I was now in a much larger space, almost enough room to stand up in. The rocky ceiling was in the shape of an almost perfect dome. Gone was the dust that had been choking me. Strangely, the air was completely clean.

What had caused this? Rather than a cave in, the passage had... caved out? I would've died had the rocks not fallen in such a miraculous way.

I pulled myself up off the ground, picked up my light and crouched so as to not hit my head. The equipment had been freed; it was sitting in some loose rocks at the edge of the dome. Picking it up with ease, I turned back to where the tunnel had been but it had vanished.

I put my hand with the light onto the wall and felt around it. I leant forward and pushed as hard as I could. The wall gave way and crumbled, and light poured in through the cracks.

The loose stones fell down on the other side, revealing a mix of worried faces staring in. The quaking restarted behind me, as though the dome was collapsing.

'It's him, he's alive! Help me get him out,' I heard one of the older men say.

A hand grabbed mine and pulled. The others grabbed onto my wrist and forearm, pulling me through the new hole and out into the cavern again. Once I was on the other side, I knelt down onto the ground, dropped the light and the equipment, and inspected the fresh gash on my hand, which was still dripping blood.

'Barely a scratch,' one of the guards said as she walked over and picked up the item and examined it, then looked at me. 'And the boy seems fine, too.'

The other guards laughed as she returned to them with the equipment and they inspected it together. Most of the workers resumed their duties, clearing away rubble. The long-haired boy from earlier and another man knelt beside me. The man had grey hair and, like the other older men around us, a beard. Both had dark brown skin.

'Are you okay?' the boy asked as I brushed small stones off my shoulder with my good hand.

I nodded, still looking down at the cut on my hand.

'I'm Toroi, and this is my dad, Turen,' the boy said as his father glanced over his shoulder to the distracted guards. 'And you're *very* lucky.'

'I'm Eno,' I replied. 'I don't feel lucky.'

Turen dipped into his tattered suit and pulled out a small piece of fabric. He brought it to my hand, wrapped it around, and tied it tight. 'It's like they have it out for kids here. They make my son do the most dangerous tasks, too.'

Toroi nodded. 'We'll help you, Eno. Just stick with us.'

Fourteen: A Tap on the Glass

The Military Quad
Sacet

The doors in front of us opened, revealing a vast, silver mess hall. It was filled with soldiers eating at long row tables, and relaxed chatter and laughter. We entered and many gazed at us. I looked down at my clothing and sighed. I felt embarrassed for wearing a military uniform so soon after being captured.

Iya marched off ahead of us, leaving Malu and Tau to guide me through the table rows. Although a few soldiers were middle-aged, I couldn't help but notice that most of them were only youths. Occasionally, a child initiate was mixed in with the regulars. My memories of being in a place like this when I was younger were slowly returning.

Many wore full combat armour, while others wore a simpler set of fatigues like mine. Most of the soldiers' streaks were either blue or red, and most of their tips were blue. It didn't seem like promotions happened very often.

As we strode down the middle of the mess hall, I locked eyes with some of the sitting soldiers. When they spotted me, they prodded the closest person on their tables and pointed. Was it because I didn't have streaks like them, or... did these people somehow know about me?

The soldiers folded their arms and shot me nasty looks as I passed. One of them stood and mocked me by imitating and exaggerating my walk. I tried to ignore the jeers and sniggers, fixing my eyes ahead.

Tau glanced back at me as we walked between the tables. 'This is the mess hall of the Military Quad; you'll eat with Malu at her place, so you won't have to worry about coming here.' Tau had noticed the heckling from the crowd, too. 'I won't hold it against you if you don't come to visit me here, either.'

Malu quickened her pace. 'Give a tour later, she's already late for training. Apparently, your trainer was flown in this morning, last minute. Let's *not* keep her waiting.'

We both sped up to match her pace. I was feeling much better than I was earlier, and I seemed to have a handle on this new power. It felt more natural, no longer constantly inducing sickness, and also increasing the range of my situational awareness. It was like I was able to anticipate things before they happened because I was able to see my surroundings both with and without my eyes. Everything felt slower, yet time had not slowed.

We reached the end of the hall, leaving the derisive soldiers behind. As we stepped through the door, my jaw dropped at the sight of a large arena. The ceiling was high, the outside was lined with seats, and in the centre was what appeared to be a sparring ring, its enclosure walls made of some kind of transparent plastic. Two soldiers were fighting in unarmed combat in front of a cheering audience.

Malu tapped me on the shoulder to get my attention. 'I'm not sure where we're supposed to be meeting your trainer. I'll find out. Wait here and enjoy the show for a bit, okay?'

Tau nodded. 'I'll stay with her.'

'Great,' Malu replied as she made her way down the steps, before turning back to us again. 'And make sure you show the proper respect when you meet her, okay? Don't move!'

I nodded and she trotted off towards the far side of the stadium. I didn't mind waiting. Watching the two girls in the arena punch each other senseless was interesting enough, although their forms were sloppy. As we watched, I couldn't help but analyse their mistakes.

It was so long ago now, but the memory of waking up to a desert sunrise and sparring with my grandfather was still fresh in my mind.

'Hey, sand scab!'

Tau and I turned to see a group of young soldiers approaching.

Tau positioned herself between them and me. 'Just ignore them. Let me handle this.'

A smug-looking woman strutted forward with her arms akimbo. 'All settled in, are we? So much better than hiding in caves like a coward, right?'

Tau raised a hand to stop her. 'Kian, in case you didn't know, Sacet is our superior.'

Kian pushed past Tau and tried to flick my fringe, but I leant away. 'Not yet she's not, not until she gets her streaks.'

A crowd of smiling soldiers was starting to gather around us. Iya was among them. She grinned like the others. Had she put them up to this?

Kian moved even closer. Her breath reeked of decay. A brief smirk revealed some of her teeth were missing.

'You don't belong here, filth.' She shoved me in the chest and I stumbled back. The crowd jeered and laughed. 'Stupid savage. You going to run away? Little baby want to go back to her sandbox?'

What was a sandbox? The entire crowd called out similar nonsensical insults.

Tau frantically looked around, as if desperate to regain control of the situation. 'You know you're messing with an acolyte, right?'

'Whatever, *killer*,' a different girl called out, eliciting more laughter.

'No one cares what you think, nomad-lover,' another added.

We were outnumbered here. I didn't seem to have anyone on my side other than Tau. And I couldn't just kill them, as much as I wanted to.

Their behaviour reminded me of how desert bandits would act in a settlement, intimidating weak townspeople and merchants to get their way. Aberym trained me in how to deal with their kind. I looked over Kian's shoulder; the arena was now empty. I glanced at Tau. 'Sorry, but I have to do this.'

Kian smirked. 'Do what, scab?'

I opened a portal under both Kian's and my feet, and we fell through to the arena. The crowd above blurted confused murmurs. Once everyone had caught up with what had happened, the entire arena erupted with cheer. I took one last look up through the portal and gave Tau a reassuring nod, before closing it.

A surge of soldiers poured through the doorway from the mess hall, filling the seats. They must have heard the commotion coming from inside the small stadium.

'I take it back, you're not a coward,' Kian said, raising her fists and cracking her knuckles. 'Just incredibly stupid. I'm going to make you bleed.'

I shook my head at her and smirked. 'You talk too much.'

We assumed fighting stances. I didn't recognise hers, but I could guess she'd fight like all the other Female Dominion soldiers.

She sprinted at me. I raised my arms to defend and she leapt into the air. The power of her kick to my stomach drove me to the arena wall. The crowd cheered.

She was stronger than she appeared. Both my arms stung. I couldn't take hits like that. I needed to be smarter and put all those cycles of Aberym's training to good use. My concentration shifted away from the booing crowd. I tried to focus my new second perception on Kian. It was as if time slowed again.

She closed the gap between us and attempted another kick. I sidestepped as her foot whizzed past my shoulder. She continued to spin, each time kicking, but I dodged them all. When the moment was right, I shifted and thrust a double open-palmed push to her chest that knocked her off her feet and onto the ground.

The crowd exploded with taunts and scoffs, but I tried putting them out of my mind again. Kian rose to her feet with a look of pure hatred. She hadn't figured out that I was too fast for her yet.

She dashed at me again, this time with a volley of punches. Still too slow. As one of her punches brushed past my cheek, I shifted my hips close to hers, grabbed her arm, and threw her body over mine. She fell onto her back and stared up at me in surprise.

I would beat her in a fair fight, not kick her while she was down, so I walked away and gave her room.

Again, she rose to her feet. She wiped her sweat from her forehead, and her anger faded. She smiled and nodded, as if impressed, before looking over to her friends and beckoning them. The crowd stood and roared as another two soldiers entered the ring behind me. What? Three on one?

I gestured at her friends. 'You think this is fair?'

Kian grinned. 'You started it. You're obviously using your powers somehow. Besides, we're not leaving here until we see your blood.'

All three girls charged, and I tried focusing on all of them at once. Kian approached from the front with an uppercut, but I ducked and grabbed hold of her wrist. I used her momentum and threw her into one of the other attackers. The third was still moving in.

My two perceptions worked in tandem now, allowing me to react far quicker than usual. I dodged the third attacker's punches and countered with a barrage of jabs to her torso. She clutched her ribs and bent forward.

While she was stunned, I smashed my closed fist on the back of her neck like a hammer, putting her on the ground. I heard a crack, probably from having hit her a little *too* hard.

The other two girls were back up. Kian stomped towards the ringside entrance. She opened it and gestured for others to enter, too. Five more soldiers poured in through the doorway, one coming to the aid of the girl I had just felled, pulling her up.

This was insane! I pressed back up against the wall as all eight edged closer. They quickly surrounded me. Being able to process everything around me at once wouldn't help now.

'Enough already, she obviously won!' I heard someone scream from the crowd. It sounded like Tau.

Kian threw another punch, and as I dodged, one of their kicks connected with my stomach. I doubled over in pain and received two more hits to the face, forcing me back into the ring wall. I placed my hands in front of my face and braced for another hit.

A draught picked up around me. An elderly, armoured woman materialised between us, stopping the girls in their tracks. She wielded a long sword, which shone an iridescent blue.

'Touch my student again and you'll pay with your hand,' she snapped at the attackers.

Fifteen: Living Legend

The shocked soldiers gave the woman a short bow before quickly exiting the arena. The stadium of onlookers ceased their cheers and began to disperse. The old, scar-faced woman sheathed her sword into what appeared to be a walking stick, and glared at each soldier as they left. Where had she come from?

She faced me. 'Take my hand!' she ordered, stretching one out to me. I struggled to my feet and grasped my fingers around hers. The crowd's droning subsided into a muddled low tone.

My head started to throb and the crowd's faces blurred and warped grossly. My feet left the ground and the weightlessness made me feel faint. The sight of the arena faded and morphed into another room. This was her teleportation.

My second perception was making me ill again. It wasn't used to such a rapid change in the environment. Still holding the woman's hand, I crumpled to my knees.

This room was much smaller than the arena. There were weights, punching bags, benches and mirrors lining the walls, and in the centre of the room was a large, padded floor.

As I rose, the old woman let go and shuffled to the middle of the room. She sat down on the cushioned floor with her legs crossed and placed her walking stick to the side. Her time-worn face was misshapen with hideous scars upon it. Her short, grey hair lacked any coloured streaks, and although she gave off a commanding presence, her body appeared frail.

The uniform she wore wasn't the same as that of the other soldiers; it was still mostly silver but the configuration was different. Was this woman my trainer?

A door opened behind me, and Malu and Tau rushed into the room. They froze and dropped their jaws at the sight of the woman.

'You're... you're...' Tau began.

'You're Esprit Matriarch Marid!' Malu finished, equally as starstruck.

'It's just Colonel now,' Marid corrected, rolling her eyes. 'Thanks to Verre. Did you bring what I asked?'

Malu nodded. 'Ye–yes ma'am.' She reached down to her belt and produced a small pair of tongs. 'And might I just say, ma'am, you are... a living legend.'

Marid shook her head. 'Don't call me ma'am, I'm retired,' she said before pausing for a moment and letting out a sigh. 'At least I *thought* I was. Well? What are you waiting for? Get to it!' she said to Malu and pointed at me.

'Right! Sorry. Sacet, sit down please.'

Malu knelt beside me as I sat and brought the tongs up to my hair. They had small gadgets at the end which Malu used to clamp onto my hair and gently pull down along some of my fringe. Meanwhile, Tau took a seat along the side of the room.

Marid stared up at the ceiling and smiled. 'So, there I was, sitting in my beautiful manor, sipping on a cold hapoyo juice. This war was over for me, I had earned my rest. When wouldn't you know it, the *renowned* Matriarch Verre came upon my screen spouting something about a teleporting prodigy in need of my expertise. The less said about that matriarch, the better.'

She glared at Malu, as though expecting her to already be finished with my hair. 'I wasn't particularly fond of her idea, either, Malu. So, of course, after I travelled a long journey, from the next province over no less, I arrive to find that this notorious neophyte is a nitwit.'

I shrugged as Malu finished the first streak and moved onto the second. 'What are you talking about? That fight?'

'You shouldn't have fought them, Sacet,' Tau interrupted.

Marid raised an eyebrow at her. 'Excuse me, who asked *you* anything? The acolytes are talking.'

Malu finished the second streak. She pushed a small switch on the device and then brought it back up to my hair again for the tips.

Marid shot a look back at me. 'How did they convince you to not use your powers? Is your gullibility going to be an ongoing problem, I wonder?'

I glared back at her. 'No, but I–'

She waved her finger and interrupted. 'I'm *not* finished talking! How could you, an acolyte, let those feeble and weak fools order *you* around? Do you *not* understand your position in this place?'

Malu stood up now that my streaks and tips were complete. I could see the white-tipped, purple streaks on the edge of my periphery.

'Leave us!' Marid yelled at the other two.

Malu glanced at Tau. 'But, *uh*, we've been ordered to stay–'

'I said leave us! Or are you stupid, too? Perhaps she learned that from you?'

Malu gave a quick bow, and left the room with Tau in tow behind her.

Marid locked eyes with me again and took a deep breath. '*Never* let a subordinate tell you what to do. You, of all people, have earned the right to command over those weaklings. You are superior to those people, and you must remind them of that every chance you get. Next time one gives you disrespect you will put them in their place. Understand?'

What did she mean I had 'earned the right'? She seemed to be waiting for a response, so I gave a quick nod.

'Now that that's out of the way, let's begin,' she said, picking up her cane and standing up again. 'Do you know who I am?'

'Only your name.'

She paced with her free hand behind her back. 'I'm a war hero, battled for decades on the Muta frontline. In my time, I've saved hundreds of lives, and killed many thousands more. You're lucky to benefit from my experience.'

Marid stopped and bent over me. 'Now, tell me what you can do.'

'Well, I create portals…'

'Yes, yes, yes… I know that part. Verre has already filled me in, but the question is: what can you *do* with those portals?'

Did Verre get her to ask this? I still needed to be careful not to mention how far my portals could really go, which included into every village I had ever visited.

'I've used my portals to hide myself in the desert, and I've used the ground as a weapon a couple of times to push and... impale. I've used them to travel and survive.'

Marid stopped in her tracks and glanced back at me. 'And? What else?'

'There is no *else*. That's it,' I said.

She sighed. 'Such gifts are wasted on the youth. The way I understand your power, there are so many more applications, like levitation perhaps. Have you tried to fly yet?'

'What? How – how would I even – I –'

Marid raised a finger to her temple as though in pain. 'Spare me the brain damage for a moment and just *listen*. Put one portal flat on the ground face down, and the destination on top of it face up.'

I didn't understand where she was going with this, but I supposed it was worth a try. I stood, concentrated and spun my fingers. My portals opened almost instantly this time. I was taken aback; my powers had improved overnight.

'Good, now hold it.'

Marid dematerialised from where she was standing and rematerialised near the side of the room. She bent down and grabbed onto one of the huge weights. She wasn't serious, was she? As if she was going to lift that.

She looked back over to where I had created my portals and dematerialised with the weight. She reappeared again, but this time the weight transported with her on top of the portals.

Marid backed away a couple of paces. 'Okay. Now... listen very carefully so you don't make a fool of yourself again. I want you to keep the bottom portal stationary, but lift the top portal up, slowly.'

Her insults were getting on my nerves. She was basically a female version of Aberym. I was going to shut her up with this. I raised the second portal towards the ceiling, which caused the weight to levitate upwards, but it began to wobble.

'Slowly, I said. Slower!'

I tried adjusting the balance of the portal, but it was no use, it tipped to the side, and I lost control. As the weight came falling down to the floor, we both braced our hands around our ears. It crashed with a loud thud, shaking the ground.

Marid brought her hands back down again, and picked up her walking stick. She disappeared from where she was standing, and I felt a strong smack to the side of my head. I fell to the ground, brought my hand to the welt and cringed.

Marid stood over me and whacked her walking stick along my back repeatedly. 'Incorrect! And every time you make a fool of yourself, you will be punished. Do it again, slowly this time.'

Even Aberym never hit me like this. I rolled away from her and stood. 'I don't have to take this abuse from you. Go and leave, go back to your stupid manor! I would rather train myself.'

She was speechless. I wasn't going to give her another chance to hit me. I ran towards the door. As I was about to reach it, she materialised in front of me and swung at me again, but I ducked just in time.

She stomped her cane on the floor. 'You're not going anywhere until I say you're done! Now get back there and levitate that weight!'

Nope, no way. My second perception sought what was beyond the closed door, and I sensed Malu and Tau waiting outside. I concentrated and opened a portal behind me.

I took one last look at the decrepit face of my tutor and stepped back, portalling myself to Malu and Tau, then closing the portal behind me. The girls were startled by my appearance.

'Sacet? What are you doing? You can't be finished already,' Malu said as I stormed down the corridor. 'And what happened to your head?'

My fists were shaking. 'I'm never coming back here!'

'Wait!' Tau called out from behind. 'What happened? *Talk* to us.'

I could hear their steps behind me as they tried to catch up. I rounded the corridor's corner and entered back into the mess hall. Looking left and right for the main entrance, I spotted it and strode through the gaps between the long row tables. As I walked, all of the soldiers followed me with their eyes.

Whatever. Just leave me alone, I've had enough.

A lone soldier stood up from her table and strolled into my path. I stopped in front of her. She grinned at the crowd of soldiers to her sides. 'Looks like she's had enough already. Our training too hard for you, huh?'

I forced a pair of portals under her feet and launched the now screaming woman into the air. It levitated her and smacked her into the roof. I closed my portals and the whole room watched as she fell from the high ceiling back down to the floor with a loud crack. She shrieked and clutched at her leg, which was probably broken. Everyone else went silent.

I walked over to where she was writhing and pulled her up by the collar. 'If any of you disrespect me again, I'll end you!' I shouted into her crying face.

I dropped her back to the ground again. The soldiers around me were stunned. Marid had entered the hall on the far side and observed me as well. She had a disturbing smile on her face. *Was that what you wanted? Was that what you meant by levitation, you old crone?*

'Stop!'

Several soldiers were running towards me from the entrance of the mess hall. Their masks and armour glistened with a mixture of silver and gold. They held long spears, at the end of each were not only the sharpened tips but gun barrels, too.

They trained their weapons on me. 'Initiate Sacet, come with us.'

Malu never told me about these types of soldiers. Was I being punished for putting this other one in her place? That's what I had been *told* to do.

'Fine,' I muttered. 'Get me out of here.'

I would be happy if I never had to come back to this awful place. As I walked towards the soldiers, they parted and allowed me to continue out of the silent hall.

Sixteen: Everyone Uses Everyone Else

The pathway outside the Royal Citadel was lined with royal guards facing inwards every few paces. They wore the same gold and silver garments and carried the same spear-like weapons as my captors. The Royal Citadel was surrounded by them. As we walked, I studied the lush garden surrounding the path.

The Citadel tower was up ahead. The tower's bright, luminous surface stood in stark contrast to the darkening evening sky behind it. The massive skyscraper had thousands of glass windows, and the tops of the windows were arched. Balconies protruded from the upper levels and were supported by more pillars. The colossal, golden tower reached into the sky higher than any of the other buildings in the cityscape behind it.

We reached the end of the pathway. Immense golden doors opened as we approached. The hall inside was lined with yet more ornate pillars. The floor glistened and reflected the light from around the room. A bright red carpet led down the centre. A large throne was built into the wall at the end, above some steps. My eyes were drawn upwards to the second story, for the city lights poured in from its windows. There were automated gun turrets in the highest corners of the ceiling, and each one of them traced my movement as I entered.

The chamber was filled with guards; some were on the second floor, their weapons trained down on me. Near the throne, six more women stood wearing military armour. Their exposed fringes revealed purple streaks with yellow tips; they must have been the six acolyte colonels.

I was ushered through the chamber and brought in front of the empty throne. There was a strong kick to the back of my legs and I fell to my knees. One of the colonels broke formation and approached. She was maybe in her late twenties, had short, black hair and an ugly sneer.

'When the queen graces you with her presence, you must bow. Only speak when you are spoken to, end everything you say with "my Queen", show absolute respect, and don't try anything stupid.' She pointed to the soldiers and turrets. 'It would only take us an instant to kill you.' The colonel leered and stepped back into formation.

Why exactly was I here? Was I being punished? If the queen herself was going to be right in front of me, they were obviously confident I wasn't going to try and kill her. It wouldn't change anything even if I did, another person would just take her place. Aberym would probably lay down his life to have a chance to kill her, but me? I just wanted Eno to be safe.

A set of double doors on the edge of my periphery opened. The colonels and all of the other soldiers surrounding me snapped their feet together and stood to attention. By the doorway was an older woman dressed in a long white gown. Her oversized sleeves hung down to her knees. Her torso was wrapped in layers, the design elaborate and golden-trimmed. Her shoulders were padded and golden, and behind her back was a gold circular arc that extended over her head, connecting the two pads. The radiant aureole shone around her, giving off a bright glow. Although old, she was also beautiful, something the rumours about her got right.

A strong smack to the back of my head forced me to look down, but I could see the queen out of the corner of my eye. The soldier held my hair so I wouldn't move.

My second perception noticed that although the queen's feet were hidden by her long, dragging gown, she was floating just off the ground. She gently hovered over to us and stopped in front of me.

'Rise, rise,' she insisted.

The soldier released her grasp on my hair and gripped the back of my collar, pulling me up with her.

She smiled warmly. 'Sacet, is it? How very nice to meet you finally.' She gestured to her goons. 'Come with me, I want to show you something. Guards, you can remain here.' She began to hover back to the doorway.

With widened eyes and an anxious expression, the colonel who spoke to me earlier broke formation. 'But, my Queen, she is dangerous. She was just seen assaulting one of the troops. I strongly suggest keeping us with you.'

'I can take care of myself, Korin. I'm fully aware of what she can do, and I'm sure she'll show respect while she is here.' She then turned back to me. 'Sacet, come. This way.'

I was just as confused as Korin. But I followed the queen all the same, smirking back at Korin when we reached the doorway. Korin obeyed the command, albeit with a look of scorn towards me.

The queen and I passed through the doorway and strolled down a wide corridor. She must have been at least sixty. Walking alongside her as she hovered was quite surreal. And her behaviour was even stranger. Was she always this kind and relaxed with her subordinates?

Ahead of us I could see a large clear tube that came out from the floor and stretched upwards through the ceiling. An elevator?

'Welcome to the Citadel, Sacet,' she began as we walked towards it. 'I apologise for the roughness of my guards.' She must have noticed my confusion. 'I heard you're having a bad day?'

'What?'

'Marid is a good friend of mine. I spoke to her not moments ago about your little, shall we say, *incident*. Perhaps I might have a word to her about training you a bit more gently?'

'Oh, uhh... thanks?'

She stopped and raised a finger. 'Hmm, we still need to work on your manners, too, I think. Make sure to address me as "my Queen", yes?'

I nodded. 'Thank you, my Queen.'

We reached the elevator and paused. A circular panel came hurtling down the tube and stopped at our level. The transparent doors parted and we both stepped in.

I had thought the queen, the brutal ruler of an evil empire that covered half the planet, would be ruthless and cruel. Why was she being so friendly?

She looked up. 'Queen's chambers.' The panel beneath our feet shook and rocketed upwards through the tube. Once we had cleared the ceiling, I observed a magnificent view of the city out through the tube.

'I realise Marid can be a bit harsh,' she said. 'But I'm sure you will learn much from her if you give her another chance. Does that sound fair to you?'

'Uhh, yes... my Queen?' I said. 'I'm sorry, why am I here exactly?'

She gave a little laugh. 'You're not being punished, if that's what you're afraid of. I actually encourage little rivalries. It's good for troop morale, just so long as you don't take it too far.'

The panel lurched and slowed as we approached our destination. We elevated through the floor of another room, and the city view was obscured. We stopped and the doors parted to reveal the queen's personal chambers. It was filled with extravagant furniture. At the far end of the room stood a desk that overlooked the city below through a large window. The queen sat in the chair behind it, and then gestured at the cushioned seats near me.

'Please, sit.'

'Uh, okay.' I did as she instructed, feeling incredibly awkward. 'Sorry, but I don't really understand what's going on. I'm not sure what the rules are here. I don't even know your actual name.'

She grinned. 'My name is Antwin, but I would appreciate it if you called me by my title like everyone else. We mustn't forget our place after all, for we each have a role to play.' She reached for a bottle that sat on the desk and poured its contents into a glass. 'Drink?'

I declined, shaking my head. 'You're nothing like I expected.'

She laughed, picked up her glass and looked out at the amazing view, which stretched beyond the city and into the desert. 'Well, the public sees what I need them to see. But as you and I both know, sometimes we must hide our true selves from others, for their own good.'

My thoughts travelled to Eno. I had lied to him his whole life.

My second perception noticed something strange. Out of all the rooms here in the peak of this tower, this was the only room with furniture. The others were all bare, completely empty.

Antwin took a sip from her glass. 'The reason I brought you here was to discuss your future. You see, I have *high* hopes for you. And I'm willing to make your life easier when you cooperate with me. Visits to your brother, for example. Making sure his living conditions are acceptable, wealth, power –'

'I don't want to be used as a weapon… my Queen.'

She grinned coyly. 'I would be lying if I said you weren't here because of your power.' She swished her glass about. 'But everyone in this world uses everyone else. That is life. Don't look it as *being* used, look at it as service to the people of this city. *Innocent* and kind people who deserve your protection.'

'I would never hurt innocent people either, my Queen. But –'

'Oh, I know you wouldn't. But still, it might put them at *ease* a bit, if they saw you doing your duties. Serving the people.' She clasped her glass tighter and stared at the liquid. 'Now, it just so happens that one of these duties is fast approaching. A grand annual tournament, with competitors from all over, hosted right here in our stadium.'

She pointed out at the cityscape to one of a dome-shaped building. It wasn't the tallest building, but it was definitely the largest. The arena must have had tens of thousands of seats.

'A tournament?'

'Yes, and as an acolyte, you're required to participate. So, we need to train you up before then. Our people are always worried when we try to assimilate an acolyte. They're afraid of you. This tournament is the perfect way for you to prove that you're not here to hurt them. That you're on *our* side, just like you used to be. Right?'

My mind raced. What could this tournament entail? What if I had to fight other acolytes?

Wait, what if I did go along with this? If they trusted me, then I could walk throughout this city with impunity. I could work out how to remove this tracking device, and then how to bust Eno and I out.

Antwin looked at me expectantly.

I glanced at the stadium for a moment, then back to her. 'Okay, I'll cooperate.'

'Good!' she said, putting her drink down and clasping her hands together with excitement. 'Now we've got that out of the way, I'm afraid I must meet my next appointment. I'm sure you can find your own way out of here, yes?'

'Yes, I should be fine. Um, goodbye?'

Antwin raised her finger up to the air. 'My Queen. Goodbye, *my Queen.*'

'Oh. Right, sorry,' I said as I pictured the Citadel's entrance in my mind and twirled my fingers to make a portal appear in front of me. 'Goodbye, my Queen.'

She took another sip of her drink. 'Thank you, Sacet. Train hard.' As I was about to leave, she cleared her throat. 'Oh, and Sacet?'

I paused.

'Don't disappoint me.'

I turned and stepped through the portal.

Malu's Apartment

It was getting dark outside the windows; I had been sitting alone at the desk and staring at a poster of the queen. After the day I had, I needed the space to sit and think.

The poster was an accurate representation of what I had met earlier, smiling bright.

'Sacet!' Tau yelled from the apartment door.

I glanced at the entrance and saw Malu and Tau enter. They rushed over.

'So, *this* is where you've been?' Malu asked. 'We had no idea where you were taken.'

'We were worried,' Tau added. 'What happened?'

I took a sip of my drink and placed it back on the desk. 'I met the queen.'

'What?!' they both squealed.

'The queen wanted to meet with me... and talk.'

Malu's eyes looked as though they were about to pop out. 'I've only seen the queen up close like... twice in my life, and I wasn't allowed to speak to her.'

Tau shook her head and approached the poster. 'I've never seen her in person. What did she want to talk to you about?'

I shrugged. 'Making sure everything was okay with Marid. She said she would help.'

Tau's face scrunched up. 'She's going out of her way to help you? The queen? Is helping *you*?'

'I know, I don't get it either,' I said. 'She was really nice. It was weird.'

Malu rubbed her chin. 'That was all?'

'No, she said she had high hopes for me, and something about a tournament. Making sure I was ready to participate.'

Malu leant against the nearby couch. 'Did she tell you what you'd be doing exactly?'

'I assumed I would be fighting other acolytes. I hope it's Iya, she could stand a little public embarrassment.'

Malu puzzled for a moment. 'Hmm. I don't think you're... ready... for the tournament.'

Tau nodded. 'Sacet, you can't do it. But I wouldn't be able to either.'

I shrugged. 'Can't do what?'

Tau sat as well. 'Okay, ah... well... Malu?'

Malu sighed. 'The first event is an execution of an unarmed prisoner.'

I shot up from my chair. 'What? How barbaric! What is wrong with you people?'

Malu averted her gaze from me and lowered her brow. 'It's better than the alternative, Sacet.'

I began to pace around the room. 'What possible alternative is worse than that, Malu?'

Her nostrils flared and she shot up, too. 'A quick death is a mercy.' She pointed a finger close to my face. 'Better than a prolonged imprisonment. You have no idea what it's like in those mines. My dad and my brother would be better off dead.'

I shook my head. 'I can't believe what I'm hearing right now. Tau? Is this how you think, too?'

Tau nervously shrugged. 'I... I can see both your points of view.'

Malu copied my body language. 'Would you prefer the people you captured to be tortured and worked until they were nothing but a sack of skin and bones?'

What was Malu talking about? How could she possibly want her family members dead? Then it hit me; it was her brainwashing. She still loved her family, but she had been forced to think of men as evil, as 'better off dead'.

I clenched my fists and stared her down. 'I'm never giving up on Eno. I'll find a way to free him. And I'll free your family, too, because it's clear I'm the only one that cares.'

My harsh words had cut into Malu. She turned away.

Tau glared at me. 'Malu loves her family, Sacet. She just doesn't want them to be in this pain anymore.'

'No, let her find out the truth herself,' Malu interrupted. 'One day she might get to visit Eno. Then she'll see.'

I shrugged. 'Either way, I'm not going to kill anyone.'

Malu stormed towards her bedroom. 'Good luck on tournament day, then.' She slammed the door behind her.

Seventeen: Rows and Columns

The Prison Quad Cafeteria
Eno

Pilgrim, Toroi, Turen and several others I had come to know all shuffled along the queue, waiting to be fed. A large, steel grate separated the servers from the lines. There was a small opening at waist level to collect our trays.

Even here, we couldn't escape the red lines on the ground, which led along designated paths to and around the tables. They had been everywhere we went since we got here. Lines led to places we could sit, stand, sleep, and even pee, but only when we were officially escorted to those locations.

Everyone needed to be in neat little rows and columns wherever we went. Even though it had only be a day, I had witnessed numerous times that going 'off line' meant you were killed, no matter what reason you gave.

Gunshots echoing throughout the mine was common and usually was swiftly followed everyone working even harder. It was so common that there was a duty just to collect and dispose of the bodies down an even deeper, darker shaft somewhere.

Toroi turned back to me. 'Best part of the day.'

As our group moved up, I took a look at one prisoner's food as he walked back. 'Is that even food?' I asked in disbelief. It was nothing more than a paste-like gruel.

'Not really, but that's not why this is the best part of the day,' Turen said, shuffling forward again.

'Look around, Eno,' Pilgrim said. 'This is the first time today that we've been allowed to talk to one another.'

Catwalks above us had guards patrolling along them, like every other section of the prison. And yet, all of the prisoners talked freely along the long row tables. It seemed like this was the only place where that was allowed.

We finally reached the front. Toroi went up first and took one of the trays from the hole. I was up next, and the woman dumped the tray down next to the hole so hard that some of the gruel splattered out of the bowl and onto the tray. I inspected the food; it appeared more spit than sustenance and had no smell to it.

'It's not going to get any better if you stare at it longer,' Pilgrim said, bending down and giving me a slight elbow to the ribs.

I picked up the tray of odourless food and a rusty spoon, then followed Toroi back through the lines. We sat at one of the empty tables. Pilgrim, Toroi's father and the others joined us shortly after, plonking their trays down, too.

As the others scooped up their sticky food with their hands and shovelled it into their mouths, I gazed around the chamber. A soldier stood next to our ugly overseer, and whatever she was saying to the overseer was making her smile and laugh.

The woman was younger; had short, black hair, with yellow-tipped, purple streaks coming from her fringe. She had a small, see-through device in her hand, which she inspected closely. It lit up with colours and shapes whenever she touched it.

Pilgrim bumped me in the arm. 'Don't look at them so obviously.'

'What?'

He dug a fork into his food. 'You're asking for trouble by staring them down, just don't look at them.'

'He's right,' Toroi said, chewing. 'If you want to survive here, you have to mind your own business. Every single one of us wants to beat that overseer's head in with a rock, so believe us, we know how you feel.'

'Rock? A *boulder*, more like.' I quipped.

'Two boulders,' Toroi replied with a smile, the first I had seen, '*and* a mine cart.*'*

'Don't be ridiculous,' Pilgrim corrected. 'Neither of you can even pick up a boulder. And second, go for something slower and more painful.' He held up his spoon. 'Like this.'

Turen's eyes darted around nervously. 'So how do you two know each other. Don't tell me you're father and son, too?'

Pilgrim patted me on the back. 'We're from the same village. And that's the same as family to me.' He scooped up some gruel, placed it in his mouth and his smile disappeared. He screwed up his face before swallowing. 'The Male Dominion assaulted our village. There were some survivors, and we hunkered down. But only a day later, the Female Dominion found our exact position.'

I averted my eyes from Pilgrim. 'About that night... my sister and I went back for Tau.'

Pilgrim narrowed his eyes at first, but then he relaxed. 'You two really did trust her, didn't you?'

I sighed as I played with my food. 'I don't know what to think now. When her kind showed up, she sided with them. But... I could tell she didn't want us to get hurt. Their acolytes were... intense. There was one that could lift Sacet without touching her, and another turned things to water.'

Toroi and Turen exchanged a look.

'This water acolyte,' Turen said to me. 'Nomadic descent like us?'

I nodded. 'Uhh, yeah. How did you know?' I put some gruel into my mouth and regretted it.

Toroi shook his head, as though disappointed. 'Because she's my big sister, Malu.'

I spat out the wretched paste back onto my tray. 'That's your sister?'

He nodded back. 'She came to visit last night, asked us to take care of you. Got any idea why she's trying to protect you?'

I shrugged. 'I'm... just as confused as you are.'

Toroi rolled his eyes. 'She said she joined the military to make it easier on the family, but really she joined to make it easier on herself.'

'Toroi...' his father started.

'It's true,' the boy continued. 'She probably has it all, everything she could want.'

'She's confused. There's no telling what they've done to her brain.'

I glimpsed the overseer and her friend out the corner of my eye. The small device the other woman was carrying glowed with a list of words. The two women started walking towards our table, so I averted my eyes.

'This is the one here,' the overseer said stopping next to our table and pointing at Turen. 'I have good news for you, 225. You're moving up in the world. We have a special job for you in the Commercial Quadrant.'

Turen locked eyes with his son before looking down at the table. Toroi's mouth was aghast.

'It's okay, you have permission to speak. You can show us some gratitude if you'd like.'

He closed his eyes and gave a small bow towards the overseer and the black-haired woman. 'I am honoured I have been chosen.' Despite his words, he looked as if someone had just died.

The other woman grinned. She inspected the list on the thin device she was carrying again and looked back up. She pointed at Pilgrim. 'I want that one, too.'

'That one?' the overseer said. 'But I just got him. At least let me get some use out of him in the mines first.'

'No, he has been specifically requested by Matriarch Verre herself,' the black-haired woman said, bringing her free hand to her chin and examining Pilgrim more closely. 'Guards, these two.'

Several guards had been waiting near the cafeteria entrance, and they approached our table as the other two women parted. Turen hugged Toroi.

Pilgrim stood. 'Keep your head down, Eno, alright?' He walked over to the guards, nodding grimly. 'Stay with Toroi.'

Toroi began to bawl and squeezed his father tighter. The overseer's smile shifted a look of disgust, and gestured the guards towards Toroi. The guards pulled on their shoulders, attempting to separate the father and son, gently at first, then forcefully.

'No, please. Don't kill him! Don't kill my dad!' Toroi screamed as he tried to reach out for his father, grasping at thin air.

'Stop it, son. Please, for your own sake.' Turen glanced back at the overseer briefly. 'There's no need to worry, I'm just going to be working in the Commercial Quadrant now.'

Toroi's eyes were filled with tears.

'Enough of this,' the overseer said. The guards collected the two men by their arms and led them out of the cafeteria.

All of the other men had stopped eating. Although some appeared furious, they all looked down at their food, trying to ignore what was happening. The overseer stared me down, and so I did the same as the others.

'I'm sorry, son,' Turen yelled back as they forced him and Pilgrim along and around the corner.

Eighteen: One Last Look

Two days later
The Science Quad
Sacet

The smooth laboratory table was cold. As the scientists prepared me for another assimilation procedure, my mind drifted. Every morning after, I awoke stronger and healthier than before.

Malu was pouting by the entrance, doing her best to avoid eye contact. For the past couple of days, other than ferrying me around to my various duties, she had barely interacted with me. She fed me, made sure I was on time for my assimilation procedures and weapons training, but that was it.

Aside from Tau visiting us for dinner each night, I had been left alone with my thoughts. I had been spending my free time wandering around the city, trying to see all the major locations. Of course, my clearance didn't allow me into most of the facilities, but that didn't stop my second perception from taking a peek through some of the walls.

All I wanted now was to rescue Eno and leave this place. Aberym had told us many stories of how dangerous it was being a prisoner of the Dominion, and unless you were an acolyte, your life expectancy was short. The longer I waited, the more danger Eno was in. But unless I worked out how to remove this thing in the back of my neck, neither of us were leaving this place alive.

Maybe there was a way I could stop it from transmitting? It would be safe to assume the city drew its power from somewhere in this Science Quad. Maybe everything depended on that power, including my tracking device?

The range of my special vision had increased tenfold since I woke up that first day in Malu's apartment. I was far more comfortable with it now, the environment wasn't so shaky and sickness-inducing. I saw inside people's pockets, through solid walls and even underneath the ground.

The scientists around me were looking at readouts and preparing drugs. I wasn't really paying attention to them.

I let my second perception fly off around the room. It bounced around a bit before delving beyond the walls and ceiling. I scouted the facility, searching for things I hadn't already seen.

Inside the adjacent building, there was a colossal, ring-shaped metal tube. The tube was closed off, and inside it the floor and ceiling glowed. The air inside the tube glowed, too, as if being heated. Outside the tube, at least a hundred scientists scurried about, examining readouts on screens and adjusting various mechanisms. Could this be what was powering the city?

Before I had a chance to think about it, one of the scientists by my side injected me with another sedative.

The Military Quad

The next day, the massive, sleek mess hall loomed in front of us. Malu and I walked up the steps in silence. Nearby soldiers noticed me passing like last time, but they simply nodded at me. I nodded back, confused.

I shrugged at Malu. 'So, are you just going to never talk to me again?'

Malu ignored me as usual, instead focusing on Marid at the top of the steps. Malu gestured to my trainer. 'Off you go, I'll pick you up here after training.' Without even looking at me, she turned and went back down the stairs.

Well, fine then, why would I want to be friends with the acolyte that captured my brother and I anyway? Eno's life was in danger because of her, so good riddance.

Marid hadn't seen me yet. She was leaning heavily on her cane, anxiously looking around. She wore a far simpler, rustic get-up today, closer to what a nomad might choose to wear, making her seem even more out of place here. She spotted me approaching and her worry turned to a smile, which didn't suit her.

When I reached her, Marid sighed and glanced over her shoulder through the mess hall doors, as if embarrassed. 'Sacet, I... apologise for the other day. I promise to be a more patient instructor.' She gestured to the doors. 'Please, this way.'

Antwin had spoken to her, as promised. Still, that was no guarantee she was going to be this nice from now on.

We went through the doors and strolled through the hall. Even with her cane, Marid's pace was quite slow. The hall wasn't as full as the other days I had come, but we still caught the attention of a few soldiers. I locked eyes with one sitting nearby, who glanced away and seemed suddenly very interested in her food.

'I'm sorry, too,' I started, breaking the silence. 'For what I said. I appreciate you trying to help me. I just don't work well under that kind of pressure.'

Her eyebrow cocked. 'Oh, is that so? What about the pressure of a real battle? How long are you going to last if you're not conditioned for fighting?' She gestured at the eavesdropping soldiers around us. 'How do you think the rest of the soldiers here are trained? They live a disciplined life.'

She continued ahead of me, tapping her cane with each step. 'When I'm done with you, you'll be the most feared acolyte in the Female Dominion.'

As we walked, she glanced back at the main entrance. 'Didn't you have a full escort last time? Why isn't anyone here holding your hand?'

'Malu brought me here, but we haven't exactly been getting along,' I replied.

Marid shrugged. 'Well, boohoo. Make new and better friends.'

The tables we passed were quiet, no jeers and slurs anymore. Almost all of the soldiers had their heads down or were turned away. Was it fear, or was it because I had a rank now?

We reached the end of the hall and entered a corridor. As we continued we saw through into numerous chambers. One was a firing range, another was a dormitory filled with beds. One corridor led over to the hangar, and another led to a briefing room.

Finally, ahead of us, was the same training room from the other day. I pointed at the closed door. 'You know, we could have just teleported here?'

She approached the door to open it and then glanced back. 'Of course we could have. But I wanted those soldiers to see you, and you also to see them. Did you see how afraid they were of you?'

'I guess?'

She smirked. 'Well, *that* is *true* power.'

We both entered. The room hadn't changed, still with fitness equipment lying about on the sides.

'Marid,' I began as we stopped in the centre. 'Do you know why they're making such a big fuss over me? I mean... the queen herself...'

She shook her head. 'At first I didn't understand it either. There are hundreds of acolytes in this city alone.'

'At first?'

She hesitated. 'They see something special in you, that's all I can say.' She cleared her throat. 'So, let's talk about what you can do so far.' She held out her fingers to count. 'Teleporting yourself and objects, levitation, crushing things and some basic optical illusions. Did I miss anything?'

I shook my head.

'I've had some ideas that we can try,' she continued. 'Have you ever tried to make more than one set of portals at a time?'

'Hmm, no.' Until recently, making one set was hard enough.

'Why don't you give it a try now? Make one set to your left and another to your right,' she suggested, pointing at the walls on both sides.

I approached the centre of the room and tried to concentrate. The left set of portals came quickly, but I struggled to focus on an additional set. How could I look both left and right at the same time?

When I was about to quit, an idea came to me. Instead of trying to look at both at the same time with my eyes, I would use my normal eyes for the left and my second perception for the right. As soon as the realisation came to me, a second set of portals formed.

I smiled. 'I did it!'

Marid gave a nod and I could have sworn I saw a hint of a smile. 'Very good. You got that much faster than I thought. I don't think I need to tell you the benefits of having more than one portal out. I want you to practise that in your own time. And now for your next lesson.'

She placed her hand on the hilt of her sword, which was still in its walking stick sheath. 'My powers allow me to quickly move up to an enemy...' She vanished from where she was standing. Her glowing blue sword was suddenly below my chin. '... And end their life with ease. But you? You're too slow-moving for that. So, what happens when someone gets in close to you? You can't crush or levitate everything. You need a quicker attack.'

She lowered the sword and switched its handle to me instead. 'Here, try this,' she said as I reached out and grabbed the sword handle. 'See the tip of the blade? Make a small portal, and then put the entire sword through it except for the handle. The other side of the portal can float in front of you.'

I remembered doing something similar to this with my knife, but I said nothing. I was interested to see what she had in mind.

I raised the sword to eye level and darted my fingers back and forth, attempting to create a much smaller portal. When it opened, I inserted the sword through the small hole, and saw the entire blade hovering through the other end of the portal. Success!

'Now, leave the sword handle you're holding by your side, and only use the teleported blade. You can practise chopping this bag in half, but, uh, wait until I'm out of the way.' Marid teleported to the far side of the room. 'Now.'

With my left hand outstretched to the hovering sword, I flicked my hand to the side. The hovering blade followed through and the bag's contents spewed onto the ground. The sword came to an immediate halt mid-air. It was so quick, so easy.

I admired the sleek weapon. 'Are you giving me this?'

'What? No! That's my sword. You can get your own, you scavenging fool!'

Well, that got my hopes up for nothing. But it felt good to do some real damage. I hadn't thought to use my powers in this way before. I was surprised how helpful this was.

She teleported to my side and snatched her sword back. 'Next we–' A loud alarm sounded from overhead. The room was bathed in swirling, blue light. Marid sheathed her sword back into her walking stick. 'Here's your chance for practice, girl.'

'What?' I asked. 'What do you mean? What's going on?'

She placed a hand on my shoulder. 'I'll show you.'

Marid teleported us. Although instantaneous to outside observers, the extended kaleidoscopic warping of reality couldn't end soon enough. My stomach churned, as though disembodied in a mixing bowl.

When the effect was finally over, I looked around the vast chamber we'd arrived in; we were inside the hangar. Although I'd never been here, the enormity of the place and the lines of aircraft made it obvious where we were.

Hundreds of soldiers stood to attention, already assembled in their formations. Hundreds more were piling through the various hangar entrances. Pilots were climbing into their cockpits, flicking various switches until their crafts began to hum.

A second hangar was visible from this chamber. It was mostly empty aside from a single, gargantuan aircraft. I recognised it from the billboard I'd seen on my first day. Malu called it the Coda. Numerous storeys tall and longer than a nomad village was wide, it was so large that it took up most of the sub-hangar. Was it even possible for something that big to fly?

I glanced back at Marid. 'Uhh, what are we doing?'

She let go of my shoulder. 'It's an emergency operation. You're going to war.' She sighed. 'You're not ready.'

'What? No, no.' I shook my head. 'I can't. I'm not going to fight!'

'You've got no choice! You know what they'll do to your brother if you refuse.' She pointed at a large door at the edge of the hangar. Almost all of the soldiers were coming and going out of it. 'Go to the armoury and get suited up.'

My hands shook. I couldn't move. 'I told you I... I can't. I won't kill.'

Marid grabbed my face with both hands and forced me to look at her. 'Just survive. Do as you're told, but survive this.' She pushed me away and gestured to the armoury again. 'Go!'

My lips trembled, but I complied, turning to the armoury and spinning my hands. I opened a portal next to me and ran through.

I was soon surrounded by hundreds of others, most of whom were shocked to see a portal open beside them. There were so many in such a small space that we were all shoulder-to-shoulder. Everyone was frantically getting armour fitted, grabbing weapons from massive, long racks, then rushing back out into the hangar.

A small child with white-tipped, red streaks picked me out from the crowd and rushed over. 'Follow me, quickly,' her tiny voice chirped. She grabbed my hand and pulled me over to the racks. 'Put this on.' She passed me a thin, silky suit.

I took off my regular combat fatigues and put on the suit she had handed me. Meanwhile, she went to collect various pieces of armour. As I pulled my legs through, she strapped pads onto my shins and knees. She pulled the straps tight and then procured a small tool from her belt. She brought it to my knee pads and twisted one of the bolts, which tightened it further.

'What weapon are you using? LR17? CSR? An Interloper-50? What?'

I had only just started my weapons training, so I had no idea what she was on about. 'Uhh—'

Her eyes narrowed. 'Autonomous Lancing Drone? A freaking Acid-Cannister Mortar? What?! Hurry up and tell me!'

'Sword,' I replied.

'What? Sword? Are you stupid?'

'Are you calling Marid stupid, too?'

'Yes, I'm saying you're just as insane as that has-been.'

'I told you what I want, kid.'

'Fine!'

I pulled my arms through the sleeves of the suit as the girl ran off to find me my chosen weapon. I tried fastening some of the pads myself, but I was failing at it. As quickly as she left, the girl returned with a large sword.

I was disappointed; although sufficiently sharp, it wasn't glowing or anything. I reached out and took the steel blade from her. The symbol of the Female Dominion was on the weathered hilt. As I examined it, she continued to reattach more pads to my frame, cursing at my poor efforts.

Another woman came over, again with red streaks, and handed me a helmet. I took it with my free hand and held it out in front of me for a moment. Not long ago I remembered throwing one of these into the depths of Teersau. Now, I was about to wear one myself, to don the symbol of my enemy. I hesitated, but eventually placed the helmet on my head and stashed the blade into the sheath around my new belt.

The little girl shoved me in the side. 'Go! Get yourself killed with your stupid sword. Move! Next!' She ran off to another unarmoured soldier who had entered the room.

I made my way through the wall of soldiers still arriving and walked out of the armoury. But I was clueless as to where I was supposed to go next.

'Sacet,' a voice behind me at the armoury entrance said. It was Malu, already fully armoured. She looked me up and down and smirked. 'It suits you.'

'Malu? Uh, I don't suppose you know where we need to go, do you?'

'Yeah, hurry up. Follow me,' she said, striding away down one of the runways.

I followed, trying to catch up and walk alongside her. We briefly locked eyes, before continuing to walk in silence.

We reached the line of idling aircraft. Some soldiers were already piling into them. We seemed to be heading towards one specific group of soldiers. As we got closer I saw they had purple streaks in their hair.

Colonel Korin was in the centre, marking off names on a checklist using one of those glass pad things. Iya was here too; she inspected my armour and folded her arms.

Korin noticed us and approached. 'Ah, Sacet.' She pushed passed Malu and got in my face. 'I didn't think you were going to show up at all, and then we would have had to punish you. A sword, huh? Marid rubbing off on you already?'

The other acolytes chuckled; everyone else had firearms. I remained silent and gripped the sword tighter.

The colonel returned to the centre of the group. 'Listen up! Iya and Neva, you're accompanying AS12. Aki and Nito, AS03. Malu and Sacet, I want you two in AS06,' she said. As her instructions continued, I glanced back at Malu.

Malu rolled her eyes and pulled on my arm. 'This way.'

We marched over to one of the aircraft, which was already loaded with soldiers. They were strapped into seats along the sides of the craft. We climbed the ramp and the aircraft's occupants looked over to us.

I awkwardly moved to the closest empty seat and tried to strap myself in. Malu sat in the seat opposite me. I felt like everyone was staring at me.

'We're full. Go!' a standing woman screamed to the front.

There was a loud whirring noise as the ramp rose, about to seal us in. The turbines were building up power outside. We jolted, and the craft tilted to the side as it turned. I took one last look out into the hangar before the door closed, leaving me entombed with blinking lights, darkness and staring eyes.

Nineteen: Just Survive

The aircraft took off, going straight up. I was pressed down into my chair. My second vision looked outside the craft as it travelled to the hangar's ceiling, a hatch on the top opening to let us through. The turbines' high-pitched shrieks increased their intensity. The acceleration caused the compartment to quiver. My heart was thumping as we left the hangar.

The lights inside the cabin turned back on, but the dim, blue light barely illuminated the other soldiers inside. There was a storage slot for our weapons and accoutrements above our heads. I still had my sword by my waist, and it was digging into my hip in this tight seat.

I was blinded by a bright image in front of me. As my eyes adjusted, I saw my helmet had projected an image onto the face panel. The other soldiers in the cabin had the same picture cast onto their transparent faceplates. There was some writing: Standby to receive message from Matriarch Aellix.

A woman's face appeared. She was middle-aged and had blue streaks with black tips.

'Please look to your sides to see if this transmission is being received by your comrades. If not, then hail the attention of the nearest superior officer,' she said as her face on the screen minimised into the top left corner, now only taking up a fraction of the visor. 'I will inform you of the situation. Afterwards, your transmission will cut to your detachment's specific matriarch, and you'll be briefed on your individual orders.

'Citeer, our neighbouring province, is under attack. The Male Dominion have laid siege to the region's factories at Usre. Your primary objectives are to drive back the forces attacking the city, muster any remaining soldiers to your squads for assistance, and to protect the manufactured weaponry. Protect the facilities at all costs. Use any weaponry you may find to your advantage and push the filth back!'

As the matriarch spoke, a map of the city appeared on my visor with various areas highlighted in blue. But I closed my eyes, and the matriarch's voice trailed off, instead replaced by the humming of the aircraft's engines. My perception focused outside on the sand-covered ground that whizzed past us below. There were hundreds of aircraft flying alongside our own. They were faster than I thought possible.

My breathing accelerated. Why have they sent *me*? Don't they know I've only just started my training? I'd do my best to help others survive, but that's it. Had Tau been deployed as well? Would she land near me? I opened my eyes again and saw Verre's face staring back at me on the screen.

'Acolytes, you heard the matriarch. We must save our factories and our fellow sisters. This attack is foolhardy of our enemy, striking so close to our home and so far from theirs. It's possible that the facility is not their true objective, so stay alert and be prepared for an ambush.' Verre's face disappeared from my visor.

Our aircraft's loadmaster walked between our seats, holding a handle on the ceiling for support. Her streaks were yellow with blue tips. 'Listen up, AS06,' she began, her voice being transmitted straight to our helmets. 'You will be landing on the far edge of the residential terrace. Make your way through the streets and enter the factories, then await further orders. The entire city is assumed to be overrun, so stay in cover. We drop in twenty. Good luck.'

A minimised and see-through map remained at the top right of my view. It rotated as the aircraft turned. The small dot that indicated our position passed rectangles on the map that I assumed were buildings. Now that we were over the city, we began to slow.

I closed my eyes again and tried to focus on what was outside. The ramp lowered as the aircraft hovered in mid-air, allowing a gust of black smoke to enter the compartment. The dim blue light switched off, and strained daylight entered through the ramp's gap.

Much of the sky was blanketed by thick smoke, and it wasn't clear whether this was from the siege or from the factories' pollution. The sky that was visible was a deep orange, as though the sun were already setting on this forsaken place, or as though the city was in flames. Perhaps it was both.

Although there were some apartment buildings nearby, the majority of the structures here were factories, just as we had been told. The sounds of distant laserfire, explosions and screams layered on top of one another endlessly, and from all directions.

The others unbuckled their straps and so I copied them. The aircraft rocked as it landed. We stood, and as the ramp continued to lower, the soldiers sprinted down it to the concrete. Compared to the others, Malu strode down the ramp with an air of calmness.

'Hurry up! Get off!'

I was the last soldier left beside the loadmaster. I ran down the ramp and stumbled onto the concrete. The area was surrounded by tall apartment buildings and pathways that led in every direction. The rest of the squad had assembled and crouched beside a nearby wall. As the aircraft began to take off, I sprinted over to join the others.

One of the soldiers peered around the closest wall.

'See anything?' Malu asked as she prodded her from behind.

She turned back. 'Looks like a straight shot to the next waypoint. No activity, but the whole area is bombed out. Plenty of ruins and craters to use for cover.'

Malu faced the only soldier with red tips. 'What do you think, Corporal?'

'We have our orders,' she replied. 'If there was an alternative route, we would have been told about it.'

I couldn't go through with this. It was completely against what I stood for. I nudged Malu in the side. 'Malu, I can't do this. I can't kill people.'

'Is she kidding?' one of the soldiers grumbled.

Malu rolled her eyes like before. 'Of course you can't.'

Another soldier glanced at the corporal. 'Is she not assimilated? Why is she here?'

The corporal groaned. 'We don't have time for this. Malu, she's *your* responsibility. If she disobeys one of my commands, I'll shoot her myself.'

Malu grabbed my collar and forced me in front of her face. 'Kill or capture them alive, got it?' She seethed. I nodded and she let me go.

The kneeling corporal waved her hand towards the corner. 'Stay in a single line and watch for explosives. Let's go!' She stood and rushed out around the corner. The others followed and I trailed at the rear.

I was greeted with a disturbing sight. Every apartment building in the long residential street was rubble-covered ruins. Fires were still spreading. There were craters and dead bodies littered around everywhere. I slowed, in complete disbelief of the revolting scene, before forcing myself to catch up.

In the distance there was a giant facility; its shadow loomed over the ruined street. From the beacon on our maps and the way it was highlighted, it must be our destination. The soldiers in front of me were running from cover to cover, pausing only briefly each time to check if the street was still clear.

None of this felt right, so I unsheathed my blade and held it out in front as ran. I weaved a small portal, and then stuck my sword through it, leaving the handle at my side. Like in my training earlier, I now had a hovering blade accompanying me, which I could whip about as I pleased.

My squad passed bodies and great dirt craters. These unarmoured people were most definitely civilians, but their clothing was drab and brown compared to those from FDC. On closer inspection, the bodies didn't seem to be burned in any way, not from fire, bombings or lasers. They looked like they had been ripped apart.

I stopped in my tracks. I sensed something. I broke formation and strode over to one of the craters, then visualised what was under the surface. Poised to emerge from the dirt, a hidden necrolisk. This wasn't the aftermath of an artillery strike... they were burrows!

'Necrolisks!' I screamed at the squad, who stopped to look back.

'What? Quiet! What are you... Ahhhhhh!'

The corporal was impaled by a claw midsentence. She had been standing next to one of the burrows.

Malu sprinted over to the surfacing necrolisk and it tried swiping at her with its other claw. She dove, slid along the dirt under the claw, and grabbed one of the creature's needle-like legs. The instant it was in contact with her fingertips, the monster burst into a deluge of water, which sprayed all over Malu and the soldiers, who were now eyeing other rising necrolisks.

The ground rumbled. I turned back to the burrow. The closer necrolisk launched up with a trail of rubble and landed back onto the ground. I flung my left arm across, and the sword sliced through the creature's abdomen. Green slime oozed and splashed about, some into my face, and the top half of the necrolisk slid and fell backwards. Its legs leaned and toppled over.

The squad opened fire, laser and flame, peppering the encroaching swarm, but there were too many of them.

'Retreat!' Malu ordered, and everyone ran back towards me without argument. 'Sacet, get us out of here!'

I panicked. Where was I going to teleport to? I closed the sword portal and looked up at the apartment buildings. The closest building would do. I concentrated on its roof and opened a new portal to it, waving the others through.

The horde stampeded closer. One after another, the girls leapt through the portal, with Malu and I rushing through last. I closed the portal just as the necrolisks converged.

Although only several storeys high, we could see most of the city from the roof. The lack of life we had encountered suddenly made far more sense. The others approached the roof's edge and watched the necrolisks crowd around our last known position. When they realised we were no longer there, they bent their heads back and roared.

One of the younger girls threw up her hands. 'I thought it was a Male Dominion siege, not a necrolisk infestation?'

Malu walked over to an even taller connected building, its windows were accessible and easy to climb through.

'It's both,' she said, mounting the windowsill. 'I've seen this before; they're being controlled by an acolyte. He'll be watching from nearby.' She clambered through and turned back. 'We need to find him and kill him.'

'Or capture him?' I suggested, and the others groaned.

Malu's face contorted. 'Sacet, can you not sense the danger we're in?'

Something had stirred the creatures below. Did they hear us? They rushed to the base of our building and began scaling the wall by puncturing it with their massive claws.

A soldier pulled on my arm. 'Move!'

One by one we jumped through the same window as Malu and ran through the ruined corridor. We could hear the necrolisks entering the lower floors, squealing and slashing. Malu busted down the nearest apartment door and scanned the room for any signs of life. The other soldiers ran down the corridor and did the same with the other rooms.

This was going to take too long; the necrolisks would find us before we found this acolyte. I closed my eyes and tried to calm myself. My perception darted through the apartment floors. I sensed civilians hiding in their rooms, innocent women and children.

Farther down the corridor and on the floor above, a single male soldier was looking down at the streets through a shattered window. Like other Male Dominion soldiers, he wore dark armour and his helmet was a mask that covered his face. Only his eyes could be seen through it. He was thin, lanky even. He was the only man about, so it had to be him, right?

I focused behind the man and opened another portal. Leaving the other soldiers in the corridor, I entered with my blade drawn and snuck up behind him.

I didn't want to kill him, so I jabbed the tip of my sword into his back. 'Call them off. And turn around, slowly!'

The man didn't say anything but did turn around to face me.

I jabbed at him again. 'And hands up, too!'

I couldn't give him the chance to try anything. He complied with my instructions, raising his hands as I brought my blade to his neck. His calm eyes looked back at me through the slits in his mask.

A stream of sizzling fluid shot from his fingertips and straight into my visor, obscuring my vision. I swung at him with my blade but he ducked and kicked at my feet. I landed on my back. Moments later, I heard a crash of glass. The man must have jumped through the window.

Some of the other soldiers had entered through my portal to assist me. 'Was it him? Where is he?'

I sprung to my feet, ripped off my acid-covered helmet, and threw it to the floor. It hissed and splattered as it rolled, the corrosive fluid eating through the armour. I felt so stupid, I should have teleported him to us instead.

I ran over to the balcony and peered over the edge. He had landed on one of his necrolisks one floor below. It had been scaling the building's side. It wasn't the only one; the other necrolisks clambered along the walls towards him, too. The creature he stood upon stayed still to ensure its master did not fall.

He glanced up at me as he balanced, but then looked back at the window in front of him. Malu crashed through it, flinging water and broken glass everywhere. The necrolisk didn't know what to do. Malu flew towards it and reached out to its head. Its head exploded, and Malu and the man grabbed onto the creature's body for dear life as it plummeted off the side of the building, down into the street.

I opened another portal to the ground by their side and stepped through, and the other girls followed me.

Malu and the man were fine; they had used the necrolisk body to cushion their fall. They struggled, and Malu snatched the man's helmet off, drew her gun from her waist, and pointed it at him. The face of a pasty, gaunt, frightened young man stared back at us.

He put his hands up, but it wasn't long before hundreds of necrolisks had latched off from the building and surrounded us. They all came in close, but stopped, as if sensing their master was in danger.

Malu stood on his stomach and pressed her weapon closer to his cheek. 'Make them leave or they won't have a master to serve anymore.'

The pale man, who appeared to be in his twenties, was wheezing. 'You FD trash. If you hurt me, there will be nothing to stop my family tearing you to shreds!'

Knowing how savage necrolisks were, I didn't doubt his words. I sped over to him. 'Let me try something,' I said to Malu before dipping down and grasping his collar.

A glimpse of a smile appeared on the man's guise, clearly not intimidated by either of us.

Remembering the sky overhead, I opened a portal underneath his upper frame, with the destination high above the city. The wind picked up, and the necrolisks squealed again, frightened for their master's safety.

As the man's body began to fall through the impressive pitfall, his eyes widened in fear. His arms flailed as he lent back. With my squatted stance firmly on top of him, and my hands clutching his neck, I was the only thing keeping him from certain death.

His eyes darted about. 'Don't drop – don't you dare drop me!'

'Send. Them. AWAY!' I yelled.

The necrolisks edged forward, tightening their circle.

I shook him, causing him to desperately clutch my wrists. 'Do you think I'm playing with you?' I screeched. 'Send them away now! Otherwise, we'll both drop through with you, and I guarantee we'll live, and you won't.'

'Alright, alright!'

The frightened man locked eyes with me and then over to the creatures. They shrieked and hissed as he raised his hands towards them. They started to retreat, scurrying back through the streets and alleys. Many more burst out of the windows above and joined them. When there wasn't a necrolisk in sight, he lowered his arms again.

'There. No need to erck-azzzzt!' he said as Malu's shock dart hit him in the neck and rendered him unconscious.

Malu holstered her weapon. 'Thanks. You get your wish. We take him alive.'

'Who is he?' I asked, pulling him back up and closing the portal.

'He's called Colony,' Malu said as the other soldiers jumped out of one of the windows on the ground floor.

'Is everyone else okay?' I asked as they walked over to join us.

'We lost our corporal,' one of them said. 'But it could have been worse if you hadn't warned us. What tipped you off that it was an ambush?'

'One of their claws was sticking out of the ground,' I lied.

'Where's your helmet?' Malu asked.

'This guy shot something corrosive at me,' I said, looking back down at his fingertips. There were small pipes leading down to them from his back. 'I had to get rid of it – it would have melted my face otherwise.'

'Alright, fine.' Malu turned to face the other soldiers as well. 'I'm the highest rank here now. We need to get to the factory for our next orders.'

Malu pointed at three soldiers. 'You three, take the prisoner to the pickup zone for extraction and then catch up with us afterwards.'

The three soldiers she pointed at nodded and began dragging Colony's body back towards the terrace at the top of the stairs.

The rest of us continued along the street again, going from cover to cover. As we paused behind one of the benches, Malu faced me.

'Good kill by the way,' she said and nodded over at the distant burrow where the dead necrolisk lay in two pieces. 'I've never seen that side of you. Colony was practically wetting himself.'

'Thanks. Malu, are you and I... okay now?'

'I don't know yet. Now's not the time.'

We both stood up and ran for the next bench with the remaining soldiers following behind us.

I sighed. 'I'm trying to understand, I promise.'

'None of that matters right now. Just have my back.'

I nodded. 'Alright.'

We reached the end of the street where the large facility towered over everything in the area. In front of the entrance was a set of stairs with numerous pylons along its sides. We moved in and ran up the stairs.

There was an explosion at the entrance. The doors burst off their hinges and hurtled through the air over our heads. We ducked behind the pylons for cover. There was a bright line of red light coming from within the facility. A familiar heat drifted through the doorway and onto my face. A high-pitched humming noise and a sickening burning smell saturated the air.

Twenty: Untouchable

Malu gestured for us to follow. 'Keep low and stay close!'

I could barely hear her voice over the sound of laserfire. I didn't need to use my second perception to know who was on the other side of the facility entrance.

Malu continued up the stairs and entered the facility. We all followed close behind. We walked along a large catwalk that overlooked the factory floor beneath us. Colossal machines were suspended from the ceiling via large chains.

Steaming bodies were scattered along the catwalks and down on the factory floor. A gunfight between black-clad Male Dominion soldiers and a dwindling Female Dominion force was taking place on the far side of the factory. Thankfully, there was plenty of cover around: metal pillars, machine debris, boxes, and so on.

Aiding the males were the two men I saw back in Pilgrim's village. They wore black armour, not that they needed it. A muscular man was firing the red energy beam from his fingertips, and was again shielded by his partner.

As the beam left the shield that was surrounding them, the white hexagons making up the shield's shell disappeared to allow the laser through. The energy blazed towards the women and melted through their cover and armour, disintegrating their bodies.

'Sacet!' Malu yelled. 'Get over here!'

My squad were sitting with their backs up against the waist-high catwalk railing. I rushed over and knelt down with them.

'I'll contact command,' Malu said, pressing a button near the faceplate of her helmet. 'This is AS06, we have encountered The King's Wrath. Our squad is outmatched. Please advise.'

The King's Wrath? Is that what these two acolytes were called?

A woman's face appeared on Malu's screen. She started speaking, but the rest of us couldn't hear. We waited patiently, making sure we remained low. Malu's face was sullen, as though hearing bad news.

'Understood,' Malu finally replied. 'AS06 out.' The picture disappeared and Malu closed her eyes for a moment.

'Ma'am?' one of the girls prompted.

The younger girl next to me was shaking. There were screams from our allies below as the red beam swept through another wave of them.

Malu's expression hardened and she peeked over the railing. 'We've been ordered to engage and proceed to the central hub.'

'This is suicide,' one of the girls said under her breath.

'How do we beat them?' I asked as the others stared at the catwalk floor in despair. 'King's Wrath have killed hundreds!'

One black-haired soldier shuffled closer and pointed left to one of the hulking machines hanging from the ceiling. Unlike the rest of the vehicles, it was like a giant person. It had legs and two giant cannons instead of arms. 'I can see a MASU over there. Looks operational.'

Malu raised her eyebrows, impressed. 'Good. Here's the plan.' She shifted closer and we huddled together. 'We're going to lure them under one of the hanging drones still under construction. When they are below it, I will liquefy the supports from above and drop it on their heads.'

She pointed at the others one by one. 'You pilot the Mech, and you five will approach through the middle using the pillars as cover. You three will provide suppressing fire from this catwalk on my signal. Understood?'

The group was silent.

'I said, is that *understood*?' Malu yelled.

'Yes, ma'am!' the others yelled back in unison.

'What about me? What do I do?' I asked.

'You? Get me on top of that drone, teleport yourself behind them, and do whatever you can to disrupt their fire.'

Staying low, our squad split and shuffled along the railing. I peeked over the rail at the unfinished machine hanging from the roof. I focused on the top of it and opened a portal. Malu and I entered. From the top of the drone, we peered over the edge at the firefight still raging below.

'I'll stay here,' May said. She pointed at another catwalk on the far side of the factory. It was above and behind the two acolyte men. 'See over there? Use that vantage point. Go!'

I closed the first portal, opened another and walked through. From this catwalk I peered over the edge. None of the men had noticed me flank them. Their soldiers were taking cover behind crates and pillars, firing occasional pot shots at the women. The King's Wrath brazenly moved up the centre, completely unafraid.

My squadmates rushed over to assist the other women in the centre of the chamber, firing back in the men's direction. The acolyte's energy beam countered, obliterating one of the women. The men cheered at the horrific explosion of blood and gore.

'Great one, Noor! There, another one to your right,' yelled the man maintaining the shield.

I could see Malu peering down at them, too. The two men were moving closer and closer to the trap. She began running along the drone's roof, liquefying some of the thinner metal cables that supported it.

My face was sweltering. I didn't want to kill them, but after what they did to Pilgrim's village, maybe they deserved it?

No, no more death. Find another way.

I concentrated and pictured a portal inside their bubble-like shield, but nothing happened. What was going on? This shield wasn't just blocking laserfire, my powers had no effect on it either.

There was a final splash and a loud creak. The colossal mechanical drone came crashing down through the air towards the acolytes.

'Tetsu, look up!' the one referred to as Noor shouted before firing into the falling drone, splitting it in two.

The machine still slammed onto the shield, sending a shockwave of dust and shrapnel flying in all directions.

The catwalk I was on jolted. There was a metallic snap. I felt my stomach give way as the catwalk lurched forward off its supports. As it fell, I opened a portal to safety, on the ground not too far away. I jumped through and hit the ground hard, tumbling into some nearby boxes. The catwalk smashed onto the ground behind me. Where the drone once was, Malu held onto a cable hanging from the ceiling.

One of the male soldiers pointed up. 'Up there.' They aimed their weapons at her.

I opened a portal and frantically moved it under all of the male soldiers' feet. One by one they all fell through, flailing their limbs as they tripped into the hole and landed in the desert just outside the city.

The pile of soldiers in the sand on the other side quickly grew into a heap. One tried reaching up to the portal's rim. After the last soldier was swallowed I closed it on them.

The cloud of dust dissipated to reveal that The King's Wrath were unharmed. Their shield remained intact. They noticed Malu, too, and Noor aimed at her. She let go of the cable just as the beam appeared. She plummeted. The beam caught and instantly disintegrated one of her hands. She scrunched up her face in agony. The beam followed her down, intent on finishing the job.

I threw my hands out and created a portal below her. She launched out of the portal to my side, tumbling until one of the metal pillars stopped her momentum.

Malu's cauterised wrist steamed. She screamed, the noise catching the attention of the two acolytes.

'There, there! That one!' Tetsu yelled as he pointed at me.

'I see her,' Noor muttered, raising his hands.

I, too, raised my hands. A portal opened in front to shield me. The exit faced down, above their shield.

The energy blast came towards me and through my portal. It exited down onto their shield, but the beam shattered, splitting in all directions.

The beam grew wider, wider than even my portal. The intense heat stung my extremities. I smelt my own flesh burning. A fragment of the laser grazed my shoulder. I screamed.

I shifted the portal exit to a pillar on the other side of the factory, then leapt forward into my shield. I closed the portals and scrambled behind the pillar, hoping they didn't see me. I slumped and grasped my singed shoulder.

'Come out! We just want to talk!' Tetsu said.

Noor laughed. 'No way, brother,' he said. 'Something tells me she's not that dumb.'

As I sat there trying to catch my breath, I could still hear gunfire from the rest of the squad. More enemy soldiers must have engaged them from the factory's side. Behind the pillar, I sensed Noor and Tetsu still searching for me.

'Maybe you're here?' Noor said as he fired on some nearby crates.

I needed to move, or he might fire on me next. I couldn't think of anything. Where could I move to?

There was a whirring noise, followed by another loud hail of gunfire coming from where the soldiers were fighting, and then nothing. Noor and Tetsu also stopped to check out the silence, but their view was blocked by the wreckage of the fallen drone and some lingering dust.

But I sensed it: the mechanical walker forced its way through the debris and rubble, before adjusting its sights on the acolytes. Its giant gun-arms started to spin up again.

The machine fired upon the men with a barrage of bullets. They ricocheted off the shield, falling harmlessly to the ground. The men stood still, Noor with his arms folded, as if unimpressed by the assault.

A volley of rockets left the MASU, bombarding and enveloping them in an inferno. The smoke cleared. The shield was still up. The two men laughed.

Noor shrugged. 'Are they serious?'

'It's cute when they try. Show them how it's done.'

That pilot was going to get killed if I didn't act now. But I still couldn't think of anything. Wait... whenever they fired, there was an opening in the shield. The gap between the shield and the exiting laser was tiny, but perhaps that's all I needed?

Noor was already raising his arms.

'No!' I yelled. I darted out of cover towards them, summoning a portal on each hand.

Noor fired and the beam sliced through the centre of the machine. Its fuel tank exploded in a firestorm.

I raised my portals to shield myself and continued to run. The two men turned towards me. I wasn't going to fail this time. I gritted my teeth. 'Enough of this!'

Tetsu tilted his head. 'Must have been a friend of hers.'

'Back for more?' Noor said, aiming at me again and firing.

I held out the portal in my right hand and received the laser. I widened the portals so they were far larger than my body. The laser exited from the portal in my left hand, which was currently aiming off to the side and melting the factory floor. The heat was so intense that the air itself distorted around me.

Noor didn't let up, perhaps thinking my portals could be worn down. My second perception eyed the small gap between the shield and the laser. I could do this. I held my breath.

I sidestepped out from cover and aimed my left portal back along the same path as the first laser, but this time slightly lower. The laser backfired through the small gap in the shield, towards the ground and their feet. The laser melted through Noor's kneecap and one of Tetsu's ankles. Both the laser and the shield instantly dissipated, and the men fell to the ground shrieking.

I closed my portals and took a deep breath. The remaining female soldiers were making their way through the wreckage. They stopped just short of us, weapons at the ready.

'Don't kill them!' I said as the two young men continued to squeal. I wasn't going to be responsible for more deaths. 'Take them prisoner!'

'But they just killed my friends,' one woman protested.

I glanced back to where I had last seen Malu. She was still on the ground, not moving. Then I examined the streaks of all the soldiers around me. 'Malu is out of action. I'm now the highest rank. I order you to capture them.'

Tetsu gripped at where his feet once were. 'Why... did you... shoot... my feet off?' he yelled at Noor, gasping between each word.

'I didn't,' Noor yelled back in agony. 'It was her!'

'She... doesn't... shoot... lasers!'

Noor was clutching his steaming knee with one hand and raising the other towards me. A shower of shock darts covered both of their bodies, rendering them unconscious.

The woman who complained now scoffed. 'Taking orders from an initiate, how depressing.'

'Hey!' one my squadmates shouted. She approached the other woman. 'That *initiate* just saved your life. Show some respect!' She turned to me and nodded. 'Go ahead, ma'am.'

I nodded back appreciatively, just as two soldiers appeared from behind a pillar. They were dragging Malu on a piece of sheet metal. I ran over and knelt beside her.

'Malu! Malu?'

Malu's hand and wrist were completely gone. Her armour had shattered and peeled back to reveal grisly burns and tears in her muscles. She clutched her burnt elbow and groaned, her breaths rapid and shallow. Like the boys, her wound was cauterised, so the bleeding had stopped.

'She's in shock, ma'am,' one of the soldiers explained. 'She needs to be evacuated.'

I reached out and held Malu's free hand for a moment, before standing and inspecting the nine remaining soldiers. Was I really going to do this, take command? I had to get out of here alive, not die a hero.

'AS06, do you read?' a quiet voice said from all of my squadmates' helmets.

The girl that had defended me gave me a nod, then raised a hand to her ear. 'We read you, command. Status update: King's Wrath have been knocked out. Malu is in critical condition. What are our orders?'

'Status confirmed, AS06. Send a team to evacuate the wounded and prisoners immediately. The rest of your squad, check the south offices for survivors.'

'Understood,' the girl replied, and she looked at me expectantly.

The woman who had complained earlier shrugged at me. 'Well?'

I turned back to my new subordinates and pointed at them at random. 'You two, grab Malu. You four, grab the men!' I watched as they complied with my orders.

I thought back to where we had first landed, just before the gardens, and spun my fingers. As the six women dragged Malu, Noor, and Tetsu closer, a portal opened. 'Go, get out of here!'

They carried the unconscious bodies through the portal, and I closed it, leaving three soldiers behind. From the wear on their armour, they seemed older, more seasoned than the ones I had sent away.

One pointed at a massive doorway on the side of the chamber nearby. 'The south offices are that way.'

The three of them checked their weapons and surrounded me.

'Okay, we're ready, ma'am. Shall we search for survivors?'

I sensed a dark passageway through the door. 'Must we?' I was already feeling the effects of combat. I just wanted to get back to Eno.

She raised an eyebrow at me. 'Those are our orders.'

I faced the doorway and took a deep breath. 'Alright, follow me.' I trudged forward with the women in tow. The sooner we got this over with the better.

Twenty-One: Dead End

The lighting to the offices had been cut, but I sensed more dead bodies in the darkness. We ran around a corner and jumped over a small gap where the floor had caved in. At the end of the corridor there were small shafts of light peeking through the concrete cracks. I put my hands on the blockade and tried pushing against it, but it wouldn't budge.

'Dead end,' one of the women noted. 'Is there another way around?'

'Wait,' I replied.

I closed my eyes and scanned through the fallen debris. A rubble-filled area was just beyond it, crater-like in shape. The floors above had collapsed, allowing the apocalyptic, smoke-filled sky to bathe the area in orange. Numerous floors of the facility were exposed. I was shocked at what I saw; there must have been over a hundred bodies lying on the ground, many of them in pieces or buried under concrete. Most were civilians, but plenty of soldiers were in there, too.

In the centre of the devastation there stood a gargantuan man, sheathed in armour. He was at least double the size of any regular person. He didn't wear a mask like the others.

He held up a female soldier a fraction of his size in his two gigantic hands. She was trying to break free from his monstrous grip. I gasped when I saw her face. It was Tau.

I pulled out my blade, opened a portal to the next area and ran through with the others. As we arrived on the other side, I created another portal, stuck my sword into it and threw the exit towards the man. He didn't notice the flying sword coming straight for his face.

As it hit his cheek, the blade bent and was deflected. I pulled the warped sword from the portal and threw it to the ground. He slowly turned his head, spotted us, and grinned.

'About time, I was getting tired of playing with this one,' he bellowed.

Tau screamed. 'Sacet! It's—'

The man tightened his grip around her waist. 'That's enough out of you.'

The other women raised their rifles.

'Wait!' I commanded, giving them pause. 'You might hit her.' I looked back at the man. 'Let her go, monster!'

An amused look came over his face as if he was delighted to hear the words. 'Oh! Oh, but of course.' His smile changed to a look of bloodlust.

He tightened his grip once more and Tau screamed again. There was a sickening snap, Tau stopped screaming and instead lay limp in his hand.

My jaw dropped and I began to shake. 'No!'

The man tossed her broken body towards us. Tau sailed through the air and came to a stop on the rubble. Her torso was covered in blood and there was what looked like a rib protruding from her chest. My eyes welled with tears.

The man examined his giant fist. 'Whoops.' He lowered his brow and flashed a malicious grin, filled with misshapen teeth. 'My mistake.'

'Ma'am, focus,' one of the soldiers said. 'We're still in danger. What are your orders?'

I wiped away the tears with my hand, my sorrow turning to wrath. 'Mistake? You killed her! So I'm going to kill you!'

He raised his massive fists. 'That's what we like to hear.'

I had tried to crush Malu when I met her, I would do the same here. But this time, I would succeed. I put a portal on the ground nearby. The destination I put above the man's head, and with one strong plunge of my arm, it came crashing down onto him. The ground near me cracked from the force on the other side.

My attack had smacked him prone, but he remained unharmed. I raised the portal up and slammed it down again and again. I kept smashing it down, hoping to see his blood. I roared louder with each hit.

Rubble from the ground portal was flinging about from the impact. I breathed heavily. He was getting crushed deeper and deeper into a hole. I didn't let up, hitting him until I my arm was tired and my voice was hoarse.

One of my squadmates put her hand on my shoulder. I stopped and seethed back at her, then closed my eyes and took a moment to catch my breath. He was surely dead by now. I closed my portal. The girls coughed and waved their hands about because of the dust cloud.

'That was your only free shot,' I heard a muffled, gravelly voice say.

My eyes widened. I glanced back at the hole in horror. The brute rose from the crater, unharmed, the only indication of damage some scratches on his armour. He lifted his knee high and climbed out, sauntering closer.

'Ma'am?'

'Fire!' The soldiers unleashed a barrage of laserfire, but each projectile only damaged his armour, deflecting off his seemingly invincible body. 'Kill him!' I screeched.

He started to sprint at us, the ground rumbled with each step. Despite his gigantic size, he was frighteningly fast.

I dove to the side. His fist rocketed into the nearest soldier with a terrible thwack. Her body careened into the air and collided into a distant wall, splattering it red. The other two continued firing to no avail, he simply laughed.

I backed away, trying to think of a way to kill him. After what he had done to Tau, I was not going to let him live.

He hammered his boulder-like fist down onto another soldier, flattening her and breaking her bones with a cacophony of crackling snaps.

My fingers twirled, making a portal out of desperation. I placed one on the ground and flung the other towards him. He leaped into the air to avoid it, then landed next to the final soldier.

'No, get away!' she shouted, but he quickly snatched her and squeezed. Another snap, she groaned, slumped forward and let out her final death rattle.

The man dropped her, glanced over, and shook his head at me. I was no match for him, I had to escape. I was trembling with equal parts fear and anger.

Before I knew it, he had stormed over and grabbed me. He lifted me up, as he had the others, and frowned. 'Come now, over so soon? I haven't had my fun.'

He pulled his arm back and threw me towards the side of the clearing. I flew up into one of the exposed floors above, then hit the floor and tumbled.

I staggered to my feet and clutched my ribs. He had winded me, I could barely breathe.

The man jumped from the rubble and landed on the ledge in front of me. He drew his arm back, ready to strike.

I opened a portal in front and another along the wall to his side. As his fist came crashing through, it burst out of the wall next to him and struck his own face. He staggered backwards and brought his hand out of the portal.

He gave his biggest laugh yet. 'You made me punch myself? How fun!'

He raised his fists above his head and then slammed them onto the floor, causing a cave in. Both of us fell into a dark room along with the collapsing rubble.

I landed hard, unable to get up off my knees. I coughed and spluttered, unable to breathe. I frantically looked around, squinting in the dusty darkness.

Then, from behind, I felt his hands clench around my waist and lift me into the air again. I tried turning around to see his face but was stopped short when he squeezed. I shrieked as he constricted further. He laughed at my cries.

'Any last words?'

Why was he toying with me? No matter.

I made another levitation portal to the side and forced it to fly into both of us. The portal smacked into our side and drove us both into the nearby wall. I pressed the portal up against us and also squeezed; we were both stuck between the wall and the portal now.

He remained unfazed. 'Call me crazy, but I'm sure I'll crush you before you crush me.'

He was right. My efforts had no effect. I used my second perception and looked up into the empty sky. I changed the destination of the portal that was crushing us so that it instead led straight up. I then pulled the portal closer so that it forced us through into the sky on the other side.

We were directly over the caved in offices, high above the city. The wind picked up as we fell back towards the surface.

'That won't work either,' he yelled over the whipping wind.

The ground was fast approaching. I opened a portal on the ground and another over my head. I tried pulling myself through it, and like an article of clothing, I squeezed it over my head, my chest, my hips, then my legs, until I was free of the man's loosened grasp. I closed the portal and crawled through the rubble, still gasping for air.

I quickly closed the portals behind me and glanced up. The man was still plummeting. As much as I wanted to, I couldn't kill him. But maybe I could trap him?

I opened a portal as wide as I could, below where I expected he would land. The second portal was placed above the first, and I waited for his body to pass it before I opened them both. He fell through the first portal, but instead of hitting the ground, he continued to fall through the second portal, then through the first again, then the second again, over and over in perpetual free-fall. As long as I kept these portals open, he wasn't going anywhere.

'Damn you, runt!' he thundered. 'Fight me properly!'

I felt foolish for not doing something like this sooner. I paid him no attention, crawling over to Tau instead. Her body was covered in blood. It had pooled underneath her, spreading among the rubble. The dirt and debris had absorbed much of it, darkening the grey dust.

Why had they done this? She wasn't like the others, she was a kind person. My body trembled. These men would pay for what they had done here.

I knelt beside her and placed my hand around the back of her neck to support her. There was a slight tingling sensation on the end of my fingertips, then throughout my whole hand. I gently let go of her neck and brought my hand up; the tingling had stopped. I placed my hand onto hers and felt the strange sensation return.

Her skin was beginning to glow. Her hand turned a resplendent white. Visible silvery, light-blue licks of air emanated from her body like flames. I closed my eyes as the sensation overpowered me.

Twenty-Two: We Are a Family

Tau was still sleeping in her bed and if she didn't get up soon, she'd probably be punished.

'Tau. Tau!' Vanu yelled. 'Wake up or you'll get in trouble again.'

I looked around the room at the other bunk beds. The other children were already up and getting changed into their uniforms.

Reliu pushed past her. 'Let me.' She punched Tau in her side. 'Get up!'

'Urgh... oww! Why did you hit me?' Tau moaned as she pulled off the sheets.

'Hurry up and get dressed,' Vanu said.

'Okay, okay,' she replied as she put her arms through her undersuit sleeves.

The door at the end of the room opened and Corporal Tallu walked in. She towered over us.

'Attention!' she yelled, her voice carrying down to the end of the bunk line.

The chattering of the children silenced. There was a loud pattering as all the kids ran to the front of their bunks, including me. Tau still wasn't dressed. She kicked her feet through her leggings and hopped over to her bunk.

The corporal strode between the beds and stopped in front of her. 'You know what? I don't even mind that Initiate Tau woke up late, as usual.' Her frown turned to a smile. 'I have some good news for all of you. You have all graduated and you've been requested at the Atrasian province.'

The whole room cheered.

'Get all of your things together, quickly! We need to make our way over to the hangar for your deployment, right now. They're waiting for us.'

Our things? Did she mean our trunk of clothes? I watched as the others pulled on their trunks' handles and followed the corporal out of the door and into the hallway. I picked mine up too, as Tau continued to put on her uniform.

'You go, I'll catch up,' she said.

I made my way out of the room and caught up with the rest of my squad in the corridor.

'You'll like it in Aero,' the corporal yelled back at us over the sound of our rolling trunk wheels. 'Don't feel bad that you're leaving the capital city; Aero is almost as big and has everything you could need.'

All the girls were excited. A new place meant a new life. We were bored of the same training drills every day. This was going to be fun.

It wasn't long before we entered through the doors into the hangar. Waiting for us at the end of the runway was a lone transport, its turbines idling over in preparation for take-off.

We pushed and shoved our way up the ramp, laughing as we went. We locked our trunks to the floor using the latches at our feet.

'Cara, where's Tau?' the corporal inquired of me.

Tau came running through the entrance to the hangar with her trunk in tow. 'Wait!' her little voice chirped. 'Wait for me!'

'Ah... never mind.'

We took our seats and helped one another strap in. These seats were too big for us, so we had to make sure the straps were tight. Tau rushed up the ramp and locked her trunk into place with the others. She took a seat in my row and smiled at everyone.

The corporal was standing at the top of the ramp. 'I'm very proud of all of you.' The cabin silenced. 'I promise I'll visit once you've settled in.'

We all looked a little shocked.

'But Corporal, you're not coming with us?' one of the girls asked.

She laughed. 'Not yet. But thank you for thinking of me.' She pointed at each one of us. 'Watch each other's backs, and never forget, you are sisters. And that is a bond stronger than anything in this world.' She gave one last smile, turned, and walked back down the ramp.

The ramp rose, leaving us in the dark, blue compartment. The engines whirred louder. The craft swayed as it sped up, launching into the sky. The other children cheered and laughed as we all felt an unfamiliar lurch in the pit of our stomachs. Sunil was crying and Medi actually yelped.

'Do you think it will be different there?' Vana asked me. 'Or the same?'

Medi was shaking in her seat. 'I don't like this. I want to go back on the ground.'

I closed my eyes and focused on the now-steady humming of the turbines. As I rested, I tried imagining what was waiting for us when we touched down. Was Aero as beautiful as the capital, I wondered? What about the people? I hoped they were friendly. And hopefully I wouldn't need to shoot anyone while I lived there either.

There was a loud swish outside of the aircraft. I awoke to my squad sisters now silent; they were trying to recognise the noise, too. An explosion shook the cabin and ripped a hole along the side of the aircraft, causing the children's seats opposite me to fly out into the sky.

I shielded my face from the bright desert light, then gripped the sides of my chair for dear life. An alarm sounded. There was a gaping hole now where some of the children had been sitting. One of the wings was missing. We were spinning and spinning, and falling towards the empty dunes far below.

We screamed, but were drowned out by the chaos. My seat wobbled. I stretched out and tried to grab the hand of the girl next to me. My seat lurched forward and broke loose. It rolled along the cabin floor with me still inside, then the wind ripped me out through the hole and into the hot desert air. The seat spun sickeningly until it eventually settled so that I was facing the clear blue sky above.

The back of the seat crashed into the sand and tumbled down the dune before coming to a stop. It was a miracle; I was still alive. I pulled on the buckles and straps until I was free. I convinced my shaking, shocked body to climb out of the seat and stand on the dune.

The aircraft continued to spin into the distance, before crash landing into the desert. Were they okay? My squad was everything to me, my family. Was Sunil okay? What about Reliu? Would I ever see Tallu again? Why was this happening?

I ran up and down the dunes, approaching the smoking wreckage. Rocks jutted from the ground between me and the crash site, and I weaved and climbed over those blocking my path. Upon reaching the peak of one of the boulders, I had a clear view of the crash site.

I quickly ducked, for a large group of people had beaten me here. They had tan-coloured clothing. Their faces were covered by cloth masks, hiding all but their eyes. They had their rusty brown weapons ready, pointed at the downed craft. Nomads. I couldn't tell if they were men or women. I had only seen men in pictures before, never up close.

I peeked over the boulder for a better look. Aircraft pieces were everywhere. The main cabin was intact, aside from the massive hole in its side. Some of the girls inside were slumped on the floor, and others were still stuck in their chairs, were they unconscious or...?

My eyes shifted back to the nomads. One of them had a much bigger weapon, like a huge metal tube over his shoulder. What was that?

The nomads ducked their heads through the hole in the cabin and stepped inside.

'Children!' one shouted with a very deep voice. 'They've sent *children* at us?'

'It doesn't matter how old the enemy is, they're going to grow up to be monsters anyway. Make sure they're all dead,' another man ordered.

They pointed their weapons down at my sisters and shot them in the head, one by one. The gruesome sight made me sick to my stomach, but I couldn't look away.

One was still moving. I think... yes, it was Tau. She was still alive. Her body twitched. She opened her eyes slowly and saw the nomads. She squealed and wriggled in her seat, trying to free herself.

'Hati, this one's awake. Should we take her prisoner?' one of the nomads suggested.

'Too risky. Tracking devices, remember?' another said. 'Kill her.'

The first man raised his weapon and fired into Tau's head. The exit wound splattered blood onto the back of her seat. I let out a shriek but placed my hands over my mouth to muffle the sound. I ducked back down behind the boulder as the nomads spun in my direction.

'I heard something. Go check it out!'

I wiped my tear-filled eyes and ran as fast as I could.

'There's one over here!' I heard a man yell from behind.

Gunshots followed, ricocheting off the rocks to my sides as I fled. I left the rocks and ran back into the dunes. There was nowhere to hide. I wouldn't be able to outrun them out here. I had no choice. I ran up and down the dunes again, away from the rocks and my pursuers.

I must escape. I must live. Please let me live. Please let me leave this war. I don't want to kill. I didn't want any of this. I wanted to leave this desert and never return, back to the safety of the city walls. No... I didn't want... I needed. *I must escape.*

There was a loud pop, followed by a whoosh. Something hit me in the back, a hot tingling sensation that travelled to my extremities. I fell down into the dune, rolling into a crevice and hitting my head on yet another rock.

As I lay there staring up at the sky and bleeding onto the sand, I pictured my home again. I peered over to the sand dune where I expected my killers to appear, but nothing. I closed my eyes. I slipped in and out. The clouds drifted away.

I opened my eyes again just as they arrived – two desert nomads walking down the dune. The sun was setting. The couple knelt beside me and brought a canteen to my lips. As I drank the cool water, two heart-warming smiles beamed back at me. I swallowed and then fainted back into the soft sand.

I shot up from the bed in a daze. 'Stop it!'

I was in a cave. Sunlight was peering in through holes in the ceiling. The bed had tattered, mouldy sheets, and no pillow.

'But we're not doing anything?' a man's voice replied.

There was a man and woman on the other side of the cave. I recognised them; it was the same couple who had found me. They were both leaning over a metal cauldron. A fire was lit underneath it, and something smelled... pleasant. Like herbs and maybe meat.

The man was middle-aged, had black hair and tanned skin.

'She's awake!' the woman said before scowling at him. 'Don't tease, Azua.'

Azua smiled back. 'How am I teasing?'

They wore rags and robes, nomadic clothing. I was wearing rags, too.

I stood up on the flimsy bed with my back to the cave wall. 'What's going on here? Where am I?'

The woman stood, too, and gestured to my bed. 'Please sit, dear. You've been asleep for a whole day now. You shouldn't be moving too much. Just rest on the bed.'

She had flowing blonde hair that reached to her lower back. She placed one of her hands on her stomach, which was ballooned up more than I thought was possible. No, wait. Was she pregnant?

I began to sob and eyed the cave's exit. 'Who are you people?'

'You're safe here,' the woman said. 'We're not going to hurt you.'

I continued to eye the exit, but my body was frozen.

The man noticed the direction of my gaze. He was still smiling. 'It's dangerous out there. And dinner's almost ready, too. It's Enni's favourite.'

The woman called Enni smiled back at Azua and then to me. She calmly walked over and sat at the end of the bed. I edged farther away and hopped off my end, shuffling along the wall.

'Try to remember what happened,' Enni said.

It didn't seem like she was going to hurt me. She was kind. But the man... men couldn't be trusted.

A tear trickled down my cheek and onto my chin. 'There was a crash,' I said, struggling to piece my memory together.

Enni placed both hands on her stomach. 'Yes, go on.'

'My sisters... wait.' I backed away from her. 'It was you! You nomads shot us down. You killed them.'

Enni raised her hands to try and calm me down. 'That wasn't us, I promise you. When we got there, it was too late. We found you and brought you here.'

Azua cleared his throat. 'If we hadn't, you'd be dead.'

They saved me, but why?

I looked down at the sandy floor. 'I don't understand.'

'Azua and I don't want to be a part of this war,' Enni said. 'We saw you and... we *knew* we had to save you.'

I shook my head, flinging tears about. 'But... you nomads shot me?'

Enni stood up. 'Shot? You have no bullet wounds or laser burns.'

Confused, I quickly felt my back underneath my rags, checking for the wound, but felt nothing.

Enni coolly made her way over and gently rubbed my cheek. 'You don't have to worry about that war anymore. You can stay here with us; we can be a family.'

Azua chuckled as he stirred the pot. 'You've always wanted a daughter.'

I shook my head and furrowed my brow. 'But you're my enemy? Why would–' I groaned and glanced at the exit again. 'Just let me leave! Take me back!'

Azua stared at Enni expectantly. Enni puzzled for a moment, taking her hand off my cheek and instead tenderly pulling on my hand. She guided me back to the bed and sat down.

'Come sit with me,' she asked.

I wanted to run, but her warm smile put me at ease. I did as she asked and sat next to her. I had stopped sobbing, but my eyes still welled with tears.

She gestured down to her stomach. 'Right now, I have a baby inside of me.' She rubbed it and smiled. 'He or she is an innocent person, so small and cute that they couldn't possibly hurt someone. Is my baby your enemy, too?'

'Well... no, but–'

'And what if my baby grows up and wants to live peacefully?' she continued. 'Would they still be your enemy? Those people that raised you are evil, and soon they would make you do *very* evil things. Wouldn't you rather live a happy, free life?'

I looked away. I realised what she was doing. She thought she was helping me. And they still wanted to take care of me, knowing what I was? She locked her kind eyes with mine and nodded.

'Don't you want to have a little brother to protect?' Azua said.

Enni raised an eyebrow towards Azua, and he gave the biggest smile yet. 'Or sister?' Her eyes widened in surprise. 'Oh, quick, come feel the baby kicking!'

She reached out to my hand and placed it on her stomach. Sure enough, I felt a small nudge.

'Wow... that's...' I said, wiping away my tears with my free hand. 'That's a baby?' There was a silence in the cave as we watched her stomach, and nothing but the flickering flames and the bubbling cauldron could be heard.

My sisters were dead, there was no changing that. And it seemed as though I had gotten my wish: to leave the war, to not have to kill. And if I went back home now, there wouldn't be any of my friends waiting for me.

I shrugged, deciding to play along. 'Maybe I'll stay... for a little while?'

'And while you're with us, we'll be your parents, alright?' Enni said.

I wiped the rest of my tears away. 'I've never had parents before.'

Azua scooped some of the broth into a bowl and stood. 'First time for everything. Speaking of, try this.' He walked over.

I let go of Enni's stomach and took the bowl with both hands. Azua quickly reached out to my head. Shocked, I tried to duck. He gave my hair a gentle tussle before standing up straight again, beaming down.

Relieved, I gave a quick smile back. This was the first man I had ever met. He was so friendly, I didn't understand. The food smelled delicious.

Azua knelt down beside me. 'Whatever the Dominion made you think and do, that's all gone now. Leave everything about them behind, including your name. The three of us can pretend... that all never happened. Okay?'

'Like I don't remember?' I asked.

Enni nodded. 'Exactly.'

I looked back down at the baby. 'Um, what are you naming it?'

'Well, if it's a boy, then Eno,' my mother said, rubbing her stomach. 'I did think of a great girl's name, but—'

'I think she should have it,' Azua interrupted, pointing at me. 'She needs a new name.'

Enni gently gripped my wrist. 'How would you like to be named... Sacet?'

I nodded. 'Saaa...set?' I said, sounding it out. Both Enni and Azua grinned.

Azua passed me a small, wooden stick and gestured at the food. 'Eat, you're probably starving.'

Twenty-Three: Revenant

The present

My eyes continued to well with tears. 'My... parents.'

It had been so long since I'd remembered my parents' faces. What they looked like and how they acted. I always knew the basics of what had happened back then, but never key details like what I had just experienced.

Tau's rib cage was fusing back together. Each broken bone snapped and crackled inside of her back into its correct position. The pool of blood around her regressed until the rubble was left unstained once more. Her hair had turned a very light-blue, almost white. The flickering streaks of silvery air grew in intensity, gently whipping around her body.

I was unsure of whether I should let go of her. The tingling sensation throughout my body was euphoric, and her body was healing. I was afraid to change that now.

My body was healing, too. I watched as colour returned to my formally seared shoulder. I brought my free hand to the back of my head, for an old lingering scar was tingling, too, now gone. My energy had returned, as though I could go toe-to-toe with the falling man all over again.

More early childhood memories were flooding back, of my little sister squad and our time in FDC. I already had a few memories of the buildings and training, but this was different. It was like completing a puzzle. I remembered that time Sunil and I tried running away from the barracks and getting caught. It was all coming back to me.

'Sacet?'

I had been so distracted that I hadn't noticed that Tau was alive once more and looking up at me. The flickering air ceased, her skin changed back to normal and her hair faded from white to auburn again. Even her blue streaks returned.

'Tau! You're okay!' I leant down and hugged her tight. 'But... you were dead?'

Tau saw the colossal man in continual free-fall.

'Is he... are we safe here?' she asked.

I let go and glanced back at him. 'He's not going anywhere. But that's not important right now. Why didn't you tell anyone you were an acolyte?'

She sat up with a bewildered look. 'I... wait, what? Me?'

I helped brush bits of rubble off her. 'Tau, this isn't the first time you've died.'

She took a deep breath. 'Sacet, I have no idea what's going on right now.'

'This power of yours... it healed me. I remember things, memories I forgot I had. I know why you hate bandits so much, because I was there. I'm Cara.'

Her eyes widened and stared into mine. 'What?'

'Or I used to be. When we met, you seemed familiar to me. We both didn't recognise... because we've grown up so much since then.'

She gasped and shot up to her feet. 'Cara? I... I remember you, too! You do look a little like her. But they told me I was the only survivor of that crash...'

I stood as well. 'And I thought I was the only one.'

Tau facepalmed. 'I feel so stupid.'

I grabbed both her arms. 'But Tau, this is amazing! Why didn't you tell anyone you could do this?'

'I don't know.' She turned away. 'How did I die the first time? I don't remember.'

I let her go. 'After the crash. You got shot in the head.'

Her gaze drifted into the distance. 'I was stuck in my seat...'

'Look, I suppose it doesn't matter. Come on, we should get out of here.'

We both wandered closer to the falling man, who had thankfully ceased his shouting.

I glanced at the multitude of other bodies lying on the ground. I was so shocked into submission that it hadn't really clicked how much death had surrounded me today.

Tau stared at the falling man. 'Sacet, there's something you should know about him...'

'Well, well, well,' a voice said from behind.

Iya and another acolyte strolled through the rubble towards us. I believed the other one was named Neva, she was one of the colonels I had met in the queen's chambers. She had long, golden hair, like Verre but was much younger. Her hair looked perfect, as if she hadn't been fighting at all.

Iya started clapping. 'Good job, Sacet. You beat every challenge that was thrown at you today.' She gestured at the falling man. 'Although this one isn't dead yet.'

I twisted my lips, attempting to keep my mouth shut, but it was no use. 'Well, why don't you finish him off yourself, Iya?'

The blonde stomped forward. 'Watch your tone, initiate!'

I ignored and gestured to all the dead women. 'Is this your squad? Where were you two? Why did you allow this massacre to happen?'

Neva stormed up close until she was in my face. 'You say one more word and I'll kill you where you stand.' Her intense stare locked with my own. 'We can take things from here. Be a good little initiate and head back to the pickup zone.'

At that time, as if by coincidence, three of our aircraft glided overhead in the direction I came from.

Neva pointed at the ground. 'Tau, you stay here. You need... debriefing.' She then glared at Iya. 'Iya, secure the prisoner.'

Tau stared at one of her dead squad members sprawled on the ground. Her lower jaw trembled.

Iya raised her hand in front of her eye and brought the falling man to a jolting stop. The man fell oddly quiet, not even struggling against her grip.

Neva pointed towards the factory. 'Well? What are you waiting for? The battle is over. The city is clear. Leave!'

I didn't like the idea of leaving Tau with them one bit. I'd dealt with four enemy acolytes today; what could these two have possibly been busy with that they neglected to protect them?

'I'll be fine, Sacet,' Tau said under her breath as she passed me to join them.

Fine? She was kidding, right? I was about to protest, but Neva was still staring me down.

I closed my portals and thought back to where the aircraft had first dropped us off. I opened a new portal and glanced back at Tau one last time before stepping through.

Twenty-Four: Going Off Line

Eno

Toroi seemed to thrust his laser drill into the cave wall harder with every hit. He hadn't cried since they took his dad. But he was done with crying, now he was just angry. Every so often he shot a vile look back at the guards. It was the only way he knew how to fight back against them without being killed.

When he pulled out the drill, I bent down and picked up one of the stones he had cut loose. I wasn't strong enough for this one. I could barely even roll it. Toroi dropped his drill and helped. Together, we carried it over to the hover cart and dropped it in. It tumbled against the walls inside the metal container before coming to rest halfway down with the other rocks.

'That's full enough,' a guard said to me, pointing at the cart. 'We need this cart topside. Take it back up.' She pointed her clicker at me and it beeped. I was free to leave the area without proximity alarms going off.

I placed both hands on the edge of the cart, stepped up onto the footrest, and pushed the same buttons as last time. The machine rumbled to life, beginning its slow journey up to the surface along the electric track.

As I pulled away from the work area, I glanced back at Toroi and the other men. They were silent and stone-faced. I rounded the track's first corner, and they were out of sight. I was alone.

The cliff path was narrow, steep, and very high up. One wrong move and I'd plummet to my death in the dark abyss below. Luckily, the cart could hover over loose stones as well as the narrowest ledges. So as long as I didn't slip off the footrest, I would be fine.

The expansive view of the misty cavern below was impressive. There were thousands of workers below, each carving up the ground without speaking.

The guards patrolled along the catwalks overhead. Whenever I was spotted, they'd watch me with contempt, waiting for me to make the slightest mistake so they could punish me.

One guard on a catwalk on the other side of the abyss trained her weapon on me. A bead of sweat rolled out of my armpit. My arms shook. I tried to focus on the cart controls, like a good little male.

'Bang!' she yelled, chortling and continuing her patrol away from me.

The path ahead wound around and up. I heard more footsteps above on yet another catwalk.

'Come on, Iya. Just put me down,' I heard one low, booming voice say. 'If any of them see, we can kill them.'

'Iya?' I whispered to myself.

I pressed a red button on the control panel and stopped the cart; I didn't think they knew I was below. Iya, I'd heard that name before. She was that acolyte girl who helped capture my sister and I.

'Relax, we're almost at your cell,' a younger voice said. It must have been her.

'How long am I expected to stay in it?' the man said. 'It seems like a waste of my time. I'd rather torture that portal girl a little longer.'

Portal girl? Was he talking about Sacet?

The voices passed over me and were getting farther away. I had to hear what this was about, but the only way I could follow was if I was on the catwalk with them. If I climbed to the top of the cart and jumped directly up, the underside of the catwalk might just be within reach.

My arms were still shaking. What if I was caught? Would they torture me? Whip me? Maybe I could sneak up there and then sneak back? So long as no one saw.

I clambered up the steel frame and looked up. I took a deep breath, bent my knees, then leapt as high as I could. My fingertips touched one of the catwalk's support bars. I fell back down and thankfully landed safely back where I started.

No good, do it again. Bent knees, and jump! This time my fingers wrapped around the bar.

'You could be in there for a while,' a different, feminine voice said. 'We haven't contacted Overwatch, yet.'

As nimbly as I could, I swung from bar to bar, getting closer to the edge of the catwalk. I grabbed onto the ledge and pulled myself up and over the rail.

Then I saw them walking away from me. Iya had one hand in front of her eye in a pinching shape, like she had done to Sacet. The enormous man, fists as big as boulders, was hanging in the air in front of her. There were two more women I didn't recognise escorting him.

'What if we staged a prison break?' the man asked.

If I was quiet enough I could hear the rest of their conversation and be back before anyone knew. I tiptoed along the metal catwalk and followed them around the path.

'The Matriarch wouldn't risk something like that,' one woman replied, her voice growing more distant. 'It would inspire too much hope in these losers.'

'Speaking of losers,' Iya added, 'those other acolytes of yours nearly screwed up everything. They weren't supposed to be in those positions. If they had have killed Sacet early...'

The man laughed. 'What do you expect? Sometimes pawns go off script.'

The path turned a slight corner, leading to a section of the mines I had never seen before. Only by using the catwalks could I have gotten here. Should I turn back? I steadied my shaking arms. No, I had to find out what happened to my sister.

Large stones jutted out from the sides of the path along the catwalk, so I raced over to the nearest one and peered over it. Their group had stopped in front of a large metal door.

One of the girls escorting them had long golden hair and was really pretty.

Iya lowered her hand, releasing the man to the ground. His crash shook the entire catwalk.

'Sorry,' Iya said insincerely.

The pretty one gestured at the door. 'You've got everything you could want in there. Plenty of entertainment. Even a live feed on tournament day.'

The hulking brute brought himself to his feet.

Iya stepped forward to the metal door and smashed the keypad with her fist, causing the door to shoot open. 'Get in.'

'Fine, but... uh... say, would any of you lovely ladies mind keeping me company for a little while before you leave?'

The two older girls burst out in laughter and a small smile came over Iya, too.

'Oh. You're serious? No,' the pretty one said. 'Just get in there, prisoner.'

'And don't look at me,' Iya said to him. 'Ever.'

It seemed they were almost finished with him. I needed to get off this catwalk before they came back and caught me. As I turned around to head back to the cart, I bumped into someone's armoured chest.

I staggered back, looked up and saw the grotesque face of an angry soldier. It was the black-haired woman who had taken Pilgrim away. Her hand shot out and grabbed my wrist, and her expression turned to that of amusement.

'Come with me,' she said as she pulled me out from the jutting rocks and along the catwalk towards the others.

'There you are, Korin,' the pretty one said. 'Who's this you have with you?'

'An eavesdropper,' the ugly woman said, throwing me to the ground between them all and blocking the catwalk.

'What's Sacet's brother doing here?' Iya asked as I stood back up.

The big man changed his expression to that of fear. 'Er – oh no! These women are just awful, aren't they, boy?'

'Shut up, Kalek,' Korin said. 'He was there long enough to know.'

'Then what do we do about him?' the other girl said, who had been quiet up until now.

I was shaking in fear, unable to move. There was no escape. The women stared at each other, unsure of what to do with me.

I focused on the ugly man. 'What did you do to my sister?'

He stopped acting afraid and instead bent down. As he smiled, his revolting breath wafted up my nostrils. 'I say we kill him.'

Korin grabbed my ear and twisted it until I squealed. 'No, this little excrement pile is our only leverage over Sacet, so Verre will want him reset.'

Iya raised a hand. 'I agree with Kalek. He should die.'

I shot a hateful look at her. To think someone my age could be so awful.

The blonde gestured to Iya and smirked at Korin. 'Check out *Your Highness* over here, thinking she's in charge.'

Iya rolled her eyes. 'Idiots, think about why we're here. The Harrowing will be a lot faster if we put him in the tournament.'

The blonde crouched down beside me, inspecting me like some sort of curiosity. 'We'd be eliminating the only thing keeping her under control.'

Korin stared at me in thought, considering Iya's words. 'Verre might not like it.'

Iya shrugged. 'Verre doesn't need to know.' She exchanged looks with each of them in the circle. 'How many cycles do you want to be here for? You know I'm right.'

They went silent for the longest time. I had no idea what they were talking about, other than them discussing killing me.

'Alright,' Korin finally answered. She bent down and grabbed my wrist again. 'You're coming with us, Eno. You've got a new job to do over in the Commercial Quad.'

Twenty-Five: A Missing Piece

Sacet

Iya and I entered the mess hall the next day and were greeted with a familiar sight: the benches were filled with girls of all ages sitting down for meals and discussions.

Iya strode ahead. 'Hurry up. I've got better things to do than to play babysitter.'

'Then why don't you just go?' I replied as we marched. 'I can get there by myself. Much faster than this, too.'

Iya scoffed. 'You think you've earned enough trust to just teleport anywhere you want, do you? Just because you captured a few men yesterday, doesn't mean you're one of us yet.'

She confirmed my suspicions, that I was still being watched. But what didn't make sense to me was why Iya and Neva betrayed Tau and her squad like that. And how could I prove it? Who would even listen to me?

I focused in front. 'Ironic, *you* lecturing *me* about trust.'

She stopped in her tracks and faced me. 'What was that?' She looked up at me and prodded me in the chest. 'You have something to say to me, initiate?'

'You heard me.'

We stood in silence, our gazes locked. Both of us refusing to back down.

A smile grew on her face, and she giggled. 'You know, I liked your little sob story the other day.' Her smile faded to a grimace. 'But it isn't until you've lost everything that you'll know true pain. And you're so... so close to losing him.'

The crowd around us started to murmur and stare over at us. But no one was jeering, there were only smiles. A young woman nearby cheered. Many others stood and joined her. Some came over and gave me an approving pat on the back. What was going on?

Iya took a couple of steps back, sneering. But she seemed just as confused as I was.

On the far side of the room, soldiers hopped up on their tables to join in. The entire mess hall was cheering for me now. Was it because of yesterday's battle?

Iya groaned, then gestured down the hall. 'Move!'

'That's alright, Corporal,' I said, gesturing for those around me to give me space. 'I think I'm close enough to get there on my own.'

While still receiving random words of encouragement from the crowd around me, I thought to Marid's training room and opened a portal behind me.

Marid was pacing around inside, and she looked over to the portal with a smile. 'Ah, there you are. Come through, come through.'

I took one last look at the continuing ovation, then to a disgruntled Iya. I gave a wave, stepped backwards and closed the portal.

Marid and I were alone.

She put a hand on her hip and smiled. 'So, I see you survived?'

I gave an exasperated sigh as I approached. 'I did, yes.'

She raised an eyebrow. 'You don't seem happy about it? I heard you did very well.'

I sat down cross-legged and placed my face in my hands. Where would I even begin? Could I trust Marid with what I knew? It'd probably be best if I didn't spread it around yet.

Noticing my hesitation, Marid tapped my shoulder gently with her cane. 'I know it's hard: becoming something new. You need time to process things. So today, let's focus on the lesson itself and try and get your mind off it, hmm?'

Like in yesterday's session, Marid was again acting friendlier. Stranger.

I nodded. 'Sure.'

Marid stayed up and paced with her cane. 'We'll begin by addressing a major problem of yours. You teleport too slow. You have to open the portal and then step through it, making you vulnerable. Stand up.'

I rose from the mat and Marid pointed at a spot on the ground. 'Now, listen carefully. I want you to make one portal under your feet, facing up. The other end will be on the floor nearby, facing down. Oh, and do it without using your hands... another weakness of yours.'

I didn't argue. I left my hands by my side and tried focusing on her directions. It felt unnatural. I couldn't move my hands, but I had to at least strain my fingers to pull it off. The portal pair opened, albeit far slower than usual.

'Don't worry,' she said, noticing my difficulty. 'Now, again without your hands, raise both of the portals at the same speed.'

I looked down at the portals and did as she asked. As the portals rose past my feet and ankles, my feet and ankles then appeared from under the other rising portal. I continued raising the portals higher and higher past my waist and chest until it was above my head. I was now repositioned where I had put the exit.

I was quite proud of what I had just achieved. Marid and I smiled at one another.

'See? Much smarter,' Marid said. 'Practise in your own time and you'll be lightning fast.' She paced around the room again. 'Moving on, I had another idea. Is it possible for you to make a set of portals where the exit is larger than the entrance?'

I shook my head. 'I – I don't think I understand. What do you mean?'

'Just imagine, you walk through a small portal and come out larger on the other side. A giant version of you!'

The thought of it did seem incredible, but surely it wouldn't work, right? It couldn't be that simple?

I opened a small set of portals, both in mid-air. I clenched my fingers in the left hand but spread those in the right. Nothing was happening.

My hands were shaking. 'I can't. It's too–'

'Don't give up,' Marid interrupted. She hobbled closer with a look of anticipation.

I strained for a few more moments before dismissing the portals. My arms fell to my sides.

She placed her hand on my shoulder. 'It's… okay. It's okay to fail sometimes. Keep practising it and I'm sure you'll get it.'

I was fed up with her act. 'Okay, stop. What is with you, Marid? Why are you acting so strange? You've gone from the world's meanest trainer to – to – this?'

She backed away. 'Is that a problem?'

'What did the queen say to you?'

Marid turned away, considering her words. 'Only that I was to take very good care of you.' She turned back. 'Looking back, in our first meeting I may have vented some of my anger on you that was meant for the Matriarch. Would you prefer I go back to that?'

I walked to the bench on the side of the room and sat. 'I'm sorry, I'm just having trouble trusting anyone after yesterday. And now I can't even trust myself to not go on a killing spree. I captured those men, sure, but I was so close to breaking my promise to myself. I wanted to kill him for what he did to my friend.'

She wandered over and sat beside me. 'Traumatic moments like that, and how we act afterwards, often define the rest of our lives. In that moment, a great need washed over you. And it felt right then, so what stopped you?'

I shrugged. 'Oh, I tried to kill him, but he was invincible.'

'Ahh, that one.'

'Yep, that one.'

She leant forward onto her cane. 'Well, next time you feel that need, whatever it is, don't deny it. How else would acolytes get their powers in the first place if we did that?'

I was nodding at first, but then raised an eyebrow at her. 'What do you mean?'

Marid closed her eyes. 'I see. You're not aware of how we gain our powers, are you?'

I shook my head. 'I thought it was just a random chance at birth?'

'Allow me to tell you a story then. When I was a child, my whole family was fighting against… we'll say some *bad* people. We were imprisoned by them. They did terrible things to us, the agony lasting for cycles. They fed us and kept us alive, but only barely.'

Her lip briefly trembled, but she composed herself before continuing. 'They almost broke me. We were just objects to them. My family members disappeared one by one. I didn't know if they were dead or just sent away. To this day I still don't know what happened to them.'

She forced a grin and pointed at me. 'But I picked myself up. I had but one wish, one goal: to escape. It drove my every action, became my obsession. And then one day, I just... disappeared. I vanished from my restraints. My first teleportation.'

I still shook my head. 'But how?'

'Acolyte powers are born from trauma, and a great need. I had a very traumatic experience, but my will stayed strong. Over long periods of time, people evolve to cope with their surroundings. Our bodies listen to our most basic needs and respond, sometimes to a far greater level.'

I cleared my throat. 'So you're saying that fear gave you your powers to escape?'

'Not just fear. To gain powers, the *soul*, if you will, must suffer. The mind and body then adapt in some way because of the person's sheer will for survival. I imagine that something similar may have happened to you?'

I nodded back and sat back down with her. 'Is that why some people don't discover their powers until much later?'

Marid pondered this for a moment. 'There are no powers to discover before that point. It's not like it's lying dormant in their system, as far as we know anyway. It's also much more likely that powers will manifest inside of a child than in an adult. The powers can even reflect their parent's trauma.

'Your friend Malu, her family was in the desert, dying of thirst. Generation after generation. Shortly before they were picked up by the Dominion, she acquired the power to change anything into water.

'Colonel Korin can manipulate any exposed blood she can see. When she was a child, she was found desperately trying to scoop handfuls of blood back into her dead sister's open wounds, hoping to make her whole again. And the list goes on...'

I looked down at the floor. 'I remember running away from the nomads. I needed to escape, too, to get away.' I shook my head in disbelief. 'But we're in a war, almost everyone is experiencing trauma of some kind, why don't they have powers, too?'

Marid frowned. 'Well, perhaps there is an element of luck to it. But I believe that only those with the strongest will to survive ever gain powers.'

I thought of my own powers, particularly the ability to see my surroundings.

'Does anything happen when you have more traumatic experiences after the first?' I asked. 'I mean, is it possible to have more than one power?'

She shook her head. 'No, it doesn't work that way. One person, one power. That power might be able to be used in many ways, though. But further trauma could make an acolyte even stronger than before.'

I nodded. 'I think I understand. Thank you.' I smiled at her. 'Did you ever get revenge against those bad people?'

Marid took a deep breath and looked away. 'No. Too afraid of what might happen.'

I nudged her side. 'What does your great need tell you?'

She beamed back at me and laughed. 'I've taught you well.'

In the hospital

The door opened for us. Iya and I stepped into Malu's room.

'Malu, how are you feeling?' I said.

Malu was propped up in her hospital bed, wearing a gown. She had the whole room to herself, with a beautiful view of the city outside the window. What was left of her arm was wrapped in bandages.

Tau was by Malu's bedside, avoiding looking at us.

Malu noticed us and smiled. 'Hey! Thanks for visiting. And you, too, Corporal? I didn't know you cared so much.'

Iya folded her arms and gestured at me. 'It was *her* idea.'

Tau refused to look up, instead focusing on Malu's sheets.

Malu pointed at me with her remaining arm. 'Sacet, I heard you... saved me.'

I nodded. 'Yeah, I did.'

She grinned. 'Well, thank you. And I'm sorry for the way I acted. Friends again?'

I moved closer and brushed her good arm. 'Friends.'

Malu peeked over my shoulder to Iya. 'Corporal, did she get her assimilation session done last night?'

Iya waved her hands dismissively. 'Yes, yes.'

Malu nodded. 'That's great.' A pained look came over her and she raised her wrist with the missing hand. 'It still feels like my hand is there, even though it isn't. Every time I try to move it...'

Malu was oblivious to the friction between the rest of us. Tau glanced up at Iya before averting her gaze again.

Iya tapped my arm and made her way to the door. 'That's enough time, come on.'

'Already?' Malu asked. 'But you just got here?'

Iya groaned at the ceiling. 'Fine, I'm getting a drink.' She turned to me. 'Stay here until I get back, understand?'

I nodded. Iya locked eyes with Tau for a moment. We stayed silent until she left.

I went over to the door and closed it, then turned back to the others. 'What did they say to you, Tau?'

Tau turned away from me and we both stood frozen for a moment.

Malu looked confused. 'Am I missing something here?'

'No, no,' Tau said. 'It's nothing.'

I scoffed. 'So being abandoned by the acolytes in your squad is nothing?'

Malu raised an eyebrow and looked up at Tau. 'Er, what?'

I pointed at Tau. 'The acolytes in her squad left them for dead. It was a slaughter.'

'Is this true?' Malu asked Tau.

'Look, I don't want to talk about it. I'm not here for that. I just want to get on with my job, okay?' She gruffly sighed. 'I've been testing this new power throughout the hospital, working my way up from small wounds. I'd like to try something on you.'

'You think you can heal me? Heal an entire missing hand?'

'I don't know. That's why I'm here. Are you up for it?'

'Of course. Fire away!'

Tau closed her eyes and brought her hands to the stump of Malu's bandaged wrist. Like the other day, small silvery, light-blue flickers of air engulfed Tau's whole body like a silent coat of flames. As her skin turned a pale white, the bandages on Malu's wrist shifted and bulged as if something was prodding them from underneath.

I ran over to the bedside and brought my hands to the bandages, too. Even with my assistance, it was like they were unravelling themselves to reveal the healing flesh.

'Wow, can you feel this, Malu?' I asked.

'Yeah, it's like... tingling, kind of. It's weird. But there's no pain.'

But there was pain, at least for Tau. She winced as though healing Malu brought her great discomfort. She didn't let up.

All the bandages fell away and the bones reconstructed themselves in front of our eyes, followed by an overlay of muscles and ligaments. The small bones that made up the digits appeared from thin air and held themselves in place as the finger tissue wrapped itself around them. Finally, the muscles and skin formed around the creation in a sickening, yet fascinating way.

Malu pushed up off the pillows. 'I can't believe it. Tau, this power – it's going to change the course of this war for us.'

'Maybe,' Tau said with a smile.

'It hurts you?' I asked.

She nodded. 'When I heal others, yeah. I've worked out I feel the same sort of pain they had when they received the wound. Sometimes it's not so bad...' Tau backed away but was grabbed by Malu's new hand.

'Don't misunderstand me, I'm grateful for this,' Malu said. 'But you have some explaining to do. The acolytes, give me their names.'

Tau struggled against her. 'I've been ordered not to speak about what happened. I'm sorry.'

'It was Iya and Neva,' I interrupted. 'They acted like they had more important things to do while Tau and her squad were exterminated.'

Tau stared down at the foot of the bed and closed her eyes.

Malu jumped up from her bed. 'That can't be,' she said in a hushed tone.

Tau wandered to the adjoining bathroom and gestured for us to follow. We walked in and shut the door behind us. Tau leant against the sink. Malu and I huddled closer.

'Tau,' Malu said, her eyes wide. 'Tell me Sacet is wrong.'

Tau shrugged. 'I was told not to speak about this, otherwise I'd be branded a traitor. I don't know – I just – I want to forget all of it. I'm going to stay here and help with whatever I can and hope everyone leaves me alone.'

'Tell us,' I whispered.

She shook her head. 'When my squad first walked into that place, Iya and Neva were behind us. They just said, "Good luck", and made one of the walls collapse, sealing us in...'

'They could be executed for this!' Malu shrieked, before Tau and I shushed her. 'Are you absolutely sure?'

'I bet Verre is involved,' I interrupted, leaning against the sink with Tau. 'This must go all the way to the top. They must have been ordered to do it.'

Malu nervously checked outside the door to make sure no one was listening in, then looked back. 'Our matriarch? You're saying the acolyte matriarch sentenced an entire squad to their deaths for no reason?' she said.

I folded my arms. 'Oh, I'm sure there's a reason, and I'm going to find out what it is.'

Tau shook her head. 'Please, Sacet, don't do anything. I don't want to pursue this further.' A tear rolled down her cheek. 'I don't want even more of my friends to die.'

Malu raised a hand at me. 'Just leave it to me, okay? I'll clear this up with Iya myself. It's probably just a misunderstanding.'

Tau and I nervously looked at one another; she, like me, probably knew it wasn't a good idea. Malu opened the door and gestured for us to leave.

'There's one last thing,' I said to Tau. 'Before we were interrupted, you were about to tell me something about that man. What was it?'

Tau watched the door closely and kept her voice barely above a whisper. 'He came and killed everyone, but he purposefully left me last. And when I was begging for my life, he lifted me up, and he stood there in silence as I struggled against him. It was like he knew you were coming, and he was waiting, for *you*.'

Twenty-Six: One of Us

The next day
The Military Quad

Malu entered the amphitheatre first, the sleek doors parting as she approached.

The massive circular room was filled with women sitting in seats surrounding the centre. There must have been hundreds of us there. Every one of us had purple streaks. Conversations echoed off the high ceiling and skylights above. Like the arena, the rows of seats were built at an incline. An illustrious lectern stood in the middle of the circular room.

We made our way down the aisle steps and found ourselves some seats next to the other acolytes. Back in the centre of the room there were six empty seats around the lectern. A number of doors lined the walls that occasionally opened to admit more acolytes.

I searched around and spotted Iya on one of the higher rows, sitting in silence. She was watching me with her usual smug smile.

I also spotted Marid by the entrance. She was looking around for someone. When she saw me, her eyes narrowed and she teleported to my side.

She sat next to Malu and I, then leant over. 'You came on time, good. It's your first war meeting, so don't do or say anything.'

Malu nudged me and pointed out some of the women. 'These are some of the deadliest people on the planet.'

'There are so many,' I said, my voice unintentionally trembling.

'Yep,' she said, looking me up and down, as if she were proud. 'And you're one of us now.'

One of the doors on the opposite side of the meeting room opened and in strode Matriarch Verre, followed by her six colonels. Everyone rose from their seats in silence. Malu tapped me on the shoulder and I did the same. The matriarch approached the lectern and stood behind it. The colonels positioned themselves in the six empty seats around her.

'Thank you for your patience everyone, take a seat,' Verre's voice boomed over the speakers from above. There was a loud shuffling as the collective sat back down. 'Before we begin, I would like to officially welcome our sisters from neighbouring provinces, who have arrived three days early to compete in the upcoming tournament. Those women, stand up now.' More than half of the audience stood.

'I would like each of my own acolytes to help out the closest standing woman at some point today. They can do this by giving them a tour of the city after the meeting and just generally making them feel welcome. Thank you, ladies, you may sit.' They obeyed.

'The focus of today's meeting is on yesterday's conflict in Usre. Overall, we suffered a tremendous loss. If the enemy's objective was to halt production in the factories, then their mission was a success. However, thanks to your valiant work, the attacking force suffered enough losses that they decided to withdraw.'

There was light applause throughout the chamber, until Verre raised a hand for it to cease. A holographic image appeared above her head displaying a list of scrolling faces. Most were blue, but some were red.

'There has been an estimated five thousand casualties so far, which includes over three thousand civilians and three of our own acolytes. A service will be held later tonight to honour their loss and the sacrifice they have made for the people of Usre. On the enemy's side, we have found roughly eight hundred bodies so far, and have captured thirty-eight prisoners.

'Now, some good news. I would like the following acolytes to come down and form a circle around the lectern for their promotions: Aki, Ameli, Cerui–' One by one, girls from the audience stood up and made their way down the aisle to the centre of the room. '–Iya, Nako, Ralu, Sacet–'

Malu gave me a reassuring grin. 'Good work. Come on, get down there!' She gave me a little push towards the aisle. Marid patted me on the back as I squeezed past to get to the steps.

'Taleu, and Tiana–'

I made my way down and was met by Colonel Korin, who guided me to where I needed to stand. As I stood there, more soldiers came down the steps and formed a circle facing inwards around the lectern. Iya had also joined the circle.

'My colonels are going to recolour their tips for them, and while they're doing that, I'll recount the deeds that have earned them this honour.'

Colonel Korin approached the girl to my left and brought a set of hair-dying tongs towards her. The other colonels did the same with others in the circle.

'We'll start with the newcomer, Sacet.'

There were murmurs in the audience as Verre descended the podium where the lectern was. She walked over to me, beaming.

'Although only an initiate, she has already proven herself in her first encounter, and today will join the trooper rank,' Verre said as she looked around at the audience. 'She was able to capture three high-level enemy acolytes alive on her own and aided with the capture of a fourth. Among her captives was the seemingly unbeatable pair of Noor and Tetsu, as well as the indestructible Colonel Kalek.'

The crowd applauded again, and some even gasped. I knew I was supposed to feel proud, but that would've been a lie. I wanted to leap towards Verre and strangle her to death.

Verre noticed my look of loathing and her eyes narrowed. She turned and walked to the next soldier.

'Another amazing performance came from Aki, which is why she will be promoted to officer,' Verre said as she placed her hand upon the shoulder of a smiling soldier. 'Her abilities alone propelled her squad through the most dangerous area of the battlefield. It is estimated she killed over a hundred men by herself!'

A swell of cheers grew throughout the audience. The colonel to my left had finished and walked towards me with the tongs. As she raised them to my hair and clamped them onto my white tips, Verre continued to read out our deeds.

'Lastly, I would like to make a comment about young Iya over here. Yet again, she has set another record. This time, it's for becoming the youngest officer ever.'

The audience continued the applause for Iya as Verre made her way back up the podium. 'The actions of all of you in yesterday's battle will not be forgotten by the citizens of Usre or by me anytime soon. Once you have your tips, take your seats.'

Korin finished with my tips and moved onto the next girl. I turned back to the steps and began climbing. I pulled on my fringe, bringing one of the purple streaks to my eye; it was now tipped blue.

'Out of the ashes, this battle gave birth to some glimmering hope in the form of a new acolyte,' Verre said. I stopped on the steps and stared at the floor. 'A young soldier named Tau was killed by Colonel Kalek. But miraculously, she brought herself back to life with the first-ever display of self-resurrection since Queen Elysia!'

Many in the crowd erupted in gasps. The screen had updated and now showed a picture of Tau. Her hair was cyan, like the other day, and she was surrounded by an aura of harmless flames.

'I personally invited her here today to receive her new streaks, but she insisted on helping the wounded in the hospital. Her healing powers have already restored over a hundred women to perfect health. Malu, where are you? Stand up.' Malu stood up from her seat and raised her healed hand in the air. 'Malu had one of her hands blown off, but Tau was able to fully restore it. Amazing!'

My body shook. I turned back to the lectern and seethed. She dared bring her up? I had to say something. Surely, if the others knew the truth...

'Tau is quickly becoming the talk of the city with many of our citizens visiting her to cure their ailments. She is taking her celebrity status well, humbled by the loss of her squad sisters.'

'She wasn't "humbled". You tried to have her killed!' I yelled and pointed at Verre. My words echoed through the amphitheatre. 'You ordered Iya and Neva to betray them. Her whole squad died because of you.'

The crowd of shocked acolytes murmured in outrage, staring at me with lowered eyebrows. Malu and Marid shook their heads at me, silently indicating for me to stop.

I glared back. 'I was there. The acolytes escorting the squad trapped them, and then they were ambushed by Kalek. The acolytes did nothing to help them!'

Verre stared at me and smiled. The colonels made their way over to the stairs and started to climb. 'Wait,' Verre instructed them, before focusing back on me. 'Your accomplishments in yesterday's battle have clearly imbued you with a stroke of confidence. But it appears that the horrors of war have left you quite confused.'

The audience laughed. What was happening, why did no one believe me?

'I'm sure you've thought of a very creative reason for why I would have my own people killed, but perhaps that's something you and I can discuss when you've reclaimed your sanity.'

The jeers continued. When the laughter finally died down, Verre leant over her lectern and scowled. The audience silenced.

'It is treason to speak to me the way you have,' she continued, 'but seeming as I am in a generous mood and you're new here... I will forgive your outburst. Sit down and do not speak again.'

The whole room was against me. I sighed, then made my way back to my seat. The only sound in the room was made by my quiet footsteps.

'I was planning to reward you in private,' Verre continued, 'with a visit to your imprisoned brother. But you can forget about that now.'

I sat down and the audience finally broke their gaze from me.

Verre cleared her throat. 'Now, where was I? Yes, the tournament. The stadium is ready and all of you have arrived in the city. The queen has personally told me she is looking forward to the event and wishes you all good luck. Although the capital has the most acolytes, there will be a fair points system in place to see which province impresses the most.'

I buried my head into my arms on the bench in front of me. Verre's voice faded as she spoke about trivial details. I shook my head against my arms in frustration.

Was I wrong about what happened? Was Tau? No, I remember what she said. And that man was toying with me for a reason, but why?

It was becoming more and more likely that I would have to kill others to protect Eno. But the question was, who? Should I play nice and kill who I'm told to kill? Or should I kill everyone in my way of freeing Eno? I didn't want to kill, period!

A hand pressed on my shoulder, it was Marid. She grimaced. I brought my head out of my arms. The meeting was over. Everyone shuffled through the rows of seats towards the aisles. The doors along the sides of the room opened and the acolytes were leaving. Still standing at the lectern, Verre stared at me.

Malu stood up and leant towards me. 'I told you I was going to take care of it.' She made her way past and out towards the aisle.

Verre withdrew from the lectern and made her way up the stairs. The six colonels accompanied close behind. She stopped in the aisle beside Marid and faced us.

'Marid? Do you mind?' she asked.

Marid stood and gave a stern frown. She dematerialised from the room, and I was alone with them. I avoided eye contact, instead crossing my arms and staring at the empty lectern.

Verre waited until the last of the acolytes had left. 'Now, you listen to me. I have spoken with Tau already about the horrible incident she was in. She admitted to me that perhaps she may have been a bit quick to lay the blame on others for the upsetting loss of life around her. She has calmed down now and is fully aware of how ridiculous she sounded accusing her fellow soldiers of such a thing.'

My second perception, which hadn't been paying much attention to my surroundings up until this point, spotted something peculiar. On top of the roof of the building was Marid, peering down through the skylights. I didn't look up. Instead, I kept focused on the lectern in front of me.

'As for you... look at me when I'm speaking to you!' I broke away and locked eyes with Verre. 'When you first came here I asked you to prove to me you were worth keeping. You have certainly shown you have talent, but your commitment to our cause is lacking. Clearly your assimilation procedures aren't intense enough. Or perhaps I should just get rid of the last piece of your nomadic past...'

She gestured at one of her colonels, who raised a small glass device in front of me. I could see Eno on it. He was sitting on a dirty floor of a dark room. He looked miserable, far thinner than the last time I'd seen him many days earlier.

'Are we clear?' Verre said.

I submitted, dipping my head. 'We're clear.'

Verre continued up the stairs to the exit. Her colonels followed close behind and smirked as they passed. I looked back at the lectern as I sat waiting for them to leave. The door shuddered and closed behind them. There was a whoosh of air as Marid rematerialised by my side.

She took her seat again. 'This is what you were talking about?' she asked, but I didn't respond. 'Why didn't you tell me about this?'

'Like *you* would have helped... or believed me for that matter. Why would I trust someone like you, who has probably killed hundreds of my people?'

'Who? The nomads? Sacet, there are bigger things going on here.' She shook her head and sighed. 'I'm looking out for your best interests.'

I stood up. 'Why do you care what I do? Just leave me alone!'

I tried squeezing past Marid but she put out her arm to stop me. 'I know it's hard for you, but I want you to put all of this behind you. You have training every day leading up to that tournament.'

I jerked my arm away. 'You can't make me kill an innocent person.'

'You don't have a choice.'

I pushed past her and up the stairs. 'I'm no one's executioner,' I said.

Twenty-Seven: Lines of White

Somewhere under the Commercial Quad
Eno

The dark underground chamber was filled with hundreds of men. Some were standing, others sitting on the musty ground and against the corroded metal walls. Some had putrid wounds and swollen limbs. These were unwanted men, men who couldn't work anymore. They glanced over at us when Korin and I entered. She threw me forward, releasing her grip on my wrist and I tumbled onto the dust-covered floor.

Korin grimaced. 'Tell them anything you want, it isn't going to make any difference. You're all dead anyway.' She turned and left through the chamber's only door.

The guards on the outside slammed the door closed, the noise echoing in the otherwise silent room. I looked back to the men, who turned away.

'No, no. Please, don't tell me it's him. Is that you, Eno?' Pilgrim made his way through the crowd of sad faces. Turen followed with an equally unhappy expression. Pilgrim looked as if he was about to burst into tears.

He knelt down by my side and placed a hand on my shoulder. 'You shouldn't be here. You're young, you could have lived. What did you do?'

'I was nosy. I overheard something I wasn't supposed to,' I explained.

Pilgrim shook his head. 'Why didn't you keep your head down, like I asked?'

'I'm sorry,' I said as he pulled me in for a hug.

He let go and stood. 'Don't worry. Someone's going to think of a way out of here.'

Turen stepped forward. 'How's Toroi? How's my son?'

'He's angry, but he's following orders.'

'What exactly were you not supposed to hear?' Pilgrim asked.

I shook my head, trying to make sense of it. 'There was a man being taken to a special part of the prison. The guards were talking about breaking him out... and they were talking about my sister.'

'Do you remember who they were?' Turen said.

'That woman who brought me here and that littler acolyte, Iya. A few others I didn't know.'

Pilgrim brought a hand to his chin and nodded. 'We should talk to the guards–'

'Are you serious?' a nearby man said, standing up from the floor. 'It doesn't matter what you say to them, they're still going to kill us.'

'Easy, friend,' Pilgrim said, stepping towards him.

'And what do you know about it?' Turen asked.

'I'm ex-Male Dominion. We're all going to be executed by their acolytes in a tournament. It'll be in front of thousands of women. Both Dominions broadcast their executions to demoralise the other side. Open your eyes, we're cattle to them. Their entertainment.'

Pilgrim's eyes narrowed and his arms tensed, but he didn't argue. I guess deep down we all knew he was right. The man sat back down and turned away, like all the others.

The door behind us swung open and in stepped three guards. A familiar one in the middle had solid blue streaks in her hair and a solemn expression on her face.

I ran towards her. 'Tau!'

'Eno? What are you doing here?'

The two guards to her sides stepped forward and blocked my path. They raised their guns. 'Get back, prisoner!'

I stopped in my tracks and gave Tau a pleading look. 'They're going to kill us, you have to help!'

One of the guards thrust her gun forward. 'I said get back!'

'No!' Tau said, reaching out and pushing the rifles down. 'You two wait outside, I'll be fine in here alone.'

The soldier looked Tau up and down. 'You can't order us around. Your streaks aren't high enough.'

Tau pulled a pistol from her waist and she started to glow light-blue. Small silvery lines started to grow all around her body and wavered from side to side like fire. Her hair turned white and flicked around as if there was a draught. Most of the chamber illuminated.

'Get. Out,' she said, staring the guard down with her finger on the trigger.

The guards backed away, closing the door behind them. The commotion had drawn the attention of all of the men in the chamber. Many at the back stood and moved closer. I ran forward to hug Tau, and she holstered her pistol, leant down and embraced me back. Her hair turned back to normal and the silvery fire disappeared.

'You're an acolyte now? Wow!' I said.

I could tell that she was close to crying. 'Oh, Eno. You shouldn't be here.'

'That's what I said,' Pilgrim said, coming closer.

'Is that you Pilgrim?' Tau asked as I let go of her. 'You shouldn't be in here, either. I'm... really sorry about what happened. You must blame me for so much.'

Pilgrim folded his arms and contorted his face. 'Very much so, yes. I'll forgive you if you've come to help us escape?'

'I'm sorry, but no. If I could get you all out of here, I would.'

'Then why are you here?' Turen asked.

'I'm a healer. I can make you all healthy again,' she said.

Pilgrim seemed confused. 'You came to heal us? You do know we're all about to be executed, right?'

She looked down at the ground. 'I know that. That's what the guards said when I came down here, too, but they let me through, thinking it wouldn't matter. In past tournaments, I've seen the condition of the men when they're brought up, some practically already dead. I just couldn't stand by while you suffered down here.'

'You could fight them instead?' Pilgrim suggested.

Tau shook her head. 'I'm sorry, I just can't.'

'What about my sister?' I asked.

'Sacet? She's fine,' Tau said, smiling. 'But when she hears about you down here–'

'No, I mean, can't she help us?' I suggested.

She glanced at the others before looking back at me. 'I... uh. I don't know how to tell you this, Eno. Sacet has been forced to participate. She'll have to execute one of these men.'

There was a silence among us. I gritted my teeth. 'She would *never* do that.'

Tau nodded. 'I know. I don't know what's going to happen when she refuses.'

'Tau, that girl called Iya,' I interrupted, 'she and the others – there was one called Korin. I think they're planning something.'

'I know, trust me, I know,' she replied, unsurprised. 'I can't do anything about it.'

'You could tell someone in charge?' Pilgrim suggested.

'I don't think that would help,' she said.

There was an air of silence in the room again.

I grabbed Tau's wrist. 'No matter what happens; could you please tell my sister that I love her?' I tried to smile but couldn't.

'I will, Eno. I promise.'

'And tell her I forgive her,' Pilgrim added.

'And tell my daughter I forgive her, too,' Turen said.

Tau raised an eyebrow, confused.

'The acolyte called Malu,' I clarified.

Tau looked back in shock at the old man. 'You're Malu's father?'

'Yes, tell her that whatever she chooses to do in her life, I'll support her.'

Tau nodded back. 'Alright.'

'And my beloved Channa,' another man said, standing up. 'Tell her I love her, too.'

'And mine.'

Soon the whole chamber was abuzz with final requests. Tau frantically repeated the names back, trying to remember them, but was clearly overwhelmed.

The door slammed open again and in walked the two guards, accompanied by the overseer. Her again? I thought I'd at least be rid of her after leaving the mines.

'What are you doing with my prisoners?' the overseer asked, striding towards us and standing right in front of Tau.

'I'm giving them medical attention,' Tau replied, unafraid.

'You're what?'

'Matriarch Verre has personally asked me to oversee the health and wellbeing of all the tournament's participants.'

'They're not the participants, the *acolytes* are!'

'Well, I suppose I'll just go and explain to her why I wasn't able to complete my duties. What was your name again?'

The overseer's gaze was locked with Tau's. Neither of them were backing down. The old woman's sneer finally changed to a fake smile, ending the stand-off.

'Very well,' she conceded. 'How about we make your visit more worthwhile then, shall we?'

She pulled out her pistol and fired it randomly at the prisoners. The chamber was filled with screaming and the deafening fizzle of red-hot projectiles. We were all horrified, unable to do anything but back away to the walls and corners.

I looked at Tau pleadingly, but she stood frozen, mouth agape. 'Stop her!' I shouted. 'Tau, please!'

The overseer continued casually firing, not caring who she hit. Several men were already writhing on the ground.

I shoved Tau to snap her out of it. 'Tau!'

'Enough!' Tau shouted and her light-blue flames ignited once more. She brought up her own pistol and aimed it at the overseer.

The overseer finally stopped firing to look at Tau with disdain. 'You *dare* aim your weapon at a superior?'

The two guards aimed their rifles back at Tau. 'Drop your weapon!'

Tau's lip trembled. 'Why did you do that?' She lowered her pistol now that the shooting had stopped. 'They did nothing to you.'

The overseer chuckled, gesturing at the five dead bodies and at least ten more gravely wounded throughout the chamber. 'I can always get more. But now I'm more concerned about your loyalties.' She turned on the spot and made for the door. 'Looks like you have your work cut out for you, traitor.'

She paused and glanced back. 'Oh, and don't worry about checking with Verre. I'm off to see her right now.' She turned once more and left, the guards closing the door behind them.

Twenty-Eight: Hanging Pictures

Two days later
Sacet

The platform was overcrowded, with civilians everywhere. As soon as one hover vehicle left it was replaced by another almost immediately. Passengers would unload and then load, filling the vehicles before we could reach them. Finally, one pulled up in our lane and opened its doors. Malu, Tau and I climbed on as another group of soldiers hopped off.

I took the window seat. Tau sat next to me and Malu sat across from us. There was only one other seat free, but no one else came on.

I looked back at the platform and the others in line. Strangely, a lot of people were gawking at us. They'd normally keep to themselves, but several were pointing at our group with interest. It took me a moment to realise that they were pointing at Tau specifically.

As the doors closed, I felt a familiar lurch in the pit of my stomach as the vehicle pulled out of the station.

'Learn anything new in training today?' Malu asked me.

I shrugged. 'Nothing new. I practised getting quicker again. And you?'

'Same. Did some basic forms in the lead-up to tomorrow.'

There was an awkward pause to our small talk, so I stared out at the buildings flying by.

'Are you still worried about tomorrow?' Malu asked gently.

I leant back in my seat. 'Well, I still have to kill someone, so yes.'

'Do you know what you're going to do?' she asked.

I sighed. 'No.' It took me a moment to realise that she was referring to my routine and not how I was going to get out of this mess.

She dipped her head. 'Best to make it quick and painless. Forget about the points this time around.'

I smirked. 'You don't enjoy the tournament, right?'

Malu laughed. 'No, no, no. I'm not a psychopath like Iya.' This elicited laughter from Tau and I, so Malu pointed at us both. 'Don't tell her I said that.'

I shook my head. 'She is seriously messed up. What is wrong with her?'

Malu leant forward. 'I ended up asking her about what happened the other day at Usre. She looked me right in the eye and said she was going to kill me. I mean, was she joking?' She pointed at me again and quietened. 'You didn't hear this from me, but I heard that she used to live in the desert, like you and I. Then, one day, she snapped and killed her whole family. Apparently saying something about how boring they were.'

'I heard something different,' Tau said. 'She's secretly the queen's only daughter, but because the queen doesn't want an heir, she's been forced to deny the link.'

I scoffed. 'That's *clearly* fake. I doubt the queen has kids.' We shared another laugh before going silent.

'Well, how about you, Tau?' Malu continued. 'How was your day? Was there anyone you couldn't heal?'

Tau's smile disappeared. 'No, all the hospital beds are empty now. I've even been allowed to heal some prisoners in my spare time. They were very grateful.'

Malu smiled. 'That's really nice of you, but unnecessary. Elysia wouldn't have wasted her healing on her enemies.'

'Did you see my brother?' I asked, ignoring Malu's insensitivity. 'Is he okay?'

Tau sighed. 'I saw him.'

My eyes widened. 'And?'

Tau smiled but still avoided eye contact. 'He told me to tell you that he loves you very much.'

'How about mine?' Malu asked.

'I didn't see your brother, but I'm sure he's okay,' Tau explained, wincing. 'Though, I did meet your father.'

Malu smiled, but quickly caught herself and frowned instead. 'Oh? Is he well?'

'He said to tell you that he... forgives you and supports your choices.'

Malu rolled her eyes. 'Ha! *He* forgives *me*? That's rich. If it weren't for *me* the family would have died of thirst. We'd be dried-out skeletons buried in a lost patch of sand.'

The vehicle was slowing, and our station was visible around the next bend. As we came to a stop and the doors opened, we climbed out. We parted through the crowd and out towards the platform's exit.

'Is there anything else Tau and I need to know about your family before we meet them?' I asked as we made our way down some steps and into the walkways.

Malu led us, occasionally glancing back. 'I would appreciate it if you didn't mention my father or brother. It's a sensitive issue.'

Tau and I nodded. We deviated from the rest of the crowd, crossed the walkway and cut through an alley. 'Okay, we won't talk about them. Anything else?' I asked as we rounded a corner. A large apartment complex stood before us.

'Well, now that you mention it, I think my kid sister likes you, Sacet... or wants to be you. I'm not sure. So be nice to her.'

I nodded back to her as we walked to the entrance of the high-rise and proceeded through the lobby.

Malu approached the elevator and pressed a button. 'And don't talk about the military, or the war. My mother hates me for becoming a soldier.'

The elevator panel lowered to our level and the doors opened. We stepped onto it. 'Level 12,' Malu said.

The panel wobbled as we levitated up through the elevator tube. Each floor we passed looked identical, with numerous corridors and apartment doors equally spaced out. The elevator slowed as it reached the 12th floor.

A small girl was waiting in front of the tube. She looked like a miniature version of Malu, except her hair was curlier and past her shoulders. She was similar to Eno's age.

'Malu!' the girl screamed with delight as the panel came to a stop and the doors parted. 'And you're Sacet!'

'Sacet, Tau, I'd like you to meet my sister, Kowi.'

'Ooooh! I knew it was you! Can you show me your powers? Please?' Kowi pleaded as she pulled me out by the hand. 'I know! You can teleport us into our place.'

'Kowi, she can't do that... she doesn't even know which one it is. She's never been here before.'

'It's alright, Malu. Which one is yours, Kowi? Point to it.'

'That one over there down the hallway on the left, number 12-03.'

I looked down the corridor to where she was pointing and saw the door. My second perception drifted through the walls. Just behind the front door there was a living room filled with furniture, similar to Malu's apartment.

An older woman, most likely Malu's mother, was standing in the kitchen, preparing a meal on the bench. I opened a portal to their living room in front of us.

'After you,' I instructed to Kowi, who wore a look of amazement.

'Awesome! Is it safe?' she said as she examined through and behind the portal.

'Very.'

'Kowi?' the mother's voice called out from the other side. 'Is that you?'

'Mum?' Kowi said in surprise as she poked her head through and walked in. 'Mum, you've got to try this.'

We followed the girl into the living room, and I closed the portal behind us.

'Aww, why did you close it?'

Her mother was around the corner in the kitchen. 'What's that, dear? I'm busy with dinner. You can come help me by setting up the table.'

'Awwww...'

'Now!' her mother said.

The young girl plodded into the kitchen and rifled through the draws. There were some family pictures of the girls hanging on the walls, but I didn't see any pictures of Malu's father or brother.

'I didn't know you could do that,' Malu said to me. 'Teleport to somewhere you can't see?'

'I – I guessed,' I lied.

'Sorry about that,' the woman said with a big smile as she appeared from the kitchen. 'It's great to finally meet you both. I'm Hana.'

I smiled back. 'I'm Sacet. This is a wonderful home you have here.'

Hana nodded solemnly. 'Yes, well, that's the reward when you split your family in half. And you must be Tau, right?'

'You've heard about me?' Tau asked.

'Of course, my daughters have told me a lot about you both. It doesn't hurt that you're fairly famous, too. Dinner's just about ready, so why don't you all take a seat at the table?'

Malu led us to the adjoining room of the kitchen where there was a dining table and chairs. I took a seat and looked out the window at the city's colourful alleyways. Malu returned to the kitchen and helped Kowi bring in the plates and cutlery.

'So, I see you finally got your new streaks,' I said as Tau pulled out a chair and sat down next to me. Her streaks were now purple with blue tips, the same colour as mine and Malu's.

'Yeah, someone came to visit me while I was working,' Tau said.

Malu placed some cutlery on the table. 'I'm surprised they haven't jumped you to corporal for all the people you've helped. I bet you're happy that you caught up to us.'

Hana brought in two large plates of food and placed them down in the middle of the table. 'Good, good. Everyone sit.'

The family took their seats beside us and started shovelling food onto their plates. 'I've cooked up some spicy anatocarni and made a fresh mycin salad.'

I simply stared at the feast.

'I'm sorry, girls? Is something wrong? Here, I'll put some on your plates for you.' Hana reached out, took my plate and then Tau's, and started filling them with pieces of meat and vegetables.

I picked up my knife, skewered up a piece of meat, placed it my mouth and chewed. There it was again, that strange aftertaste. Ever since I had arrived in this city, there was something off about the food, delicious though it was. Maybe I was imagining it.

I gave a quick, courteous bow to Hana. 'Thank you, sorry, I didn't know where to start, it all looks so good.'

'Thank you, Sacet. Do you say that because Malu isn't feeding you properly?' Hana scowled over at her. 'Malu, what are you feeding this poor girl? She's got barely any definition on her.'

Malu finished chewing her food. 'Mother, I make sure she gets a balanced diet, I promise you. Don't I, Sacet?'

'Uh, yes?'

'Alright, fine. Malu, you should take your sister out after dinner. She hardly gets to see you lately.'

'Yesh!' Kowi agreed with a mouth full of food. She swallowed. 'You can meet my friends.'

'Do I have to?' Malu whined.

'Yes!' Hana replied. 'It's another way you can make it up to me. To both of us.'

'Make what up?' Tau asked.

Malu turned to us, also with a mouth full of food. 'My mother thinks it's my fault that they're both being forced to be in the audience tomorrow – because I'm in the military. But I keep telling her that everyone has to attend.'

'And what my daughter *isn't* telling you is that if she's in the military then she supports everything they do.'

I raised my finger to interrupt. 'Erm, I don't support the military, at all. I was forced to join it.'

'I know, dear, and I'm sorry about that. But Malu here joined it willingly. Very different.'

Malu sighed. 'And you've reminded me about it every time I come over here. You asked me why I don't like to visit, and now you know.'

'Stop being so melodramatic, Malu. We have guests,' Hana said.

'I'm sorry... back up,' I said. 'Did you say everyone is going to be there?'

Malu shook her head. 'Well, obviously not everyone in the city. A lot of people watch from their homes. The queen insists on it, saying something about inspiring our people.'

'She inspires me to put my foot up her arse is what she does,' Hana said.

'Mother! Don't talk like that. Treason is a crime. If you ever get caught–'

'Yes, yes, I know. But every time this awful tournament comes around, Kowi and I have to sit there and be subjected to that zealous drivel. I have to turn her head away for practically the whole thing. How can they consider murdering people as entertainment, honestly?'

The table went silent aside from the clattering of plates as we ate. My perception drifted throughout the home, examining the family's belongings. On the wall in Hana's bedroom there were two more hanging pictures, one of the father and one of the brother. The men were depicted against a white backdrop. They looked sad; it must have been taken when they were captured. It was the only picture the family had of them.

In the Commercial Quad

The buildings towered all around us. I had to tilt my neck to see the night sky peeking through. Billboards covered in neon lights flashed and shimmered down to the congested walkways. Every metal surface reflected the vibrant shower of colours. The smell of food permeated the streets, as did the colossal noise from thousands of pedestrians coming and going.

One billboard in particular caught Tau's eye, stopping her in her tracks. Malu and I followed her gaze. It was a giant picture of Tau, with her aura activated, standing over a hospital patient. Underneath were the words 'Elysia Reborn' in bold letters.

I jabbed her in the side. 'Quite the hero now, huh?'

Tau shook her head in disbelief. 'That's not why I heal people. I'm going to complain about this – they didn't even ask me if they could put it up.'

Malu pointed up at the billboard with a smile. 'She's not the only one.' The screen Tau's picture was on changed, now displaying a picture of me. I was in full armour, standing over Colony in the gardens. This time the words said: 'New Allies Join the Fight'.

I shrugged. 'How did they even get that picture?'

The picture changed again, this time to a soldier I didn't recognise and a new tagline.

Malu giggled. 'I remember when they advertised me up there, too. They like to show off all the newbies in the lead-up to the tournament.'

'Great,' I drawled.

The billboards were certainly doing their job. The three of us were becoming increasingly aware of how much people in the street were staring at us. Some even stopped and waved, awestruck.

'Hey, come on!' Kowi yelled from the other side of the crowd, breaking us away from the billboard.

We did our best to follow her, negotiating our way through the crowd. Why was there such a big hurry to play a game?

My mind drifted, and my second perception sped around our surroundings. Although my maximum range was only a few city blocks, there was so much to see around here.

I had been doing my best to scout the city, searching for where they were keeping Eno. This was made that much more difficult having either Malu or Iya always tagging along to keep an eye on me. And whenever I had drifted closer to the Prison Quad, they'd always redirect me back to the approved areas of the city.

I'd do anything to know exactly where he was. Without knowing his location, I couldn't help him escape.

Kowi stopped in front of a storefront. It was a large gallery of lit screens and buzzing noises. This 'arcade' they'd told me about was filled with happy kids, all of them interacting with rainbow-coloured machines and boxes. A consistent, deep thumping droned from the speakers inside, like the beating of a drum.

Two kids came out of the arcade and approached us. Kowi immediately ran over and hugged her friends. The kids beamed at Tau and I.

With a proud look on her face, Kowi gestured back at us. 'You know my sister, Malu. This is Sacet, and that's Tau.'

'Wow!' the kids exclaimed in unison.

Kowi folded her arms, nodded and smiled. 'I know, right?'

'Hi! It's so awesome to meet you,' one of the girls said, grinning with glee. 'Tau, you're amazing! Thank you so much for healing my mother.'

Tau smiled back. 'You're welcome.'

What were we doing here? Didn't these children know I had far worse things to be thinking of right now?

'Sacet – I – I,' the other child began, running over and stopping uncomfortably close to me. 'Capturing all those men like they were nothing. You're my hero.'.

'Your hero?' I replied.

'Of course!' the girl squealed. 'You're so famous. The whole city is talking about you... and Tau as well.' I shrugged at Malu, who nodded back.

Kowi impatiently gestured inside. 'Come on, we need to make the others jealous. Let's play!'

The kids led the three of us in and through the arcade. We caught looks from many of the kids, who dropped their jaws at the sight of us. Meanwhile, Kowi and her friends smugly strutted, leading us to every corner of the crowded, noisy place.

At that moment, I imagined the mass of men waiting for their execution, huddled together in the dark. When Tau told me the way they had rounded up the prisoners and practically abandoned them in a locked room under the stadium, I almost vomited. Although it was horrible for them, I was so glad Eno wasn't among them.

I couldn't let them commit mass murder like this. But how could I save them? Even if I knew where they were, Verre would know it had been me, the instant I created a portal.

Unless maybe they escaped while the event was going on with me in it? They didn't know I could see through walls, and they especially didn't know I could teleport the men as far away as I wanted to. But if the guards spotted a single portal, I would be putting Eno's life at risk again.

'Ready?' one of the kids interrupted.

'What?' I said. She handed me a plastic gun and pointed at a doorway in front of us. Inside, the dark corridor lit up like the neon lights from the billboards outside. 'What do I do with this?'

'You've got to shoot the bad guys inside,' she yelled back over the pulsating bass. 'Go for the red ones, they're worth the most points.'

The others made a circle. They were all smiling, but I had no idea what was going on.

Kowi leant in. 'We'll beat her score this time, I'm sure of it. Go for all the easy shots, unless you see a red one, got it?' She cutely acted like she was our leader. 'Now that we've got Sacet, we can't lose!'

The kids cheered, and Malu noticed my bewildered look. She leant over to me. 'Iya holds the record for this game.'

'*Iya* does this?' I replied, following our makeshift squad into the neon corridor.

We reached the end of the corridor and entered a neon-lit, smoke-filled chamber. Artificial chest-high walls were strewn about the maze-like complex. There was a loud beeping noise, and the others ran for cover. I did the same, diving for the nearest barricade.

The room filled with fake laser projectiles. Several figures appeared in different positions around the maze. They were men, enemy soldiers, but they were made entirely of light in a variety of colours. Each took cover, like we did, before returning fire on our position.

I raised the small plastic firearm and shot into the maelstrom of colours, producing a harmless red beam. I downed one of the soldiers, creating a satisfying explosion of light.

A chime rang above us. Hanging from the ceiling was a scoreboard, and its number was already rising.

'Good shot!' Malu called out to me, before continuing to fire with precision, taking out three more enemies.

Tau fired sporadically, not seeming to care too much about the game.

The kids, meanwhile, jumped in and out of cover, firing inaccurately and taking risks. A laser soldier was ready to flank them from the side, so I took aim and shot him before he could act. The girls noticed the explosion and smiled back at me.

I stopped and lowered my weapon. Maybe there was a way we could beat Iya?

I thought back to my training when Marid tried making me create an exit portal larger than its entrance. Maybe I'd been thinking about that technique all wrong. I imagined my portals as a window. What if it were more like a magnifying glass?

It clicked in my head. Without even trying, a small portal opened in front of my gun, and the exit in front of me stretched and warped. It grew as large as the room's ceiling would allow.

I pushed my gun through the small end, but its size was unchanged on the other side, as I expected. What mattered more was that the light travelling through was enlarged.

I clicked the trigger as fast as I could, firing the beam into the portal. The laser exited at least 100 times its original size and filled with the room with blinding red. The wave of light swept across the room, downing every enemy combatant, even those in cover. Strangely, the electronic sound of the gun was also amplified through the portal, now a distorted, booming mess.

As the scoreboard ticked higher, more and more enemies appeared, but as soon as I caught sight of them, I simply tilted my exit portal, and each disintegrated almost immediately upon entering the battlefield.

The enemies wouldn't stop coming, no matter how many of them I killed and scattered back into nonexistence. I expanded the exit portal even larger. I clicked as fast as I could.

I gritted my teeth and growled in frustration. 'Just die, already!'

There was a loud beep and the lights ceased, then gently faded to green. It seemed as though the game was over, so I closed my portals and took my finger off the trigger. The beeping noises continued and the scoreboard flashed above.

'Yes! We did it!' Kowi said as the kids cheered.

As our group made their way back to the corridor, Malu put an arm around me and smiled. 'Cheater... thanks.'

I shrugged. 'Don't mention it. I'm going to enjoy seeing the look on Iya's dumb face.'

A crowd of children were waiting for us back in the main arcade area. When they saw us, a swell of cheers filled the building.

One of Kowi's friends grabbed my wrist to get my attention. 'You quadrupled Iya's score! How did you do that?'

I smirked. 'A lot of skill. Malu calls it cheating.'

Tau pointed her pistol in the air. 'How about another game?'

The crowd cheered again, and many of the kids requested to join us.

Malu gave me a firm pat on the back. 'That was fun, right? Come on, let's beat your score.'

I smiled back. 'Yeah, sure.'

Everyone looked so happy, but I knew this was just a distraction. Underneath the ground was the real Dominion. Cruelty and enslavement were all this place had in store for my brother and I. And to think I thought I could live here if I just obeyed.

I still didn't know what I was going to do tomorrow, but I *was* sure of one thing. I was *not* going to kill for them.

Twenty-Nine: No One's Executioner

The next evening
In the stadium

Yet again I was surrounded by hundreds of acolytes. We all sat in organised rows on benches that overlooked the arena platform in the centre of the stadium. The platform was broken into quarters. Each steel section was elevated above the artificial grass on the stadium ground.

I'd never seen this many people in one place before. The bevy of spectators sounded like a huge, groaning mass. The crowd was divided into partitions, the front rows filled with soldiers and a sea of the queen's loyal followers. They cheered and shouted to the acolytes down in the grounds and in the pews where I was. The second and third tiers of the stadium were packed with the city's residents, who were far more reserved than the soldiers.

We soldiers wore our full armour in a sea of silver, as though ready for combat, while the civilians were every other colour one could imagine.

I prodded Malu. 'Is there any particular order to this?'

'Hmm, what? We get called up by those screens up there.'

I was breathing quickly. With so many people here, it felt like there was no air for me to breath!

Malu noticed my panicked state. 'It won't be as bad as you think it is, I promise. Take deep breaths, in and out. In... and out.'

I tried to control my breathing as she suggested for a few moments, but I didn't feel any better.

She pointed to the platform. 'You'll just go up there and do what you need to do. Then afterwards we'll go out for a nice dinner, okay?' She smiled and shrugged. 'This will be my third time. I don't even think about it anymore.'

'Please stand in silence for the queen's entrance,' a voice boomed.

The crowd hushed and gazed to the upper terrace, where a separate podium had been raised. There were seven seats, one of them a large golden throne placed between the other six. The queen, followed by her matriarchs, appeared from a cordoned entrance at the rear of the podium. She made her way to her throne and stood in front of it.

A blinding flash appeared in the centre of the arena, for several spotlights had converged to produce a giant hologram, a replica of the queen herself. Other than its towering size, it was a one-to-one recreation of the queen above.

'I, Queen Antwin, welcome you all to this glorious event,' she announced with gusto. 'The unquestionable loyalty of our armies is a testament to our power, but like steel, that loyalty must be tempered so as to not succumb to a dull edge. Our vehicles of war must be maintained, our weapons must be recharged, and our bombs must be tested. Likewise, our acolytes must prove their worth. Our enemies outnumber our people, so as a society we must show them how capable we are.'

Her hologram paced about the arena. As it did, my second perception flew over and scanned it to ensure that it wasn't there.

'Although today's demonstrations will be carried out upon the weak and feeble, I assure you, each one of these men was dissident and rebellious. May the actions of our faithful acolytes act as a reminder of our commitment to end the terror the Male Dominion has wrought. Thank you.'

The crowd around me erupted in cheers and applause, and the hologram disappeared. Even Malu stood, clapped and nodded.

I concentrated and scouted the stadium with my second perception. Watching from far above on the lip of the stadium's retractable roof was Marid. She stood with the aid of her cane.

Several of the acolytes around me stared in my direction, their eyes hungry. They didn't know I could see them. It was like they were waiting for me to slip up somehow.

My perspective shifted below the stadium, where men were being driven out of the chamber and through the tunnels. They were going to die. There was nothing I could do without risking Eno's life.

'I would like to reiterate the queen's gracious welcome to you all on this fine day,' another announcer echoed. 'Could we also put our hands together for today's medic, Tau.'

The entire audience practically exploded with cheers, the largest we had heard so far. Everyone around me, both military and civilians joined in.

Tau stood down on the grounds in the centre of the four arenas. She nervously waved a little but was mostly in awe.

'The executions will run simultaneously on four arenas,' the announcer continued. 'As always, we will start with the pride of our military, the youth.'

As the announcement ended, the crowd roared once more. Back at the benches, three young initiates stood up. Beside them, Iya stood as well. She locked eyes with me, narrowing her gaze and smiling before turning away again.

The four girls descended through the pews and climbed the steps around each of the arenas, going to their respective centres.

Malu pulled on my shoulder. 'Sacet, you might want to look away for this one.'

'What?'

My heart jolted. In the four arenas, four men from separate tubes rose from an underground platform. In the same arena as Iya, the weathered and scarred face of Pilgrim rose from its underbelly. He stared down at his bound hands and then up to Iya.

'I thought you'd be bigger!' I could hear his deep voice yell, even from here, eliciting laughter in the pews around us. He spat on the ground in front of him. 'Do your worst!'

'Pilgrim!' I shouted as a loud bell rang.

My face burned. I tried stepping out of the row but was pulled back by Malu.

'Sit! I told you not to look,' she said as I took rapid, deep breaths.

Iya raised both of her hands in front of her eyes with palms facing one another. She clapped the two palms together in one disgusting movement, and Pilgrim's body exploded into a grotesque mess of pulp. She released her hands, causing his crushed remains to sluice onto the ground in a heaping mess.

'No!' I screamed. The other acolytes eyed me with suspicion, but I didn't care. 'Pilgrim was a *good* person, he didn't deserve that.' I gripped my hot face and tried to control my breathing. 'How can they expect me to do this? I'm not doing it!'

Malu kept her hand on my shoulder, making sure I stayed in my seat. 'It was quick, that's the best he could have asked for. And if you don't kill them, someone else will.'

I closed my eyes, but I could still hear the ripping and slashing continue, followed by the shouts and applause of the soldiers. I peeked through the acolytes sitting on the benches in front of me as Iya made her way back to her seat. As she sat, she nudged one of her friends and pointed over to me.

Malu pointed towards a tall pole in the centre of the stadium. 'Look, that's how we know if we're up.' At the top of the pole there was a screen with the four participants' names listed. The names on the screen changed to another four.

Neva was one of the next participants to climb the steps. She whipped her long, blonde hair and posed for the crowd.

I pointed her out. 'She was the one with Iya. The one that—'

'Yeah, I know.'

Another group of men was raised up to the arena. The one in Neva's arena fell to his knees and appeared to be begging for mercy. The bell sounded and I watched as Neva's skin morphed and changed its texture into granules of sand. As if she was being blown away by the wind, the particles flew up and out of her armour, leaving her empty suit to fall to the floor.

Like a miniature desert storm, the plume of sand whipped over to the man and enveloped him. He screamed as his body dissolved at her touch. His flesh was shredded away from his bones.

'Since when can sand do *that?*' I asked in astonishment.

Malu shrugged. 'It's definitely not sand.'

The cloud returned to the armour and entered through its cavities, leaving what remained of the man's body clumped on the ground in a steaming pile. As if it had a life of its own, the armour stood straight up. The 'sand' refilled the missing head and hands and reformed back into Neva, who waved at the cheering crowd.

My stomach churned. I could the smell burnt flesh from here. As the four women climbed down the steps of the arenas, another four names appeared on the screen above. Aki, Herathi, Nyar and... Sacet.

Malu slapped me on the back. 'Go! Get it over with!' But I bent over and vomited onto the ground by my feet. 'Yuck. Quick! Wipe your mouth and get up there!'

I got up from my seat and sidestepped to the nearby aisle, wiping my mouth as I went. This was it. I staggered through the aisle and walked over to the arena steps.

My perception shifted back down below to the chamber. Hundreds of men were still being kept there. And then I spotted something so shocking that I almost tripped. Sitting against the side of the chamber, mixed in with the others, I spotted my brother.

'Eno?' I said to myself.

What was he doing down there? Did Tau know about this? Why hadn't she told me? My face screwed up and I shot a look over to her by the pole. She and everyone else were watching me as I walked. When she noticed my hate-filled expression, she closed her eyes and dipped her ahead, ashamed. It was like she knew I knew.

I wanted to throw up again. I didn't care what happened to me now; I had to save him. Remembering what Marid had taught me, I kept my hands by my side and focused inside the chamber. I had to get them all as far away as I could.

I could portal to anywhere I had already been. But where would be best? Where would be safest? What about Pilgrim's old village? There would be no one there anymore, surely.

As I made my way up the steps I felt the queen's gaze upon me.

The other three acolytes had already taken their places. I reached the centre of the platform, still focusing on the portal's destination. I could not afford to screw this up.

Without moving my hands, I opened a portal to Pilgrim's village in the chamber below, right next to Eno. *Run, guys! Run, Eno! Get out of there!*

The rattling platforms began to rise from below each of the arena floors. My eyes widened as my victim's head came into view. I had only seen this grey-haired man yesterday in a hanging picture. Like Pilgrim, his hands were bound, and he appeared submissive to his fate. It was Malu's father.

I turned back to the benches and saw the shock on Malu's face. She stood up and made her way down the steps. The queen's eyes were still fixated on me. It was as if the whole world was watching in this one horrible moment. The bell sounded.

The other three arenas lit up with light and fire, followed by bloodcurdling screams. The entrails of a man from one of the other arenas had flown through the air and spilled into mine. Malu's father seemed indifferent to the horrors around him. The crowd of soldiers cheered with bloodlust. But I stood there, frozen, unable to act.

I could hear some of the familiar jeers and taunts from when I first arrived here. The crowd was booing at my indecisiveness. My knees shook. My whole body went weak.

My perception shifted back to the unseen chamber below – almost all of the remaining prisoners had run through the portal. But I had foolishly waited too long before checking back. Several guards had entered the chamber to pursue the escapees, and some were running through the portal after them.

I closed the portal immediately, causing the remaining soldiers to stop in their tracks. I had done my best. Hopefully, they could overcome the three or four guards that got through to the other side.

'Do something! Kill him!' I heard someone yell from the audience.

Like I had done the previous night, I opened a small portal in front of me and stretched the exit to be as large as I could make it. I brought the small end to my mouth and pointed the exit towards the crowd.

'Silence!' I yelled, my voice amplifying many times over and echoing throughout the chamber as though I were a giant.

What now, Sacet? I needed to think of something to say.

'There is no honour in killing an unarmed man. If you want me to fight for the cause, for the queen, or for my own pride, then send me out to fight an enemy who fights back. Or bring forth a weapon, a way for him to defend himself.'

The still audience gasped and murmured. Queen Antwin rose out of her throne and approached the edge of the upper terrace's podium.

There was a lone clap in the audience. I searched for its source and saw that it was Hana. She and Kowi had been forced to sit in the upper rows with the other civilians. Those around her joined in, gathering the applause. Soon after, it appeared that most of the audience in the upper partition was clapping.

I stared back at the queen. Her murderous eyes locked onto mine and her casual grin turned to a scowl of absolute hatred.

Malu brushed past me and towards her father.

I tried reaching out. 'Malu? What are you doing?'

But she didn't stop. She kept running straight for her father. The man's face lit up and he raised his bound hands into the air as she approached. As she embraced him, he brought his arms back down around her, and the nearby audience continued to boo.

Malu broke out into a bawl. 'I'm sorry, Dad.'

'I'm sorry, too, Malu. I love you,' he said. He looked over to me as he was holding his daughter and smiled. 'Thank you.'

He turned back to his daughter and held her in a tight embrace. As he closed his eyes, his face burst into reddish water vapour, followed by the rest of his body. His liquified remains spilled through Malu's arms onto the arena floor at her feet.

Thirty: Shattering the Line

The destroyed village
Eno

'What is this place?' the overseer said as she got to her feet and drew her pistol.

The other three guards got up as well, looking around in astonishment. The rescued men inspected their surroundings, too.

We were in a large cavern, surrounded by scrap metal and demolished shacks. Daylight streamed in from the cave skylights above us, illuminating the whole village. We were standing in the centre of Pilgrim's old home, now abandoned.

'All of you, sit down where you are,' the overseer yelled, stepping forward and waving her pistol around. The men remained silent and still, so the overseer fired up at the cavern's ceiling. 'Now! Do it!'

The noise of the blast echoed off the cave walls and rang in my ears. All of the other men sat down where they were, but I remained standing, looking down at the dirt. The overseer ambled closer.

'Spread out,' she told the three soldiers, then focused her attention back on me. 'Sit down, Eno.'

Sacet didn't make that portal for me just so I could surrender here.

I clenched my fists. 'No.'

She aimed her pistol at me. 'Last chance, you little maggot.'

The chances of me escaping this were slim. The others weren't standing up with me. I was alone in my defiance.

The overseer shrugged. 'Fine, that's the way you want it? You were *supposed* to die in front of your sister. But she's probably dead now anyway.'

I looked back up at her and felt a tear forming in my eye.

'And so... are... you.' I could sense her depressing the trigger.

'No!' I screamed as loud as I could, flinging my arms at her.

She fired her gun and the laser projectile streamed through the air. The ground rumbled. Everything shook. The laser slowed until it had stopped in front of my face. I didn't stop screaming.

The hissing laser hung in mid-air, and then slowly shifted backwards with the rippling waves of force I was producing. The whole cavern quaked. The overseer and her guards were launched off their feet. They tumbled away from me, along with the nearby debris. The laser sped into the cave wall in the distance. The dirt beneath my feet rolled like waves.

The broken shacks tore further into pieces, and fragments barrelled along with the tumbling soldiers, back towards the edge of the cave. I could see the roof of the cavern collapsing, large rocky chunks breaking free and flying into the sky, allowing more light to pour in from above. I didn't stop screaming.

Lifted and taken by the force, the women smacked into the far side of the cave, and the walls around them started to crumble. Shards of metal and stone flung through the air and showered over them; one particularly large spike flew into the overseer's chest and impaled her. The rest of the wall collapsed on top of them as it all continued to push away. The ceiling was pushed away, too, extending the skylights to the point that we were now just standing in a huge crater.

I felt a hand on my shoulder, and I stopped screaming. I turned back to see one of the men, shaking from the destruction. Indeed, all of the men were shocked, but somehow the devastation had only affected what was in front of me, leaving them all unharmed. Tears were rolling freely down my cheeks, but I didn't cry out any longer.

The one holding my shoulder was the ex-Male Dominion man, the same one that had spoken out against Pilgrim's optimism. He smiled with relief. 'You got 'em, kid, you got 'em.'

Realising there were no more soldiers left, the crowd of escapees began to cheer for me, before joyously hugging and celebrating with one another. Overcome with relief, some even shed tears of happiness.

'Why didn't you tell us you were an acolyte?' one asked as he ran over to me.

I panted and collapsed to my knees. 'I – I never – never knew?'

'Well, you saved us. You're a hero.'

I looked up at the sun bearing down on us. 'No, the hero is my sister.'

'What do we do now?' another man asked, his voice mirrored by many similar murmurs.

One of the eldest of us raised his hands. 'Listen, listen to me!' He waited for silence. 'Even dead, those soldiers have tracking devices in them. We must go as far from this place as we can, as quickly as we can, or we'll be right back in that tournament.'

The crowd erupted in bickering, each suggesting their own plans.

I couldn't leave, right? How would Sacet find me again? She'd sent me here, and she'd come for me eventually. But I also remembered what happened last time I didn't heed the warnings about the tracking devices, in this very village.

The ex-MD turned back to me. 'What do you think, kid? You're the only one with powers here.'

'I have to stay,' I replied. 'My sister might come back for me.'

He gestured around at the others still arguing over which direction to move in. 'You sure? You might be waiting here alone, only to be recaptured. Your sister wouldn't want that, right?'

I shrugged and shook my head. 'I guess, but–'

The men wouldn't let up, some even going so far as to push each other in frustration. It wouldn't be long before a fight broke out.

'But we don't even know where we are?' one shouted.

'The smartest move is to scavenge for supplies first!'

'We can't scavenge if we're dead, you idiot. They could be here any moment.'

The man beside me was absolutely right: what point would there be to escaping thanks to Sacet, only to be recaptured because of my own inaction?

Too long had I been following the lines others had laid out for me. Even before I was captured, my hand had been held my entire life by my protectors. I appreciated and loved them for guiding me, but there was no one here to do that for me anymore. It was time I drew my own line in the sand.

'There is a river,' I said, but no one seemed to listen. 'There's a river!' I shouted this time, and they silenced and turned to me. 'To the west of here. I've been there, before I was captured. We are on the border of the Promised Land. There is plentiful fresh water, food and shade there. We could complete the great pilgrimage by sundown.'

They were all calm now, smiling and nodding at one another, hanging on my every word.

I stopped in the centre of them. 'And I can lead you there.'

The old man stepped forward and gave an approving smile. 'Then lead on, young pilgrim.'

Thirty-One: What Have I Done?

In the stadium
Sacet

Malu had fallen to her knees, scooping up puddles of what was left of her father. From the sidelines, Tau climbed into the arena and ran over to her. All I could hear was the booing crowd. Some of the acolytes on the benches surrounding the arena started to stand and make their way over.

The queen still glared down at me. One of her matriarchs approached and whispered into her ear.

They were going to find out what I had done any moment now. I had hoped I could rescue the men without them knowing that it was me, but it was obvious. The guards in the chambers below had seen the men escaping through a portal.

It was time for me to leave. But if they were tracing me, I couldn't lead them straight back to Eno again, right?

I thought back to Malu's apartment and pictured her living room. Using what Sula had taught me, I opened a portal under my feet and one in Malu's apartment, then lifted both at the same time. As soon as they were above my head, I closed them behind me and sat down onto the soft carpet of the living room floor.

The curtains were drawn and the lights were off. The booing still rang in my ears. I began taking deep breaths to centre myself.

The queen would want me dead now. I could never come back. That was okay, I'd find my brother, along with the other men, and we could hide out in the desert. But the tracking device was still inside of me. What if they decided to detonate it right now?

I ran my fingers over the back of my neck, expecting to feel scarred tissue from the surgery. It was instead smooth, no doubt from the healing Tau had given me. I could still feel the lump though. It was definitely still in there.

How was I going to get it out? What if it released the acid as I was trying to remove it?

The lump pulsated. Was that my blood or was something happening with the device? I had no choice, it had to go.

Using my second perception, I looked inside my own flesh and examined the device up close. I had never looked inside my own body before, it was quite surreal. Mostly dark, red, and disgusting.

The device was small and metallic. Barbed antennae anchored it into my neck tissue. I pictured a point on the other side of the room as a destination and carefully made another portal around the device inside my own flesh.

The initial portal sliced through my muscles, causing a strong sting. I was staggered by the pain. I cried out.

In one quick motion I tried to guide the portal around the device, but each pull made me jerk in pain; the barbed antennae refused to let go. The lump pounded quicker, as if it knew what I was trying to do.

I didn't care what damage it did, I wanted it out! I tried forcing it through again, this time with an almighty wrench. The portal tore through my flesh and spat the small gadget out the other side.

I screamed and lay on my side, panting from the effort. The device still had chunks of muscle sticking out of its barbs. A small red light appeared on it, steady at first and then flashing. There was a puff of air, then a spray of sizzling liquid. The green substance quickly corroded the floor, leaving a small hole.

I grabbed the back of my neck. I hadn't broken the skin, but I felt a large cavity underneath. The pain was excruciating. My head went woozy. Blood vessels drained. I tried standing, leaning on the couch for support, but my legs gave way and I fell.

No! I had to get... out... of here...

'Wake up!'

There was a strong kick to my legs. I opened my eyes and sat up. The back of my neck was still throbbing. My blurry eyes adjusted, and I saw Malu standing over me.

She crossed her arms. 'Out of *all* the places you could have run to, why back here?' Her face was pale and grim.

I pulled myself up using the couch. 'Malu? Why? Why did you do it?'

'After all you've been through, you still don't understand.'

'No! You don't understand. How could you kill your own father? I was *trying* to save him. But what you did was unforgivable.'

She scoffed. 'I'm sorry I can't live in your naïve and perfect world, where everyone magically gets along. You know, I really thought that you would come around. I hoped we could be friends, but you ruined everything. Why did you turn out this way?' Malu said as she stepped closer to me with her hands outstretched.

I slowly backed away. 'Malu, don't do something else you'll regret.'

'Shut. Up! I heard about what you did. The whole city is after you now. So, you're either going to come with me peacefully –' she jumped forward and forcibly grabbed my arms '– or you're going to die right here.' I tried squirming out of her grasp, but she was too strong.

We both heard a loud rumble outside, giving us both pause. I flew my second perception outside and across the walkway to the rooftops of the other buildings.

Iya and a squad of heavily armed soldiers pointed their weapons in our direction. I sensed Iya had used her powers to break off a large piece of metal architecture on her roof, and she flicked it towards our apartment window.

'Get down!' I yelled.

The massive piece of debris smashed through the window and into the living room, and we both jumped backwards. We landed behind the couch just as the debris tumbled through. It tore up tiles and flung furniture about, until it finally came to rest. Light now poured in through the huge gaping hole the debris had caused.

'Are they insane?' Malu screeched. 'They almost killed me!'

'Since when has Iya *not* been insane?' I yelled back.

Malu pulled me up and started to drag me towards the hole in the side of the apartment. 'Stop your attack, I have her!'

I squirmed, trying to release myself from Malu's grip.

Iya smiled, glanced at the soldiers to her sides and gestured towards us. 'That one's compromised. Shoot them both.'

Malu dropped me to the floor in surprise. 'What?'

The soldiers raised their guns and unleashed a hail of laserfire. I thought back to Pilgrim's village again and opened a portal at my feet. Malu ducked the barrage but fell back onto me, and we both tumbled through to the ground on the other side.

I scrambled to my feet, hastily closing the portal above.

The entire cave was different from when I last saw it, more of a crater now. There was dust and scrap metal everywhere. The Male Dominion really did a number on this place.

It was already night-time here, and although the sky was dark, the moon and stars bathed the crater in a soft glow.

'They – they tried to kill me,' Malu said in disbelief, still sprawled on the cavern floor. '*You*, I understand – but why me?'

I glanced around, but I couldn't see anyone but us here. 'Where are they?'

My perception flew through the cavern, and then outside to the desert. Nothing.

'What are you talking about?' Malu asked as she rose up from the ground.

'My brother! I teleported all of the men who were scheduled for execution here, but they're gone.'

'I don't know what to tell you.'

'I can already sense that they're nowhere near here.'

Malu gritted her teeth and stomped around. 'What? What have you gotten me into, Sacet? And how are we all the way out here?'

At that moment I saw a hand sticking out of the debris. I ran over, bent down and frantically dug around it, flicking rocks and dirt clumps behind me.

'I've always been able to teleport as far as I wanted to,' I explained as I dug. 'So long as I've been there before, or I can see it.'

I revealed the arm below the hand and recognised Female Dominion armour. This was one of the soldiers that had pursued Eno through the portal. The men must have taken them out.

I breathed a sigh of relief. 'I think Eno's okay,' I said to myself. 'They must have run off into the desert.'

'Wait, wait,' Malu said in disbelief. 'You could teleport... basically *anywhere* this whole time?' She screwed up her face in disgust. 'That's why they wanted you so bad.'

I nodded. 'And it's not the only power I've been keeping secret either.'

'Why the secrets, Sacet?'

I pointed at her. 'Because I didn't want to be used. If Verre found out what I could really do, then all the settlements I've visited in my life would be in danger.'

'Hmph! Nomads again?' She pointed in a random direction. 'Why don't you go back and live with them now then? Because, clearly, the way I live is crazy. No need to thank me for feeding you and giving you a home. I mean, this is what you've wanted all along, isn't it?'

'I never wanted your father to die.'

She kicked a piece of debris. 'Just leave!'

'Open your eyes, Malu. The people in the Dominion hate it there,' I continued. 'Your family's been torn apart by them, and you've been brainwashed so much that you think they would be better off if your father was dead. Wasn't there ever a Malu who thought she could rescue her father?'

Malu's eyes started to tear up. 'Once... but then I woke up. I woke up to the reality of my situation. They own the world – not the nomads – and there's nothing you or I could ever do to change that.'

I paced about the crater. 'You "woke up" to think what they wanted you to think. They've been using your family to keep you obedient, like they tried to do with me. I'm asking you, *begging* you, listen to reason.'

Malu sat down on a knee-high boulder and brought her hands to her face. 'Just go away, go back to the desert and out of my life, which you've now ruined!' She grabbed her head and shook it from side to side. 'You're wrong...'

'Think of what family you have left. Your mother, your sister and your brother. It's not too late to save them.'

'Wrong, wrong, wrong, I can't – he's a male, he can't be saved.' Her eyes fluttered as if her mind was fighting against her own words. She removed her hands, allowing her tears to roll freely down her cheeks. 'When I was first captured, I wanted to fight back, but I was only a kid. We still are kids compared to them.'

I shook my head in disbelief. 'Fine, then ask yourself this: what is your mother going to say to you when you get back? What is your sister going to think of you after what you did?'

Malu looked down and closed her eyes. 'They'll hate me even more,' she mumbled. She brought her hands to her face again. 'What have I done?'

I hated Malu for what she did, but I still felt sorry for her. I turned my back on her and started walking. 'I'm done with your Dominion, both of them. And you, too. All I care about is my brother.'

A sharp, high-pitched noise rang throughout the cavernous crater. A bullet had ricocheted off the scrap metal by my feet, so I stopped in my tracks. Malu jumped up and stood beside me.

'That's far enough,' a nearby voice said.

Several figures appeared around the rim of the crater. We were surrounded.

Thirty-Two: What I Was Meant To Do

'Don't take another step,' an elderly man's voice called out.

There were more of them than I thought. At least thirty nomads cautiously descended into the crater with their rifles up ready. I had been so distracted by Malu that I hadn't noticed them.

Malu shifted awkwardly, trying to get my attention. 'Get. Us. Out of here,' she whispered through gritted teeth.

'Don't shoot,' I pleaded. 'I'm one of you, I – Hati? Elder Hati?'

Among the nomads was the old man who had once condemned Tau to death. As before, he was frail and could barely walk. Unlike the others, he carried no weapons.

These were Pilgrim's fellow villagers, or what was left of them.

'Teelo?' I shrieked in surprise.

The closest nomad was the one-eyed boy that Pilgrim had once called his son. Based on his scowl, he was not pleased to see me.

'How does she know our names?' another man called out as they all closed in around us.

'Because she is the portalling girl, Sacet,' Elder Hati called out. 'The reason our settlement was found and destroyed.'

'And now she wears their armour,' Teelo said, gesturing to my outfit with his gun.

Now only a few paces away, each nomad stopped, forming a large circle, with Malu and I in the centre. I slowly knelt and raised my hands.

'We should kill them,' one of the women suggested to Hati. 'While we still can.'

The entire group murmured in agreement.

Malu's fists tightened, so I caught her gaze and shook my head as subtly as I could. She knelt down, too, copying my passive body language.

'Their tracking devices will lead more of them here,' another added, to yet more, louder mutters.

'No, no, no,' I said in a panic. I gestured to the back of my neck where there would still surely be a giant red mark. 'I ripped mine out, see?'

'And... I've never had one,' Malu included.

'Lies!' Teelo said.

'Truth,' Malu snapped back.

While the others stared Malu down, I scanned inside her neck, just as I had done for myself. There was a tiny, barbed, metallic object in the same place mine had been, although hers was smaller without the acid capsule. There was no scarring on her neck, but then I remembered that she had been healed by Tau.

She either didn't know she had it, or she was lying. But if I confronted her about it now, they'd probably kill her, like they were planning to do with Tau.

I focused on Hati. 'We're clean. Please trust me.' I gestured around at the crater. 'I never meant to lie to you before, and I'm sorry about what happened here. I – we – only just escaped the Dominion. I helped my brother escape, too. I sent him and others here earlier today. Do you know where—'

The nomads' expressions grew more suspicious with every word I said.

I sighed and closed my eyes. 'I just want my brother back. Please.'

Hati considered my words carefully and looked around at his tribe. 'She's telling the truth.' He concentrated back on me. 'Your mistake caused a lot of death here.'

I dipped my head in apology. 'You're right, and I'm so sorry. If I could undo my mistake, I would.'

He grimaced. 'After the attack, we survivors were ambushed yet again, this time by the women. This is all that remains of us.'

I looked around at each of them. 'And you came back here?'

'Earlier today, we saw an explosion here from afar. We waited, then came to salvage what might have remained.'

I took quicker breaths. 'An explosion?'

'A massive one. The hills themselves broke apart. I'm sorry, but if this is where you sent your brother, it's unlikely he survived.' He gestured down to the partially buried dominion soldier nearby. 'He could be buried under all this.'

No, that didn't make sense. Eno was a survivor, like me. He would have run, right? I clutched my shaking head. 'That's impossible. He – he–'

With difficulty, Hati sat on a boulder across from us. 'Look around you, there's nothing left.'

My second perception spun and twisted in a panic, diving underground at random spots, searching for bodies, for anything. I felt sick, both my mind and stomach churned. My heart was sinking, straining under the pressure.

I lowered my hands and slowly stood. 'You're wrong. He's alive, and I *have* to find him.'

I turned and tried breaking out of the circle, but Teelo rushed over and put the end of his rifle to my forehead, stopping me.

I glared at him. 'Go ahead and shoot.' My tough façade didn't last, however. I began to sob. 'Because without him, if he really is dead, then I have no one left to protect.'

'Teelo,' Hati said. He gestured for Teelo to lower his weapon and he complied. 'Sacet, you're wrong.'

The nomads all relaxed their stances. Malu lowered her hands, too.

'Before Pilgrim was captured,' Hati continued, 'he told me everything about you. Even how you were born in the Dominion and yet your parents took the risk to adopt you as one of their own. Not related by blood, and yet you became family, correct?'

I wiped away my tears and nodded.

'Well, you are surrounded by family right now. And we need your help.'

My eyes narrowed. 'He told you about Aberym's plan?'

Hati slowly nodded. 'Yes.'

I shrugged. 'My grandfather wanted to use me as a weapon, just like everybody else.'

Hati sighed and looked up at the stars. 'You're not the only one who has lost people. My beloved Pemei and I lost all five of our children. And then I lost her, too.' He then gestured to the nomads around us. 'But I found new family. And I would do anything to help them. You should, too.'

I avoided his gaze.

Hati smirked. 'I can't imagine how many settlements the three of you must have visited–'

'At least a hundred,' I replied.

'Did you visit Fort Promise?'

I nodded. 'When I was eight, yes. And Cairn's Beach, and the Sable Mountains – my brother and I went to them all. All we did was travel.'

Hati chuckled. 'All together, there must be thousands of us.'

'More.'

The nomads all raised eyebrows at one another, tantalised.

Hati closed his eyes and looked down. 'Then perhaps it's time our people all met each other, wouldn't you say? Sacet and…?' He pointed at Malu.

'Malu,' she answered.

'And Malu,' he continued. 'Now that you can use your portals again, you can unite your people. Your family. And with our superior numbers, we can bring down the Dominions.'

I thought about Eno. I didn't know if he was alive or dead, but a part of me hoped he was fine, travelling somewhere, making a shelter for himself and others. Foraging like I taught him. Yes, if he was alive, then I knew he'd be okay, at least for a little while.

The Dominion only wanted me. Eno was safer as far away from me as he could get.

I took a deep breath. 'Alright. Tonight, we will all be reunited.'

Some of the nomads exchanged smiles and took stronger stances, excited for what was to come.

I remembered back to my time at Fort Promise, the biggest, most fortified, most remote structure we nomads had. Although it had been so long ago, with my grandfather's memory training, I still remembered the place as clear as day. The portal opened as easy as any other I had made.

Elder Hati was helped to his feet by one of the nomads. He and the others approached the portal and peered through. It was night on the other side, too. We could all see the interior of the fort, lit with a few torches. Hati turned back with a delighted grin.

Fort Promise
The Chieftain's tent

Like the crowds in the stadium, the sound outside the tent later that night was a mess of indistinct speech all meshed into one monstrous voice. How many nomads were out there? I wondered. It was amazing how quickly I was able to unite them. Portalling to the villages took no time at all, and my grandfather had worded them up about the plan long ago, so they didn't require much convincing to come through.

The various chiefs and elders had gathered in the tent with Malu and I around a table. We had ditched our armour and now wore nomadic robes. I felt at home in the airy, freeing clothing again. Malu, on the other hand, kept examining them and muttering about how ashamed she was.

We were all examining a map of FDC that I had helped create. Malu helped, too, but she wasn't as forthcoming with the information as I was.

The chieftain of the fort, a large, muscly man named Orrik, opened the tent door and gestured outside. 'As much as I love to see our people together like this, it is a far greater risk.'

The chieftain from the Sable Mountains nodded. Her name was Tamil. She was quite young considering she was a chieftain and seemed to like spinning her dagger on the table. 'Agreed. The bigger the tribe, the bigger the target for the Dominions.'

Hati had been silent for some time. 'But we only just united them,' he finally said.

Orrik approached the table and pressed down on the map. 'Which is why we need to strike now, while we have the numbers and they don't expect it. It's already the middle of the night in FDC by now.'

'If this map is accurate, we should strike in multiple locations,' another said. 'What's this location here?'

Tamil stabbed her dagger into the table. 'Where's the queen hiding? I'll gut her myself.'

I gestured to the map. 'Or what if, instead, I portal our people to key points around the outskirts? They could act as diversions to draw away soldiers from the Citadel.'

Malu was becoming more uncomfortable with each passing moment. She had no choice but to play along with our side. If they found out what I knew about her, she'd already be dead.

She discreetly grabbed me by the arm and pulled me outside. 'I need to speak to you.'

The tent was positioned on top of a cliff overlooking the entire fort. The statue of the tribe's chieftain was still there in the village's centre, towering above the shacks. The fountain I remembered drinking out of as a kid still bubbled.

Malu and I could see thousands of people readying for battle, maybe even ten thousand. The number of warriors streaming through the portals outside seemed endless. They all had rifles and other rusty nomadic weapons.

It was a real army. It was truly inspiring, and all because of my grandfather and I. All my life wandering the desert, thinking these people a lost cause, but here they were now united, ready to fight. My people.

'This is insane,' Malu whispered to me. 'These people are my enemy!'

'No, these people are your original family,' I replied. 'And before we go back to the city, I need to know that you won't turn your back on them again.'

She hesitated and looked out over the masses. 'I can't betray the queen. But... my family is more important. I'll help, but only so I can rescue them.' She gestured to me. 'And what about you? How do you expect to lead a rebellion when you can't even kill anyone?'

'I've killed before,' I replied.

She smirked. 'Yeah, but you didn't *want* to.'

'No one should want to kill, Malu,' I retorted. 'But I've realised sometimes they need to.'

Malu pointed at the army. 'And what if they kill civilians?'

I pondered this for a moment. 'I have a plan for that.'

She sighed and leant against a nearby wooden post.

'What's wrong?'

'Just like that?' she said. 'You're okay with all this? Ready to assault the city when earlier today you couldn't wait to escape it?'

I took a deep breath. 'I've been training for this my whole life. I didn't like it at the time, but now that it's finally happening, it feels right. This is what I was meant to do.'

She gave a sarcastic cheer and rubbed the back of her neck, as if exasperated. 'Well, good luck to us then, I guess.'

Her movements reminded me that Malu still had a tracking device. I paused and stared at her until she seemed uncomfortable.

'What?' she said with a shrug.

I glanced around to make sure no one was listening in. 'I know you lied.' I then silently tapped the back of my neck.

She tensed and pushed off the post. 'Tracking dev...' She also looked around. 'I already told you, I don't have one.'

I smirked and shook my head. 'I'm looking at it right now. There's no point in lying to me.'

Her eyes darted, trying to understand, before locking with mine.

I gestured to the army. 'But by the time they get here with their best soldiers and weapons, it'll be too late. We'll be in the heart of FDC.'

Malu's stance went rigid, as though she were ready to fight or run. 'Why didn't you say anything to them?'

I scoffed. 'Because you're my friend, dummy.'

Her mouth was agape. 'Seriously? Even after everything–'

'Yes,' I said as I hugged her. She was stiff at first and I wondered briefly if she'd been embraced often, though I guessed most people were worried about her liquifying them. Slowly, I felt her muscles relax in my arms. 'You helped me keep my brother alive. Now I'll help you free yours.'

After sharing the moment a little longer, we turned and faced the crowd.

She slowly shook her head. 'Not just him, all of them.'

FDC Prison Quad

I stepped through the last portal with Malu. It was night-time here, just as we'd planned. It was so late that the station, the surrounding streets and the stairs leading up to the Prison Quad were completely deserted. I peeked back through the portal and gave the all clear.

Shortly after, Orrik stepped through. His tribe followed his lead, darting through in silence. I widened the portal so that it was almost the entire length of the station. Malu and I headed for the Prison Quad steps as our army piled in behind us.

The other tribes were no doubt through their portals by now, and each group would be dotted around the city. I closed all but the closest portal. Any moment now, fights would break out everywhere, particularly in the Military and Science Quads.

It was remarkable how quiet the thousands of people were. They knew that until the battle was joined this was a stealth mission. They filled every nook and cranny of the station, as well as the surrounding streets, which were curiously deserted. The younger warriors were shaking and sweating.

My second perception saw no other warriors left through the last portal, so I closed it. I turned and walked up the steps.

'Are you sure about this?' Malu asked.

I shook my head. 'No, but I'm going to do it anyway.'

I closed my eyes, focusing on the prison in front of me. The crowd waited in silence, some crouching down.

My perception flew into the prison. The same power-inhibiting cells I was once interrogated in were filled with sleeping male acolytes. They had strange collars around their necks, something they didn't have last time I saw them.

There must have been at least a hundred of them. Keeping them locked up seemed odd. What was the point in keeping them alive? Experimentation, maybe?

I couldn't seem to find Kalek, the invincible colonel who had murdered Tau.

As much as I would like to rescue every single non-acolyte prisoner down in the mines, I would need to be much closer to even sense them. And by the time I portalled each one out, the surprise of our attack would be gone. No matter, the acolytes would do for now.

I took a deep breath, then began opening portals under every sleeping acolyte prisoner. One after another they each fell onto the grass near the steps. The shock woke them, and they sprung up, gauging their surroundings.

'What happened? Who are you people?' one shouted.

As the acolytes stood, many cried out in surprise. The nearby nomads ran to greet and hush them.

I didn't let up, teleporting a few at a time, then several at a time. My perception flew through each cell, emptying them right under the guard's noses. The noise of over a hundred frightened men broke the night's tranquillity.

I sensed one of the guards discovering an empty prison cell. She was sprinting down the corridor, probably to alert the others. I put a portal underneath her and dropped her high above the prison. She plummeted down to the roof and crashed onto the concrete. The first necessary casualty.

I dropped to my knees and wheezed. Creating this many portals at a time had winded me.

Malu examined the men with wide eyes. 'What kind of training has Marid been doing with you?'

Thirty-Three: Flick of a Switch

'What's going on?' a prisoner asked.

I recognised his voice, it was Noor. His helmet had long been discarded, so it was the first time I had seen his face. He appeared similar in age to Malu. His leg had been healed by Tau. He was pale-skinned, tall, somewhat muscular, and had short, brown hair.

'Woah, a prison break,' another said with a grin, before playfully punching Noor in the shoulder.

It was Tetsu. He was also similar in age to Malu and his leg had been healed, too. He was dark-skinned with black hair and was a bit stocky. He was shorter than Noor, but still taller than me.

Some of the nomads anxiously trained their rifles on the acolytes.

Malu pointed at the acolytes' necks. 'These collars inhibit their powers, like their cells.'

I opened a portal above the crowd, and another one over my head. I carefully brought the second one down over me, which made my body pop up and out of the higher portal so I could more easily address the crowd.

'Listen to me,' I yelled, and the prisoners looked up. 'It doesn't matter if you're from the Male Dominion or a nomad, tonight you have a choice.'

Distant gunfire could be heard. The other tribes must have engaged their targets.

'I freed you because we have a common enemy.' I turned and pointed at the glowing, golden Royal Citadel. '*Her*. Tonight, the queen dies.'

The nomads started to cheer, and some of the stunned prisoners joined in, too.

I raised my hands for silence and continued. 'If you want to join us, we can take your collars off. The other option is your collar stays on, and you are free to go. If that is your choice, leave now.'

An alarm sounded, and the entire Prison Quadrant lit up. It wasn't the only one; more alarms sounded throughout the city.

I stood patiently, waiting for any of the prisoners to break away, but none did.

'I'll fight,' Noor called.

I nodded at Malu.

She hesitantly approached him and grabbed his collar. 'Well, if it isn't the infamous King's Wrath.'

'Nice hand,' he said, referring to her replacement.

Malu smirked back. 'Nice leg.' She liquified the collar and took a step back. The two narrowed their eyes at one another for a moment.

'Anyone else?' I asked.

Tetsu raised his hand. 'Me, too.'

Another forcibly pushed through the crowd to get to Malu. 'And me. Get this thing off me!'

One by one, the prisoners came to Malu and had their collars liquified. Each man reawakened his unique power and smiled with glee. The surrounds lit up with bright, varied displays of power: fire, smoke, gasses and flying rocks.

'One last thing,' I continued over the crowd. 'We are not here to destroy this city, but to free it. To make it a place where all peoples can live in peace. We will kill the queen, as well as anyone who stands in our way. But if you intentionally harm a defenceless civilian, you will have to answer to *me*.' I then looked down at Orrick and pointed at the Citadel. 'It's time.'

Orrik nodded and turned to his tribe. 'Nomads, men and women, warriors of Seron! To war!' He thrust his rifle in the direction of the Citadel.

His roar was echoed by the masses, some chanting his words, while others let out bloodcurdling shouts.

I lifted and closed the portal, feeling the ground quake as the army charged northward. Most of the freed acolytes joined, too. A small crowd still surrounded Malu, waiting to have their collars removed.

One acolyte slunk away into the shadows, rather than joining our army. A coward or two was to be expected. No matter, I had more pressing matters to focus on.

During the tournament, I had created a portal to amplify my voice. I would do it again, this time with multiple portals all around the city in the sky. With the city so silent, my voice would hopefully cut through the night air and reach everyone. This was going to be difficult, but hopefully not impossible.

I closed my eyes and remembered all the places I had visited in the city: the Residential Rim, the Commercial Quad, and the Military Quad. Then I strained and opened several small portals in front of my face.

Next was far more difficult. I stretched and strained my fingers apart to grow the destination portals. I gritted my teeth and clenched every muscle in my body.

It took a great deal of my concentration, but I made them as large as I could. From here, I looked through at each destination. If anyone was looking up at the portals, they'd probably see a giant projection of my mouth.

I leant closer and licked my lips. 'People of FDC,' I yelled. The volume of my voice was magnified many times over, echoing throughout the city.

'Today, I refused to execute an innocent man in front of you, and most of you showed your support. It's because you know this war is wrong. Female or male, we are all one people.

'As we speak, a coup is taking place. So, soldiers and citizens alike, now is the time to join us. Take up arms and enter the streets. Fight alongside your sisters and brothers. Your mothers and fathers. Your daughters and sons. And show this queen she is wrong! We will not be divided on the basis of our gender.

'And if you disagree? Then stay out of our way. Hide in your homes, in your barracks. Keep your heads down and tomorrow you will wake to a brand-new world.'

I closed the portals and took a deep breath before looking around at who was left. 'Where's Colony?'

Other than Malu and I, only a few acolytes still remained. Then I saw him. Colony was sitting on the steps. His collar was gone now, but he just sat there, motionless.

He looked up at me as I approached. 'How do you expect me to fight without my family?' He gestured to Malu. 'You two took me away from them!'

Malu had finished up with last of the acolytes, who ran off to join the nomads. She walked over to us. 'I can't help but feel I've just unleashed a terrible evil.'

I gestured at our army, still charging into the city limits. 'Malu, go with the others.'

'With the savages? Why?'

I glanced back at her. 'Because you can't help me with what comes next. Go support the diversion.'

She opened her mouth to answer back but left in a huff instead.

'Direct them to the Citadel,' I called out to her before focusing back on Colony.

Colony folded his arms. 'You've got all the meat dancing nicely. I wish I was as adept at playing with my food.'

'How would you like to have your army back?' I asked, cutting to the chase.

He raised an eyebrow. 'And in return I bet you want to use them as a weapon, right? Male, female, nomads... you're all the same.'

'You're only half right,' I said, taking a seat next to him. 'I'd rather be friends. Friends do each other favours. Seeming as I just saved you, maybe you can repay me by bringing your "family" to bear on the queen?'

I thought back to Teersau, where I first met Tau, the place where the necrolisks ambushed us. The pitch-black portal opened to Colony's side.

He looked through the portal with wide eyes. 'Is that...?'

'A nest,' I finished for him. 'Yes.'

A look of bliss came over Colony's face as he stood and peered into the nest. He was about to step in, but I grabbed his arm to stop him.

'Do we have a deal?'

He glanced back, at first with a look of revulsion towards me. 'It's not enough. You want my family's help? We're going to need more than just my rescue.'

I sighed. 'Fine. We will discuss it. *After* the battle. So? Do we have a deal?'

His creepy smile returned. 'Deal.'

'Alright,' I said, letting go of him and standing by his side. 'Summon as many as you can. When I'm ready for you, I'll open another portal in the same place.'

He nodded, but curled his lip derisively. I watched as he stepped through, and I closed the portal behind him.

I was the last one left at the station. My second perception sensed guards running all throughout the Prison Quad inside. It was only a matter of time before they looked outside to the station.

Next step. I thought back to the Science Quad. I had sent Tamil's tribe there to secure the building with the enormous, ring-shaped device. I just hoped it was what powered the city, like I assumed. In moments, a portal opened in front of me, and I stepped through.

I was met with quite the chaotic sight. The vast chamber was mostly taken up by the giant metal tube, which hummed loudly. There were both nomads and scientists everywhere, and all turned to me when I arrived.

The scientists were on their knees, cowering with their arms up in surrender. There were many older women among them, and some were crying. I could see several dead, armoured soldiers, splayed on the floor in pools of their own blood.

The nomads had all of the survivors at gunpoint. Tamil was interrogating an old, grey-haired scientist, forcing her against some nearby control panels.

As I approached them, my second perception shifted inside the massive, humming tube. It was hollow and filled with flames. The air itself was ridiculously bright. Whatever was inside, it was extremely hot.

Outside the tube was something I hadn't noticed before. Densely packed bundles of cables connected to the tube before leading out of the facility in every direction through the roof.

Tamil was backed by some of the burliest nomads I had ever seen, but she didn't need them. She had the scientist pinned against the wall and was running the tip of her dagger along the terrified woman's face.

'If you don't start speaking sense, I'm going to cut your head clean off!' Tamil shouted.

The scientist was a colonel, as denoted by her the white streaks and yellow tips in her hair. If she was here, this room *must* be important, as I suspected.

'What is this place?' I asked.

The scientist's eyes darted over to me before focusing back on Tamil. 'As I – as I keep saying, it's the binary fusion reactor!'

Tamil smacked the woman against the wall again. 'And as *I* keep saying, speak in a language we understand!'

'Please! Please!' the scientist begged. 'I told you what it is.'

I brushed Tamil's shoulder, hinting for her to let the woman down. Tamil released her but kept her dagger at the ready. The scientist remained against the wall, too frightened to move.

I pointed at the reactor. 'It's what powers the city?'

'Ye – yes,' she answered. 'But it's no use threatening me or my staff. I can't shut it down. Even if I wanted to, I *can't*. There are too many fail-safes.'

I turned away from her and focused on the reactor. 'Very well, then I'll just destroy it.' I pointed to the only door. 'Everyone get out.'

Everyone in the room had frozen, still a step behind what was about to happen.

I opened a portal inside the reactor where all the super-heated light was, with the destination on the far side of the chamber, pointing down on the thick cable bundles. A blazing cascade of lava-hot energy fired both down onto the equipment and up into the ceiling, melting and disintegrating the delicate instruments instantly.

'Is she crazy?' one of the scientists cried.

'You heard her,' Tamil screeched over the thunderous distortion. 'Move! Out, out, out!'

Both nomads and scientists fled to the exit.

I opened a second portal, and a third inside the reactor, with destinations sending more waterfalls of destruction at the cable bundles. As the first bundle melted clear through, the lights in the room began to flicker. Smoke billowed in all directions.

Eventually the last of the people left the room. I was alone. I continued slicing up the cables around the reactor using its own power against it.

The reactor itself began to warp and turn orange, clearly not designed for having the heat on the outside. The smoke was overwhelming. I couldn't see without my second perception. All the nearby control panels continued to flicker.

As I roughly cut through the final cable bundle, all the lights in the room went out. The only light was the blinding, destructive power in front of me.

My perception sensed the blackout had spread across multiple city blocks, and hopefully farther than that. Almost all electronics in the area had died, leaving everyone still inside buildings to flounder in the dark. The city had lost its power.

It was time for me to go. I pictured the Teersau nest in my mind, the same spot I had sent Colony. The portal opened and I stepped through just as a blindingly bright hole split upon the reactor's surface.

Thirty-Four: Nothing Can Heal This

The Residential Rim
Tau

Hana, Kowi and I were almost at the entrance to their apartment complex. The building was thankfully still open at this time of night. No one was around but us, thanks to the curfew. Aside from an occasional guard patrol, the streets were empty because of the imposed curfew. If I hadn't been escorting Hana and Kowi, they probably would have been detained by now.

Kowi had been crying on and off all day and night. Hana was equally as distraught, but attempted to hide it under a wall of stiff, stubborn anger.

Because all the remaining 'contestants' had been freed by Sacet, the event had ended prematurely, which I was secretly thankful for. Afterwards, Hana approached me, asking for my help to find and confront Malu. We had been searching for her since then, but no one we asked knew her whereabouts. It was like she had vanished.

What had Malu been thinking? How could she kill her own father like that?

I'd finally convinced Hana to take Kowi home, telling her I'd confront Malu when I next saw her. Hana had scoffed at my offer but was too tired to argue any longer.

As for Sacet, I completely understood her actions. If only I'd been as brave as her. I should have gone up on the platform, too, stood by her side. I wished I knew how to stand up the Dominion and tell them to stop the violence.

I was so glad she rescued Eno, and I felt terrible for not telling her about him. I'd assumed that it wouldn't have made a difference, but knowing what I know now, perhaps it would have given her a smarter way to escape? And maybe I could have even escaped with her.

Although this area of the city was deserted because of the curfew, the Military Quad was a hive of activity, on high alert, ready to respond to news about Sacet. Thanks to her portals though, I doubted they'd find and catch up with her. I hoped they *never* found them, and that Sacet and Eno could live together in their forested promised land, like they'd always wanted.

Hana let go of Kowi's hand for a moment and hugged me. She sniffled and her tears leaked onto my shoulder. 'Thank you for helping us. It's good to know someone still cares.'

I embraced her back. 'It was nothing, really. If there's anything I can do... anything at all...'

The neon streetlights shone on Kowi's wet cheeks. She sobbed and buried her face into her mother's side.

Hana did her best to comfort her. 'Thank you, Tau, but... nothing can heal this.'

A distant scream carried on the night air, giving us pause. I glanced up and down the deserted street. It wasn't just screaming, it was yelling, a crowd of people, and they were getting louder.

I pointed at Hana. 'Get inside. Take Kowi and find a good place to hide.'

They were frozen in place, eyes widened with fear.

'Mum, what is it?' Kowi asked frantically. 'Mum?'

'Go!' I commanded.

Hana nodded and dragged Kowi into the complex. The yelling was coming from somewhere to the south. The Prison Quad.

I strode towards the commotion, then sped up to a jog. I didn't have my helmet with me so I couldn't call this in. Was it a riot? A protest over the curfew?

Just as I was about to question the absence of city alarms, one sounded throughout the street.

'All civilians must return to their homes immediately,' a woman's voice resounded in monotone. The woman's disembodied voice repeated the command again and again.

I ran faster, now sprinting.

There was an explosion up around the next bend. The flames expanded into the sky above the buildings, momentarily painting the night world bright and orange. Gunfire followed, up and down the next street. Laser projectiles zoomed into nearby windows and homes. The sprinkling glass sprayed onto the walkways below.

What was happening? Who was attacking? I didn't have a weapon with me; I hadn't carried one ever since I discovered my powers, but I really needed it now.

The streetlights vanished, as did the lights in the buildings. The power must have gone out. The only things illuminating my path were the stars and the gunfire.

I ignited my healing aura, turning my skin white. A luminescent, light-blue aura of harmless flames surrounded me once more. My path was visible again.

I rounded the corner and gasped. A patrol of soldiers lay dead in the streets. Beyond them, an enormous, angry crowd of people, both men and women, were approaching.

'An acolyte!' one of them shouted, her words echoing down the residential apartments lining the street.

There must have been hundreds of them. Most wore nomadic robes and carried weapons, while others were in prison uniforms.

One of the bodies in the street twitched; she was still alive! I could still heal her. Maybe get her out of there?

I sprinted again, unafraid of what the horde would do to me.

'Take her down!' a man's voice bellowed, and the line of marching warriors fired.

The projectiles, a mix of lasers and bullets, fizzed and whooshed past me as I ran. Many struck my chest. Although I didn't feel any pain, each wound had to be healed, draining me ever so slightly.

I didn't stop. I reached the dying soldier, knelt down and grabbed her with both hands. She had a gunshot wound to her stomach and was bleeding out everywhere.

'No, stay with me – stay awake. Live!'

The incoming fire continued to strike all over my body, but I looked down and saw my own wounds heal almost instantly, tingling as they did so.

My enemies drew closer. A stray bullet pierced into the chest of the girl I was holding, near her heart. She went limp again, dead in my arms. A teardrop jostled from my eye. 'No...'

'Wait, stop!' a woman's voice said from the crowd. 'I said stop firing!'

The confused rabble parted, revealing Malu among them.

She pushed through the group with all eyes upon her. 'She's of no danger to us, move on to the Citadel.' Malu paused, getting her bearings, and then pointed to a nearby street corner. 'That way.'

The crowd turned and reignited their war cries. I still held the dead soldier in my arms as they all passed by me, heading to where Malu had directed.

'Wha – what is – Malu? What are you doing here? What are doing with these nomads?'

Malu came closer and stood over the body. Hundreds of people continued to pass as she and I stared into one another's eyes.

'It's Sacet's plan,' she began, gesturing at the horde. 'It all ends tonight.'

I wildly shook my head, flicking gentle flames about. 'What plan? To attack the city?' I gestured to the poor, dead girl in my arms. 'You've come here to kill us all?'

The passing nomads eyed me with contempt but continued on.

'No,' Malu shouted over the sound of the marching army. 'To free us.'

I slowly shook my head. 'I don't even know you anymore. The Malu I knew would never kill her own people.'

'I haven't killed any of my people.'

I clutched the woman's body tighter and scowled. '*She* would disagree, and so would your family.'

The crowd had finally marched by and around the bend. Explosions and fire followed in their wake. They must have found more soldiers like me to kill. Malu and I were now alone.

Malu turned to the city. 'Where are they? My mother and sister?'

'Why? You want to kill them, too?'

She clenched her fists and paced around me. 'Oh, enough, Tau! I'm not a monster. Yes, I gave him a quick death, but I'm *furious* at our superiors for putting him in there. I'm trying to do the right thing now.'

I suddenly felt a searing rip in my chest, causing me to screech. My heart palpitated and my limbs went numb. I collapsed over on the body with a pained groan. It was as though my heart was going to explode, like I was about to die.

Malu shifted closer. 'Are you okay? What's wrong?'

The pain finally ceased, leaving me a shaking, sobbing mess.

'You're – you're Tau–' a weak voice said below me.

I looked down and saw that the girl I was still holding had opened her eyes. Her chest wound had healed, leaving only bloodstained armour. She moaned and slowly took in her surroundings.

I gasped. 'But – you – you were dead.'

Malu knelt as well, and we both helped the girl sit up.

'I was?' she said groggily.

Malu wrenched the girl to her feet. 'Are you sure?'

'Positive,' I replied, examining the girl up and down.

The girl spotted her fallen comrades and her face contorted. 'I have to – to stop them. Where are they? The intruders, which way did they go?' she asked, picking up her pistol.

I had just raised this girl from the dead and she was already going to throw her life away a second time.

She laid eyes on Malu, noticed her nomadic robes, and aimed the pistol at her head. 'You, you're one of them. Don't move!'

Malu smirked and bent her knees, as though getting ready to dodge forward and liquefy her.

I stood between them and raised my hands. 'Stop.' I calmly approached and held her shaking weapon, pointing it at myself. 'There has already been enough death today. Right?'

Although she didn't release the tight grip on her gun, she at least didn't fire. Her streaks were pure red, meaning she outranked me. There was fear beneath her tough façade, an uncertainty. I somehow sensed it when I relived the pain she had endured in death. She had a kind soul, too kind for this world.

She glanced at her fallen comrades again, lower lip trembling, and her weapon finally lowered. Tears streamed down her overwhelmed face. 'You're right, this... is too much. I – I just want to – just want–'

I pointed at the nearest building entrance. 'Go inside and hide until it's all over. No one will judge you. We won't tell anyone.'

Malu relaxed and nodded reassuringly at the girl, who in turn backed away from us to where I had indicated. She continued to look back at us and cry as she retreated into the safety of the building, until eventually she rounded a corner and was out of sight.

The sounds of combat were growing farther away now. Malu and I stood in silence for a moment, trying to process what had happened.

Malu stood next to me and shook her head, flabbergasted. 'How did you do that? You just resurrected the dead, like Queen Elysia.'

'I know,' I slowly replied. 'It changes everything.'

All my life, I had felt conflicted with what the Dominion wanted me to do. I never wanted to kill anyone. But if I could bring them back, it didn't matter, right? Maybe I could finally help heal this world of its obsession with death. But that excruciating pain, would that happen every time? It was like I had to die like they did before I could bring them back. Could I put myself through that for every single person that had died in this war?

There was an odd slurping noise beneath us. The pools of blood throughout the street were quavering and merging, before rising into the air in big globules.

'What the...?' Malu began, before turning around. 'Korin.'

Two figures approached from down the street. Colonel Korin whipped her hands around, and the blood at our feet violently copied her action.

Malu raised her hands to defend herself. The blood hardened, crystallising into the shape of a long spear, before driving through the air. Malu caught and re-liquified one spear, but a second drove itself into her neck.

Malu choked on her own gushing blood. She flailed her arms at the second spear, but it pulled itself out and quickly stabbed in a different position, over and over again.

The second figure emerged from the dark, a giant man stomping with each step. Fear overtook me, I couldn't move. It was Kalek. The ground quaked as he charged. I backed away, unsure of where to go. He roared as he got close.

His colossal fist slammed into my petite frame, launching me across the street. I hurtled into one of the buildings, crashing through the window with such force that the walls and ceiling around me collapsed. Metal and concrete caved in, burying me in rubble.

I couldn't move or hear anything. I couldn't breathe. I squirmed and I struggled, but it was no use. But then, breathing didn't seem to matter. I wasn't choking like I expected. My aura was still activated. Maybe I didn't even need air while it was on?

There was a crumbling, scraping noise. The concrete around me shifted. It was getting lighter. Something was moving it above me.

My head was freed, then my hands, and my eyes met with one of the building's denizens. I was surrounded by women all helping to dig me out of the rubble.

'Thank you,' I said as I pushed myself up and stood. I brushed myself off and climbed through the smashed entrance.

'Are you okay?' she asked, and the group followed me.

'I'm fine. Please stay inside, it's not safe out there,' I said confidently as I marched back into the street.

'What's going on?' a young girl added. 'Tau, please – you'll protect us, right?'

The group continued to murmur as I inspected the street. Both Korin and Kalek were gone. Perhaps they assumed they had dealt with me? Their assault should have killed me, but I felt fine, no physical pain at all.

'Why was that soldier with that man?' the woman behind me asked.

I strode over to Malu's body and knelt beside her. It was too late; she had bled out.

My whole life I had known something was off in this society. When Kalek killed me in Usre the other day, it only made me more confused. Why would Neva and Iya betray me? Why were they working together with the MD? Why was Kalek waiting for Sacet with me in his grasp? And that was exactly the answer: Sacet. My death was meant to cause *her* more trauma. How high up the chain did this scheme go?

Regardless, I couldn't fight for it anymore. I couldn't conform to the insanity. For any chance at peace, it all had to come down. Sacet was right, and now Malu, too. I had to help them. But to do that I would have to betray the society that had raised me, and my fellow sisters. I made my choice.

My aura erupted, filling the street with blue and causing the surprised women behind me to shriek.

I knelt, grabbed Malu's neck and immediately felt like I was being garrotted, like sharp knives were stabbing me in the throat. I watched as her wounds began to heal.

Thirty-Five: Iya's Game

In the Teersau necrolisk nest
Sacet

My foot squelched onto the mucus-covered ground. The horrid smell of death stung my nostrils. The bright reactor explosion behind me through the portal briefly illuminated the far ends of the cave tunnel, revealing skittering silhouettes that quickly retreated into the darkness. I closed the portal, wrapping myself in pitch-black.

'I'm not ready yet!' Colony yelled somewhere from the inky blackness, his voice echoing back and forth.

Where was he? My eyes searched the chamber, but it was hopeless without a light source. How he had managed to navigate this place without vision was a mystery to me.

My second perception flew about and, although I was unable to make out how things looked, I was still able to sense their shape. It was certainly better than nothing.

I blindly stepped forward, knowing the path was clear. With each step, my feet sank into the disgusting mucus and cracked the brittle bones.

'I could easily have you killed right now,' Colony whispered.

'We're friends now, remember?' I called back. 'Remember who brought you here.'

I perceived Colony standing on the far side of the chamber. His hands were stretched out towards me. Several motionless necrolisks surrounded him, waiting for his command.

I continued to trudge through the oozing unknown substance. 'How long is this going to take? Your brothers need reinforcements.'

'Those flesh sacks are not my brothers... this is my real family. But this queen hasn't accepted my presence yet.'

As Colony spoke, the necrolisks snarled and chattered their enormous jaws. Did he say queen? I didn't realise these things even had a leader.

'How long until that happens?'

'Not long, but you being here isn't helping. It's taking a lot of effort just to keep them from eating you alive, and I'm considering letting them do it.'

'Alright, I'll go. I'll leave the portal open. Remember, the civilians are not the target.'

'LEAVE!' he bellowed. His voice echoed throughout the chamber, and the necrolisks roared, too.

The whole cavern rumbled. My second perception sensed hundreds of agitated creatures swarming in the dark, edging closer and closer.

It was time I began the true assault on FDC. While their soldiers were distracted by all the skirmishes around the city, I'd teleport to the Citadel and kill the queen. But rather than dropping right into the throne room and immediately getting shot, I'd hide in the gardens and scope the place out first. Hopefully this necrolisk army would be ready by then, too.

I thought back to the day I was escorted through the royal gardens. The beautiful bushes and flowers, the carved path and golden pillars. The portal opened, and the moonlit night sky invaded the cave's darkness. Many of the creatures squealed in protest.

I stepped out of the filth and into the gardens, scanning for signs of life. The city buildings surrounding the gardens were unlit. Fantastic, the power was still down. Thanks to the moon, the gardens were bright compared to the cave, but it left me exposed. I ran to the nearest golden pillar for cover and paused to take everything in.

In the distance, along the outer walls of the gardens, I could see giant gun turrets. They weren't turning and scanning for targets anymore, which meant they, too, had powered-down. The towering Citadel, normally with its golden surfaces lit up, was nothing but a dark silhouette taking up a good portion of the sky.

There was a thundering explosion somewhere beyond the wall, in the streets of the Residential Rim. More eruptions and gunfire followed where the nomads and acolytes were still battling. They had advanced surprisingly close in a short amount of time.

Something on the path in front of me caught my eye. There were five royal guards marching down it towards me from the Citadel. Had they seen me? I shifted the portal to Teersau behind a nearby pillar and hid next to it.

Would I have to kill them? Personal guards to the queen herself were probably unwaveringly loyal. My second perception noticed their march become a sprint. They had *definitely* seen me. It looked like I had my answer.

It was then I spotted a much shorter girl among the guards. Iya darted out to the front while the others charged with their spears. Laserfire erupted from the spear tips, showering the pillar I was hiding behind in flames.

I darted out and took cover behind another pillar, focusing on the ground underneath them. Effortlessly, I opened a portal where they were about to take their next steps, with the destination high above in the air.

It collected the first few, who plummeted down with screams. They continued firing their lances, frantically sending bolts every which way in the sky. Some tried to dodge or jump over it, but in vain, as I simply readjusted it and enveloped them, too.

As the first of the guards hit onto the ground nearby with a crunch, the pillar I was hiding behind groaned. It had been fired upon to such an extent that its base was melting. The whole column teetered, shaking the ground around me, before eventually tipping over towards my hiding place.

I leapt to dodge as it crashed onto the ground. The resulting force blasted me clear away. I rolled away and got to my feet just as a second pillar collapsed nearby.

Iya could see me now and she was close. I readjusted the portal a final time, putting it under her. She tripped in, but unlike the others, she was remarkably calm as she plunged back down.

Rather than flailing about, she kept her body as upright and focused on one of the pillars. When she was closer to the ground, she brought her hands near her eyes and brought them together, presumably using her power on the pillar.

It was as though she were trying to slide down a pole, and somehow this slowed her descent. The pillar's edges crumbled slightly, as though two enormous invisible hands had grabbed it. Eventually, she came to a stop, hanging mid-air just off the ground. She let go and landed on the grass, unharmed.

I stood and watched the spectacle in amazement, before shaking out of it.

'That isn't going to work on me!' she shouted.

She took advantage of my momentary stupor, sprinting forward and using her power on one of the fallen pillars. The heavy mass groaned. It rose for a moment and was then hurled at me. It smashed down into the dirt in front of me, before rolling.

My reaction was like second nature: raising a portal from beneath my feet and instantly teleporting myself to a nearby spot farther down the path, only narrowly avoiding being flattened. I ran behind another pillar.

Iya laughed as she strolled closer to the path. 'I've been waiting for this! We finally have the green-light to kill you, and it's going to be me. As soon as you're dead, I can leave this stupid place. You hear me, you sand-munching bumpkin?'

I glanced over to my first portal. Colony still hadn't come through. What was taking him so long? I could see movement inside the dark portal. An amassing horde of necrolisks scurried back and forth.

'Hiding again?' Iya yelled, still searching for me. 'Hiding *and* cheating. Quite the spineless reprobate, aren't we?'

Was she referring to that time in the arena, or to that stupid laser game? And after all the brave things she'd seen me do? I wasn't going to let that stand. This had been a long time coming, anyway. I wanted to see her face up close after she realised I had won.

I confidently strode out onto the path until I was opposite her. I knew exactly what she was about to do. I was ready.

She noticed me and stared me down. 'Gotcha.'

We both raised our hands at the same time, she in an attempt to crush me, and I to create a pair of portals on either side of me to block her. Our two powers clashed, but hers were stronger. We both strained as hard as we could.

Her power had my portals clenched around my body tightly. If I didn't fight back, I'd be crushed. Her smile turned to a scowl as she strained and squeezed her fingers even tighter.

'Everyone can't stop talking about you, fawning all over you. But you're just a cheating weakling!'

I gritted my teeth as a swell of energy sparked inside of me. 'I'm not... weak!'

I pushed back against her grip until Iya finally gave out. She repositioned her fingers, trying to crush me into the ground instead. But before she could get a proper hold, I took one of my portals and flung it towards her.

The portal enveloped her, and she appeared through the other end, by my side. I punched her in the face with all my might, sending her sailing through the air.

She landed back on the path among the rubble. She rolled closer to the Teersau portal then struggled to her feet. She had a large gash on her face, and it was spitting blood at an alarming rate.

'I'm a weapon,' I added with a smug smile.

'Cheap shot. You think you h – hurt me? This is nothing to me!'

She was tearing up – she was only a child after all.

My attention shifted to the portal behind her. One of the necrolisks wandered through and onto the path. It went straight for Iya.

She was still scowling at me and hadn't noticed the new danger. The creature drove its claw into her back and impaled her small body with ease. It raised its limb into the air with Iya on it. Her body sank down the spike.

It was horrific. Her chest had been torn to shreds and blood spilled and squirted from the gigantic wound. She coughed and more blood spat out of her mouth and down her chin. Her eyes widened and her hands trembled as she raised them to her ruined chest.

Colony stepped through the portal and sauntered over to her. 'How about this? Does this hurt?' He put his hand on the necrolisk's torso and gave it an approving pat. 'My kind hates screeching children like you.' He circled to her front and got face to face. 'But you taste just fine.'

Colony marched over to me. 'Make the doorway wider! Are you expecting them to come through one at a time?'

'Oh. Right.'

I shook out of my stupor and turned to the portal. I stretched my fingers as wide as I could, and the portal widened across the path and into the gardens. A pack of necrolisks poured through and assembled around their master.

He raised his hand and pointed to the Citadel. The necrolisks all turned to the tower and stampeded towards it. Potentially hundreds more were still to come through.

I walked over to the impaled Iya, who was, amazingly, still clinging to life.

'Cheated... again,' she muttered while coughing up blood onto herself.

'It's called having friends,' I said, gesturing to the necrolisks scurrying around us. 'You chose the wrong ones.'

She tried forcing a smile through the pain. 'I don't... have friends.' Her eyes gently closed, and her head tilted back.

I thought I'd enjoy seeing her die, but now I just felt sorry for her. I turned away.

Colony raised his arm towards the necrolisk still holding Iya. I didn't want to look but my second perception made that impossible. The creature brought her towards its mouth and crushed her upper body in its jaws, thrashing from side to side as it tore her torso away from her legs with a sickening crack.

I felt queasy as a spray of blood splattered onto my shaking hands.

Colony gestured to the nearby pillars. 'I'll take cover here. If I die my necrolisks will tear this entire city apart. What a shame that would be. And you? Are you just going to stand there?'

I exhaled and focused on the Citadel. At least a hundred necrolisks were already streaming towards it. I created a portal to my side with its destination to the Citadel's golden entrance.

'I've thought of what I want my favour to be,' Colony began. 'You're going to give my necrolisks a new home here... a nest.'

What was he talking about? A nest here in the city? What would they eat? That couldn't possibly work.

He noticed my hesitation. 'What's the matter? What happened to "friends do each other favours"?'

'I said we'd discuss it *after* the battle,' I called back as I walked through my portal. 'First, the queen dies.'

Thirty-Six: I Am a Weapon

The oversized Citadel doors were locked and the horde of necrolisks piled up against them, trying to force their way inside. One by one they smacked against the golden gates before circling around the building's sides, looking for alternative entrances.

On the other side of the gates, I could sense a large locking mechanism keeping the doors barred.

There were numerous skirmishes taking place between the necrolisks and the guards throughout the gardens. The beasts were overwhelming the women with ease and destroying the powered-down turrets on the Citadel's outer walls.

Inside the Citadel, I sensed that the throne room ground floor was devoid of any people, but in its centre was a glowing, white orb as wide as the chamber's red carpet. The second floor had at least fifty royal guards hiding in the darkness along the balconies.

The orb sparkled with light; it was like a shifting vial of white sand. Small fibres of the orb casing flicked away before folding back to their origin. The white noise speckled and glistened like brilliant starbursts.

An odd sight, and not what I was looking for. My focus shifted to the queen's chamber high up in the tower; she wasn't there either. I searched high and low for her. Throughout the corridors and tunnels, in each individual room. Nothing. Could she be hiding inside the orb? It was probably a trap. But I wasn't going in there alone.

Teleporting the necrolisks inside one at a time wasn't going to work. There were too many and even more were on the way. These doors needed to come down. Something big had to hit them, and hard.

I remembered the fallen pillars back in the gardens. I closed my eyes, focused on one and put a huge portal under it. It exited far above me and plummeted down. As the mass of rubble was about to reach the ground, I placed another portal above my head for it to fall into. The giant pillar was now in perpetual free-fall.

Perhaps sensing my intentions, many of the necrolisks backed away from the door. I waited until the pillar reached a good speed, and then pointed the top portal towards the gates.

The momentum battered the pillar into the doors, ripping them off their hinges. The ground rocked as the pillar tumbled into the throne room and across the floor. Hundreds of tiles fractured, sending sharp-edged chips flying everywhere. The pillar rolled into the white orb but was deflected to the side of the room. The rumbling stopped. The orb was unaffected.

The mass of necrolisks at my side stormed through the open doorway and filled the hall. I waited until a good number had entered before running inside with them. They funnelled through every interior door, every corridor, and even climbed the pillars on the chamber's sides to reach the higher levels. A number even tried piercing and slashing at the white orb, but their attacks did nothing.

The second floor ignited with laserfire as the guards engaged the necrolisks. Due to the sheer number of the monsters scaling the walls, the guards were already on the back foot, retreating to the rear of the hall.

The dim, grey room, until now only illuminated by the presence of the mysterious white sphere, began to brighten. The mechanical turrets that were suspended from the ceiling's corners started to whirr and swivel to life.

What? I thought I had destroyed the reactor. Why was the power coming back on?

The orb in the middle of the room was shrinking. It grew smaller and smaller, eventually disappearing completely, revealing six women within. It was Queen Antwin, along with five acolyte colonels. As the queen floated up the steps to her throne, the others ducked to the ground, bar one colonel, who stretched her arms to the sides.

Long, thin strands of a black ooze extended from her hands to the walls of the chamber. The ooze was initially shapeless, but it sharpened along its long edges like giant scythes. She clicked a pair of small contraptions on her wrists, which ignited the oil with flame.

She started spinning in place, and as she did, the long strands spun with her like a fiery turbine. The blades sliced through the necrolisk's bodies, causing a trail of green blood to follow in their wake.

I backed off a little to a safer distance. The necrolisks around me squealed and shrieked as they were chopped to pieces by the boiling oil. The colonel continued spinning as more of the necrolisks tried closing in. Their attempts to reach the women were ineffective, for the blades dismembered each creature as it got close.

The turrets in the ceiling corners opened fire. Having dealt with the guards, the necrolisks on the second level amassed near the walls to reach the turrets above but were dispatched by the rapid-fire cannons. The corpses formed a writhing mound, each piling onto each other's slaughtered bodies in their desperate attempts to reach the turrets.

The colonel in the centre of the women stopped spinning, and the others stood up. I couldn't see Verre or Korin. But Neva was there, and her body dissolved into sand, left her armour and then proceeded to attack and melt the nearby necrolisks.

Another woman stepped forward and threw her arms towards me. A bright spectrum of colours shot out of her hands, above my head, and landed at the base of the entrance to the hall. The bright purple, blue and red bands of energy morphed into a wall and blocked further necrolisks from entering. The creatures on the outside struck the energy wall with their claws but their attempts produced nothing more than bright swirls.

Meanwhile, the necrolisks above had been successful in disabling the turrets. They leapt down from the second floor to rejoin the conflict below. The oil-flinging colonel shot more strands out of her hands at the descending creatures. Rather than turning it into a blade again, she set the line of oil on fire and the creatures along with it, creating a giant web of flames. They squealed hideously.

There were two other colonels who hadn't done anything yet. They were just standing there, watching me. The queen sat in her throne and smiled. If I didn't act now, I would have no more necrolisks left to help me.

I opened a portal above Antwin's head, but it instantly disappeared. One of the colonels had her eyes closed. She was pointing a hand towards the queen. Somehow, she was prohibiting my powers in that spot.

The final colonel ran at me, jumping over necrolisk bodies. I tried opening a portal under her feet, but she leapt over it. The neutralising colonel gestured to this portal also, instantly disrupting it for good measure.

The running woman was closing in. Whatever she had planned, I'd receive it with a shielding portal of my own. I raised up my hands. She stopped several paces from me, stretched out her arms and her body turned white. A shimmering white orb expanded from her body, encasing everything near her inside it, including me.

I tried moving, but I wouldn't budge. I couldn't breathe either, or teleport myself to safety. I was locked in place. It felt as if the very blood in my veins had stopped coursing, and yet I was still left with my thoughts. I was surrounded by a partially translucent bubble of energy, which from inside was extremely colourful.

The other woman was stuck inside the bubble with me with a smile frozen on her face.

'You got her. Great! Just hold it there,' the queen's muffled voice called out from her throne. 'The rest of you, get rid of these things. Quickly!'

The others sliced and melted their way through the remaining necrolisks, while I repeatedly tried to move my hands to make portals.

Rather than reforming inside her suit again, Neva reformed without it. Her sand moulded some robes around her. They glistened in the light.

The other colonels, except for the one maintaining the energy wall, ran over to the both of us frozen in the orb. The oil colonel created a pair of long sharpened scythes, clicked the mechanisms on her wrists and lit them ablaze.

I couldn't be sure, but by now the Teersau portal outside would have probably closed. This fight was taking all my concentration, so I had probably lost it.

Although I couldn't move, I didn't need to if I wanted to create portals, thanks to Marid's training. Also, though my eyes were locked in place, I could still use my second perception to see outside the orb.

'As soon as she lowers that orb, kill her!' the queen commanded.

I pictured the Teersau nest again from my memories. The neutralising, sand and oil colonels closed in around the orb.

The oil colonel raised her flame scythes above her head in preparation to strike. 'Wait for my mark.'

She wasn't going to get the chance because I was going to send her to her grave. I opened a portal beneath her feet. She lost her balance and fell through. The hooks of her hardened scythes caught the lip of the portal on the way through and she hung there with the cavern below her. A look of terror spread upon her face. The shadows below writhed faster.

Before she had a chance to pull herself back out, I closed the portal and cut the oil scythes in two, causing her to fall again. The tips of the scythes splattered onto the ground, bubbled for a moment, then dispersed. The other two colonels stood in disbelief.

'Release her and kill her now! Do it, Neva, kill her!' Antwin shouted from her throne.

'Now!' Neva said, exploding into a shower of sand and surrounding the orb.

The orb shrunk. I was released. I quickly opened a portal above my head and flew it down over my body. But before the portal had completely transported me, Neva's sand caught on my ankles.

After the portal closed, I fell onto the second floor and screamed. The sand was still dissolving the flesh around my foot. A pool of blood formed. My screams were heard by the three colonels below, who faced my new hiding spot on the balcony above.

I was losing this fight. I needed a better strategy. If I dealt with the one creating the shield, the necrolisks outside could assist me again. My mind shifted over to her. Picturing Teersau again, I opened a portal under her feet and she fell through. The colourful shield fell.

I tried standing but as soon as I put pressure on my right foot, I fell back down, shrieking again. There was a soft sprinkling sound. Neva's cloud form loomed above me. I hurriedly teleported away again, back downstairs.

I landed on the floor in the middle of the main chamber. More silhouettes had gathered at the main entrance. *Good, reinforcements.* The two colonels in front of me turned around to look, as did Neva, who had reformed on the second floor.

The necrolisks that were trapped outside the entrance were now dead. Standing in their place were Korin and Kalek. Korin had a stream of green necrolisk blood orbiting her like a shield. The other three colonels turned back to face me, and Antwin cackled from her throne.

Thirty-Seven: Worth Keeping

I was outnumbered. I hobbled to the side of the throne room one painful step at a time. I hid behind one of the crumbling golden pillars, and rested against it. The queen was still on her throne, smiling at the entertainment. Neva had rejoined the others on the main floor, and I could sense them all striding over to surround me.

Korin had entered the throne room, and she spotted the trail of blood leading towards my hiding spot. She threw her hands to the side, and the green ooze she had been collecting from felled necrolisks sprayed away. 'Oh, what's this?' she said as she bent down and examined closer. 'Your blood, huh? Not long now, Sacet. Your trauma is almost over.'

I inspected my ankle, which didn't show any sign of stopping bleeding. I struggled to stand and stayed hidden behind the pillar.

'Sacet,' the queen said from her throne. 'Just give up.'

I peeked at her from around the corner.

She gave a knowing smile. 'Let go. You have proven your worth. Your death is not the end. We have so many plans for you.'

I could see through her ruse; she was distracting me. This whole time, I had felt something off about Antwin, but now I knew what. My eyes had been lying to me. She was an illusion. My second perception revealed the truth.

As she spoke, I sensed the shape of an invisible figure. It had stood up from her body's position, crept down the steps, approached me, and then raised a small weapon, aiming it at my head.

I whipped my arm at the supposedly empty air, making contact with the figure's wrist and forcing the gun upwards. It discharged and flew out of the figure's hand.

The fake queen sitting in the throne faded and the invisible figure emerged from the air just as quickly. She had long blonde hair and a scowl that could frighten the bravest warrior. Verre backed away in shock. 'Wha – what?'

'Your illusions don't work on me anymore, Verre.'

The rest of my enemies surrounded me, each now only several paces away. As they prepared to attack, Verre raised her hand. 'Wait!'

The others looked confused, but stopped nonetheless.

'No one has ever seen through my abilities,' she said. 'How?'

I was going to pass out before too long. 'Tell me your secrets first,' I said, trying to delay the inevitable. 'You've been working with the men all along. Why?'

Verre tsked. 'Oh, Sacet. Our secrets are *far* more important than yours.' She took a few steps back so that the acolytes were in front of her. 'And I know when someone is stalling for time. I'll find out your truth soon enough. Kill her!'

I grimaced. 'Do it then!'

'Fine with me,' Kalek replied. He charged at me, rattling the tiles.

I quickly made a portal shield, its exit in a nearby wall. Kalek burst through the pillar and right into my shield, collecting the portal, as well as my body behind it with his arm. I couldn't withstand it.

He smashed us through the wall and back out into the gardens. As Kalek stopped, the force propelled me like a catapult. I spun and tumbled along the grass and collided into a low stone wall.

The portal disappeared. The other colonels stepped through the gaping hole the gargantuan had created. Kalek stood over me victorious as I spat up blood onto the ground.

'You're done,' he said with a frown.

I rested my head on the soft grass and stared up at the stars. My thoughts shifted far from the Citadel to the desert where my grandfather had taken care of me all of these cycles. Where I played with and protected my little brother. I had failed, but at least he was safe out there, away from me.

The windows of the city buildings had lit back up again. They were in neat rows and columns, symmetrical. Everyone in their place.

It was in such contrast to the stars, which didn't conform to any particular pattern. The stars were individuals, able to choose their own spot in the sky. When they came together, they did so in the most beautiful of ways, as constellations. Connected not by rigid order but by a beautiful chaos.

I sensed the stars and all the empty space in between. I pictured it in my mind and felt as though I had been there before.

'This isn't fun anymore – finish her,' Korin said.

I closed my eyes and sensed Neva walking over to my broken body, ready to deliver the final blow. 'Allow me.'

There was a nearby explosion, catching the attention of everyone around me. I opened my eyes and tried to sit up. On the far side of the gardens, one of the gates had burst open, and hundreds of people were storming in. There were male acolytes, nomads, and even women from the city itself.

'More of them?' Korin said.

'More to kill,' Kalek replied with a smile.

Neva turned back to me and morphed into sand.

I gripped the low stone wall with one hand as hard as I could, and then threw my other hand towards my enemies. In the middle of all of us I created the largest portal I could manage. A rapid gust of wind whipped around us as the air was drawn into the portal. In her sand form, Neva was sucked into the vacuum of space first.

I widened the portal as far as I could, increasing the pressure. I watched as the others struggled against it. Korin had latched onto the Citadel wall. The others desperately grasped at the grass. But one by one they lost their footing and were sucked into the void, screaming. Like Korin, my legs dangled towards the portal.

As the neutralising colonel flew past and into the hole, she tried using her powers to destabilise the portal. I almost lost control at first, it trembled and wobbled, but I was able to maintain the portal. I could feel my fingers slipping on the wall.

The grass Kalek was clinging to ripped and he flew into the hole, bellowing obscenities. The orb colonel went next, but before she reached the portal, she immobilised herself in another white orb. It was unaffected by the vacuum, completely motionless, so I shifted the portal closer and enveloped her. Even necrolisk bodies from the throne room were sucked out of the hole in the wall and into the vacuum, too.

Korin still managed to hang onto her wall, but now she had pointed one arm towards me. My heart rate quickened and my veins throbbed. The blood coming out of my injured ankle floated up in front of me in a stream. Korin was pulling the blood right out of my veins.

The globule of blood took the shape of a long needle and solidified. I shifted the portal closer to Korin. The needle of now solid blood flew into my chest and stabbed me through the rib cage. I let out a shriek as the incredible pain took hold.

My control over the portal had weakened. My fingers trembled as they struggled to keep it open for a single moment longer. The portal closed and we both fell to the grass. Korin quickly rose. I tried to grab the needle protruding from my chest, but only gave myself more pain. Korin ran over and stretched both of her hands out towards whatever blood of mine she could find.

'Stubborn, even in death!' she yelled.

She raised her hands up and the remaining blood ascended before forming into a giant spear. She pointed the tip downwards and plunged it into my stomach, causing me to jolt up and whimper. I could feel my bodily fluids seeping away. I coughed, resting my head back onto the grass and closing my eyes one last time.

Thirty-Eight: A Swell of Red

In the Royal Gardens
Tau

After resurrecting Malu, we joined up with the rest of the rebels. Our raucous army bayed at the looming Citadel, crushing every shrub and flower underfoot on our way to it. It didn't matter that many of us were unarmed, our sheer number would not be denied. Malu and I led the way, with my aura illuminating our path through the dark gardens.

We numbered in the hundreds, and although it was horrible seeing so many dying on the way here, I'd make sure to resurrect them when this was all over. Our ranks were now vast and diverse, including FDC civilians and fellow soldiers. Apparently, Sacet had projected a rousing speech to most of the city. I hadn't heard it myself, but after hearing it, hundreds of women had left their homes to riot with us.

Noor and Tetsu were close behind. Tetsu's shield had been invaluable, making every skirmish a nonissue. Noor, meanwhile, was terrifying. His laser cut through one or two guards and it was enough for entire squads to surrender and occasionally join us.

As we marched along the pillar-edged path, I pointed ahead to the base of the Citadel. 'Is that Korin?'

'And Sacet!' Malu yelled. We charged ahead, and the mob followed.

Sacet's body lay lifeless on the blood-smeared grass. Her head had slumped to the side, and her face was absent of colour. Korin waved her hands and the large, crystalised sword of blood that firmly impaled Sacet's chest liquified and flowed into the air.

As we closed in, Korin backed away towards a hole in the Citadel wall. She was quickly surrounded before she reached it. Realising she couldn't escape, she instead eyed us with disgust and raised her hands.

Her gaze found me. 'You're too late. She's dead.'

At least fifty nomads pointed their weapons at her.

'Get on your knees!' Noor commanded.

She knelt, and the floating sword lost its form and splattered harmlessly onto the ground.

'Everyone, find the queen!' one of the nomads roared.

'Find her and kill her!' another added.

Most of the crowd joined in, entering the Citadel through the nearby hole, while others went around to the main entrance.

Korin's eyes widened when she saw Malu. She sighed and tilted her head at me. 'We were hoping you wouldn't work that out yet.'

I did my best to ignore her, striding over to Sacet's perforated body.

'Tau, listen to me,' Korin pleaded. 'Leave her dead. If you resurrect her, we will come for you until everyone in this city is dead.'

I paused. 'What are you talking about?'

'Don't listen to her,' a nomad said.

'They have lied to us for so long,' a civilian added. 'They lie still.'

There was no trace of smugness on Korin's face, only deadly earnestness. 'All this time we've been fighting a fake war. What do you think is going to happen when you misfits take over? The war will become real, and none of you will survive it.'

The crowd exchanged confused looks. I knelt over Sacet's body.

'Believe me, Tau,' she continued. 'Her resurrection will come at a great toll. But if you don't bring her back, everyone else can live. We just want her.'

Malu approached Korin from behind and placed a hand on her shoulder. The colonel looked up at her with widened eyes. 'Wait, wait!'

Malu shook her head. 'Shut up, ma'am.'

Korin's entire body liquified in a swell of red water, bursting outwards then splashing onto the ground.

'Fake war?' Noor asked, before looking at a shrugging Tetsu.

Malu stepped back. Her fists shook and her breathing quickened. 'I feel so... *stupid* for following their orders all this time.'

There was a low-pitched hum, one so loud that it echoed throughout the city. We turned and saw an ominous silhouette rise on the dark city skyline over the Military Quad. A massive airship powered on its spotlights and propelled itself towards the Citadel.

My jaw dropped. 'The Coda...'

'It's operational?' Malu added, just as shocked.

There was no doubt it was the giant aircraft the queen had commissioned to guarantee an end to this war. Had it been ready this entire time?

Noor glanced back at us. 'We'll take care of this. Tetsu?'

'Right!'

I laid my hands on Sacet's wounds and tried to concentrate. Malu, Noor and Tetsu all stood next to me. Tetsu brought his hands to the sides and his shield enclosed around us.

The airship hovered over the gardens with a constant mechanical droning. The hundreds of nomads and rebels still outside scattered for cover, many screaming in fear.

I took a deep breath and squeezed Sacet's hand. A warmth grew within me, tingling just as it had for the others. The feeling rushed from my stomach, up my spine and then out to my extremities. My hair flickered and turned white. My skin glowed, and a light-blue aura engulfed me.

'Rioting scum, surrender now and you will not be gunned down like you deserve,' a voice echoed from the floating fortress above. I recognised them – it was my former superior Matriarch Aellix. 'Cease this senseless destruction.'

Noor and Tetsu turned to each other and smiled.

'They're not a fan of a senseless destruction, brother,' Tetsu said.

Noor pointed his arms at the airship. 'Then maybe we should be more direct.'

A mighty beam of energy blasted from his fingertips and out of the shield. The sweltering heat inside the shield was blistering. The beam ripped through the night air, instantly making contact with the side of the craft, but it wasn't cutting through.

Over a hundred mixed rebels also aimed up and fired their weapons, but nothing seemed to make a difference.

The blood that had formed around Sacet's body creeped back inside her. And as the large wound in her stomach closed in on itself, I felt a phantom stab into my own stomach. I screamed through the unbearable pain. It was like my innards had been sliced in two.

The others glanced at me with concern but were starting to realise this is just what I'd have to endure when using my power.

Sacet's split skin converged and repaired, while mine felt like it was peeling. My ankle was on fire. I continued to scream, and I couldn't hold back the tears. I slumped over her, completely spent. No more.

Sacet's eyes fluttered for a moment, before opening and groggily staring up at me.

'Noor,' the matriarch's voice boomed. 'You didn't really think you could melt everything, did you?' They tutted their tongue disapprovingly.

Several gigantic cannons under the ship's hull strafed the gardens seemingly at random, making enormous craters and blasting many of the rebels apart. There were rapid pops, followed by a high-pitched squeal as a hail of rockets shot out from the airship. The rockets hit the ground around the shield, penetrating deep into the soil. Thin poles extended from the back of the projectiles, and they lit up with green light.

Noor stopped firing and looked down at his hands, confused. Tetsu's shield started to waver and weaken, before disappearing completely.

'Tetsu?' Malu called out.

Tetsu flung his arms out repeatedly trying to reactivate the shield. 'It's not me.'

Noor ran over to Sacet and me. 'It's an inhibitor field. Quick, get out of it!'

With Noor's help, we lifted Sacet up off the ground.

There was another flurry of pops, this time lighting up the sky in a firestorm. The rockets screamed as they tore through the air towards us, leaving blazing orange trails in their wake.

Thirty-Nine: A Great Need

Sacet

Tau and Noor were arm in arm with me, dragging me along the grass. There were many nomads and civilians running about. I looked at Tau's worried face, trying to work out what had happened.

'Jump!' Tau yelled as we passed a set of green poles.

We leapt into the air, hit the ground near Malu and rolled. Tetsu brought up a shield around us. Rockets smacked into its side and a violent explosion coated our shelter in flames.

My head spun, and I shook out of it. I leant forward and rose. Wait, hadn't I been stabbed? I frantically felt around my body to examine my wounds. There was nothing wrong with my stomach or chest. Even my ankle had been healed.

I peered through the flaming shield at the night sky. A giant airship hovered above, almost as large as the Citadel itself. It was the same airship I had seen docked in the hangar.

Noor fired his laser straight up but failed to do any damage. The others looked desperate, out of ideas.

Could I portal the threat away? No, I couldn't make a portal wide enough. But I had another idea. Noor's power had reminded me of that game we played with Kowi, and how I had amplified the light.

I left Tau's side and approached Noor. 'When I tell you, you're going to shoot into one of my portals, got it?'

Noor glanced back at Tetsu, who shrugged, before turning back to me and nodding. 'Alright.'

I closed my eyes and held my hands out, opening one portal in my right palm pointed towards Noor, and the other in my left palm pointed at the airship.

'Now!' I yelled.

He redirected the energy beam into my right hand. The beam exited out the left portal, out of our shield and blazed up into the airship, the same as before.

'Sacet, what are you doing?' Malu called out over the deafening noise.

'Wait!' I screamed back. 'Tetsu, lower the shield!'

He shook his head at Noor. 'Is she crazy?'

Noor and I caught each other's eyes over the boiling heat wave. I gave him a firm nod.

'Do it, brother!' Noor yelled back.

Tetsu complied, bringing the shield down. Now that there was more room, I began widening the left portal. As I did so, Noor's beam grew wider with it. Its heat intensified, too, searing my skin.

The far more powerful laser turned the airship's surfaces bright orange. The beam's width was now half the width of the airship. After a short time, the bright orange frame became white-hot. Clouds of smoke wafted up from the ship's engines. The ship began to list sideways, before spinning uncontrollably and careening downwards.

I nodded to Noor, and he disengaged the beam. We stood and watched as the melting airship plummeted and ploughed into the gardens. The impact quaked the earth so intensely that most of us were blown off our feet, including me.

As the ship drove into the soil towards us, it left a canyon of fire behind. Large chunks of dirt and plants launched into the air. The craft sizzled and hissed, and its engines had stopped their high-pitched squealing. The ruined airship finally came to a stop, and sat there, unresponsive, defeated.

There was a swell of cheering all around us in the gardens, and the wind carried the sounds of cheers in the distance, perhaps from all around the city.

I sat up and looked up at a smiling Tau. 'Was I... was I dead?'

She nodded and leant down to help me up.

'You saved me?' I continued. 'I didn't think you were going to join us...'

'I couldn't stand the lies anymore, *especially* the ones I told myself.'

I smiled back. 'Well, thank you.'

Tetsu and Noor were still celebrating the destruction of the airship. They jumped around, slapped each other's hands, and hooted nonsensically.

Tetsu brought his hands behind his head in amazement. 'Wooooooow! Great work, brother. That thing's gotta be our record, right?'

'In terms of size? By far!' Noor yelled back. He turned to me and cleared his throat. 'Uhh, with your help, of course.'

I dipped my back head to him.

'Come on,' Malu interrupted. She was over by the hole in the wall. 'We've got a queen to kill.'

Our group, along with several other rebels, followed her through the hole, back into the throne room. The chamber was filled with at least a hundred mixed nomads and civilians. By the throne's steps, there were male acolytes and entire squads of turned FD soldiers. Even Colony was there with some of his surviving necrolisks, which most chose to stand well away from.

'Where is she?' I asked as we strode in.

Orrik approached. 'We can't find her anywhere on the ground floor.'

'My necrolisks climbed the floors above,' Colony added. 'Nothing!' The creatures growled in frustration.

Elder Hati ambled out of the crowd. 'If she escapes to another city, this rebellion will have meant nothing.'

I closed my eyes and concentrated. My second perception double-checked their claims, quickly scanning through every room of the Citadel. There was destruction everywhere I searched, and plenty of bodies. But I couldn't find Verre.

Then I noticed something peculiar. The elevator shaft that I had once travelled up to the peak in also went down, far below ground level. At the very bottom of the shaft, almost at the limit of my perception's range, there existed another subterranean room. It was dark, lit only by holo-screens.

Malu placed a hand on my shoulder. 'Sacet? What do you see?'

There was an old man's face on the screens. I didn't recognise him. He was stern, with greyish hair and a moustache. Verre and Marid were in the centre of the room. They were having a discussion, and Marid was pointing her sword at Verre.

I sighed in relief. Not only had we found Verre, but Marid appeared to be on our side.

'I know where she is,' I addressed to the whole crowd, and they went silent in anticipation. I focused again. 'I can see her, far below.'

The dark room's screens flickered off. Marid grabbed Verre's arm and brought the tip of her blade close to Verre's stomach. Verre was oddly calm, she closed her eyes. They both exchanged more words. What were they saying?

There was a sudden whoosh of air as both Marid and Verre appeared at the top of the steps by the throne. The crowd was taken aback. Marid brought the tip of her blade to Verre's stomach, looking like she was about to finish her off.

'Wait!' Tau yelled, giving Marid pause. 'Shouldn't we interrogate her?' The crowd of others murmured, mostly in disagreement.

Malu shook her head. 'We've come this far. She needs to die.'

Still hovering her blade near Verre's stomach, Marid then turned to me. The mob quietened.

'This fight isn't over until she dies,' I said, staring into Verre's quivering eyes. 'She's not worth keeping.'

Marid grinned, then plunged her blade into Verre, who spat up blood and cried out in pain. Some of the crowd gasped, while others cheered.

Marid didn't let go of her blade, sinking it deeper. Verre fell to her knees, a shocked expression frozen on her face, in so much pain now that she couldn't even make a noise. Eventually she succumbed to her fate, closing her eyes and slumping to the side. Marid twisted her blade for good measure, then sliced it back out. The body went motionless, and the blood dripped down the steps.

My second perception homed in on the body to make sure it was real. I didn't detect any more illusions. Verre was dead.

Marid and I locked eyes. She gave a solemn nod first, that I returned.

I glanced at a group of former FD soldiers. 'Send a message to the barracks, to anyone who will listen. It's over. The queen is dead.'

A couple of soldiers nodded back. One raised her finger to a button on her helmet to record and broadcast.

'But that's not the queen?' Tetsu pointed out, and there were murmurs throughout the chamber.

'Verre *was* the queen,' Marid called out, silencing the confused mob. She pointed down at Verre with her blood-coated sword. 'The queen you all knew was an illusion, concocted by Verre long ago.'

'And how do you know this?' Hati asked, his hunched frame becoming visible as some of the nomads around him parted.

Marid flicked some blood off her sword. 'Because I was there when the last queen died, decades ago. Matriarchs from all over the world met in secret to decide who would be next to rule. To embody Queen Elysia, she needed to be kind and matronly. Also unkillable, with unquestionable loyalty to her people.'

She sheathed her sword and kicked Verre's body down the stairs. 'So Verre volunteered herself – with a carefully designed fabrication as the figurehead to keep the masses placated. I was the only one to object.'

Tamil parted the crowd, brandishing her dagger at Marid. 'And why should we trust you?' Her question elicited jeers. 'How do we know you're not covering her escape?'

'I can vouch that Antwin was an illusion,' I called out. I ascended the steps and stood beside Marid. 'In addition to portals, I have the power to see through walls, to see what others cannot. I could tell she was an illusion, that she wasn't there.' I turned to Marid. 'But what I can't vouch for are your motives. Whose side are you on?'

Many tightened their grip on their weapons. Some necrolisks snarled.

'Yours,' she replied, glancing over at the necrolisks and raising an eyebrow. 'I think.'

'You think?' I said.

Marid shook her head. 'After all I've done for you, my student, you still don't trust me?'

'How can I when you keep these secrets?'

She pointed at me. 'We all keep secrets, Sacet, *you* included.'

I groaned, conceding the point. 'Fine then, but why switch sides now? Why kill her?'

She straightened her back and faced the crowd. 'Because I've been defending my people my whole life. Like many of you, I've sacrificed so much for the fight.' She poked her cane into me. 'So, imagine my shock when I return to this city and learn that Verre and her lackeys are working with the Male Dominion, while still pretending to be in a prolonged war of attrition.'

She firmly tapped her cane on the steps. 'If that was happening for who knows how long, then why are we fighting in the first place? What a spit in the face to all of us, striving and dying for nothing!'

Some of the rebels roused in agreement.

Malu came up a few steps. 'Well, what do they want then? To what end?'

Marid lowered and shook her head. 'I don't know. But there's no telling how long their faction has been pulling the strings from the shadows.'

'I might know,' Tau said from the side of the chamber. She had been hiding behind a pillar, but she stepped out and approached. She pointed at me. 'They orchestrated my death to traumatise Sacet. To make her more powerful.'

I shrugged. 'Why me though?' I looked up and noticed the silent crowd staring at me.

The soldier who had been recording still had her finger on the button, broadcasting every word. There was no telling how many would see and hear this, or how far the message would reach.

'I suppose it doesn't matter why,' I continued, dismissing my own question. 'It won't be long until this news is worldwide. What's important is that we all stop fighting this pointless war.'

The crowd murmured again. It seemed like everyone was in agreement.

Hati hobbled over to the base of the steps. 'These are great strides forward. I'm assuming we will do away with this... totalitarianism?'

Orrik pushed through to reach the front. 'You're all crazy if you think the Male Dominion is going to rise up against their king.'

Tetsu laughed out loud and nodded. 'Ah, yep. Even a whiff of treason is met with execution there, so I very much doubt it.'

Hati rose up a couple of steps. 'Then we, a faction of peace, are still at war. The united peoples of this world need a leader that represents all of our voices.'

Malu scoffed. 'And I suppose that would be you, would it?'

Orrik ascended the steps, too. 'I will do it. Under my leadership, we will grind the MD into the dunes!'

Many of his tribe members applauded in agreement.

'We will not support another warmonger,' a civilian from the crowd interjected, and many around her cheered.

The crowd's previous agreements soured, with most now turning to others to argue.

Marid smacked her cane repeatedly on the steps, and the noise reverberated throughout the chamber to regain the crowd's attention. 'If we are to have a ruler, there is only one person here that is qualified. And it is not me, or any of you that have come to this throne room to seek power. There is only one who embodies the ancient Queen Elysia. She is kind, unkillable, and has a great loyalty to her people.'

Marid went down a couple of steps. 'And it is you, Tau.'

'What?' Tau said, pop-eyed. 'Why me?'

The entire room turned to her, stunned.

'Because while everyone else was killing each other, you were in the hospitals and the prisons, healing the sick and wounded, both women *and* men. You didn't care who it was, you just wanted to help. I even watched as you resurrected the dead tonight. Your fallen comrades stood back up and continued the fight.

'Many in the city believe you are Elysia reincarnated, but you're better than even she was. After a lifetime of indoctrination, you didn't become a warmonger. You're still a good person. This city, the entire Female Dominion *loves* you.'

When there was a pause in Marid's words, a few civilians began to clap, and that surged to echoing cheers of support.

Tau seemed dumbfounded, unsure of what to do with herself. 'Um... uh?'

Malu and I both smiled at one another. We waited for any protests but heard none.

'It should be you, Tau,' I said to her. I looked out to the crowd and noticed that while the FD citizens were cheering, most of the nomads were silent. I waited for quiet and gestured to her. 'As a proud nomad myself, I can't think of anyone better than her.'

Marid pointed Tau to the throne. The room silenced as they waited for her decision. Tau glanced around nervously. Her knees quivered as she climbed the steps. She glanced back at everyone else as if searching for objections.

Tamil was near the front, and she appeared upset. 'Wait, stop!' Everyone turned to face her. 'Will you allow the nomads to live here in your cities? Will you release all the prisoners, and stop hunting nomads?'

'Will you stop forcing hormones into our food?' a soldier asked. 'And allow us to live as civilians if we want to?'

'And stop the experiments on men,' a civilian added. 'And the executions?'

Every question generated more and more intrigued murmurs. We all waited for an answer.

She hesitated at first, but then found her confidence. 'Yes, to all of it. All of those injustices have horrified me my entire life. The cruelty ends today.'

The biggest cheer yet erupted as Tau took her place on the throne. She stared out at the throne room, filled with her new subjects, took a deep breath, and ignited her cyan aura of flames around her body. Her hair and skin went white. The golden throne's surfaces glowed brighter than they ever had before.

'Let there be no illusions from this point forth,' Marid addressed the inspired crowd. 'Your new queen shall be Tau, the Queen of Light.' She had a smug grin, as if satisfied in knowing she had made the right choice. 'Those of you who don't want to live here are free to leave. Everyone else should show respect to their new queen and bow.'

As Marid turned and knelt, most of the crowd did, too. Surprisingly, not one person broke away from the group to leave.

The nomads all turned to their own leaders. The various chieftains pondered, but they eventually bowed, and their tribes did in turn. The male acolytes all bowed, too, including Noor and Tetsu.

Colony stared at me. He had been for some time. He nodded and raised his eyebrows inquisitively. I knew what he wanted, his favour. How could I even bring that up right now? Necrolisks living with us, too? Insanity. But I nodded back at him all the same.

He grinned and bowed, and surprisingly even his necrolisks split their legs apart and dipped forward, as if bowing, too. It was peace for now, but that was a discussion I was certainly not looking forward to having.

The whole room was bowing to Tau now, all except for me. She and I locked eyes and I smiled. 'My Queen.' I bowed proudly like the others, knowing that tomorrow, the world would be a different, better place.

Sitting on the citadel roof just before dawn, the view of the city was stunning. I wasn't sure how they brought power back online, but the usual city lights and sounds had returned. It somehow appeared even more colourful than before. Even though it was so late at night, the streets were filled with celebrating civilians.

The very top of the tower was a small square platform with no railings. Tau was sitting next to me. We dangled our feet over the edge of the tallest building in the city. Marid and Malu were behind us, keeping their distance from the edge.

Marid tapped her walking stick as she paced. 'I used to come up here all the time, to think,' she said, looking out at the desert beyond the city walls. 'And also to get away from the idiots.'

'It's amazing up here,' I said, looking down at the light-filled urban sprawl.

'And cold,' Malu said, shivering. She looked at Tau, determined. 'My Queen, I–'

Tau shook her head. 'Don't call me that. We're friends, Malu.'

Malu nodded. 'My father – he – you can bring him back, right?'

Tau struggled to find the answer. 'Resurrection is very painful, I feel how they died as if it were me.' She shook her head. 'But that won't stop me. There are so many people I want to bring back: your father, my friends, and Pilgrim, too. But it might not work, because of what you did to him. That water was swept away after the tournament.'

Malu looked away as tears appeared in her eyes.

'I'll still try though, I promise,' Tau said to her, before looking at me. 'Sacet, what about your grandfather? Or your parents?'

I frowned. 'That's not going to work either. They weren't just killed; their bodies were taken away by necrolisks a long time ago. And my grandfather was blown to bits. Whatever was left of him would have been scavenged by now.'

'Oh,' Tau said, abandoning the idea. 'I'm... I'm sure we'll find a way, for both of you.'

Now that we had a tentative peace, my thoughts shifted to Eno. I imagined where he might be. When things died down here, maybe I could go search for him? But if this secret faction was still out there, would he ever be safe with me again? How long would they come for us?

Malu turned to Marid. 'Are all the prisoners free now?'

'I teleported there and made sure everything went smoothly. They'll be released in the morning and housed.'

Malu nodded. 'Then my mother and sister will be reunited with my brother.'

Tau pointed at Malu. 'You should go see them, too?'

Malu shook her head. 'No, they won't want me there, not after what I've done.'

We all went quiet again, not sure how to help her. We sat in silence, soaking in the view and listening to the distant celebrations.

'Sacet,' Marid began. 'Now that things have settled, I can tell you one more secret I've been keeping.'

I glanced back at her with a raised eyebrow. 'Only one?'

She smiled. 'When I first came back here to train you, I was told the assimilation sessions weren't having any effect. That you were... a special project.'

'Assimilation, you mean the brainwashing?' I asked and she nodded back.

'Figures,' Malu added. 'That's why you were always such a pain in my arse.'

I brought my hand to my head. 'So... all my feelings of confusion over which side I should be on, that was just me?'

Marid nodded. 'Yes. I don't know why, but they told me that your training was incredibly important. That and they were going to take everything away from you. I was told to... "sit back and watch".

'As I got to know you and started to learn their plans, I felt sorry for you. I wanted to tell you so badly, but each time I... I couldn't. It wasn't until I learned how deep their plans went that I realised I was on the wrong side.'

'But why me?' I asked.

Marid shook her head gravely. 'I honestly don't know.'

Tau looked at me. 'Speaking of *them*, where exactly did you send Kalek and those colonels? Kalek didn't die, surely?'

'I didn't kill them... I just sent them away, far away.'

Forty: The Fall of a Dominion

Seron's upper atmosphere
Kalek

I tried to grab the tiny woman as we spun in the zero gravity environment. The choking colonel didn't notice me, instead gripping at her chest. The liquid around her mouth and eyes vaporised into nothingness. She contorted and exhaled into the vacuum. A scream was frozen on her face. Her skin was already reddened from the star's unfiltered radiation. She convulsed again then went motionless, finally dead.

The body drifted away. I pitied her. No matter, she'd soon be revived.

As I didn't need oxygen, the whole experience was quite surreal for me. There was no sound in space, other than the blood pumping in my eardrums. The planet took up most of my view.

That Sacet girl, she was holding out on us. If I had known she could do this, I wouldn't have gone easy on her. Her portal was long closed.

A bright, white ball floated where it used to be. It was one of the other colonels in suspended animation. Great, how many of us were going to fall for that trick?

A hazy silhouette passed over the white light. It grew larger until it eclipsed the ball. It was Neva in her sand form. She was somehow propelling herself in the empty vacuum.

She surrounded my body. The cloud brushed my face and lips. It entered through my now widened mouth and nostrils, before trickling down my throat and into my stomach. She tickled my insides; I couldn't help but laugh.

Still caught in the planet's gravity, the dead body caught fire and burned away. Good. It would only be a matter of time before I fell back to the planet's surface.

My skin was heating further, but I wasn't worried. This was nothing, I would survive this. All of these weaklings around me were susceptible to so much. At times like this, I was truly grateful for my immortality.

My armour caught fire, but I still felt nothing, no pain. My ears popped, and I could hear the blazing flames around me. The atmosphere was starting to thicken.

The sand inside my stomach quivered; the heat was getting to her somehow. I closed my mouth and pinched my nostrils. Was that better now? She still squirmed. Well, too bad, I've done all I could do.

The burning subsided, my body was dropping in temperature. Another layer of the atmosphere?

This was taking forever. Where would I hit? I supposed it was impossible to tell from this high up. I hoped it was somewhere with civilisation nearby, I didn't want to walk all the way back. I also didn't want to contact... him.

A blanket of clouds grew closer as I hurtled. At least I wasn't landing in the ocean. It was getting colder. Neva wasn't shaking around anymore so I stopped pinching my nose. The wind blasted past my ears. *Hurry up! Come on!*

I rocketed into the clouds and was surrounded by grey mist. The spray glazed my squinting eyes. The furious wind billowed against my cheeks.

I shot through and out of the cloud and spotted the desert floor. The cloud's shadow darkened the world below. I recognised where this was. I was going to land in the middle of nowhere.

Of all the crazy things I had been through, this was the most dangerous. I wondered if I'd feel pain when I crashed. It had been a long time since I'd felt anything.

I better try landing on my feet, just in case. I waved my arms, trying to rotate my body. I was going to hit any moment now. I could make out separate rocks and cliffs below.

'Brace yourself, we're about to hit!'

The sand became heavier in the pit of my stomach, as if solidifying.

My feet plunged into the ground, rippling a wave of displaced soil away from me. The sand grated my skin as my body drove itself down and down. I was completely covered, buried alive.

I gradually raised my arms through the shifting sand until they pointed above. I then bent my knees. I gave an almighty push, springing up and out of the crater. My escape cast dust everywhere. The shockwave quaked the nearby cliffs, and they started to crumble.

My gag reflex acted involuntarily, so I bent over and opened my mouth. Neva shot up my oesophagus and out my mouth and nostrils. Her cloud hovered in front of me, before reforming back into the attractive colonel.

I chuckled. 'Did you enjoy being inside of me?'

She glared. 'You degenerate. Did you have to eat me? It was a mess in there, and you don't even *need* to eat!' She flicked a piece of undigested food from her shoulder then inspected her new, glistening robes for more.

I gestured around. 'Well, we're stuck here now. I don't suppose you can communicate with the sand or something to get us a ride home?'

'I already told you. I. Don't. TURN. INTO SAND! Got it?' she said and stomped away from me. 'Why don't you just call Overwatch and get it over with?'

I sighed. 'He's not going to be happy.'

'Oh, what's this? I thought you weren't scared of anything?'

'The only thing I fear is time. I need that promotion, and if he blames me for this, I'm not going to ever get it. This was my last shot after I... uhh... you know...'

Her laugh echoed off the cliff faces. 'After you accidentally ripped that dignitary's arm off? Fine, *I'll* talk to him. Make contact.'

I nodded, opened my mouth, and reached in with my hand. I could barely fit my stubby fingers in to reach the molar at the back, but I managed to grab hold and yank it out. As I held it in front of us, a small blue beam of light shot up from it, before widening into a holographic float screen.

Neva paced. 'I'm going to kill that girl. After this, I'll head back there and end it all.'

The screen remained blue for a while, and nothing seemed to be happening.

'Where is he?' I said under my breath.

'How should I know?'

'I wasn't asking you!'

The image on the screen changed in the corner of my eye. Overwatch General Tuloch sat down in his chair and leant forward. The middle-aged man had black, almost greying hair and a wide moustache.

'Yes? Oh, it's you two. Report, Kalek.'

'I... I...'

Neva edged closer to the screen. 'What he's trying to say, sir, is that we've failed to contain the situation. We couldn't stop her.'

The general scowled. 'You think I don't already know that? Do you think we just sit here waiting for you to tell us what's going on down there? I was addressing Kalek!'

'Sir, I apologise,' she said.

'That's enough of that. Where are you anyway? And who have you lost?'

I glanced at our surroundings. 'We've crashed back on the surface in southern Citeer. Amren froze herself up in orbit. And that other one, I always forget her name, she burned up in the atmosphere.'

Neva pushed me in the side and edged closer. 'The other was Topal, sir.'

Tuloch folded his arms. 'We'll collect them both shortly. Anyone else?'

'Uhh, yes, sir,' Neva continued. 'Rake and Saree were teleported somewhere by her, but we're not sure where.'

'Yes, we've already picked up those two. If that's all then—'

'What about the situation in the FDC, Sir?' Neva asked. 'Do you want us to head back there? I promise you, we won't fail again. We still might be able to salvage this.'

'No, you won't, it's well beyond that now. I've contacted home and they agree what's happened here is a welcome change. So, we're going to see how it goes.'

I shook my head, confused. 'But, sir, what trauma can we possibly bring her if she won't fear death? They have resurrection now.'

He laughed. 'Then we'll just have to take that away from them, won't we?'

'Sir?' I interrupted. 'What about us?'

'You're going to head back to MDC. Take her with you as – a prisoner, I guess.'

Neva looked at me with shock, then back at the general. 'But, sir, my skills are needed in the field! I–'

'NO! Your skills are needed where I tell you they're needed! If I think of something more important for you to do, I'll tell you myself. Until then, you agents all have a role to play, so make it believable. Head back there and await further orders!'

'Uh, sir? About that?' I said and glanced at the sand dunes around me. 'We're going to need a lift.'

About the Author

Inhabiting the thoroughbred, horse-loving town of Melton, J.B. Villinger is not your typical schoolteacher. By day, he's molding young students into IT super soldiers, teaching them the fine art of crafting video games that don't suck, the flashy widgetry of Photoshop, and the tedious tedium of coding. But by night, he obsessively thinks about his unwritten stories and characters, instead of… you know… sleeping.

When he's not rewriting a chapter for the 67th time, James can be found staring at his ever-growing collection of video games, wondering if he'll ever have time to play them all. The answer is no, but he likes to dream. Board games, D&D, comics and anime, is there anything he doesn't like? Yes: cauliflower. He particularly likes lying games, although his poker face is about as unreadable as a children's bathtub book.

James often thinks about the meaning of life, his purpose and his legacy. What will he leave behind on this world for his young son, Theodore? That's why J.B. proudly tells his tales, whether you choose to buy them or not. He is… I am… content.

For more content and updates from J.B. Villinger's Sisters series, contact him directly at jvillinger@live.com.au, or you can also find him on Wattpad @ JamesVillinger.

Shawline Publishing Group Pty Ltd
www.shawlinepublishing.com.au

SHAWLINE
PUBLISHING
GROUP